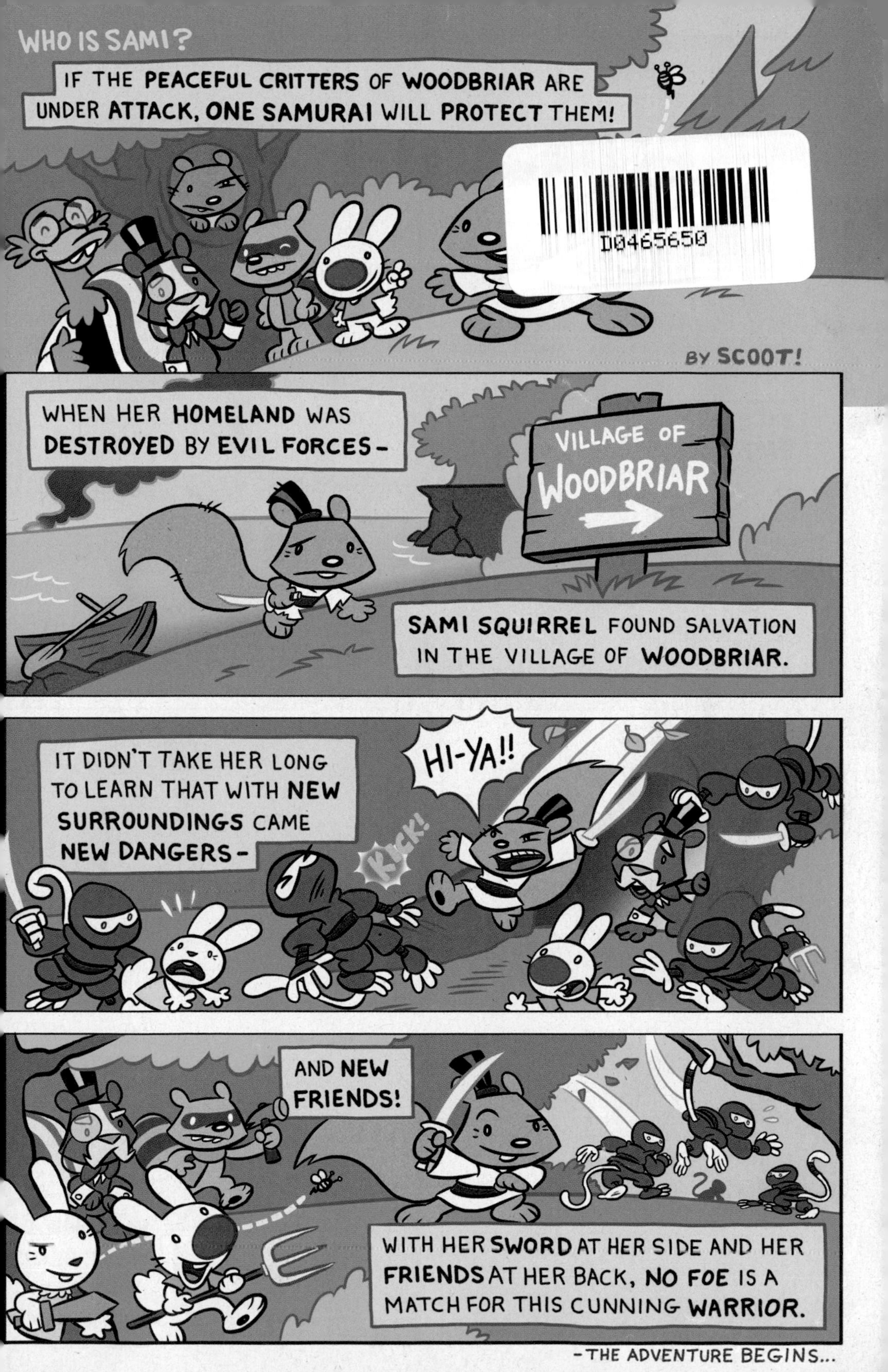

WHO IS SAMI?
IF THE PEACEFUL CRITTERS OF WOODBRIAR ARE UNDER ATTACK, ONE SAMURAI WILL PROTECT THEM!
BY SCOOT!
WHEN HER HOMELAND WAS DESTROYED BY EVIL FORCES-
VILLAGE OF WOODBRIAR
SAMI SQUIRREL FOUND SALVATION IN THE VILLAGE OF WOODBRIAR.
IT DIDN'T TAKE HER LONG TO LEARN THAT WITH NEW SURROUNDINGS CAME NEW DANGERS-
HI-YA!!
KICK!
AND NEW FRIENDS!
WITH HER SWORD AT HER SIDE AND HER FRIENDS AT HER BACK, NO FOE IS A MATCH FOR THIS CUNNING WARRIOR.
-THE ADVENTURE BEGINS...

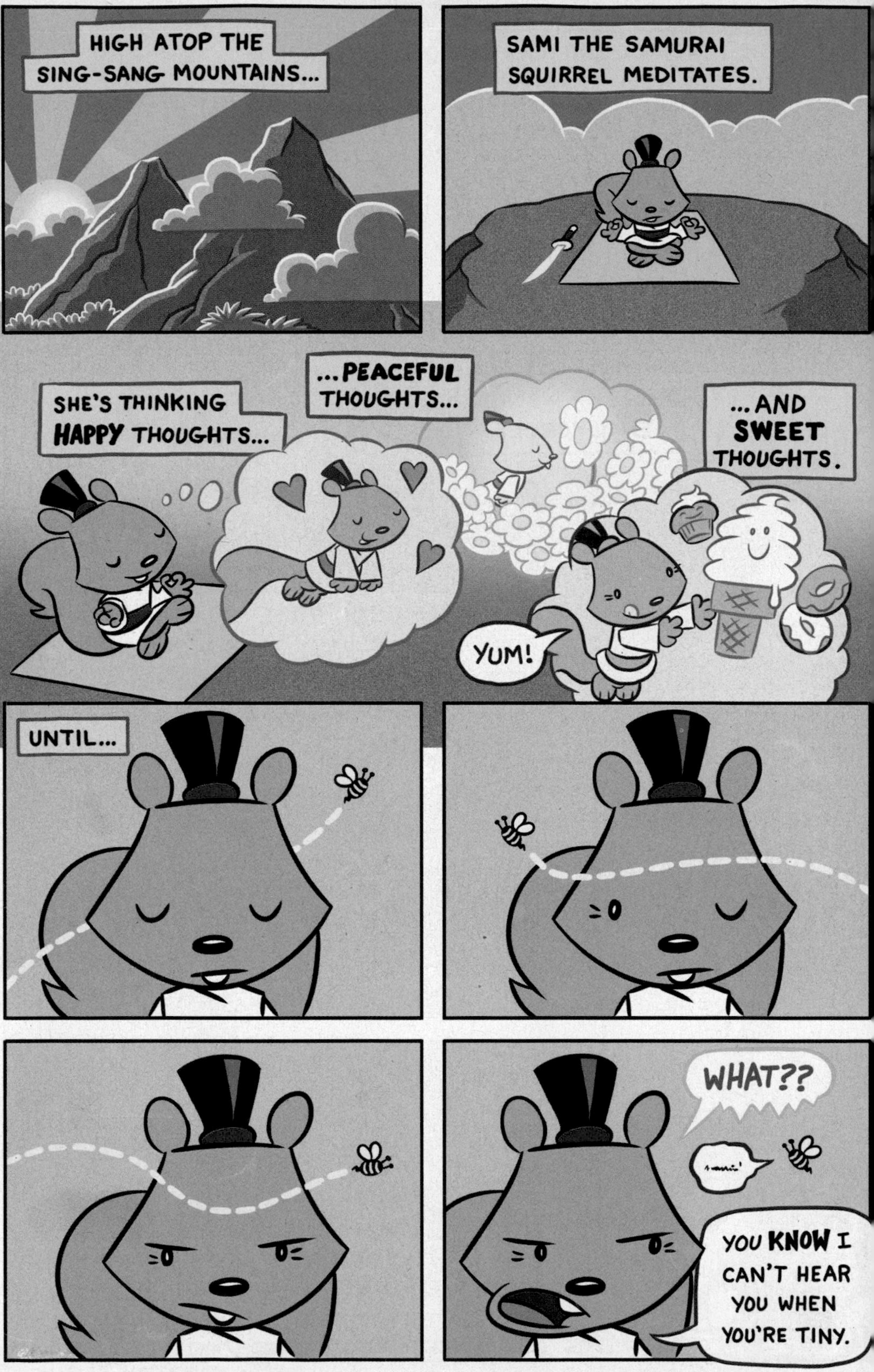
HIGH ATOP THE SING-SANG MOUNTAINS...
SAMI THE SAMURAI SQUIRREL MEDITATES.
SHE'S THINKING HAPPY THOUGHTS...
...PEACEFUL THOUGHTS...
...AND SWEET THOUGHTS.
YUM!
UNTIL...
WHAT??
YOU KNOW I CAN'T HEAR YOU WHEN YOU'RE TINY.

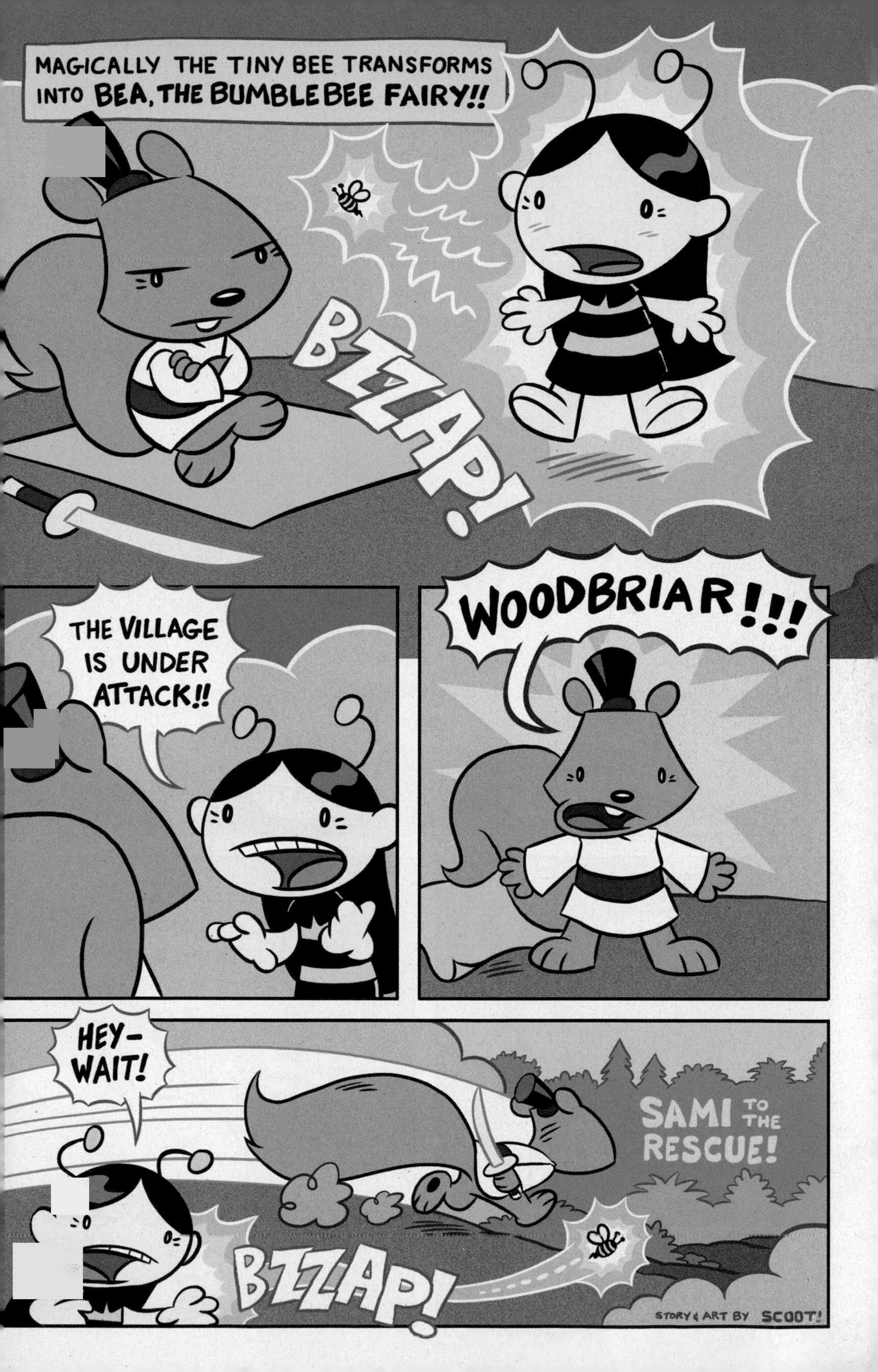

MAGICALLY THE TINY BEE TRANSFORMS INTO BEA, THE BUMBLEBEE FAIRY!!
BZZAP!
THE VILLAGE IS UNDER ATTACK!!
WOODBRIAR!!!
HEY- WAIT!
SAMI TO THE RESCUE!
BZZAP!
STORY & ART BY SCOOT!

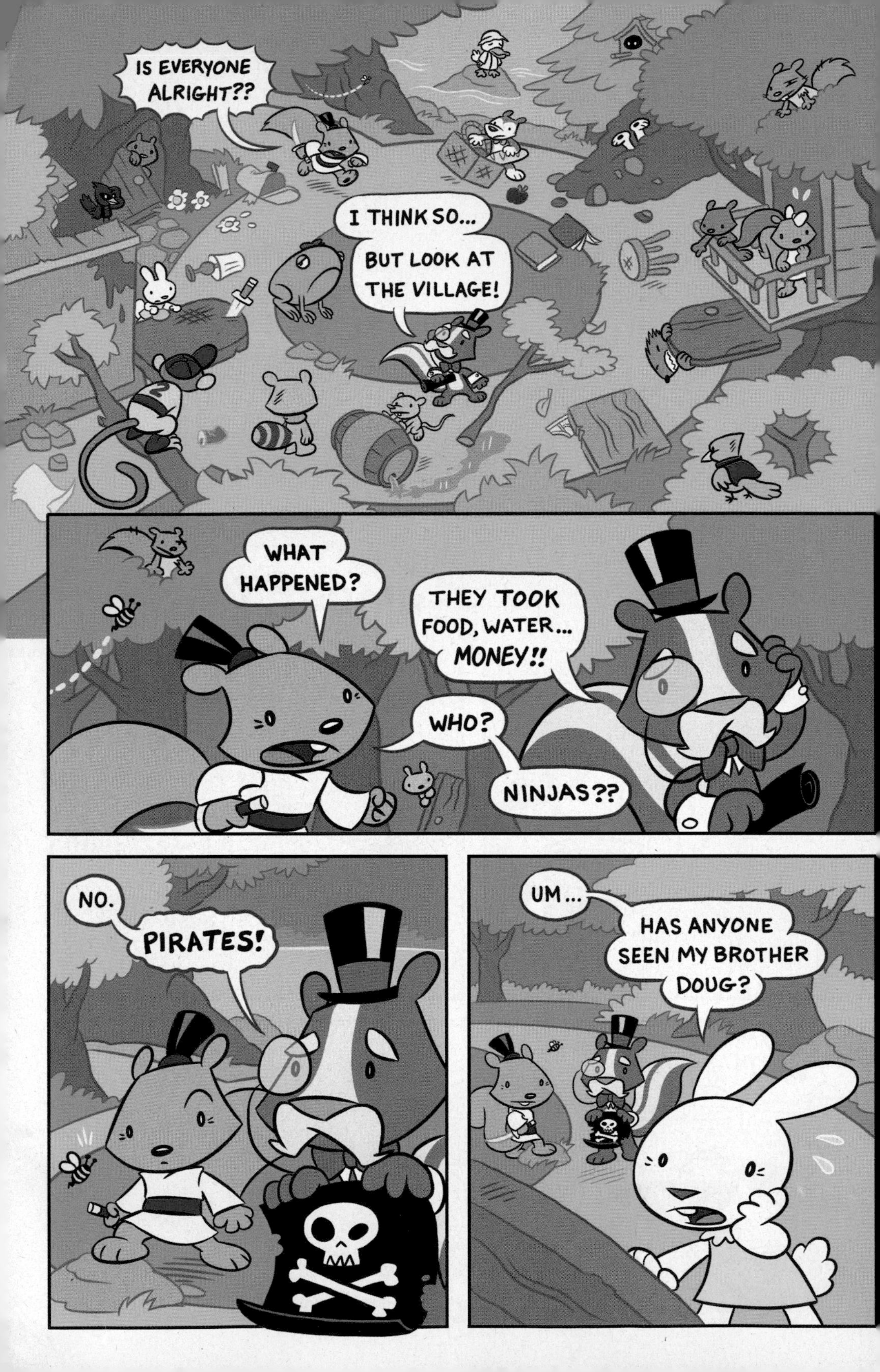
IS EVERYONE ALRIGHT??
I THINK SO...
BUT LOOK AT THE VILLAGE!
WHAT HAPPENED?
THEY TOOK FOOD, WATER... MONEY!!
WHO?
NINJAS??
NO.
PIRATES!
UM...
HAS ANYONE SEEN MY BROTHER DOUG?

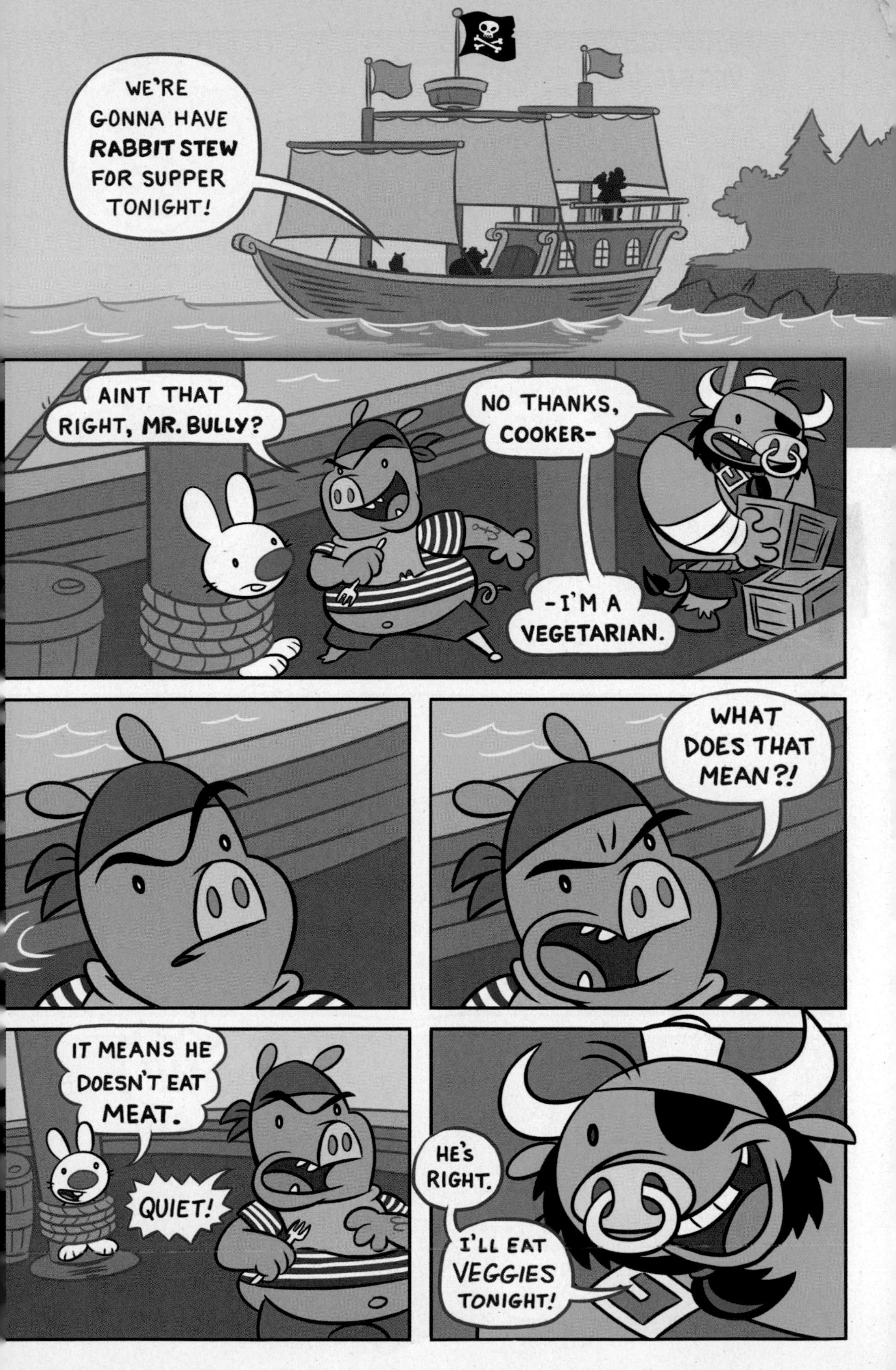
WE'RE GONNA HAVE RABBIT STEW FOR SUPPER TONIGHT!
AINT THAT RIGHT, MR. BULLY?
NO THANKS, COOKER-
-I'M A VEGETARIAN.
WHAT DOES THAT MEAN?!
IT MEANS HE DOESN'T EAT MEAT.
QUIET!
HE'S RIGHT.
I'LL EAT VEGGIES TONIGHT!

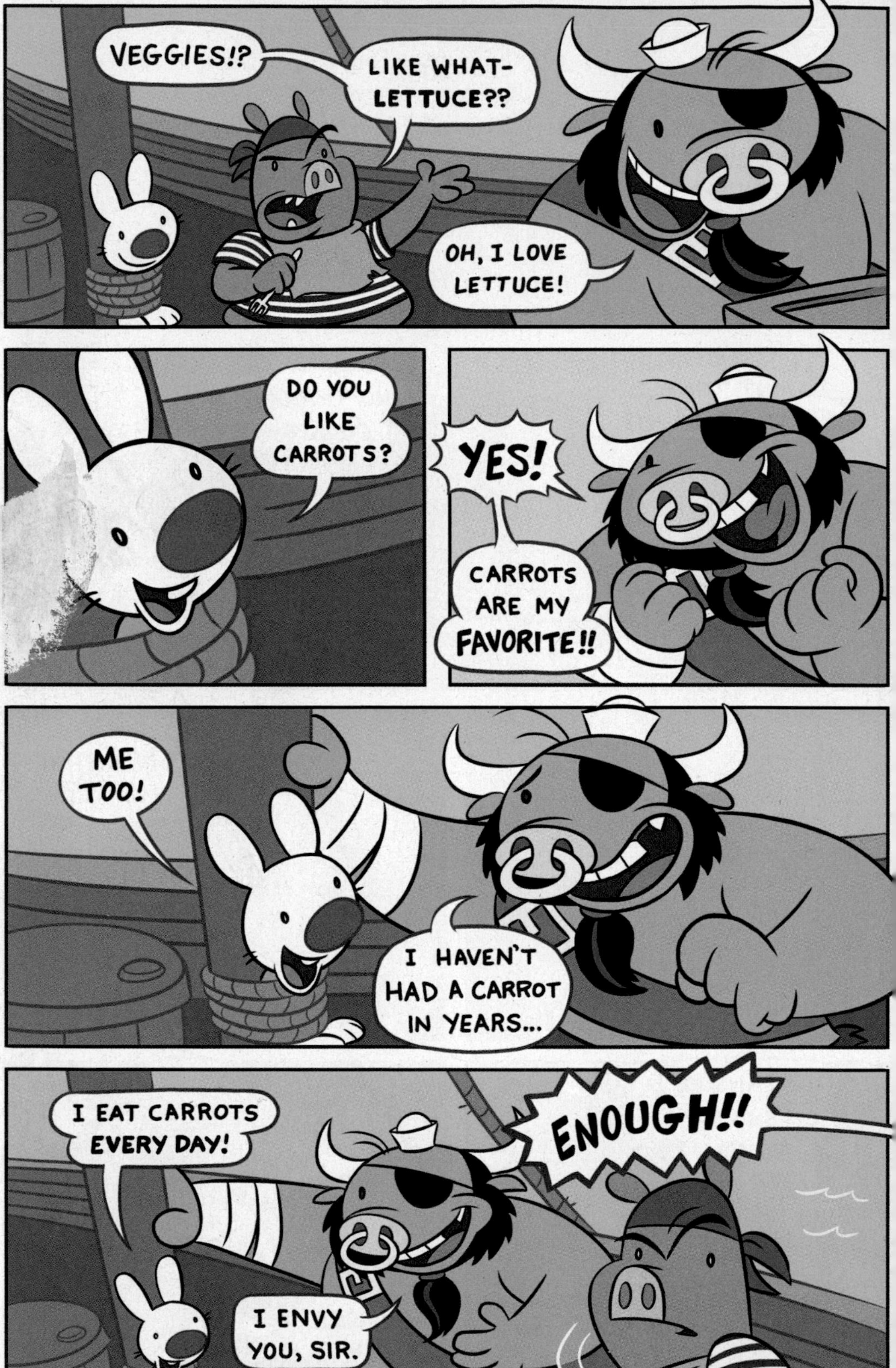
VEGGIES!?
LIKE WHAT- LETTUCE??
OH, I LOVE LETTUCE!
DO YOU LIKE CARROTS?
YES!
CARROTS ARE MY FAVORITE!!
ME TOO!
I HAVEN'T HAD A CARROT IN YEARS...
I EAT CARROTS EVERY DAY!
I ENVY YOU, SIR.
ENOUGH!!

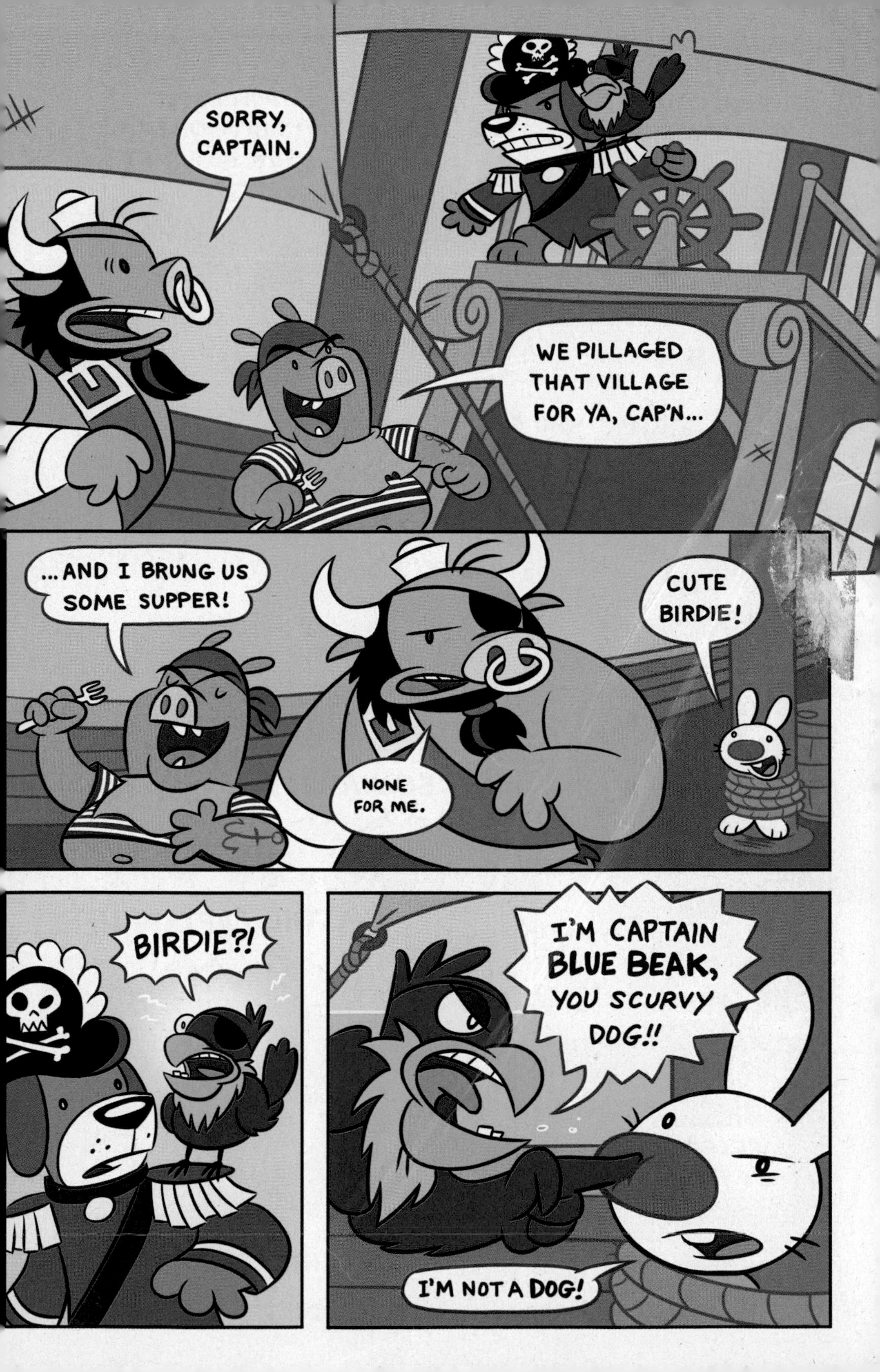
SORRY, CAPTAIN.
WE PILLAGED THAT VILLAGE FOR YA, CAP'N...
...AND I BRUNG US SOME SUPPER!
NONE FOR ME.
CUTE BIRDIE!
BIRDIE?!
I'M CAPTAIN BLUE BEAK, YOU SCURVY DOG!!
I'M NOT A DOG!

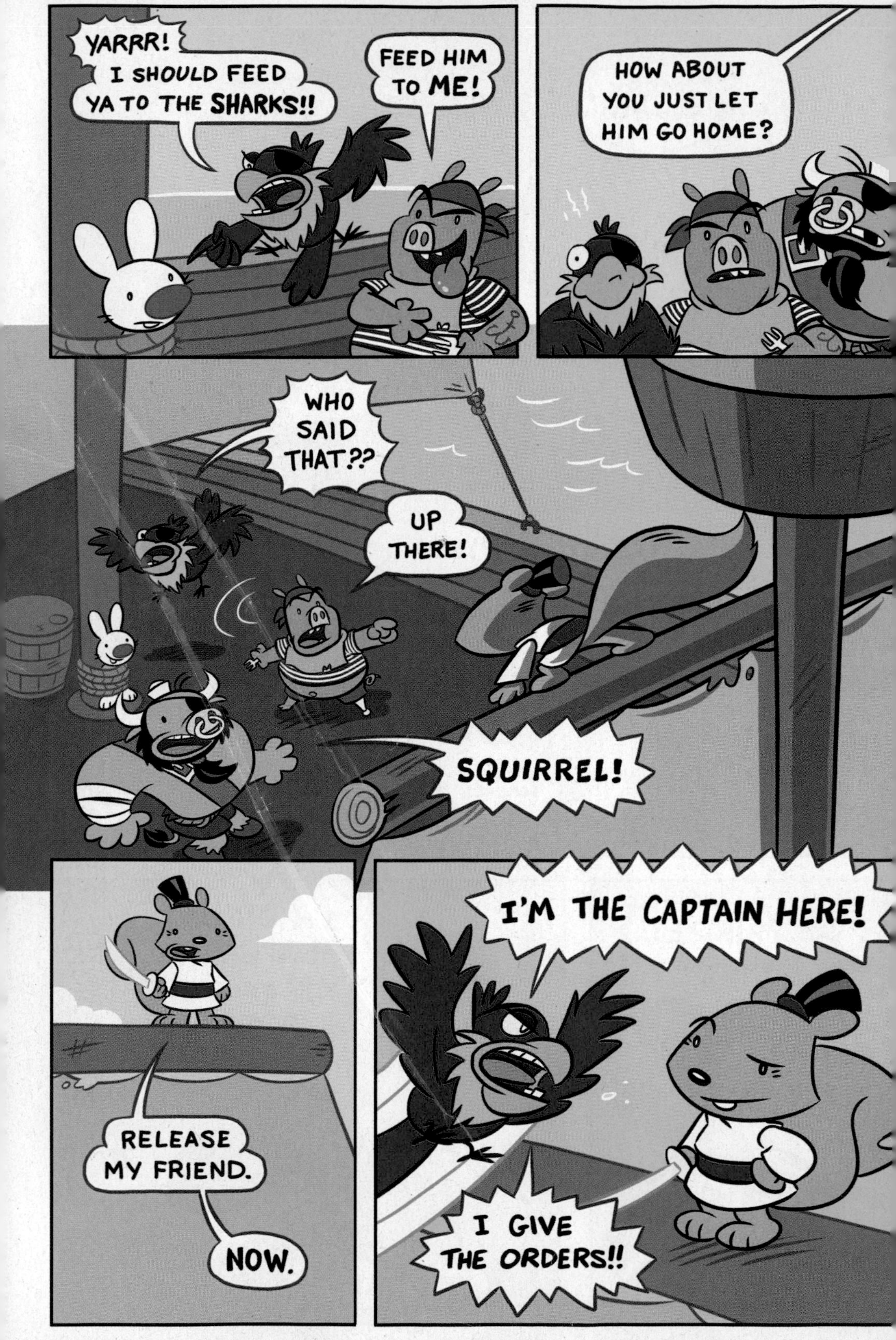
YARRR!
I SHOULD FEED YA TO THE SHARKS!!
FEED HIM TO ME!
HOW ABOUT YOU JUST LET HIM GO HOME?
WHO SAID THAT??
UP THERE!
SQUIRREL!
RELEASE MY FRIEND.
NOW.
I'M THE CAPTAIN HERE!
I GIVE THE ORDERS!!

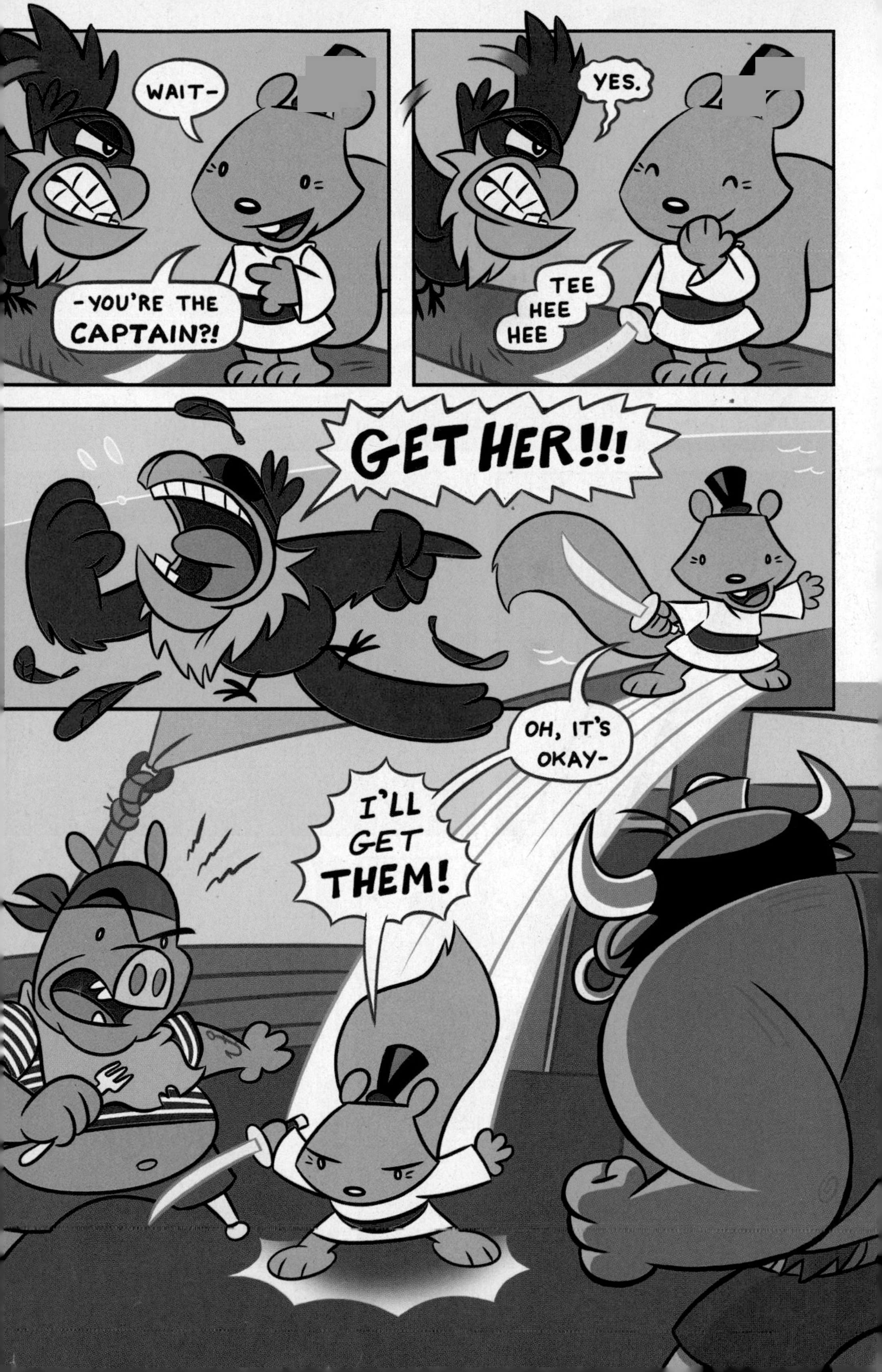
WAIT-
-YOU'RE THE CAPTAIN?!
YES.
TEE HEE HEE
GET HER!!!
OH, IT'S OKAY-
I'LL GET THEM!

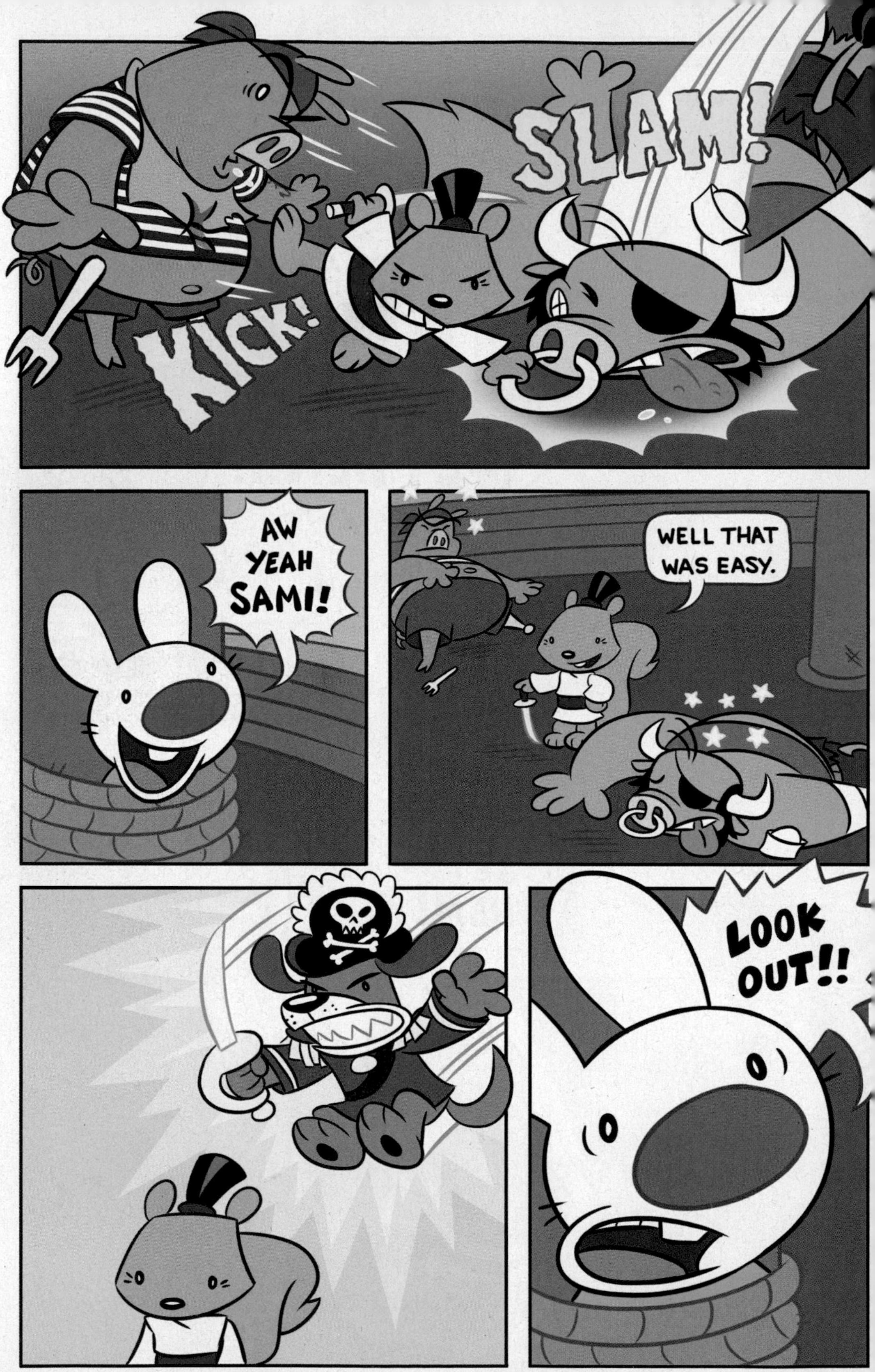
SLAM!
KICK!
AW YEAH SAMI!
WELL THAT WAS EASY.
LOOK OUT!!

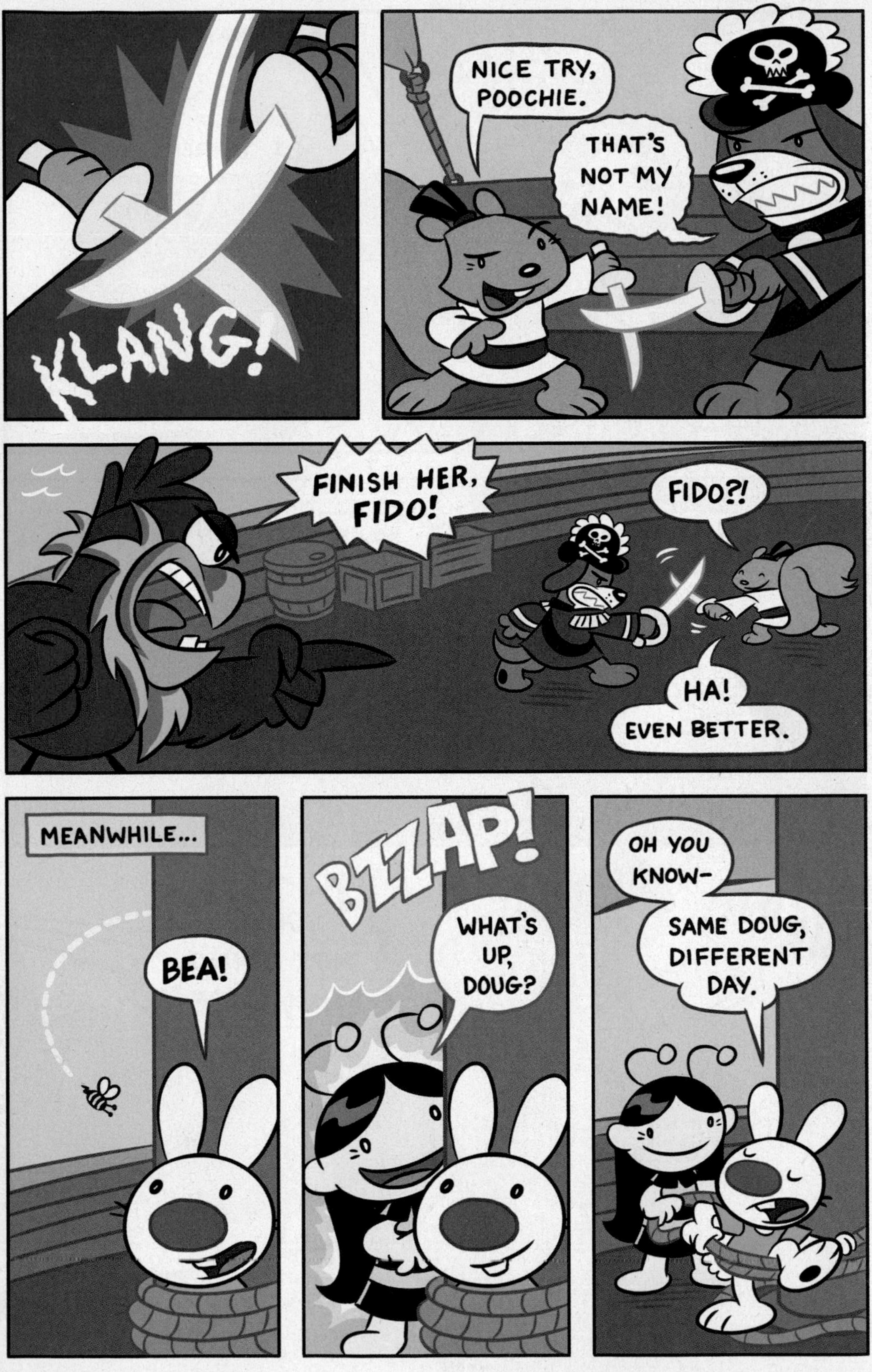
KLANG!
NICE TRY, POOCHIE.
THAT'S NOT MY NAME!
FINISH HER, FIDO!
FIDO?!
HA! EVEN BETTER.
MEANWHILE...
BEA!
BZZAP!
WHAT'S UP, DOUG?
OH YOU KNOW-
SAME DOUG, DIFFERENT DAY.

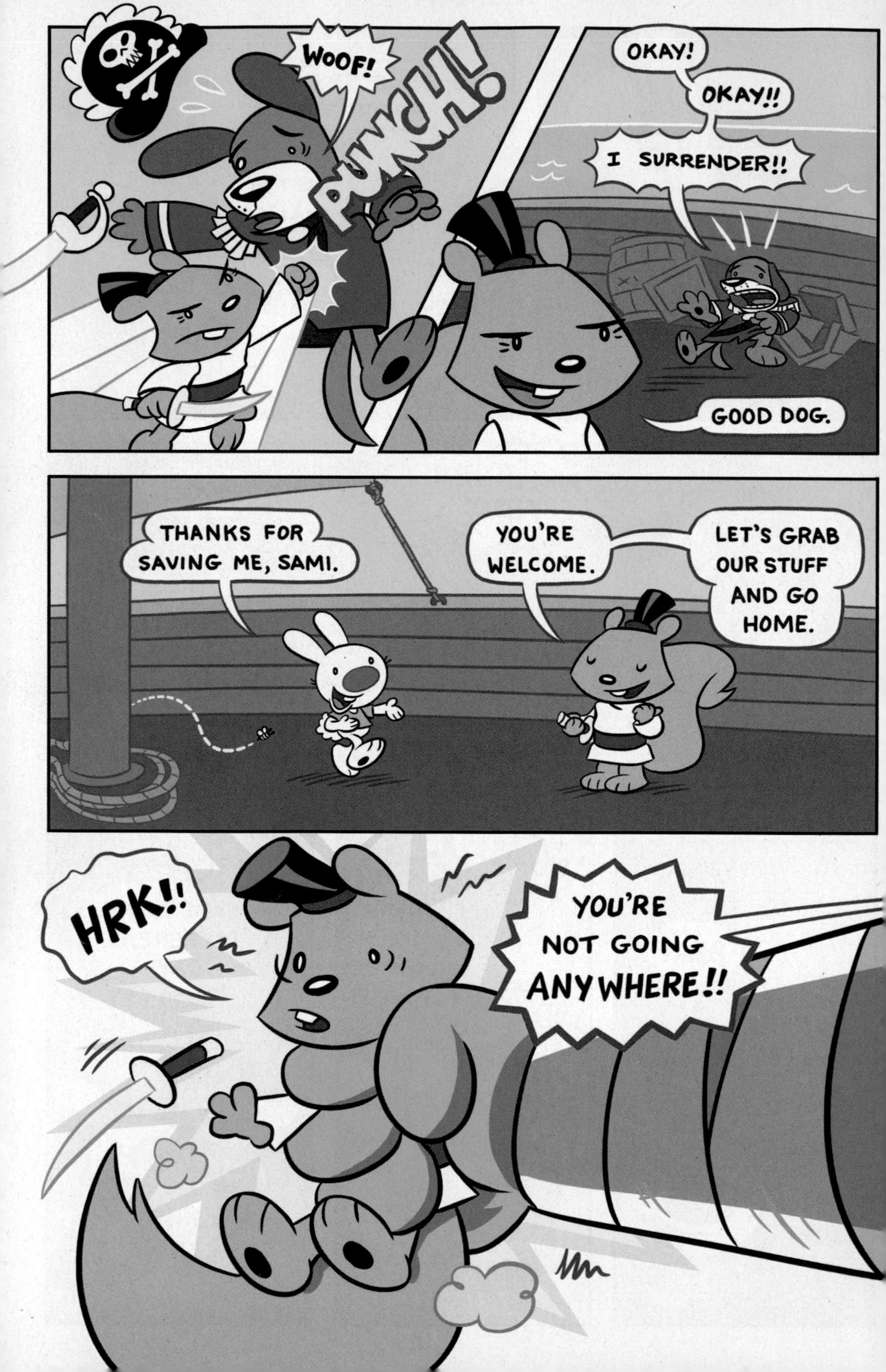
WOOF!
PUNCH!
OKAY!
OKAY!!
I SURRENDER!!
GOOD DOG.
THANKS FOR SAVING ME, SAMI.
YOU'RE WELCOME.
LET'S GRAB OUR STUFF AND GO HOME.
HRK!!
YOU'RE NOT GOING ANYWHERE!!

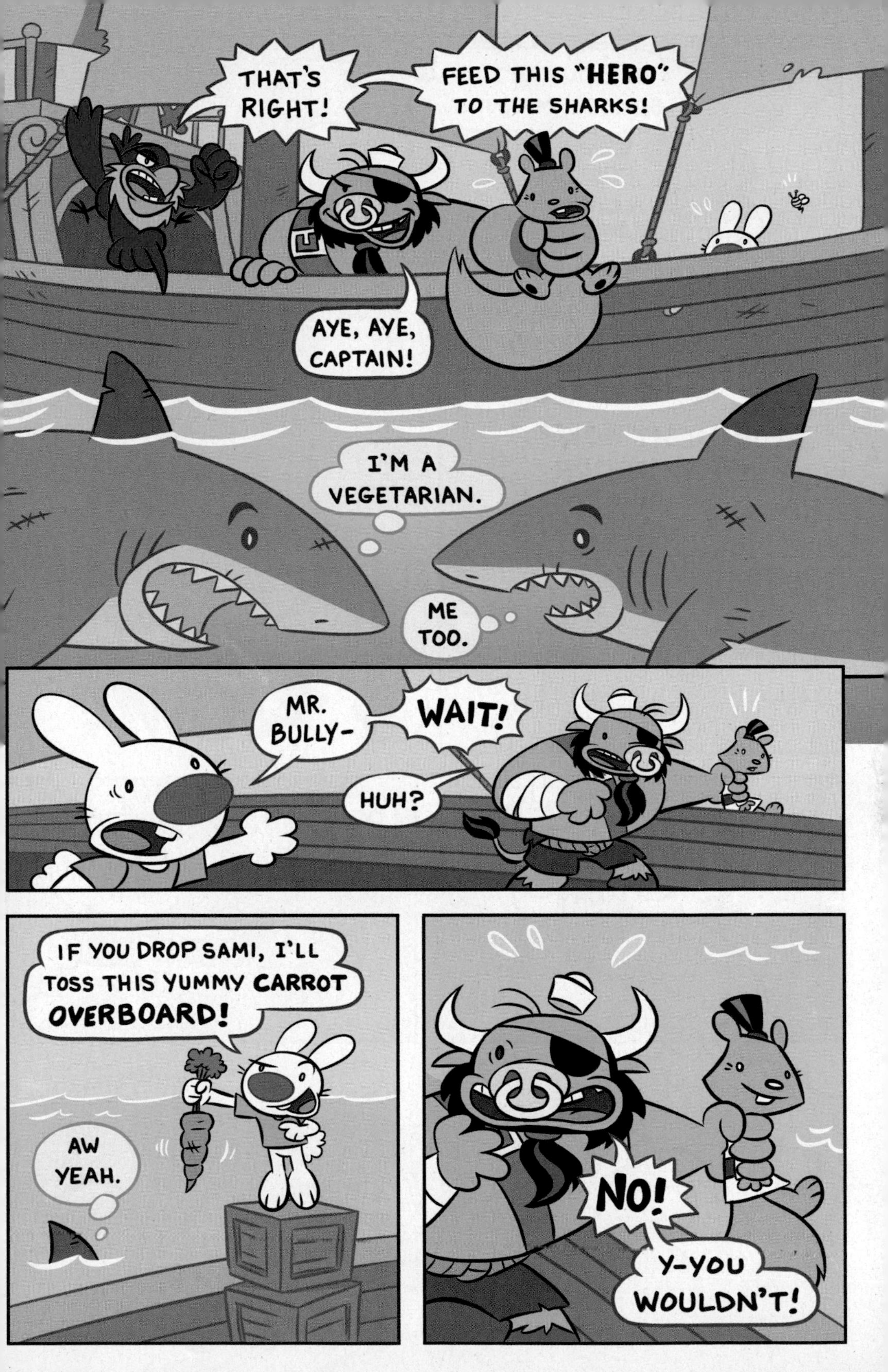
THAT'S RIGHT!
FEED THIS "HERO" TO THE SHARKS!
AYE, AYE, CAPTAIN!
I'M A VEGETARIAN.
ME TOO.
MR. BULLY-
WAIT!
HUH?
IF YOU DROP SAMI, I'LL TOSS THIS YUMMY CARROT OVERBOARD!
AW YEAH.
NO!
Y-YOU WOULDN'T!

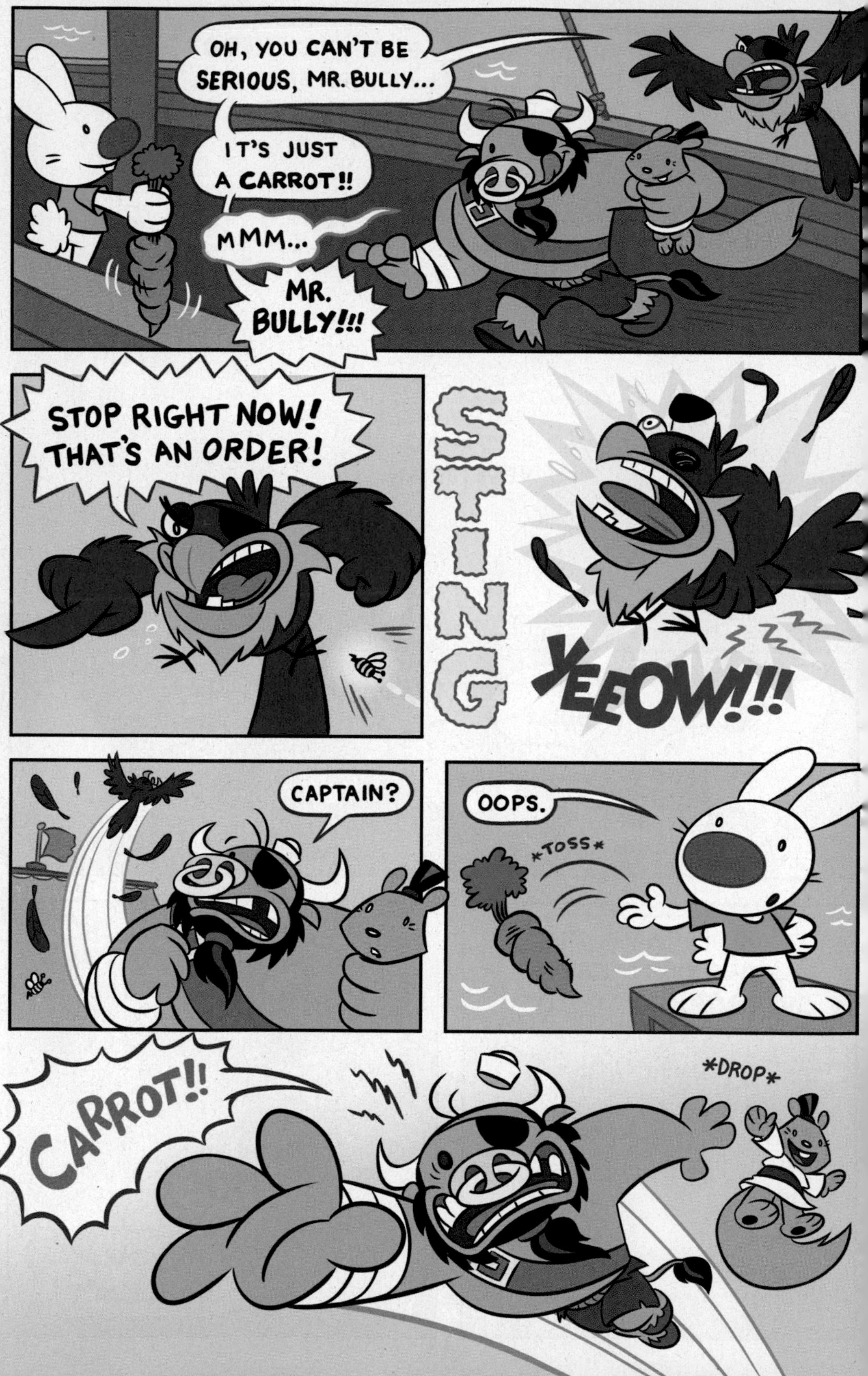
OH, YOU CAN'T BE SERIOUS, MR. BULLY...
IT'S JUST A CARROT!!
MMM...
MR. BULLY!!!
STOP RIGHT NOW! THAT'S AN ORDER!
STING
YEEOW!!!
CAPTAIN?
OOPS.
TOSS
CARROT!!
DROP

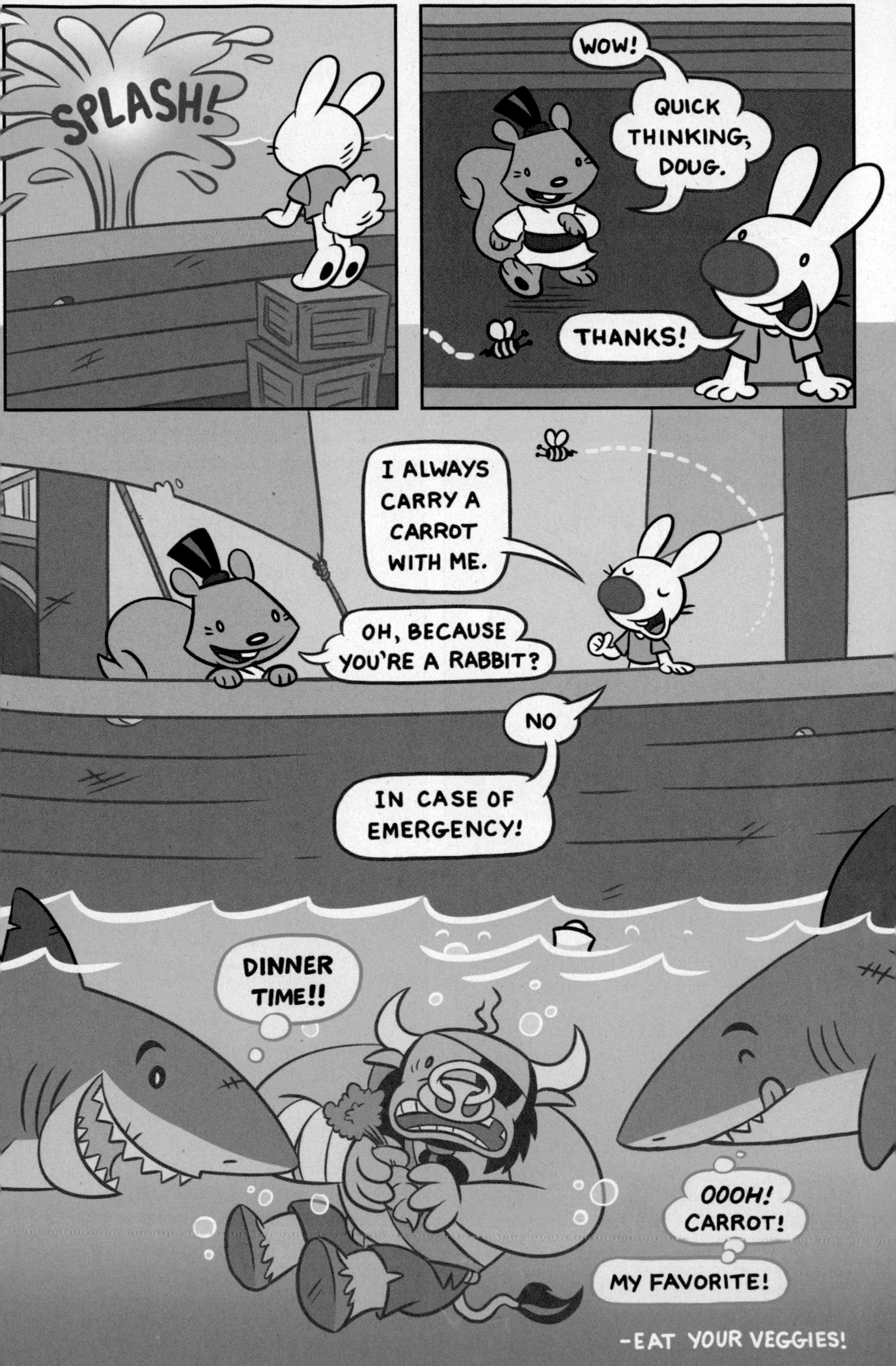
SPLASH!
WOW!
QUICK THINKING, DOUG.
THANKS!
I ALWAYS CARRY A CARROT WITH ME.
OH, BECAUSE YOU'RE A RABBIT?
NO
IN CASE OF EMERGENCY!
DINNER TIME!!
OOOH! CARROT!
MY FAVORITE!
-EAT YOUR VEGGIES!

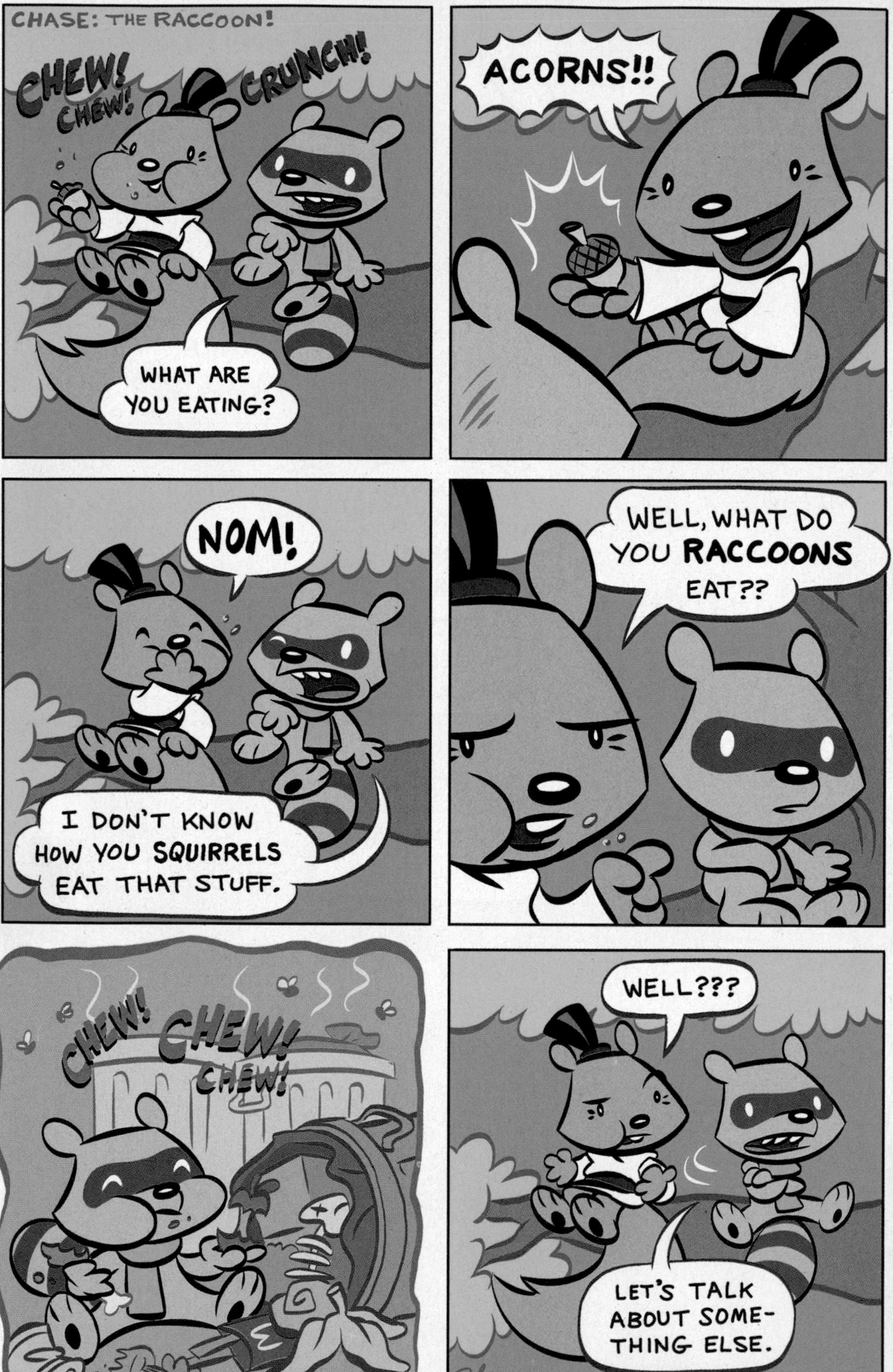
CHASE: THE RACCOON!
CHEW! CHEW!
CRUNCH!
WHAT ARE YOU EATING?
ACORNS!!
NOM!
I DON'T KNOW HOW YOU SQUIRRELS EAT THAT STUFF.
WELL, WHAT DO YOU RACCOONS EAT??
CHEW! CHEW! CHEW!
WELL???
LET'S TALK ABOUT SOME-THING ELSE.
— BREATH MINT PLEASE.

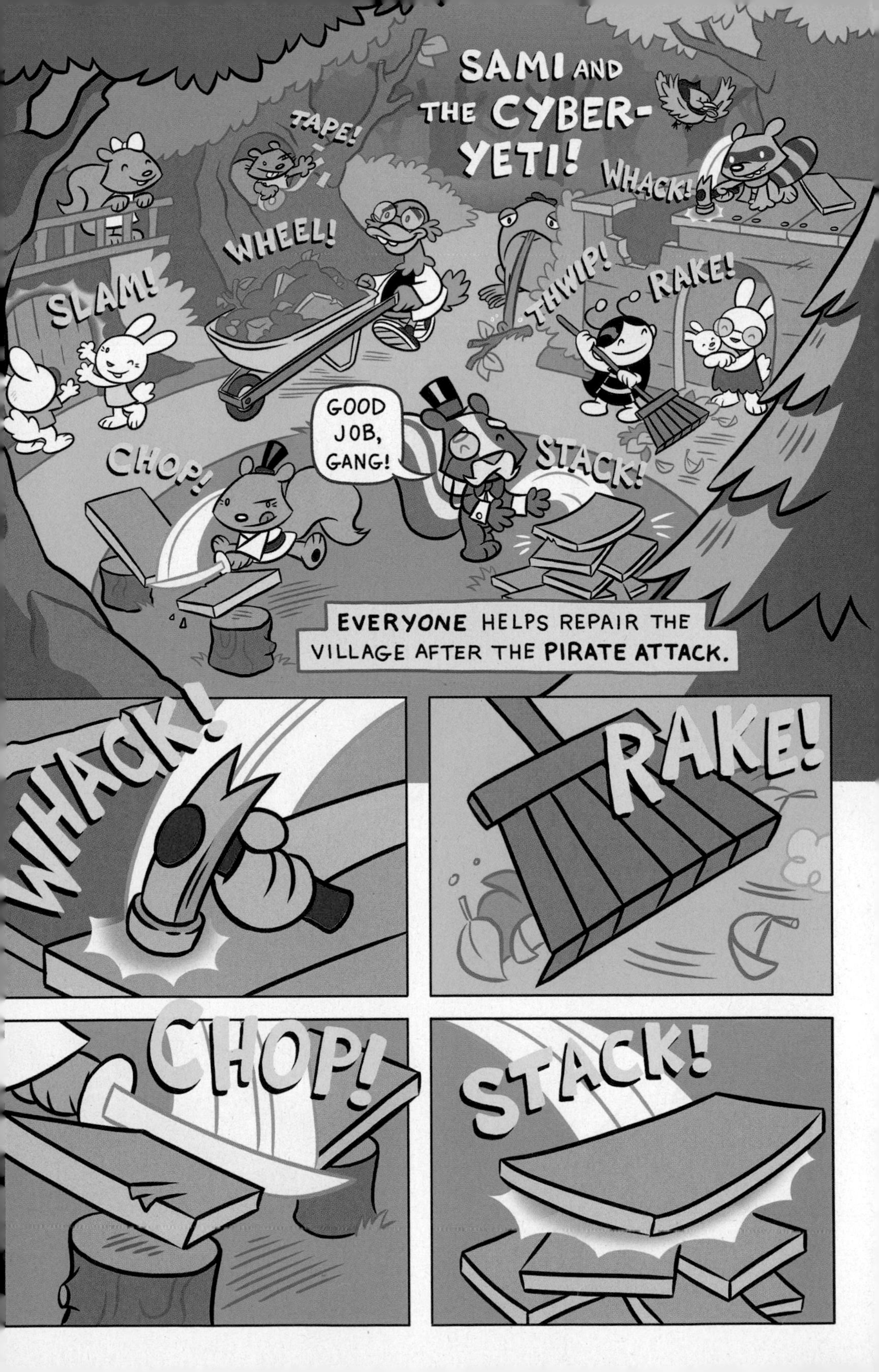
SAMI AND THE CYBER-YETI!
TAPE!
WHACK!
WHEEL!
SLAM!
THWIP!
RAKE!
GOOD JOB, GANG!
CHOP!
STACK!
EVERYONE HELPS REPAIR THE VILLAGE AFTER THE PIRATE ATTACK.
WHACK!
RAKE!
CHOP!
STACK!

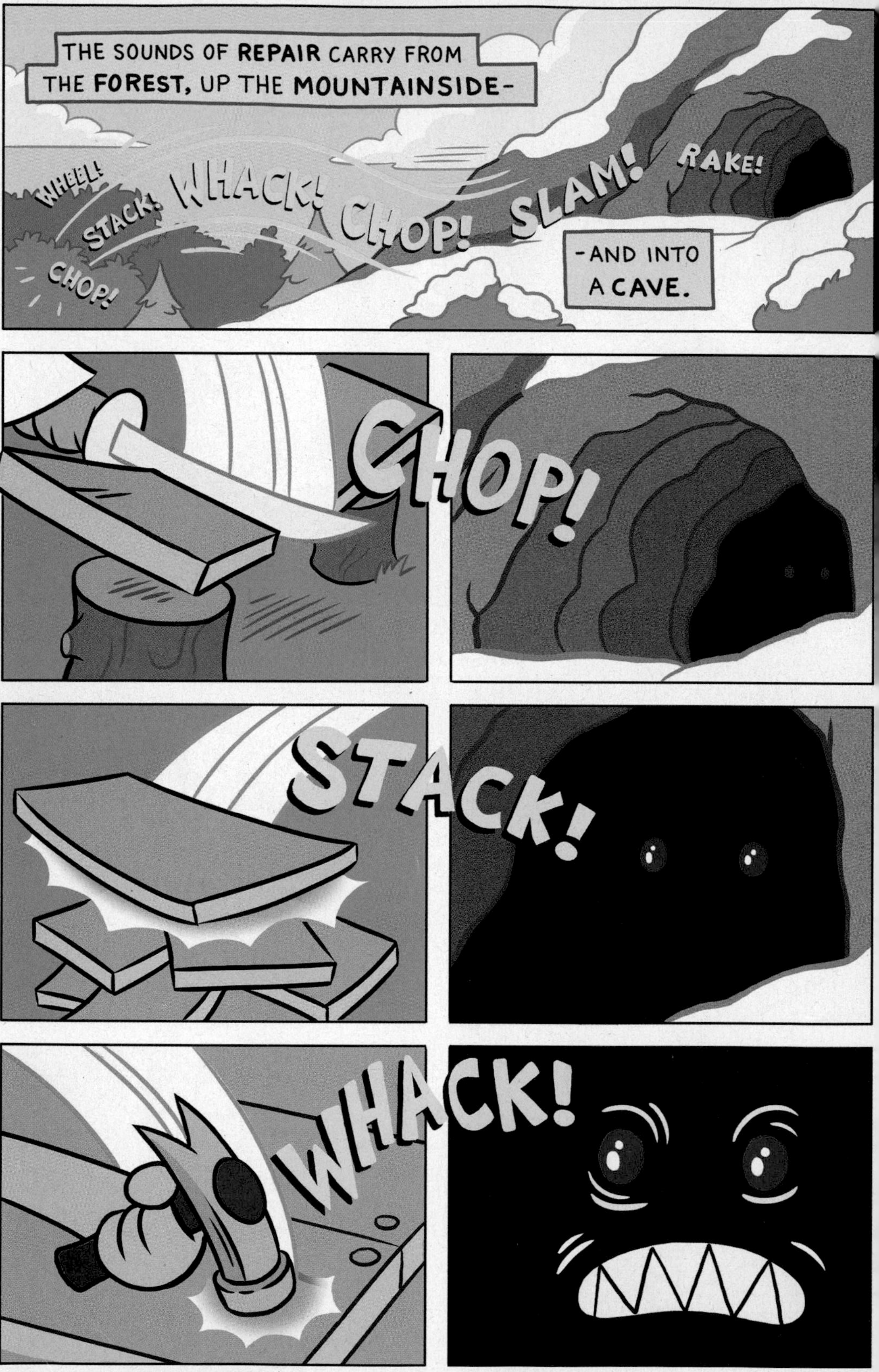
THE SOUNDS OF **REPAIR** CARRY FROM THE **FOREST**, UP THE **MOUNTAINSIDE**-
WHEEL!
STACK!
WHACK!
CHOP!
CHOP!
SLAM!
RAKE!
-AND INTO A **CAVE**.
CHOP!
STACK!
WHACK!

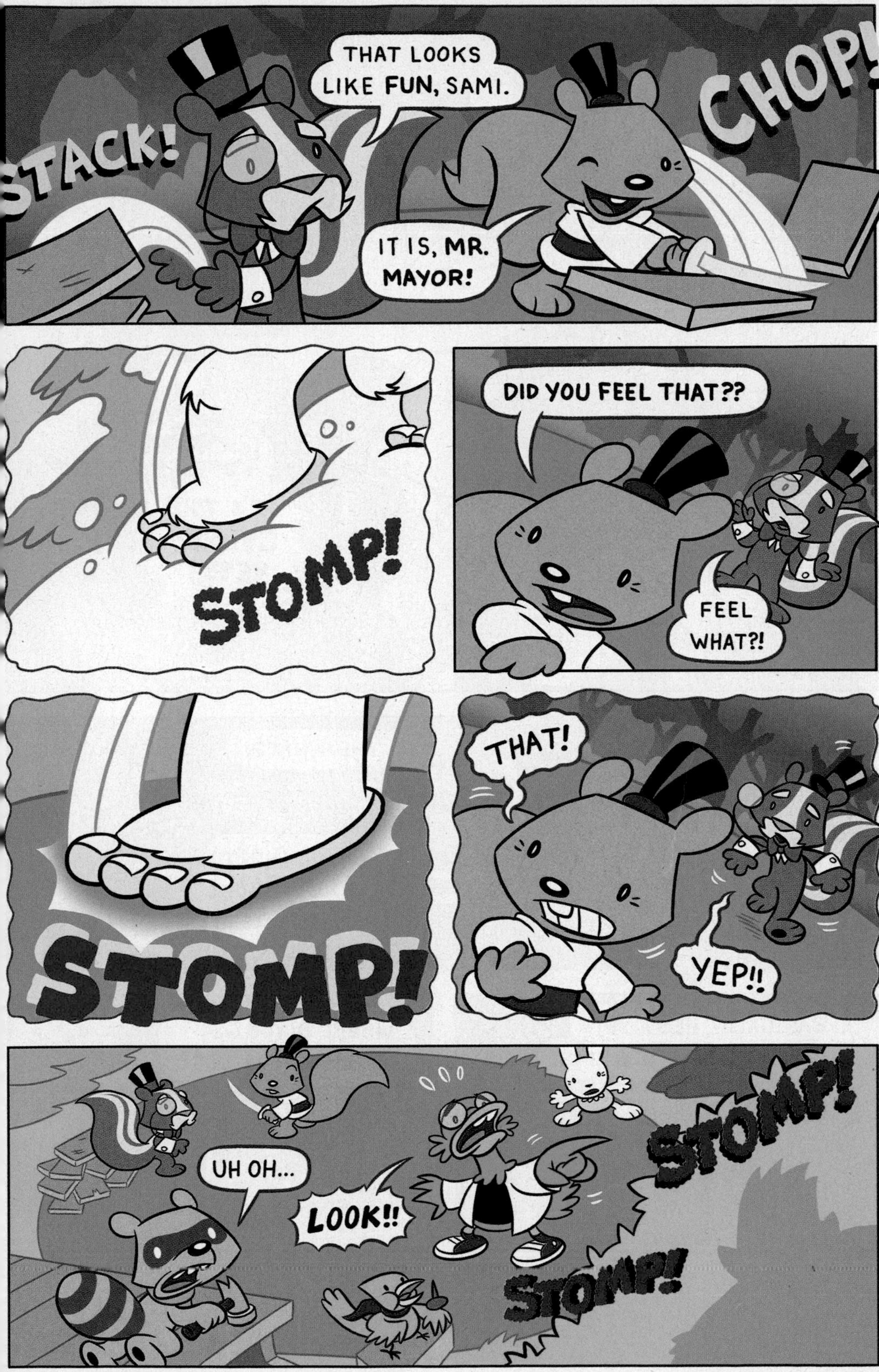
STACK!
THAT LOOKS LIKE FUN, SAMI.
IT IS, MR. MAYOR!
CHOP!
STOMP!
DID YOU FEEL THAT??
FEEL WHAT?!
STOMP!
THAT!
YEP!!
UH OH...
LOOK!!
STOMP!
STOMP!

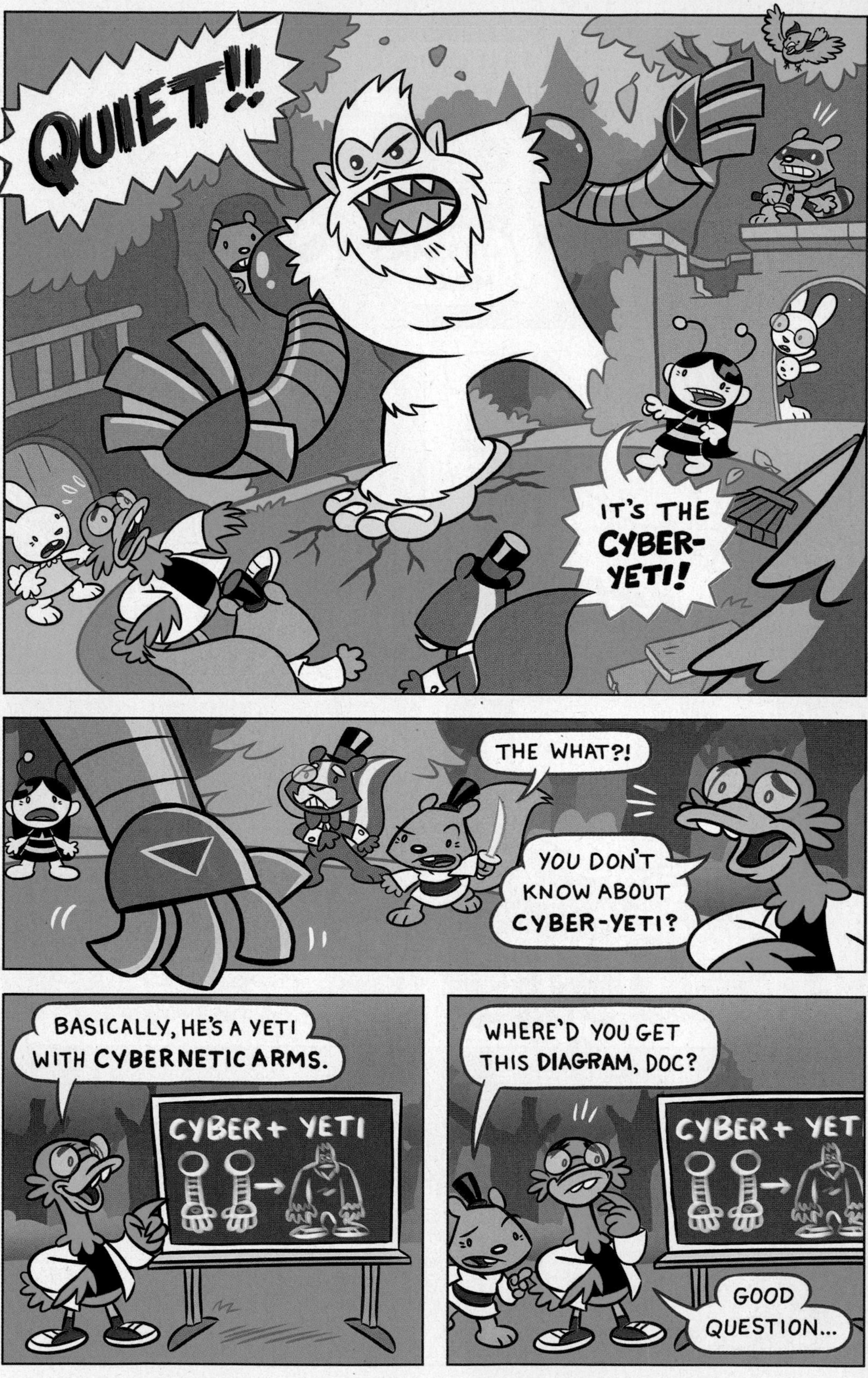
QUIET!!
IT'S THE CYBER-YETI!
THE WHAT?!
YOU DON'T KNOW ABOUT CYBER-YETI?
BASICALLY, HE'S A YETI WITH CYBERNETIC ARMS.
CYBER + YETI
WHERE'D YOU GET THIS DIAGRAM, DOC?
GOOD QUESTION...

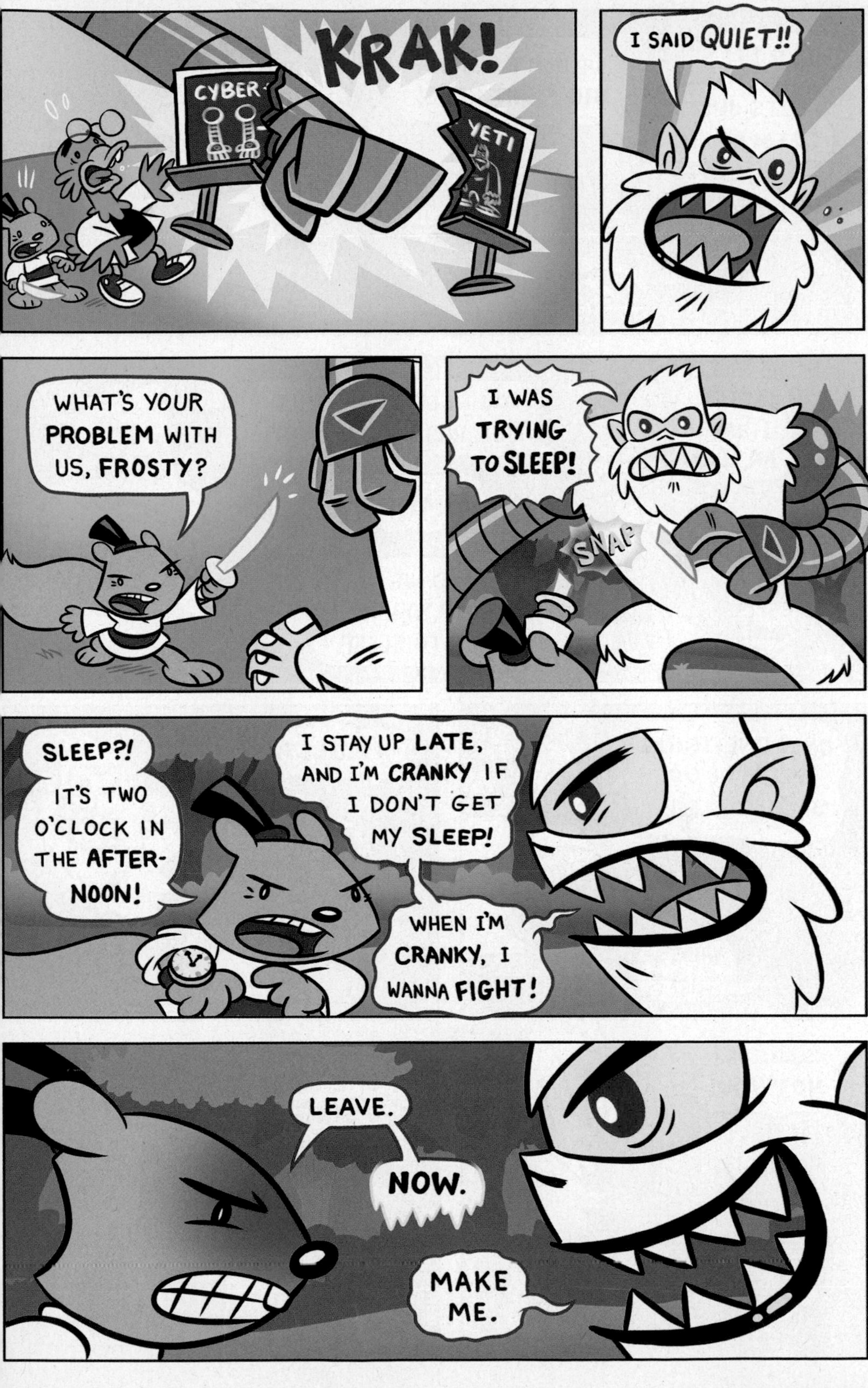
KRAK!
CYBER-
YETI
I SAID QUIET!!
WHAT'S YOUR PROBLEM WITH US, FROSTY?
I WAS TRYING TO SLEEP!
SNAP
SLEEP?! IT'S TWO O'CLOCK IN THE AFTER-NOON!
I STAY UP LATE, AND I'M CRANKY IF I DON'T GET MY SLEEP!
WHEN I'M CRANKY, I WANNA FIGHT!
LEAVE.
NOW.
MAKE ME.

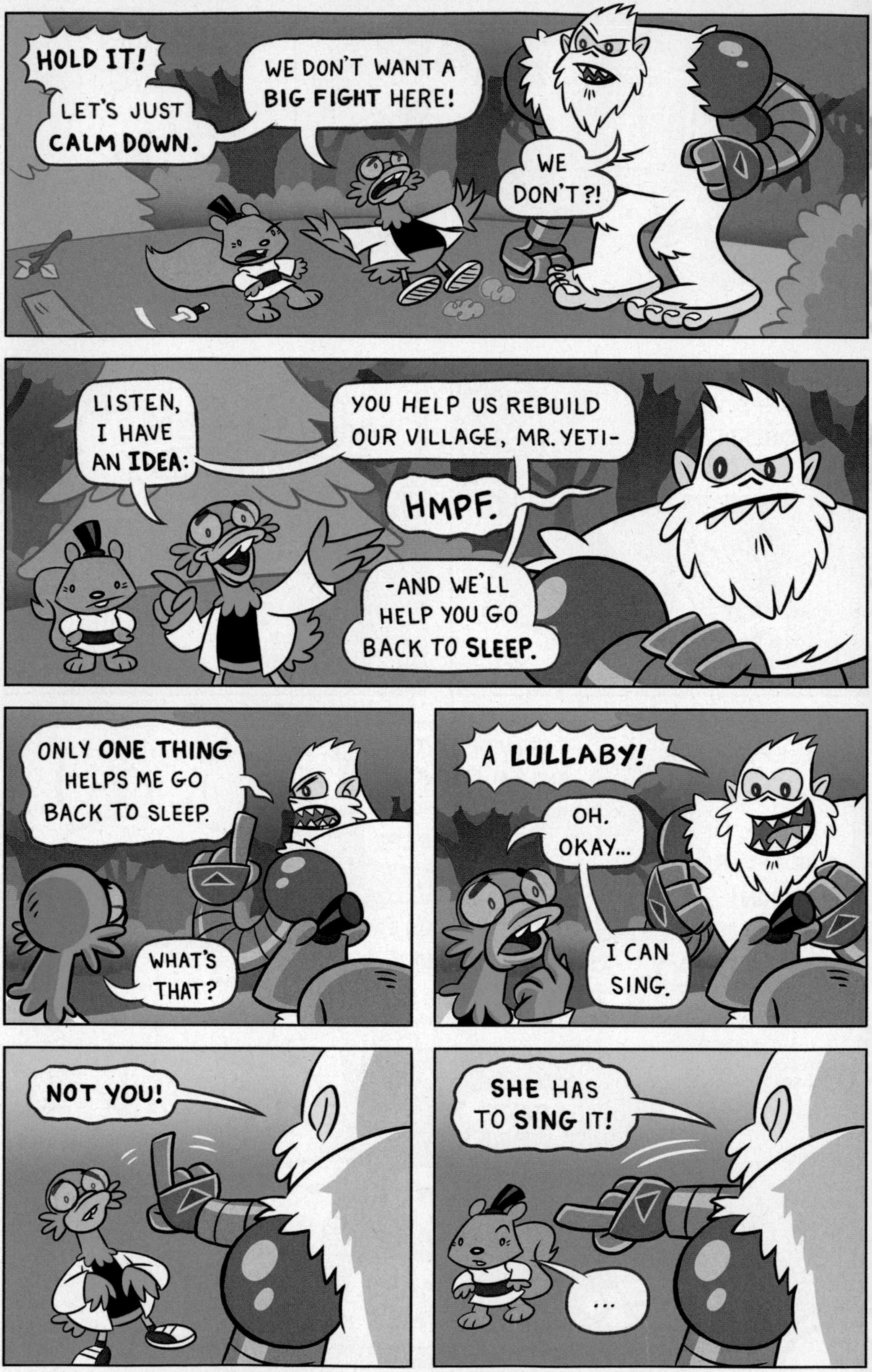
HOLD IT!
LET'S JUST CALM DOWN.
WE DON'T WANT A BIG FIGHT HERE!
WE DON'T?!
LISTEN, I HAVE AN IDEA:
YOU HELP US REBUILD OUR VILLAGE, MR. YETI-
HMPF.
-AND WE'LL HELP YOU GO BACK TO SLEEP.
ONLY ONE THING HELPS ME GO BACK TO SLEEP.
WHAT'S THAT?
A LULLABY!
OH. OKAY...
I CAN SING.
NOT YOU!
SHE HAS TO SING IT!
...

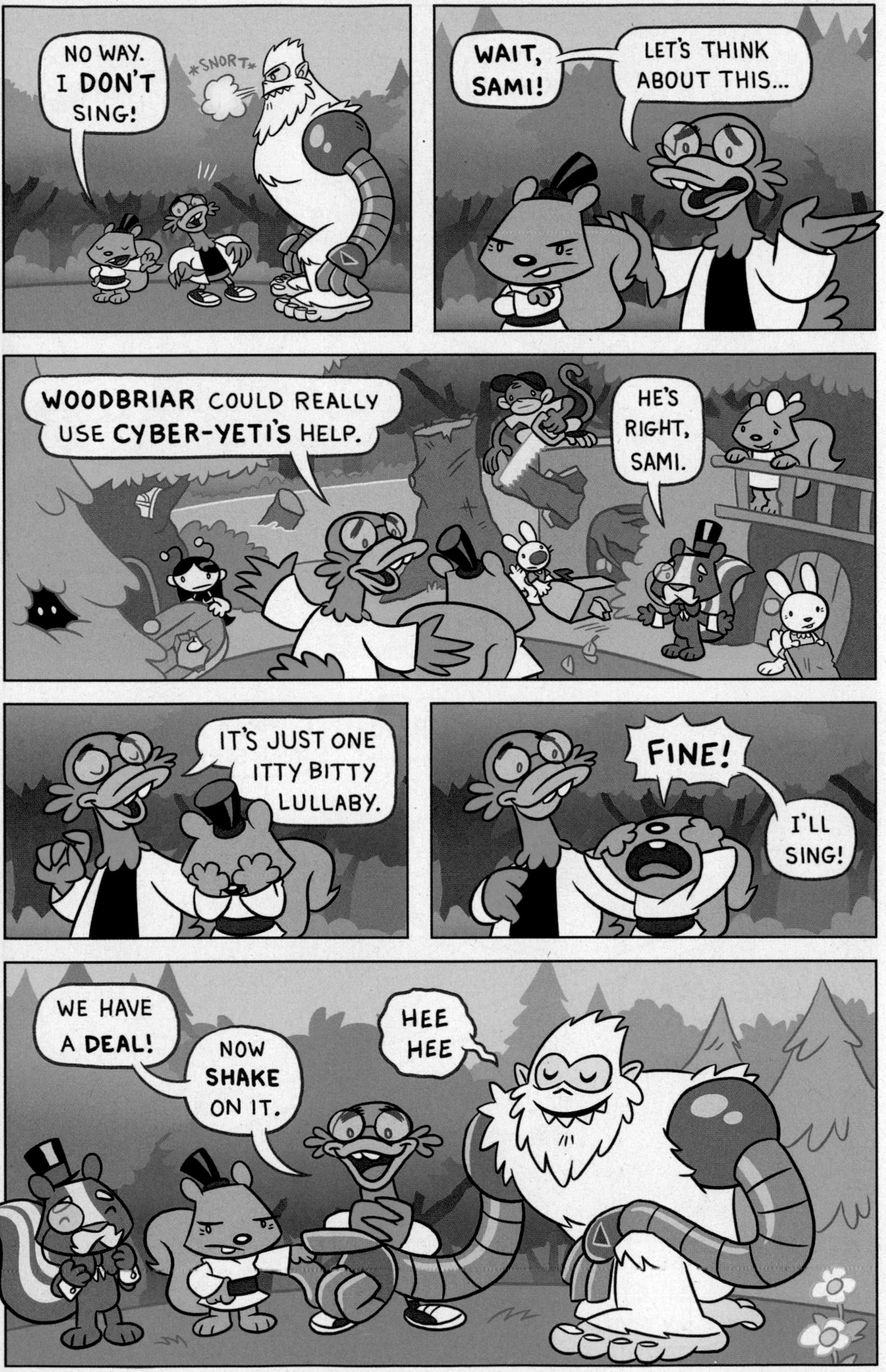
NO WAY. I DON'T SING!
SNORT
WAIT, SAMI!
LET'S THINK ABOUT THIS...
WOODBRIAR COULD REALLY USE CYBER-YETI'S HELP.
HE'S RIGHT, SAMI.
IT'S JUST ONE ITTY BITTY LULLABY.
FINE!
I'LL SING!
WE HAVE A DEAL!
NOW SHAKE ON IT.
HEE HEE

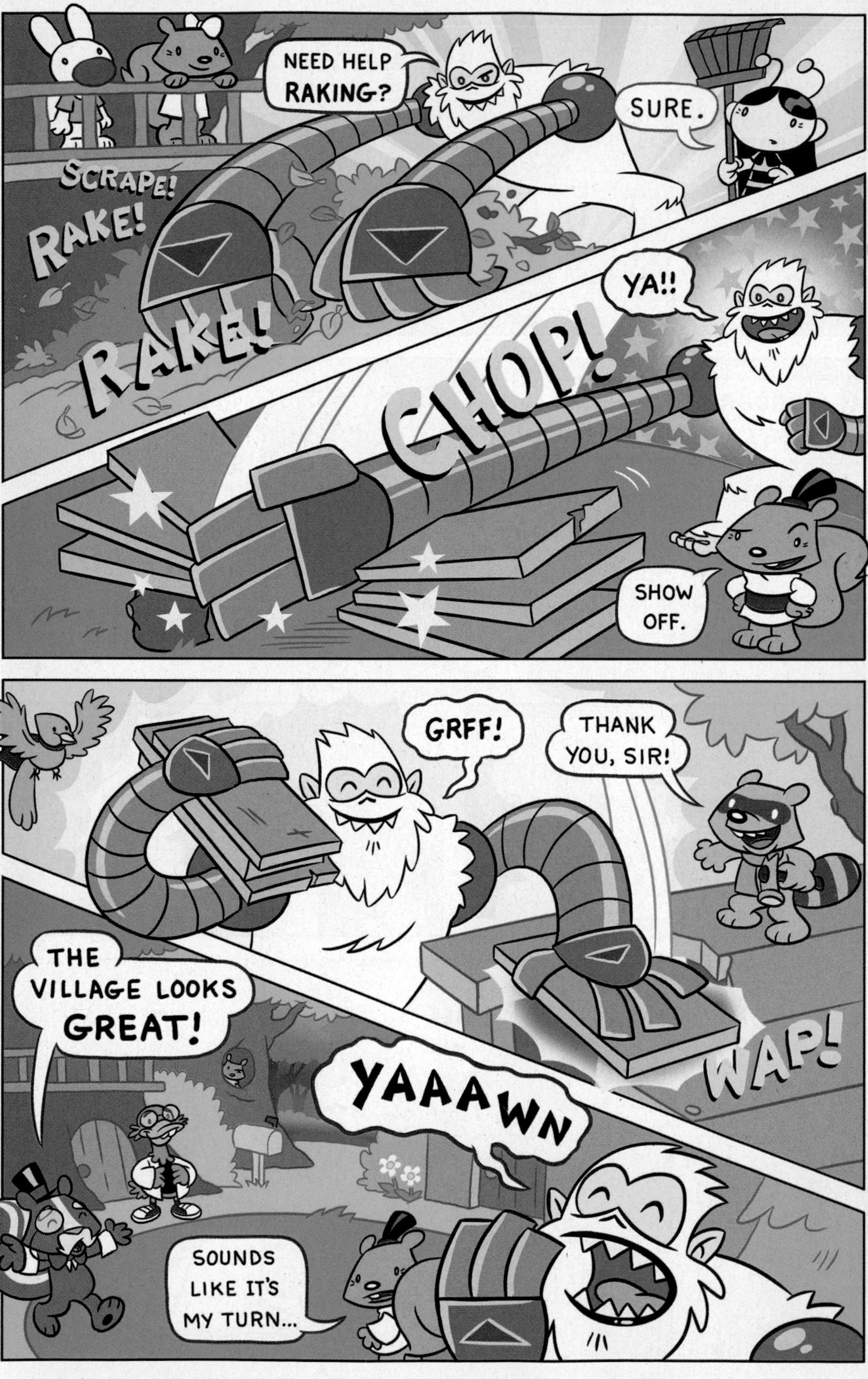
NEED HELP RAKING?
SURE.
SCRAPE!
RAKE!
RAKE!
YA!!
CHOP!
SHOW OFF.
GRFF!
THANK YOU, SIR!
WAP!
THE VILLAGE LOOKS GREAT!
YAAAWN
SOUNDS LIKE IT'S MY TURN...

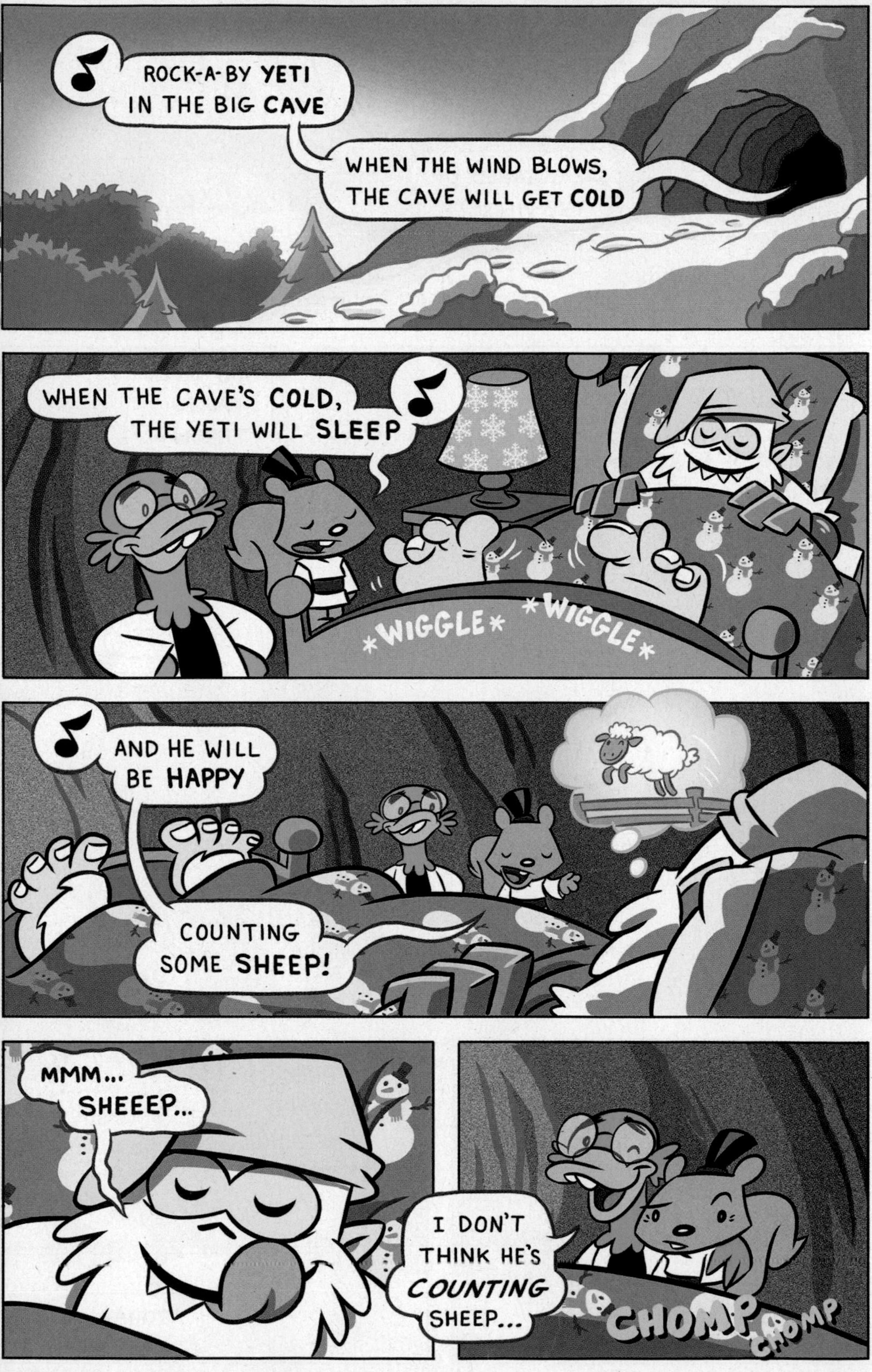
ROCK-A-BY YETI IN THE BIG CAVE
WHEN THE WIND BLOWS, THE CAVE WILL GET COLD
WHEN THE CAVE'S COLD, THE YETI WILL SLEEP
WIGGLE *WIGGLE*
AND HE WILL BE HAPPY
COUNTING SOME SHEEP!
MMM... SHEEEP...
I DON'T THINK HE'S COUNTING SHEEP...
CHOMP CHOMP

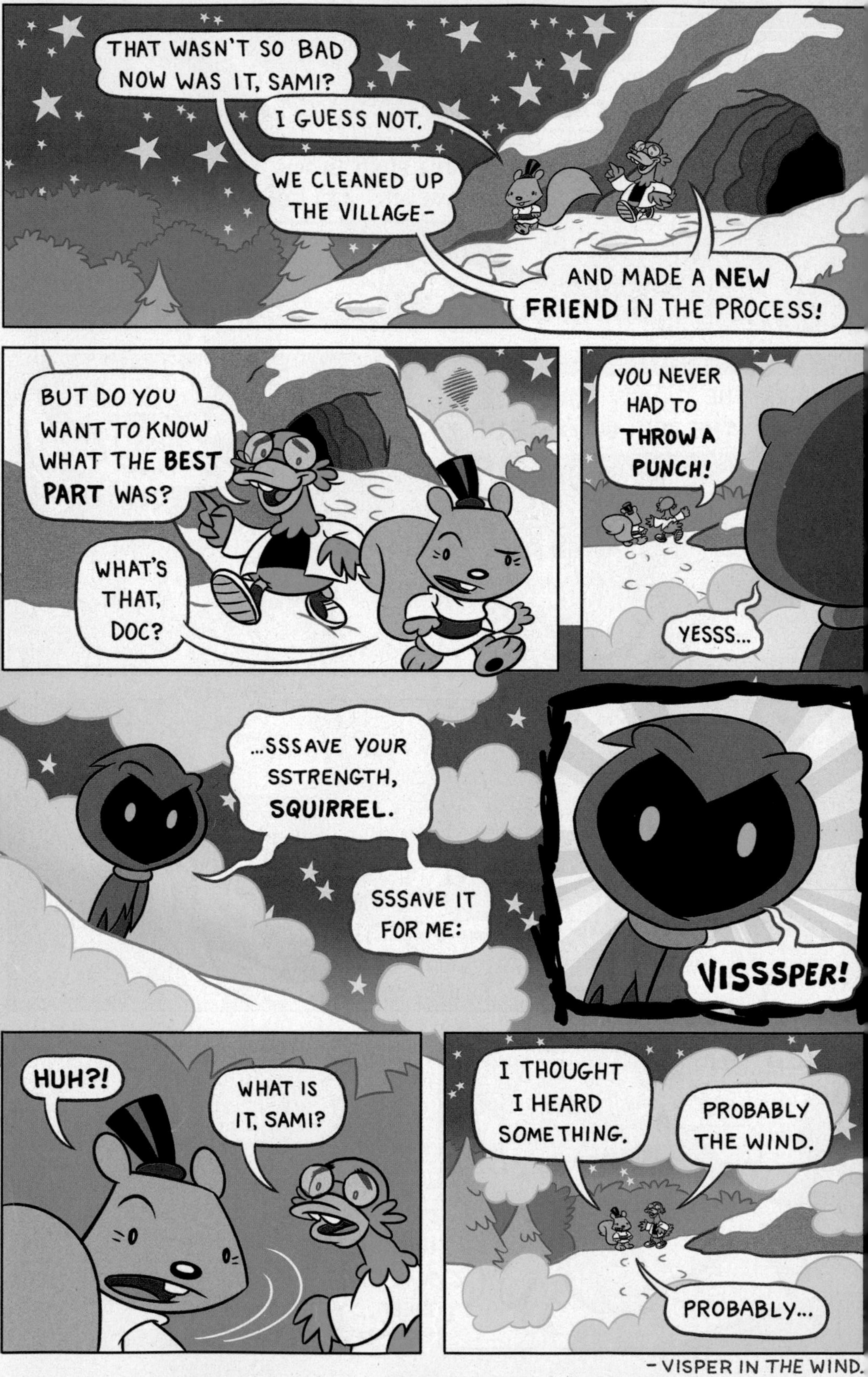
THAT WASN'T SO BAD NOW WAS IT, SAMI?
I GUESS NOT.
WE CLEANED UP THE VILLAGE-
AND MADE A **NEW FRIEND** IN THE PROCESS!
BUT DO YOU WANT TO KNOW WHAT THE **BEST PART** WAS?
WHAT'S THAT, DOC?
YOU NEVER HAD TO **THROW A PUNCH!**
YESSS...
...SSSAVE YOUR SSTRENGTH, **SQUIRREL.**
SSSAVE IT FOR ME:
VISSSPER!
HUH?!
WHAT IS IT, SAMI?
I THOUGHT I HEARD SOMETHING.
PROBABLY THE WIND.
PROBABLY...

- VISPER IN THE WIND.

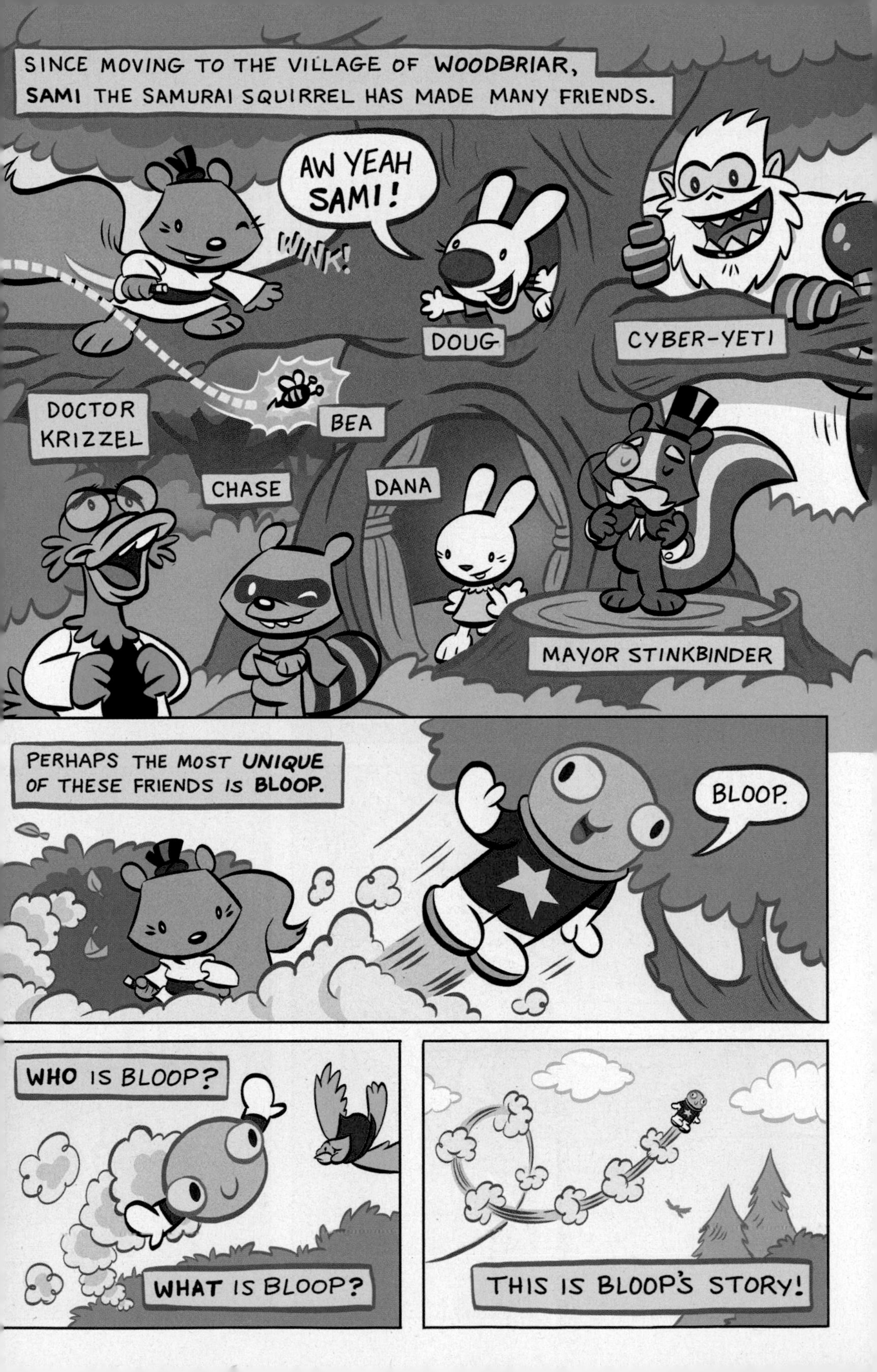
SINCE MOVING TO THE VILLAGE OF WOODBRIAR, SAMI THE SAMURAI SQUIRREL HAS MADE MANY FRIENDS.
AW YEAH SAMI!
WINK!
DOUG
CYBER-YETI
DOCTOR KRIZZEL
BEA
CHASE
DANA
MAYOR STINKBINDER
PERHAPS THE MOST UNIQUE OF THESE FRIENDS IS BLOOP.
BLOOP.
WHO IS BLOOP?
WHAT IS BLOOP?
THIS IS BLOOP'S STORY!

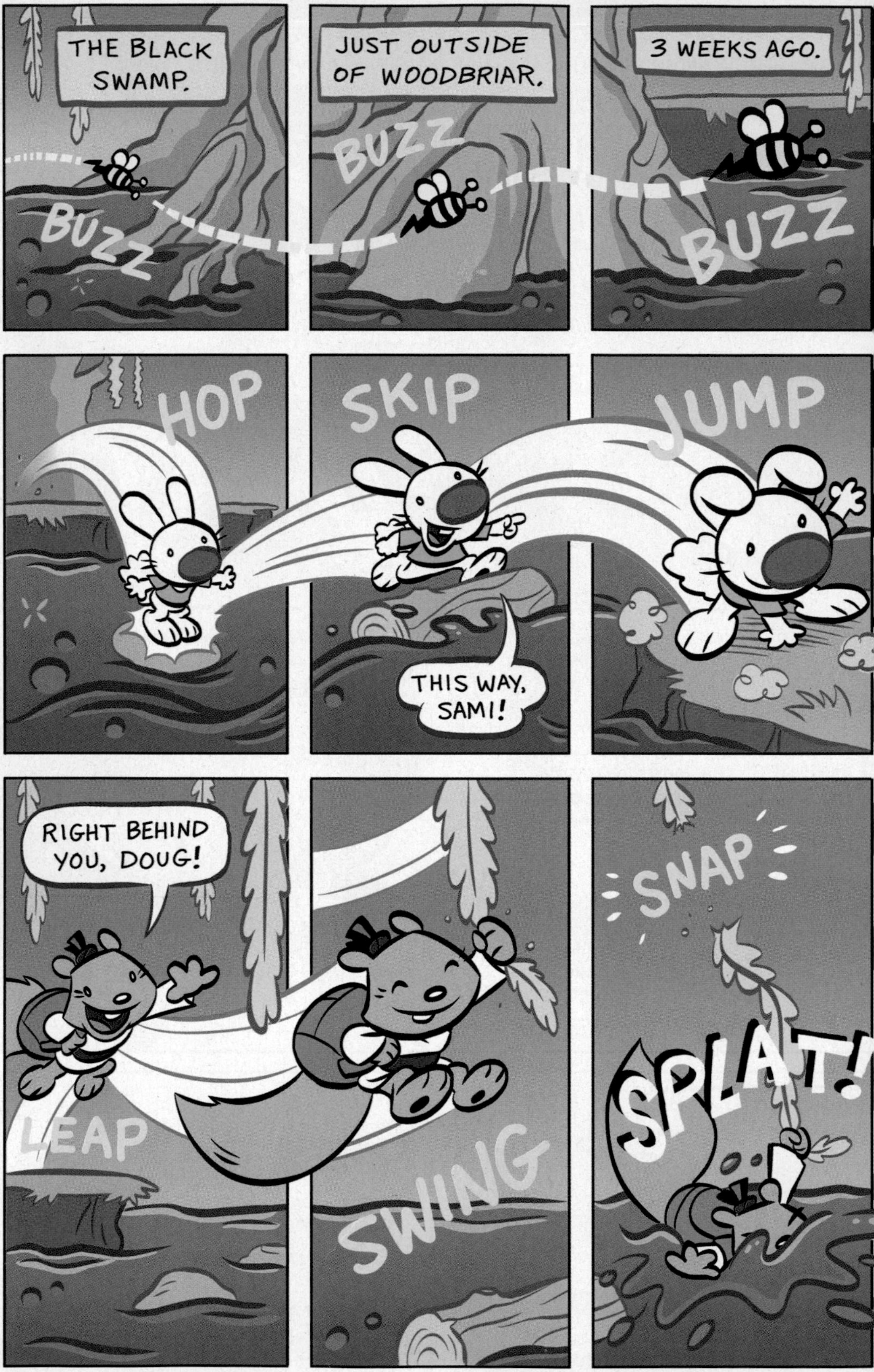
THE BLACK SWAMP.
BUZZ
JUST OUTSIDE OF WOODBRIAR.
BUZZ
3 WEEKS AGO.
BUZZ
HOP
SKIP
THIS WAY, SAMI!
JUMP
RIGHT BEHIND YOU, DOUG!
LEAP
SWING
SNAP
SPLAT!

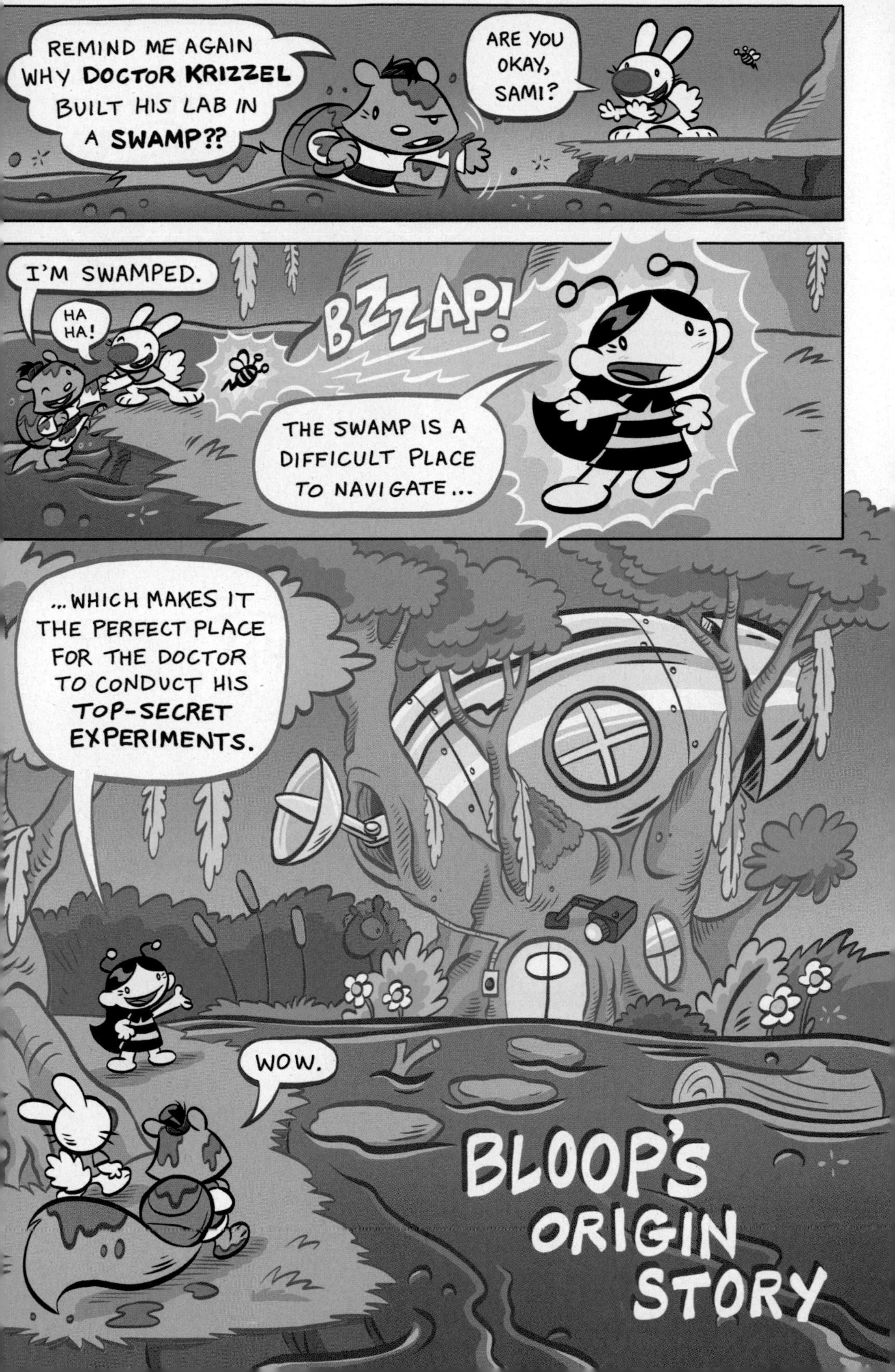

REMIND ME AGAIN WHY DOCTOR KRIZZEL BUILT HIS LAB IN A SWAMP??
ARE YOU OKAY, SAMI?
I'M SWAMPED.
HA HA!
BZZAP!
THE SWAMP IS A DIFFICULT PLACE TO NAVIGATE...
...WHICH MAKES IT THE PERFECT PLACE FOR THE DOCTOR TO CONDUCT HIS TOP-SECRET EXPERIMENTS.
WOW.
BLOOP'S ORIGIN STORY

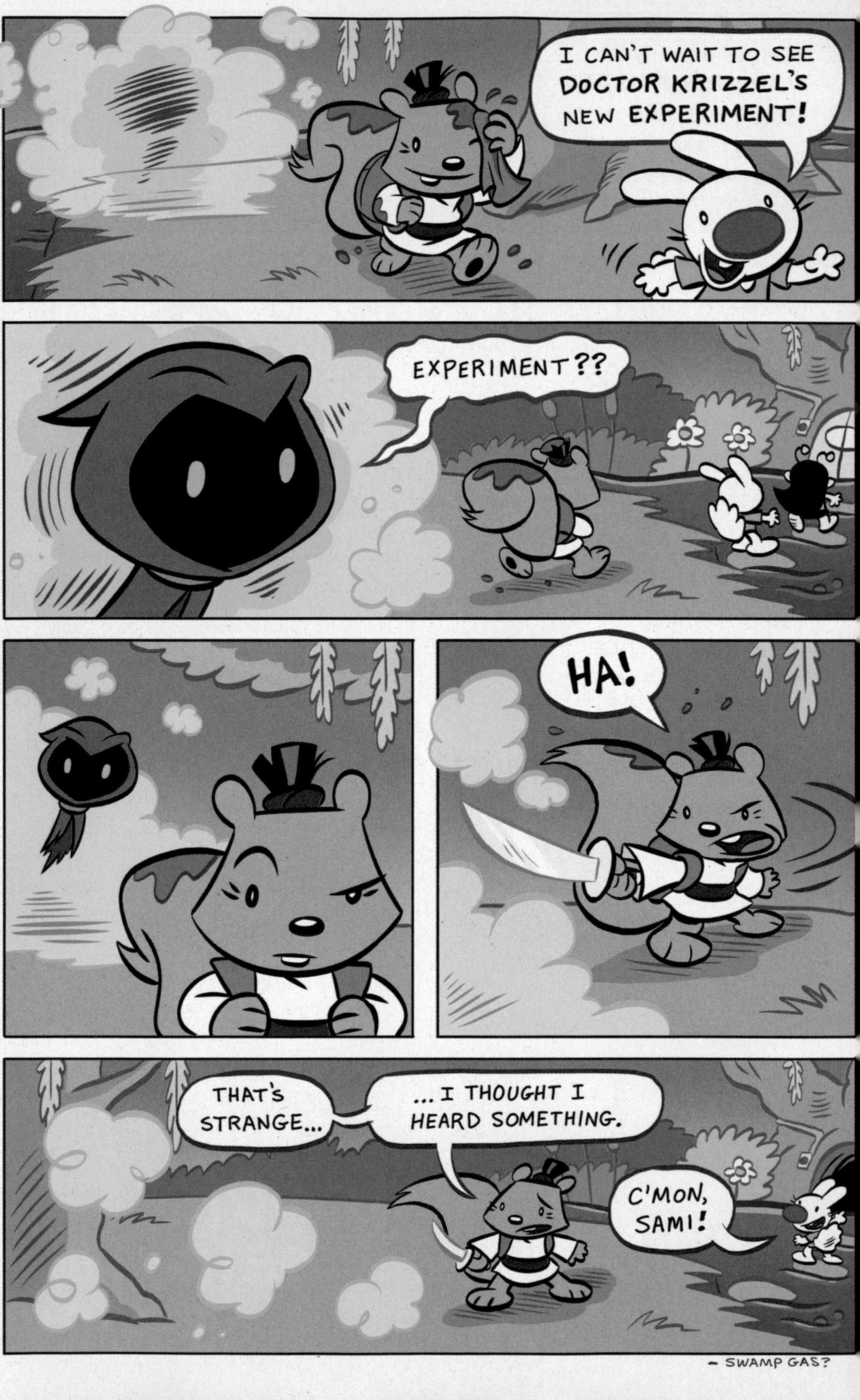
I CAN'T WAIT TO SEE DOCTOR KRIZZEL'S NEW EXPERIMENT!
EXPERIMENT??
HA!
THAT'S STRANGE...
...I THOUGHT I HEARD SOMETHING.
C'MON, SAMI!
- SWAMP GAS?

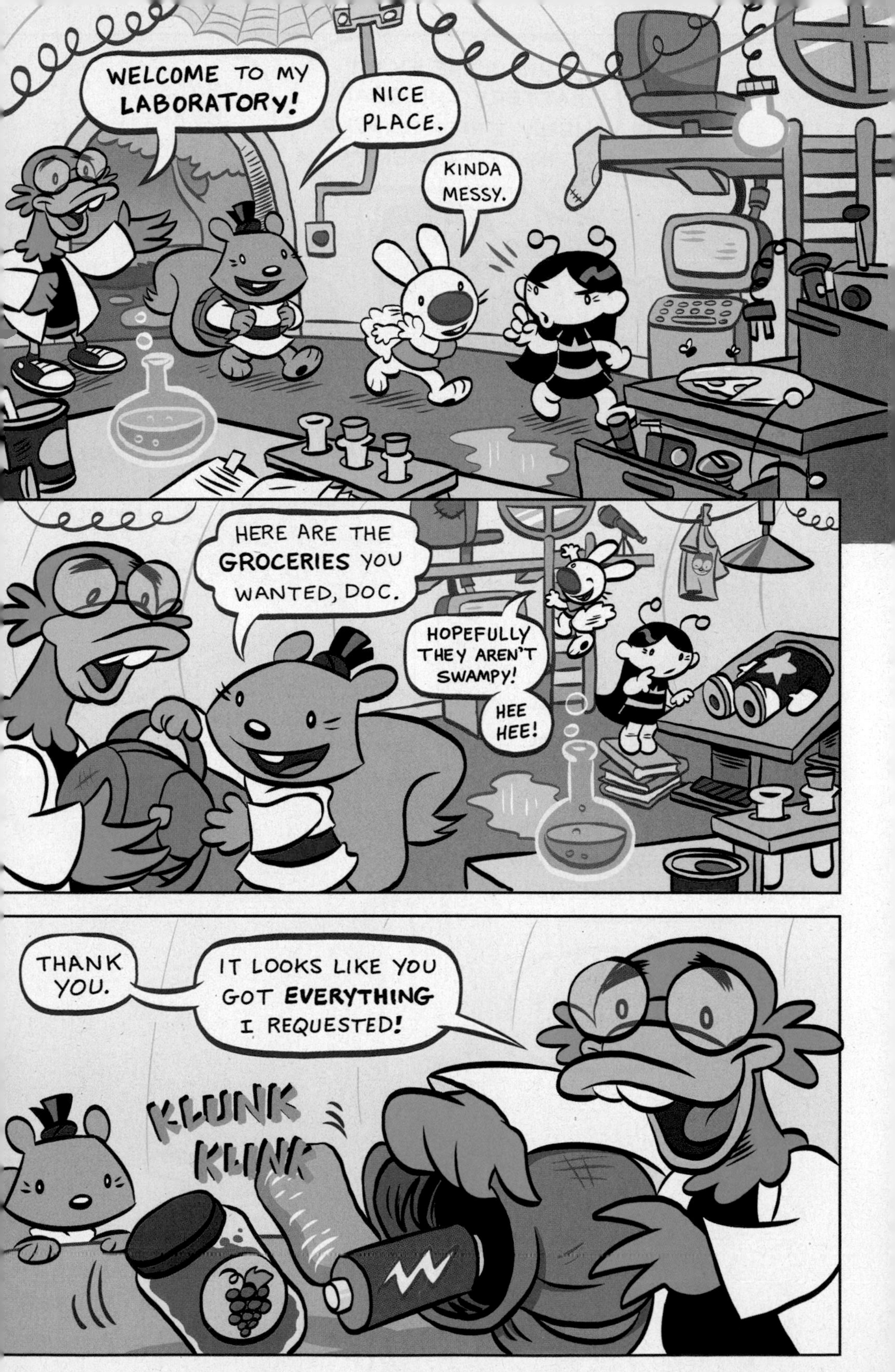
WELCOME TO MY LABORATORY!
NICE PLACE.
KINDA MESSY.
HERE ARE THE GROCERIES YOU WANTED, DOC.
HOPEFULLY THEY AREN'T SWAMPY!
HEE HEE!
THANK YOU.
IT LOOKS LIKE YOU GOT EVERYTHING I REQUESTED!
KLUNK
KLINK

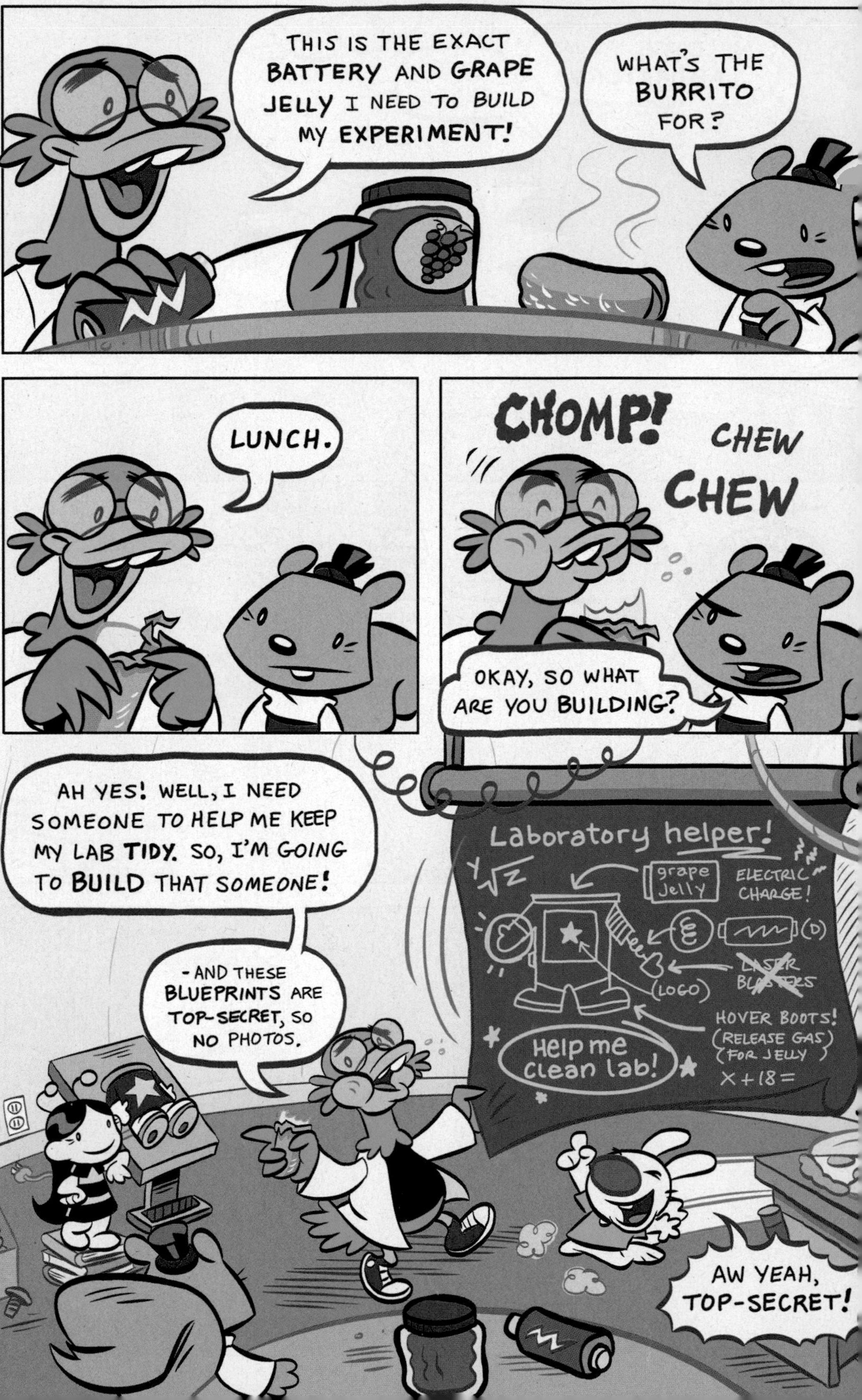

THIS IS THE EXACT BATTERY AND GRAPE JELLY I NEED TO BUILD MY EXPERIMENT!
WHAT'S THE BURRITO FOR?
LUNCH.
CHOMP!
CHEW
CHEW
OKAY, SO WHAT ARE YOU BUILDING?
AH YES! WELL, I NEED SOMEONE TO HELP ME KEEP MY LAB TIDY. SO, I'M GOING TO BUILD THAT SOMEONE!
Laboratory helper!
grape Jelly
ELECTRIC CHARGE!
(D)
LASER BLASTERS
(LOGO)
HOVER BOOTS! (RELEASE GAS FOR JELLY)
Help me clean lab!
X + 18 =
- AND THESE BLUEPRINTS ARE TOP-SECRET, SO NO PHOTOS.
AW YEAH, TOP-SECRET!

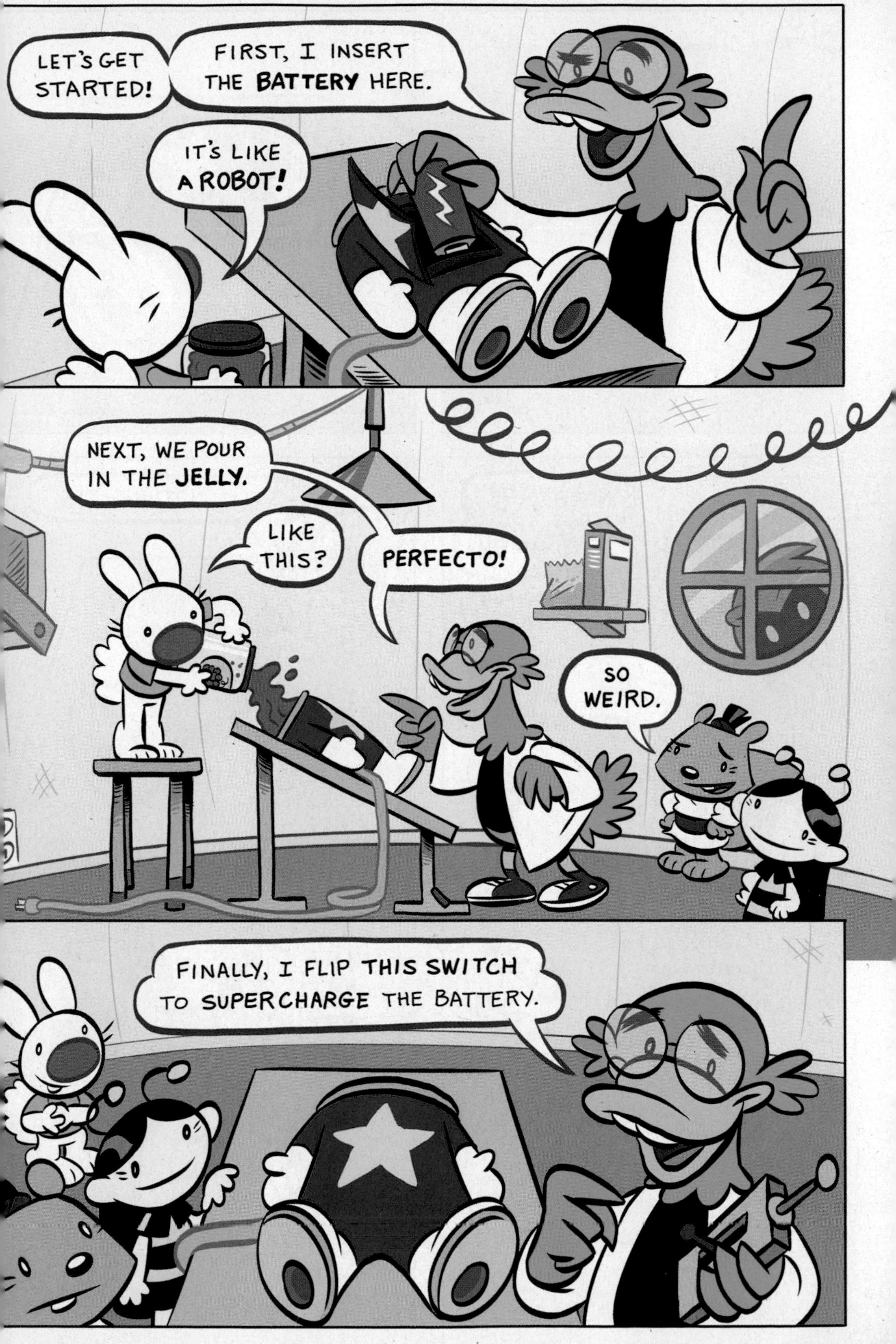
LET'S GET STARTED!
FIRST, I INSERT THE BATTERY HERE.
IT'S LIKE A ROBOT!
NEXT, WE POUR IN THE JELLY.
LIKE THIS?
PERFECTO!
SO WEIRD.
FINALLY, I FLIP THIS SWITCH TO SUPERCHARGE THE BATTERY.

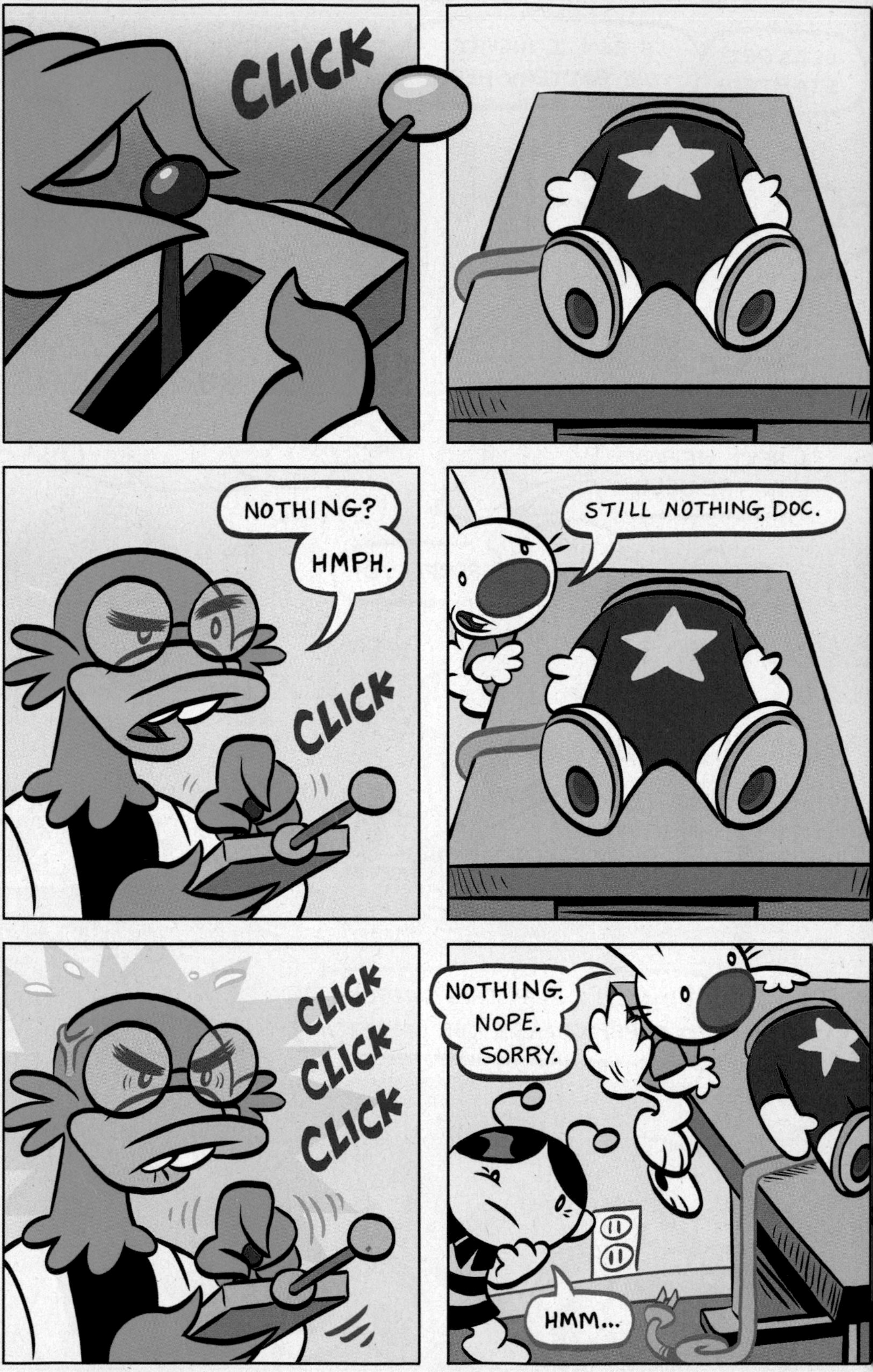
CLICK
NOTHING?
HMPH.
CLICK
STILL NOTHING, DOC.
CLICK
CLICK
CLICK
NOTHING.
NOPE.
SORRY.
HMM...

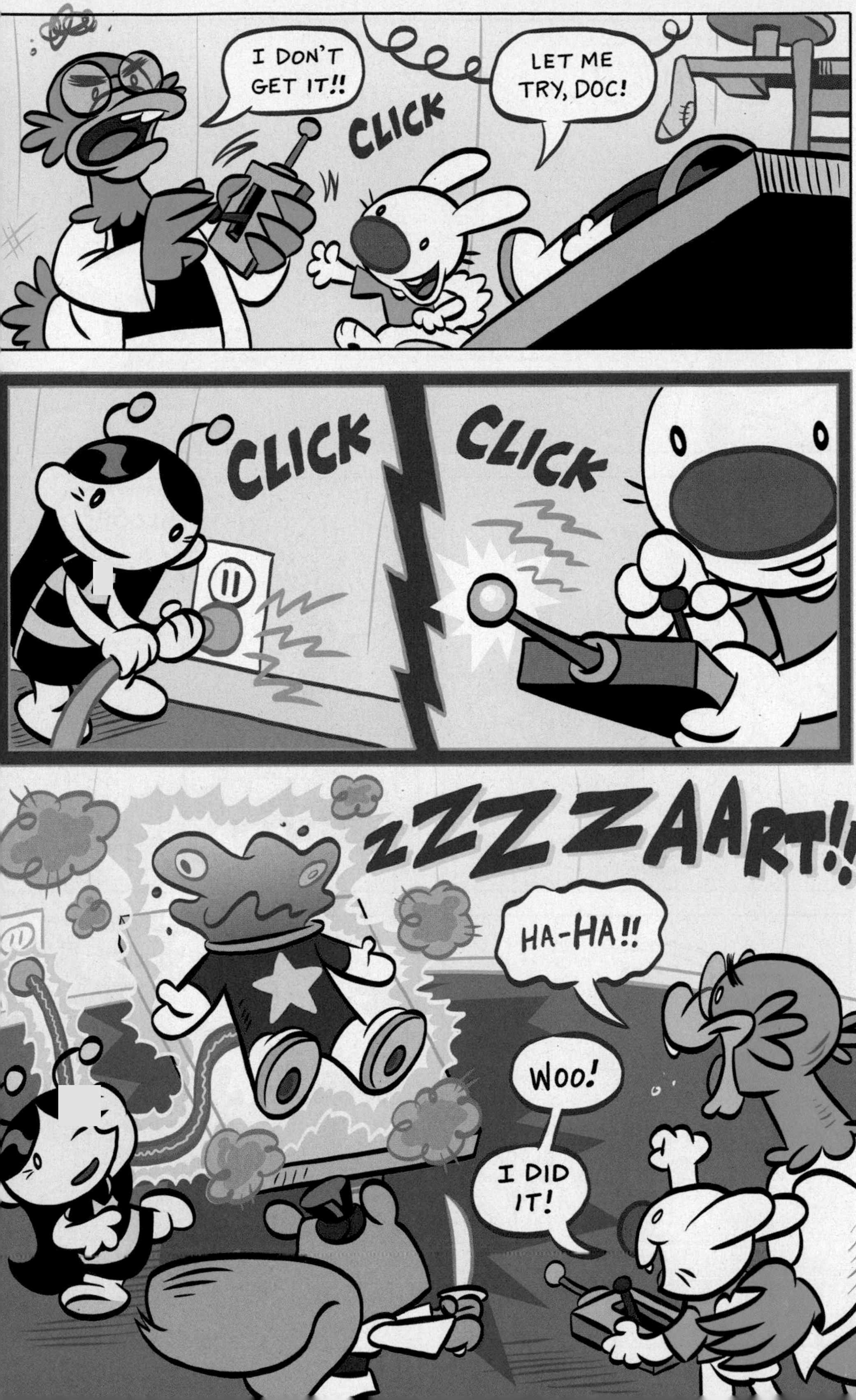
I DON'T GET IT!!
CLICK
LET ME TRY, DOC!
CLICK
CLICK
zZZZAART!!
HA-HA!!
WOO!
I DID IT!

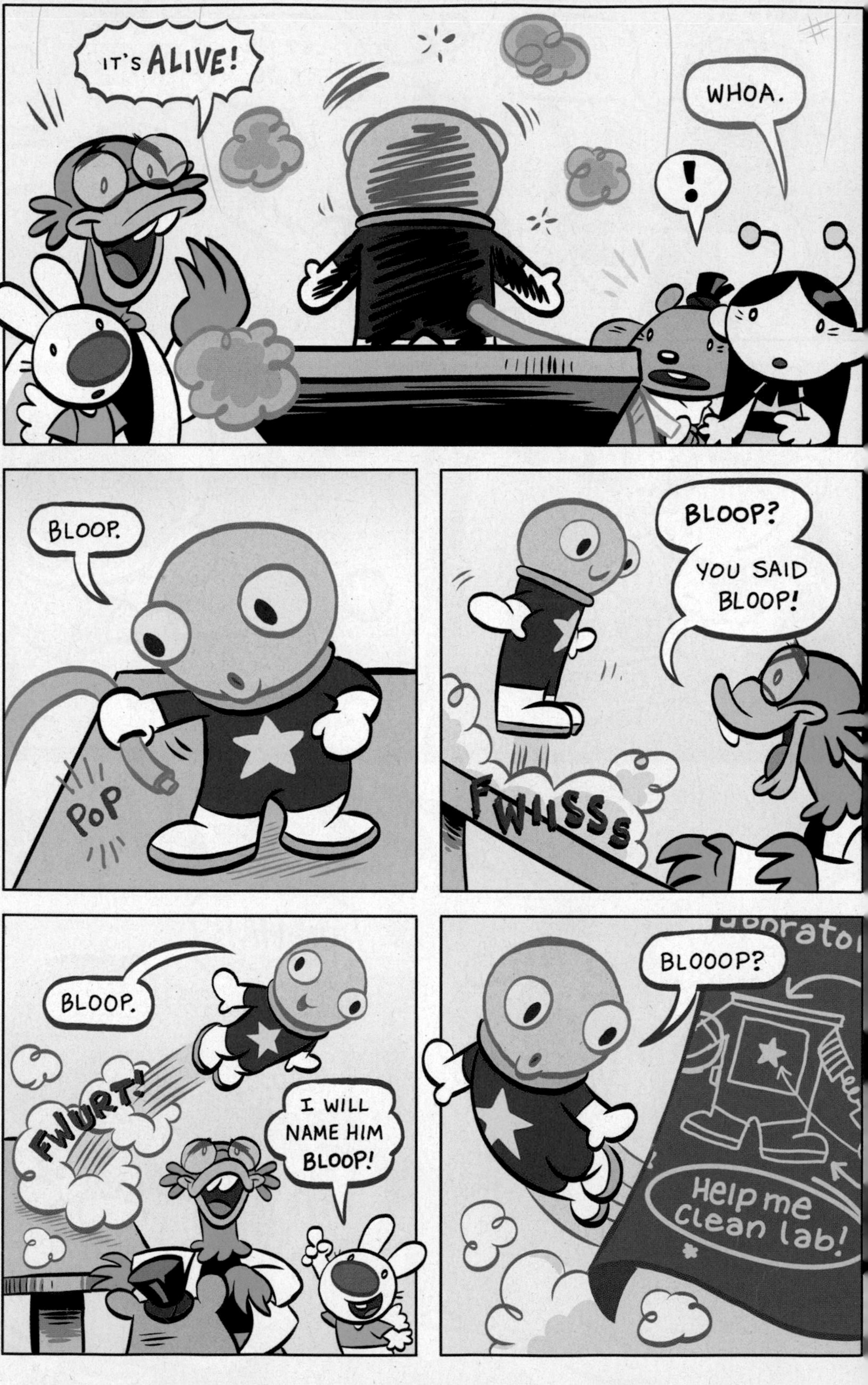
IT'S ALIVE!
WHOA.
!
BLOOP.
POP
BLOOP?
YOU SAID BLOOP!
FWIISSS
BLOOP.
FWURT!
I WILL NAME HIM BLOOP!
BLOOOP?
Help me clean lab!

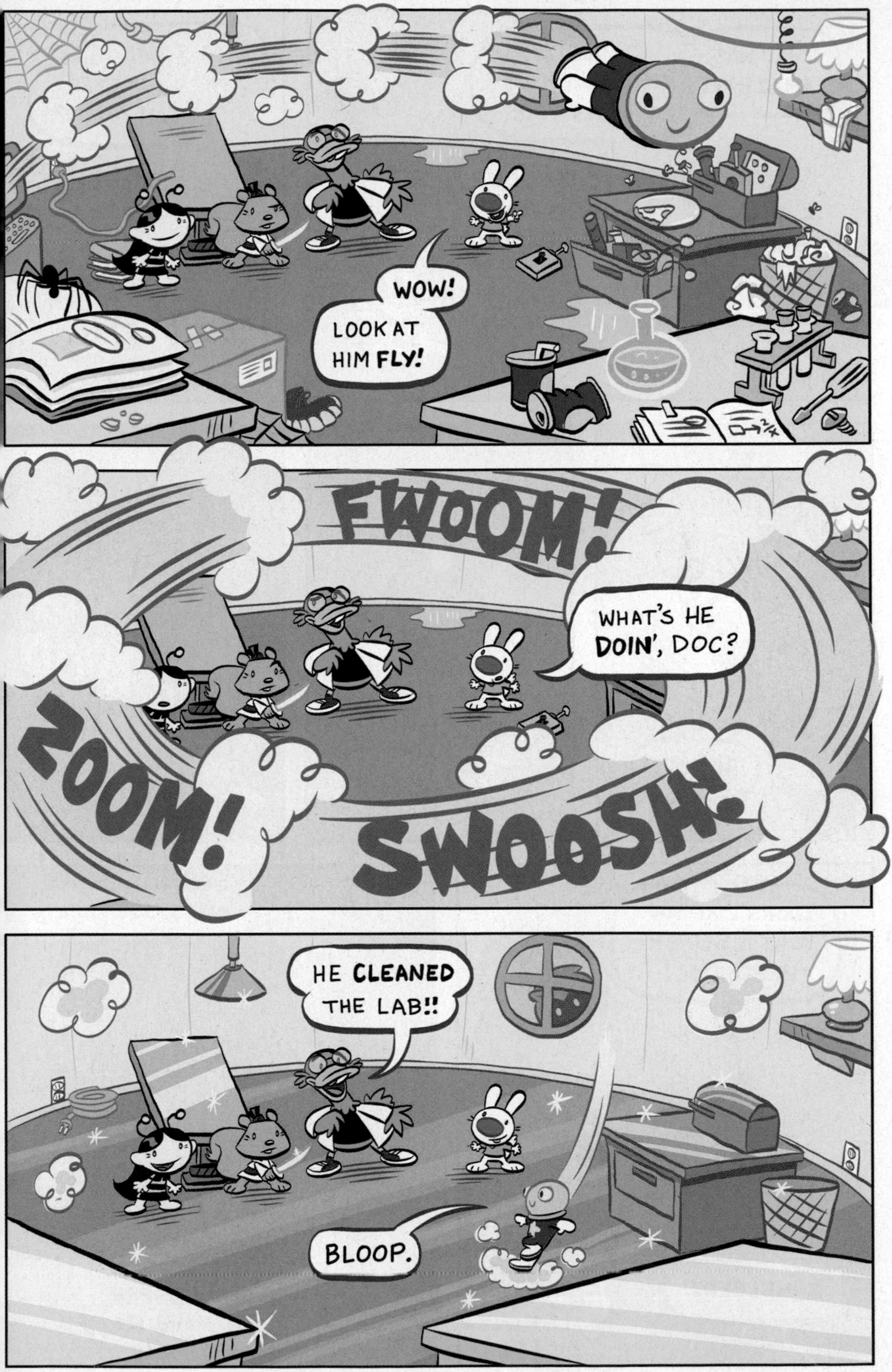
WOW!
LOOK AT HIM FLY!
FWOOM!
WHAT'S HE DOIN', DOC?
ZOOM!
SWOOSH!
HE CLEANED THE LAB!!
BLOOP.

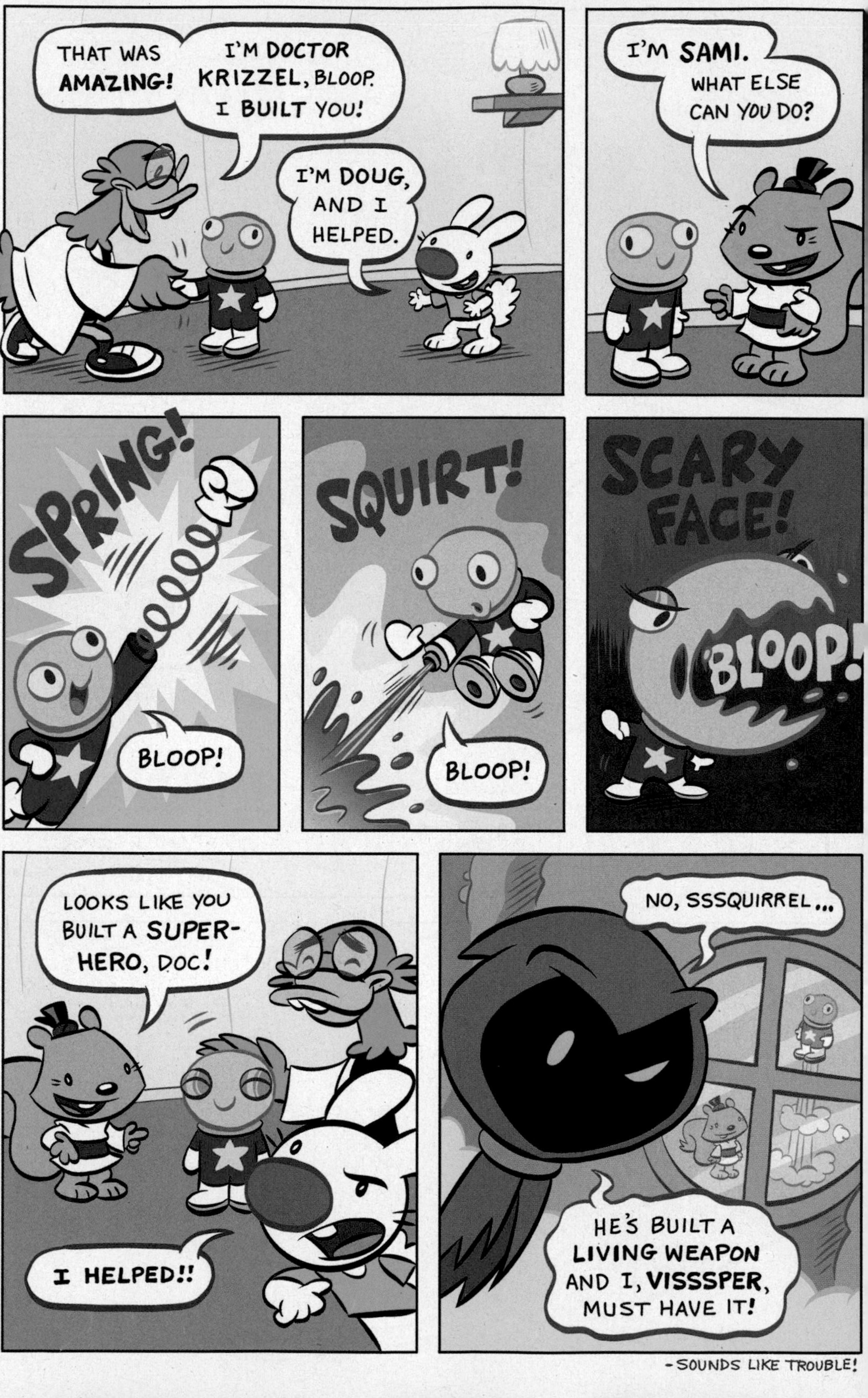
THAT WAS AMAZING!
I'M DOCTOR KRIZZEL, BLOOP. I BUILT YOU!
I'M DOUG, AND I HELPED.
I'M SAMI. WHAT ELSE CAN YOU DO?
SPRING!
BLOOP!
SQUIRT!
BLOOP!
SCARY FACE!
BLOOP!
LOOKS LIKE YOU BUILT A SUPER-HERO, DOC!
I HELPED!!
NO, SSSQUIRREL...
HE'S BUILT A LIVING WEAPON AND I, VISSSPER, MUST HAVE IT!
- SOUNDS LIKE TROUBLE!

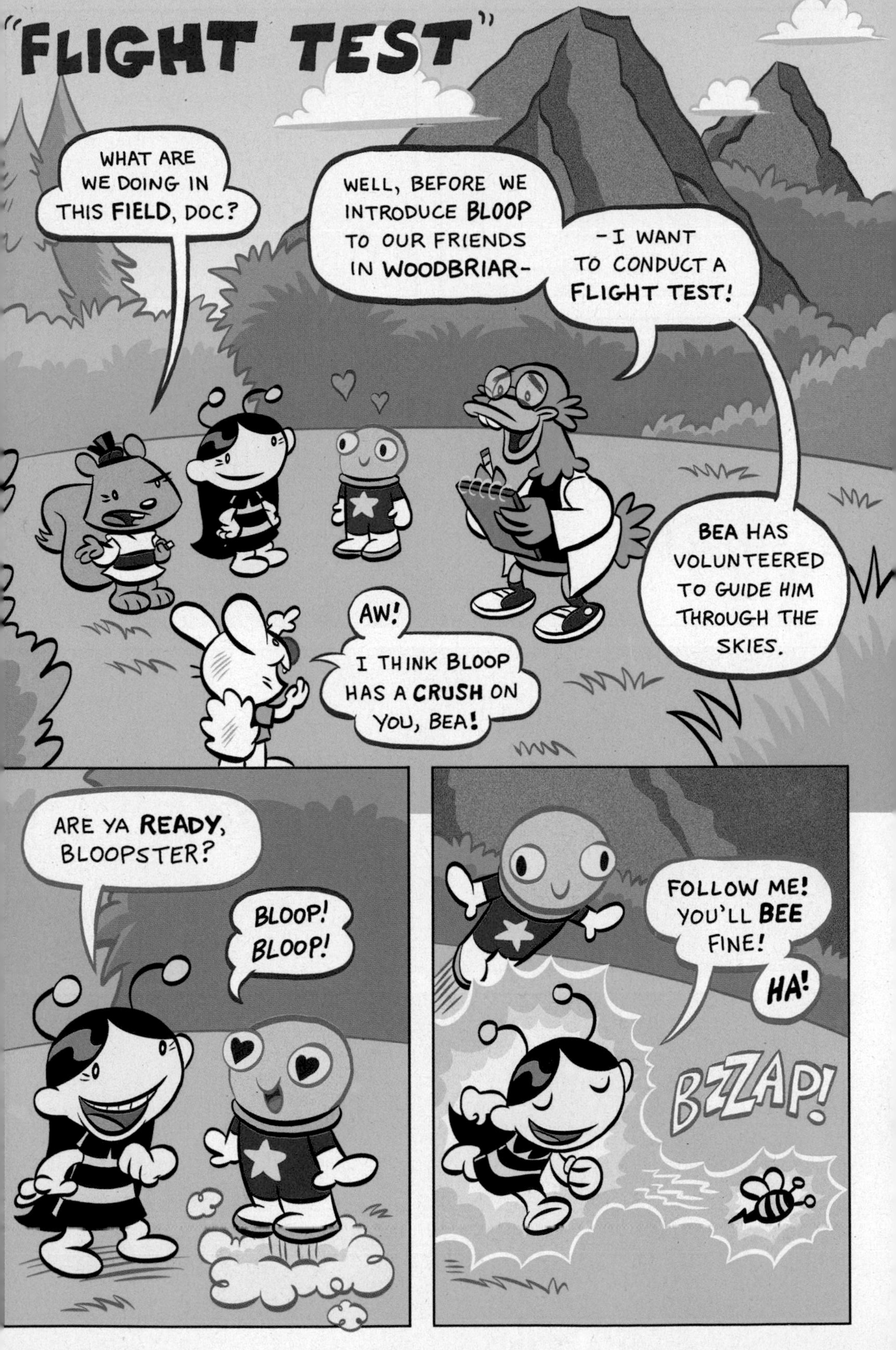
"FLIGHT TEST"
WHAT ARE WE DOING IN THIS FIELD, DOC?
WELL, BEFORE WE INTRODUCE BLOOP TO OUR FRIENDS IN WOODBRIAR-
-I WANT TO CONDUCT A FLIGHT TEST!
BEA HAS VOLUNTEERED TO GUIDE HIM THROUGH THE SKIES.
AW!
I THINK BLOOP HAS A CRUSH ON YOU, BEA!
ARE YA READY, BLOOPSTER?
BLOOP! BLOOP!
FOLLOW ME! YOU'LL BEE FINE!
HA!
BZZAP!

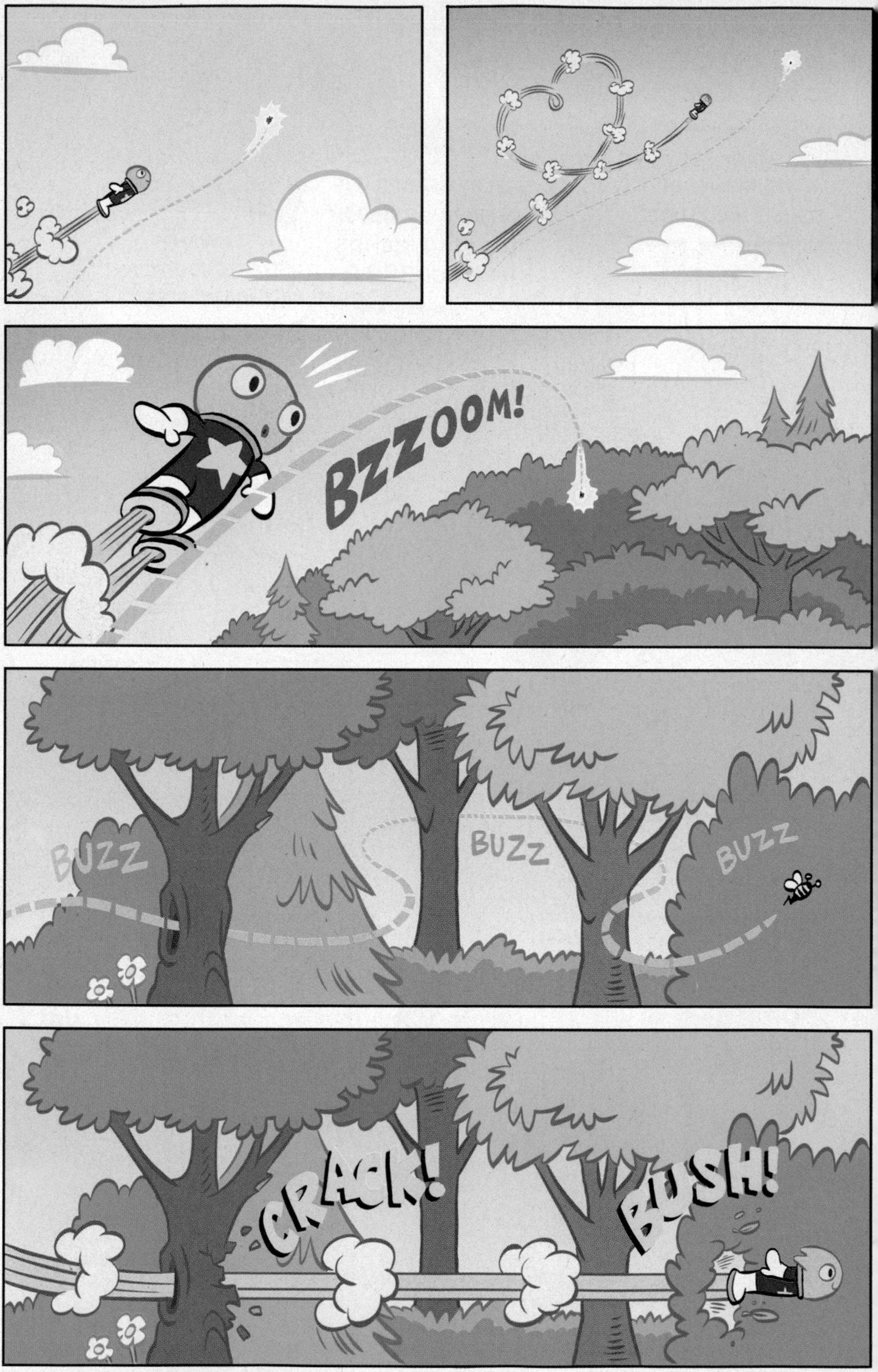
BZZOOM!
BUZZ
BUZZ
BUZZ
CRACK!
BUSH!

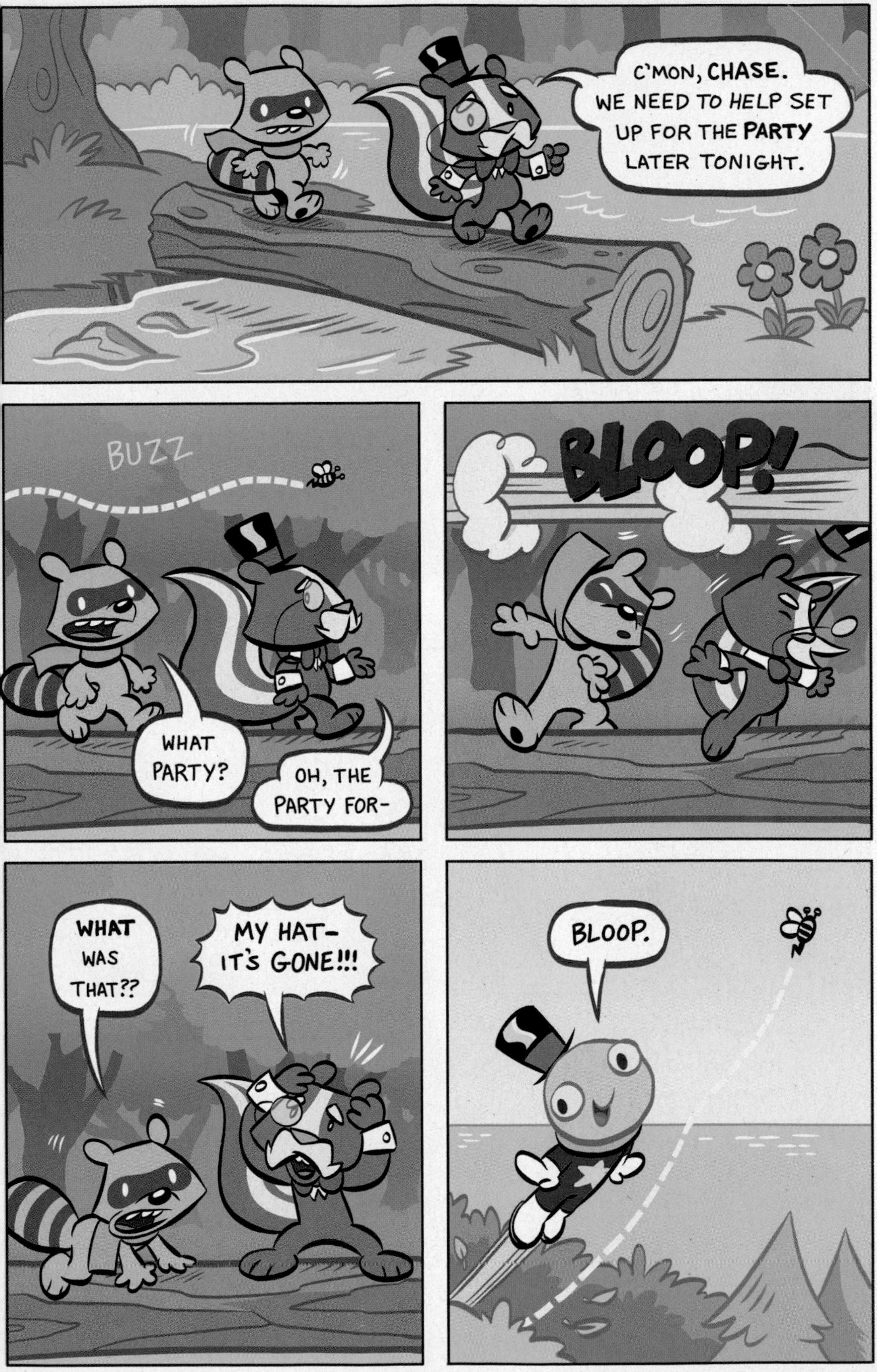
C'MON, CHASE. WE NEED TO HELP SET UP FOR THE PARTY LATER TONIGHT.
BUZZ
WHAT PARTY?
OH, THE PARTY FOR-
BLOOP!
WHAT WAS THAT??
MY HAT- IT'S GONE!!!
BLOOP.

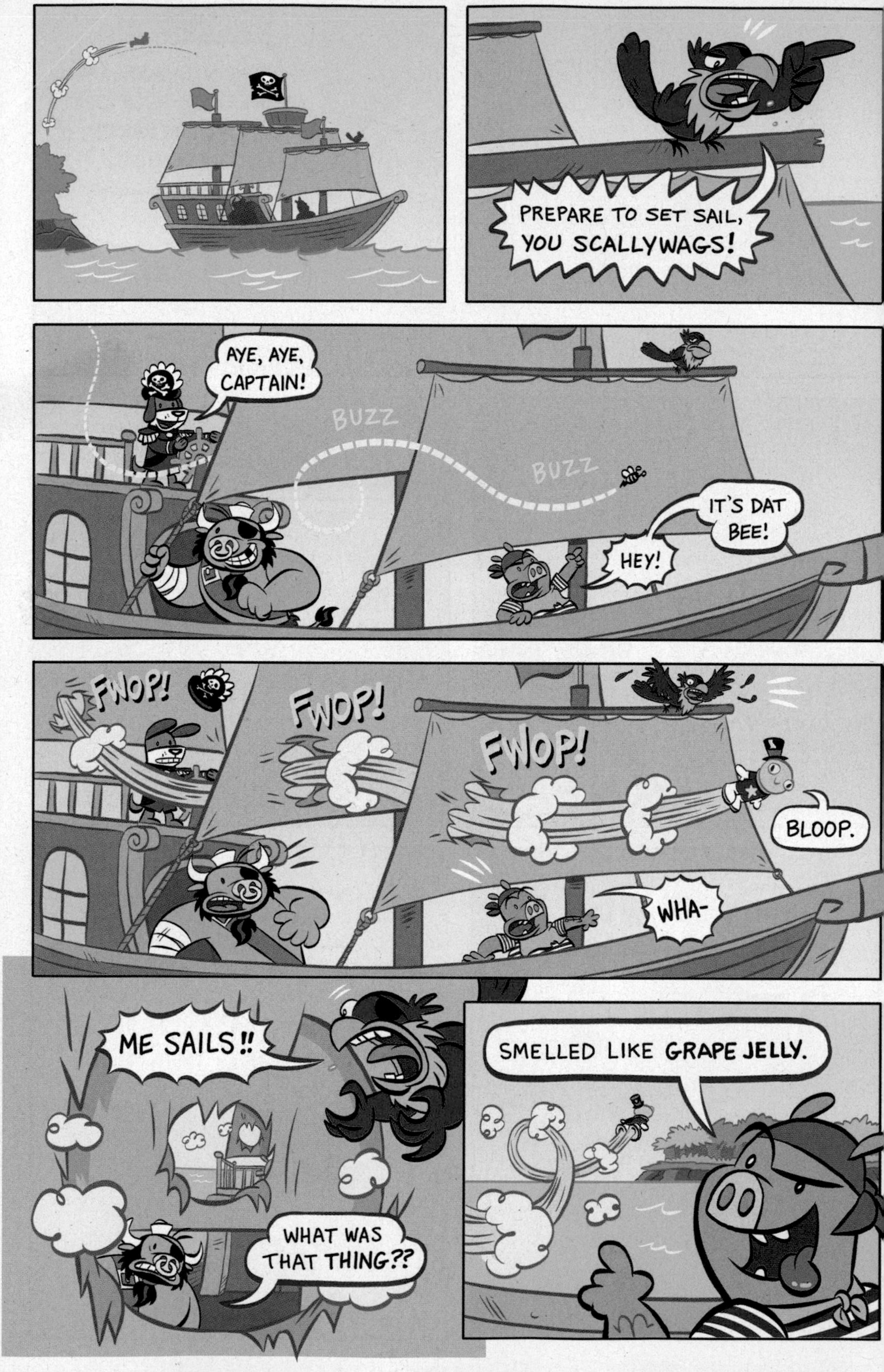
PREPARE TO SET SAIL, YOU SCALLYWAGS!
AYE, AYE, CAPTAIN!
BUZZ
BUZZ
HEY!
IT'S DAT BEE!
FWOP!
FWOP!
FWOP!
BLOOP.
WHA-
ME SAILS!!
WHAT WAS THAT THING??
SMELLED LIKE GRAPE JELLY.

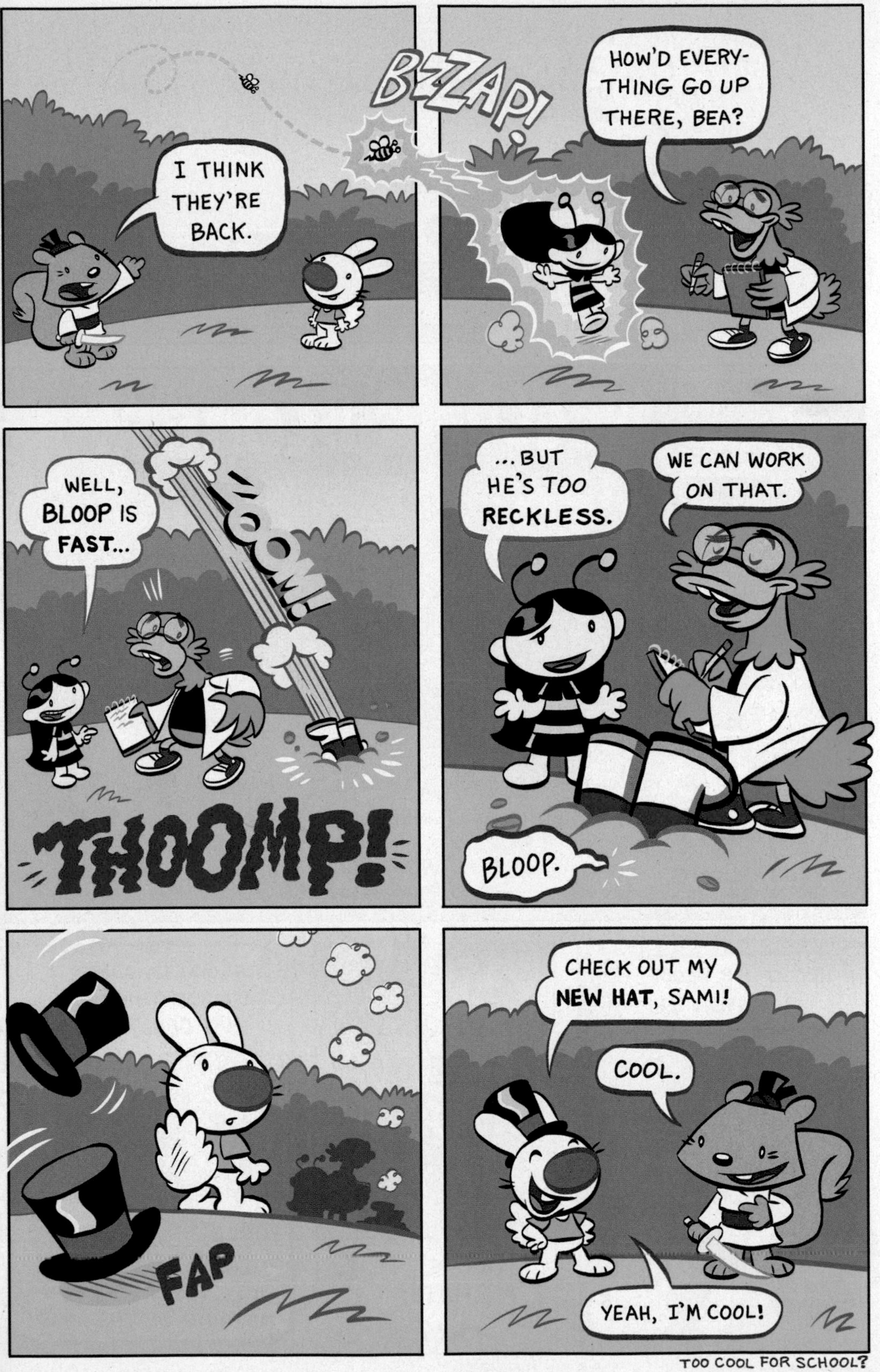
I THINK THEY'RE BACK.
BZZAP!
HOW'D EVERY-THING GO UP THERE, BEA?
WELL, BLOOP IS FAST...
VOOOM!
THOOMP!
...BUT HE'S TOO RECKLESS.
WE CAN WORK ON THAT.
BLOOP.
FAP
CHECK OUT MY NEW HAT, SAMI!
COOL.
YEAH, I'M COOL!

TOO COOL FOR SCHOOL?

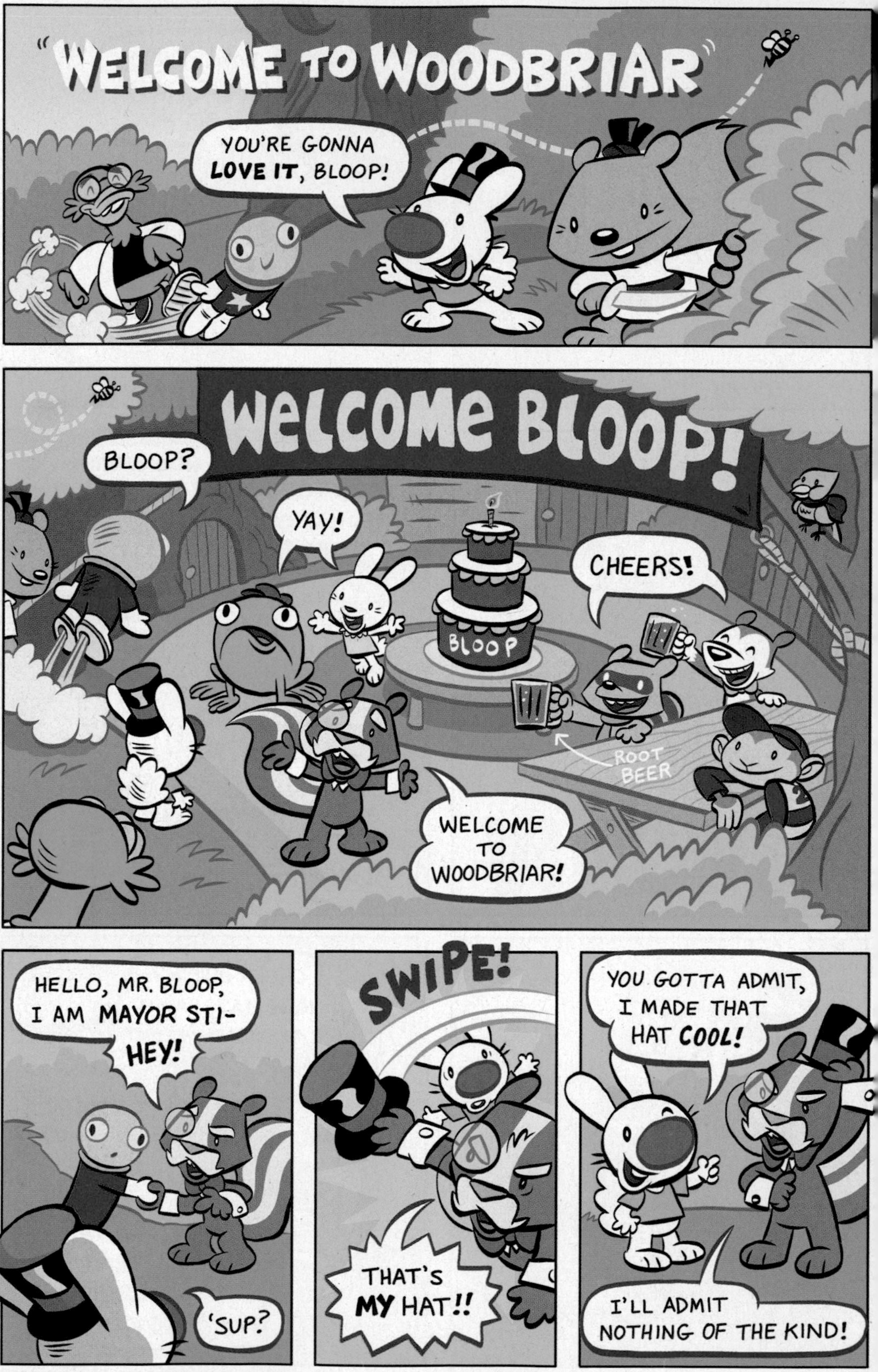
"WELCOME TO WOODBRIAR"
YOU'RE GONNA LOVE IT, BLOOP!
WELCOME BLOOP!
BLOOP?
YAY!
BLOOP
CHEERS!
ROOT BEER
WELCOME TO WOODBRIAR!
HELLO, MR. BLOOP, I AM MAYOR STI-
HEY!
'SUP?
SWIPE!
THAT'S MY HAT!!
YOU GOTTA ADMIT, I MADE THAT HAT COOL!
I'LL ADMIT NOTHING OF THE KIND!

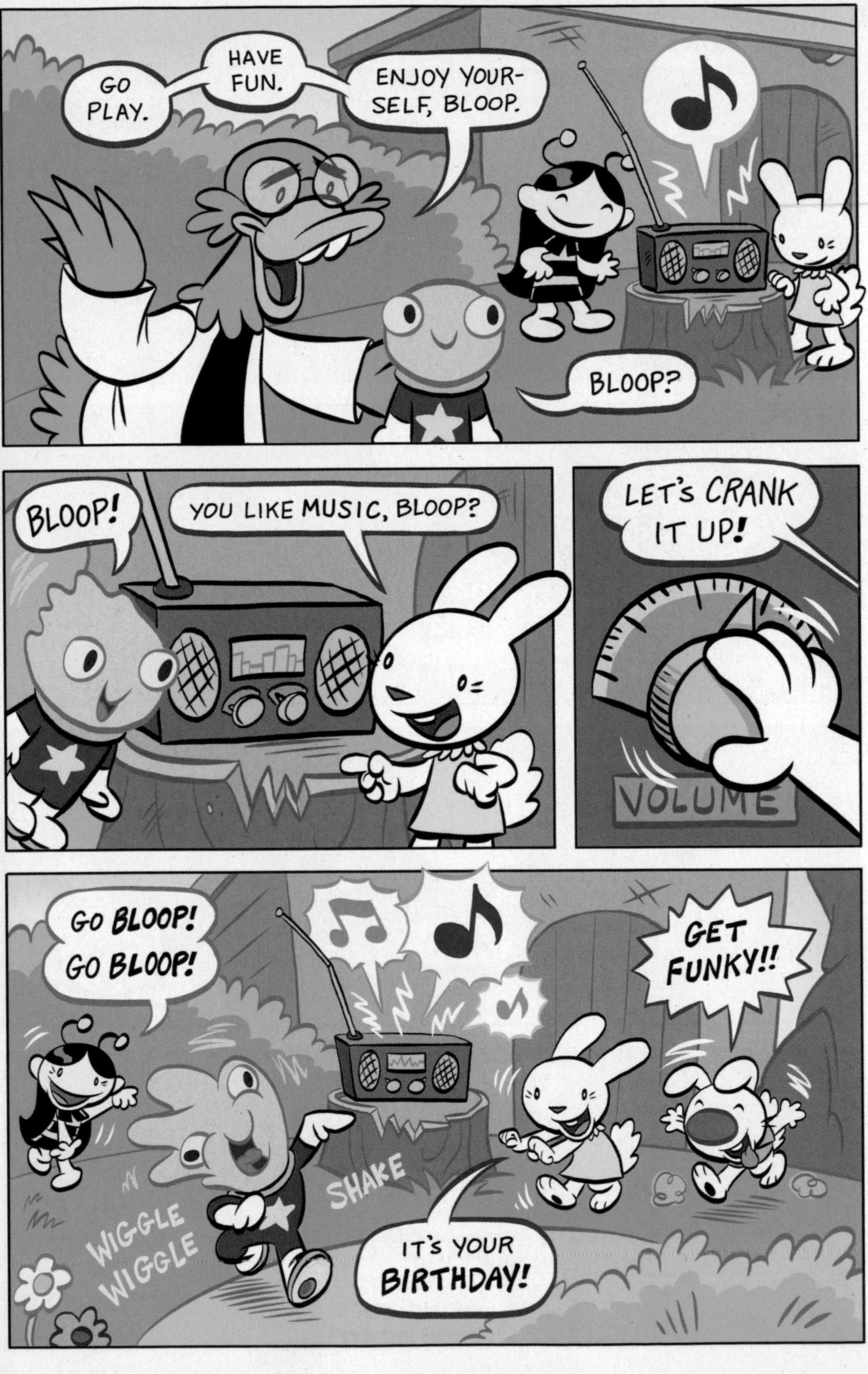
GO PLAY.
HAVE FUN.
ENJOY YOURSELF, BLOOP.
BLOOP?
BLOOP!
YOU LIKE MUSIC, BLOOP?
LET'S CRANK IT UP!
VOLUME
GO BLOOP! GO BLOOP!
GET FUNKY!!
WIGGLE WIGGLE
SHAKE
IT'S YOUR BIRTHDAY!

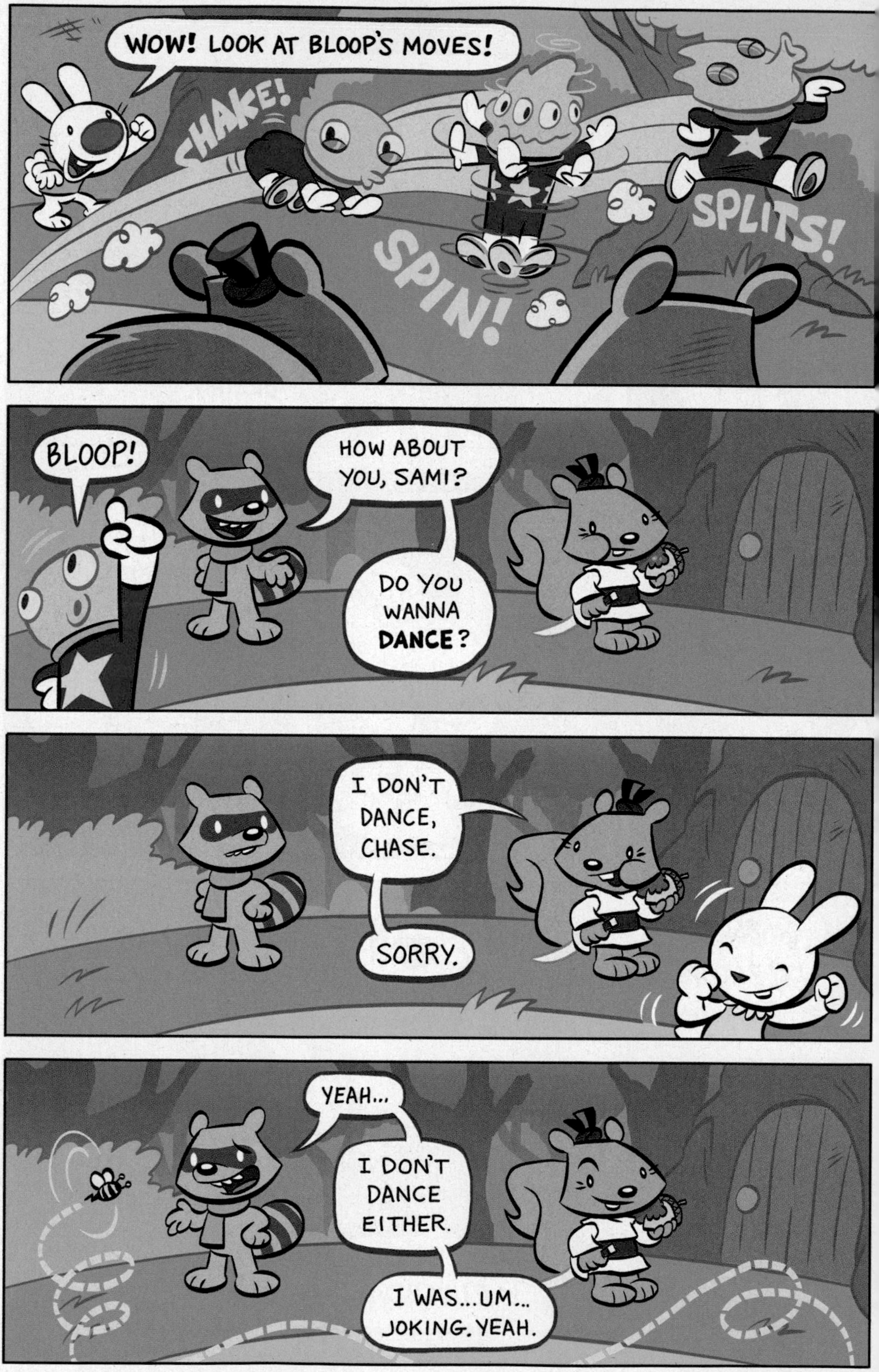
WOW! LOOK AT BLOOP'S MOVES!
SHAKE!
SPIN!
SPLITS!
BLOOP!
HOW ABOUT YOU, SAMI?
DO YOU WANNA **DANCE**?
I DON'T DANCE, CHASE.
SORRY.
YEAH...
I DON'T DANCE EITHER.
I WAS...UM... JOKING. YEAH.

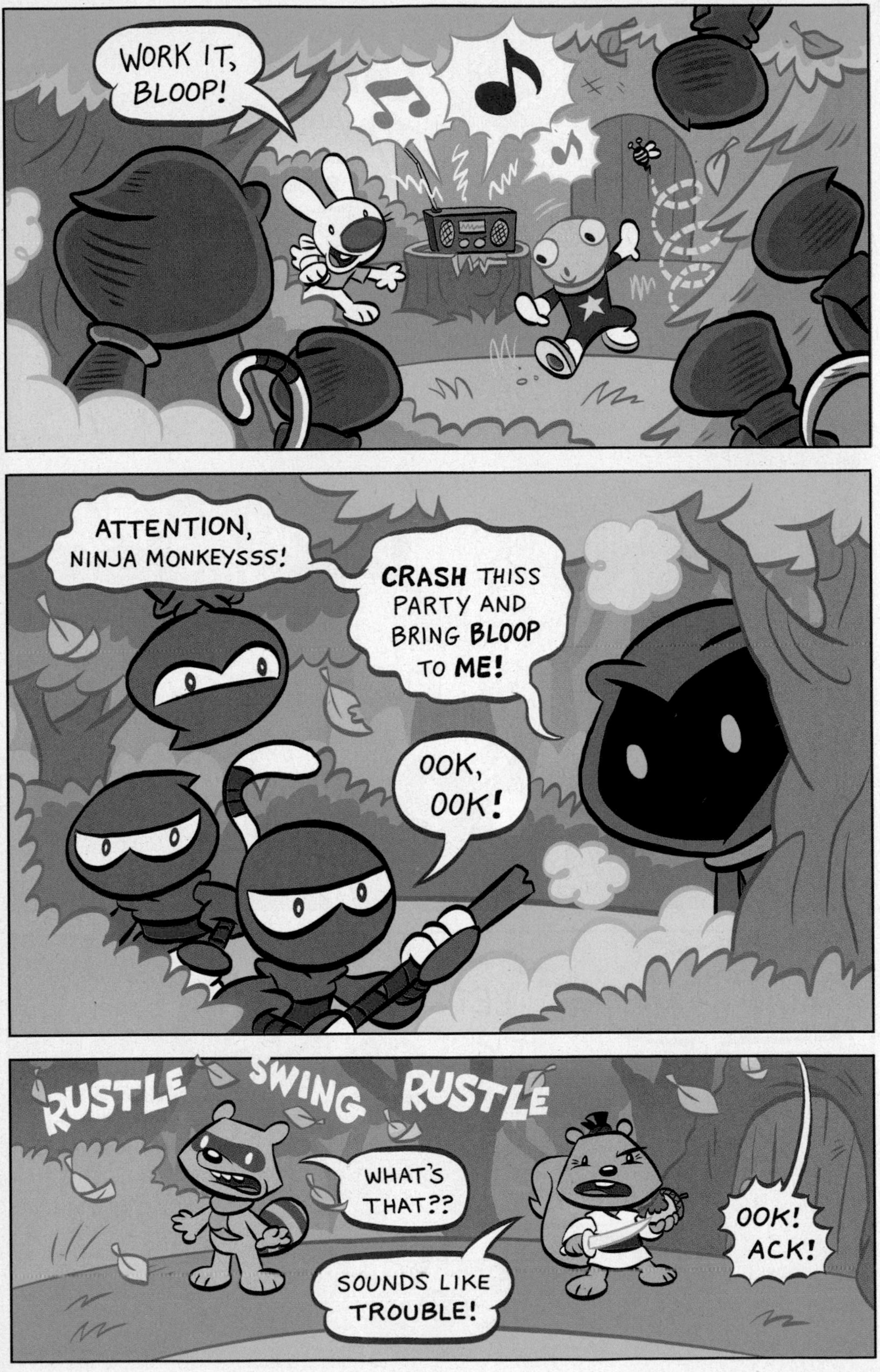
WORK IT, BLOOP!
ATTENTION, NINJA MONKEYSSS!
CRASH THISS PARTY AND BRING **BLOOP** TO **ME!**
OOK, OOK!
RUSTLE SWING RUSTLE
WHAT'S THAT??
SOUNDS LIKE TROUBLE!
OOK! ACK!

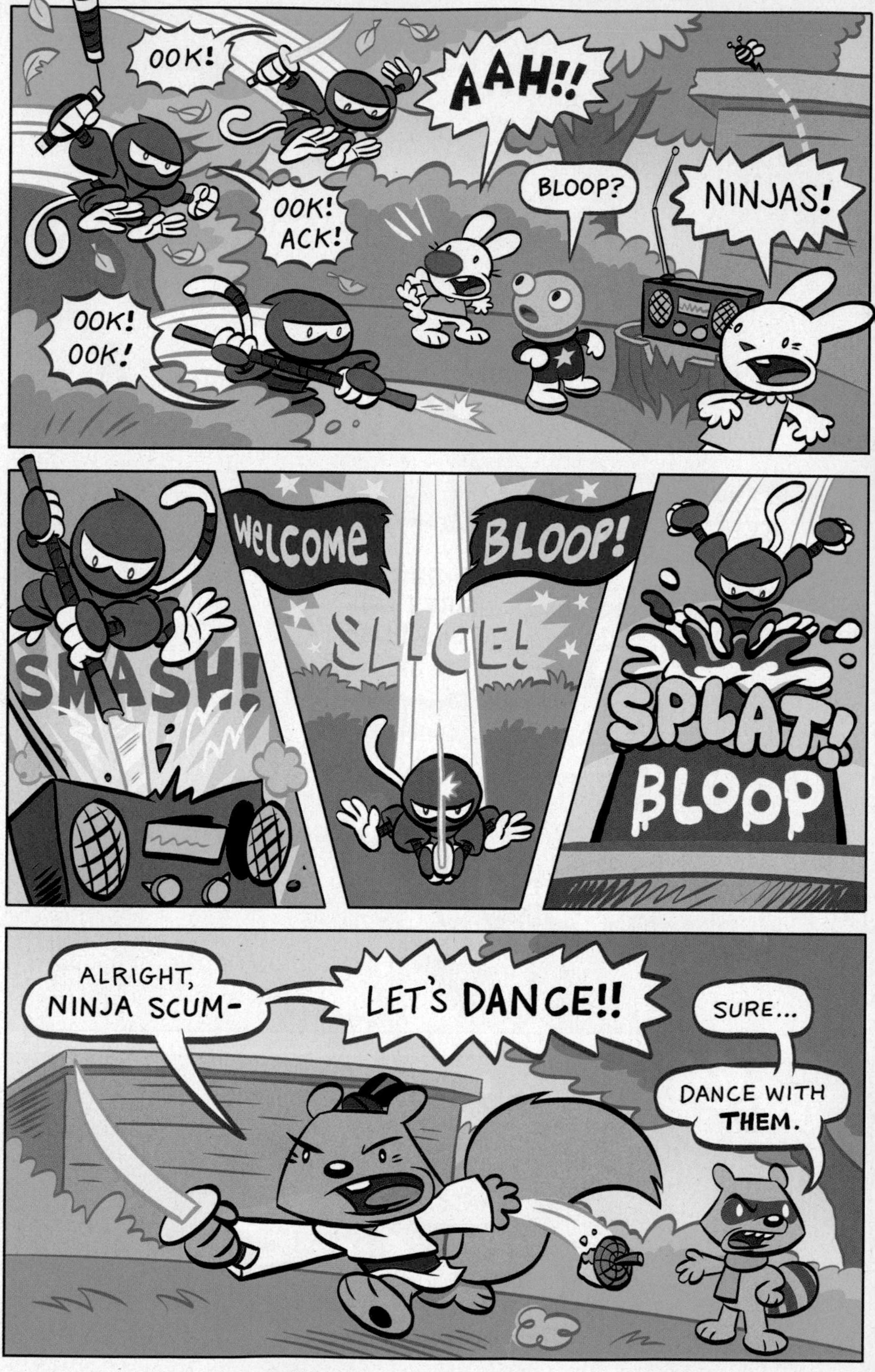
OOK!
AAH!!
OOK! ACK!
BLOOP?
NINJAS!
OOK! OOK!
SMASH!
WELCOME BLOOP!
SLICE!
SPLAT!
BLOOP
ALRIGHT, NINJA SCUM-
LET'S DANCE!!
SURE...
DANCE WITH THEM.

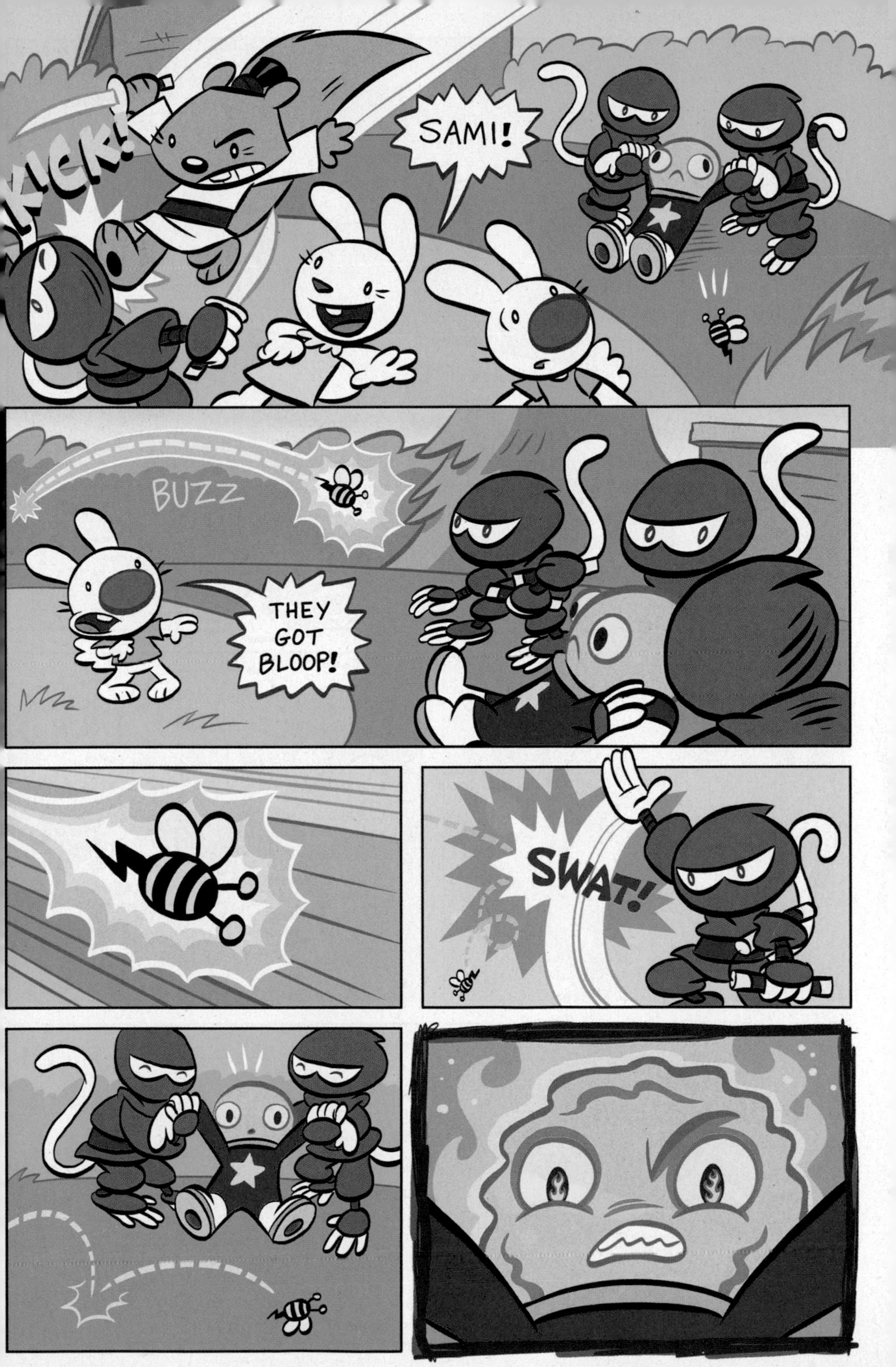
KICK!
SAMI!
BUZZ
THEY GOT BLOOP!
SWAT!

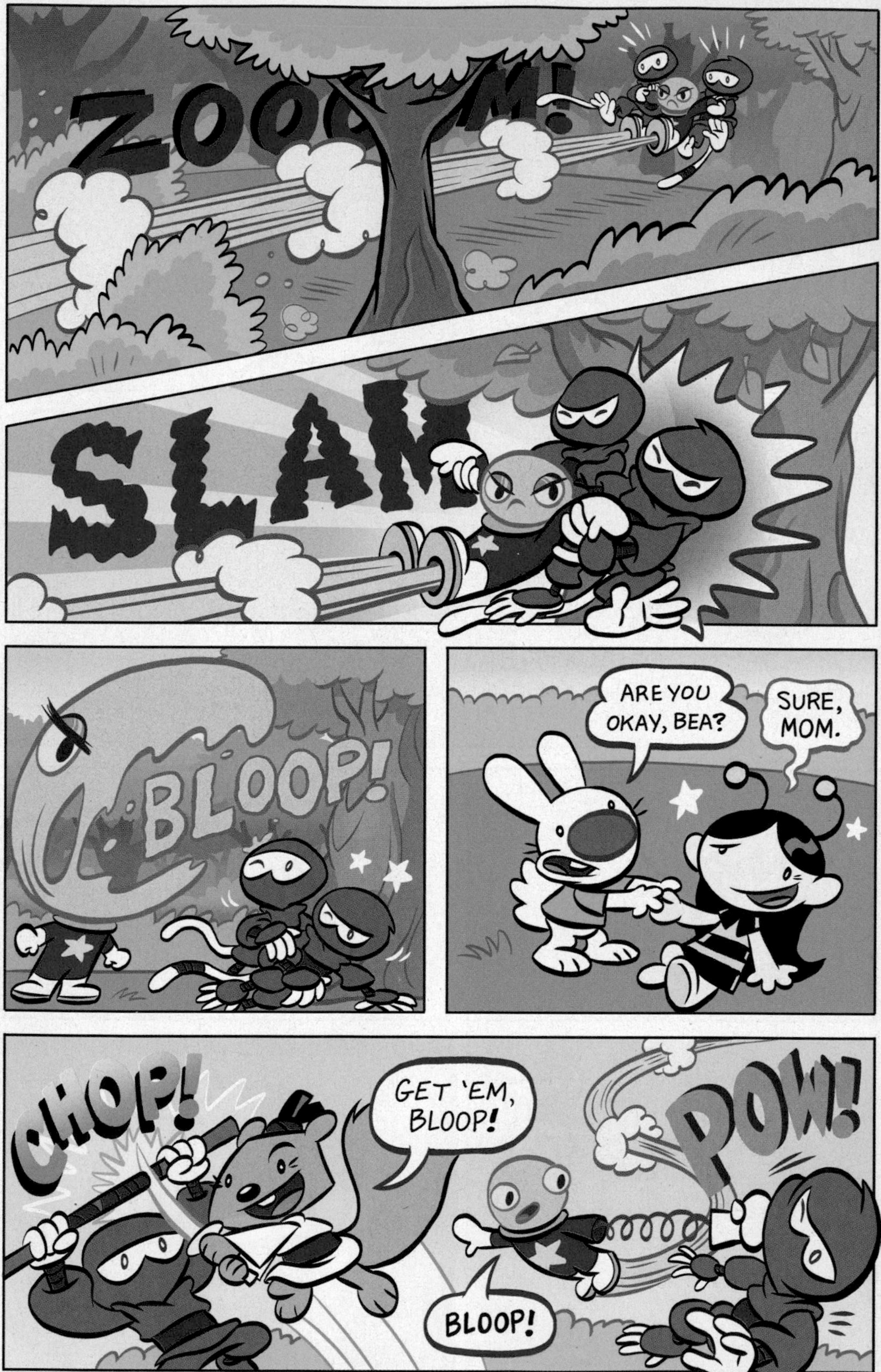
ZOOOOM!
SLAM
BLOOP!
ARE YOU OKAY, BEA?
SURE, MOM.
CHOP!
GET 'EM, BLOOP!
POW!
BLOOP!

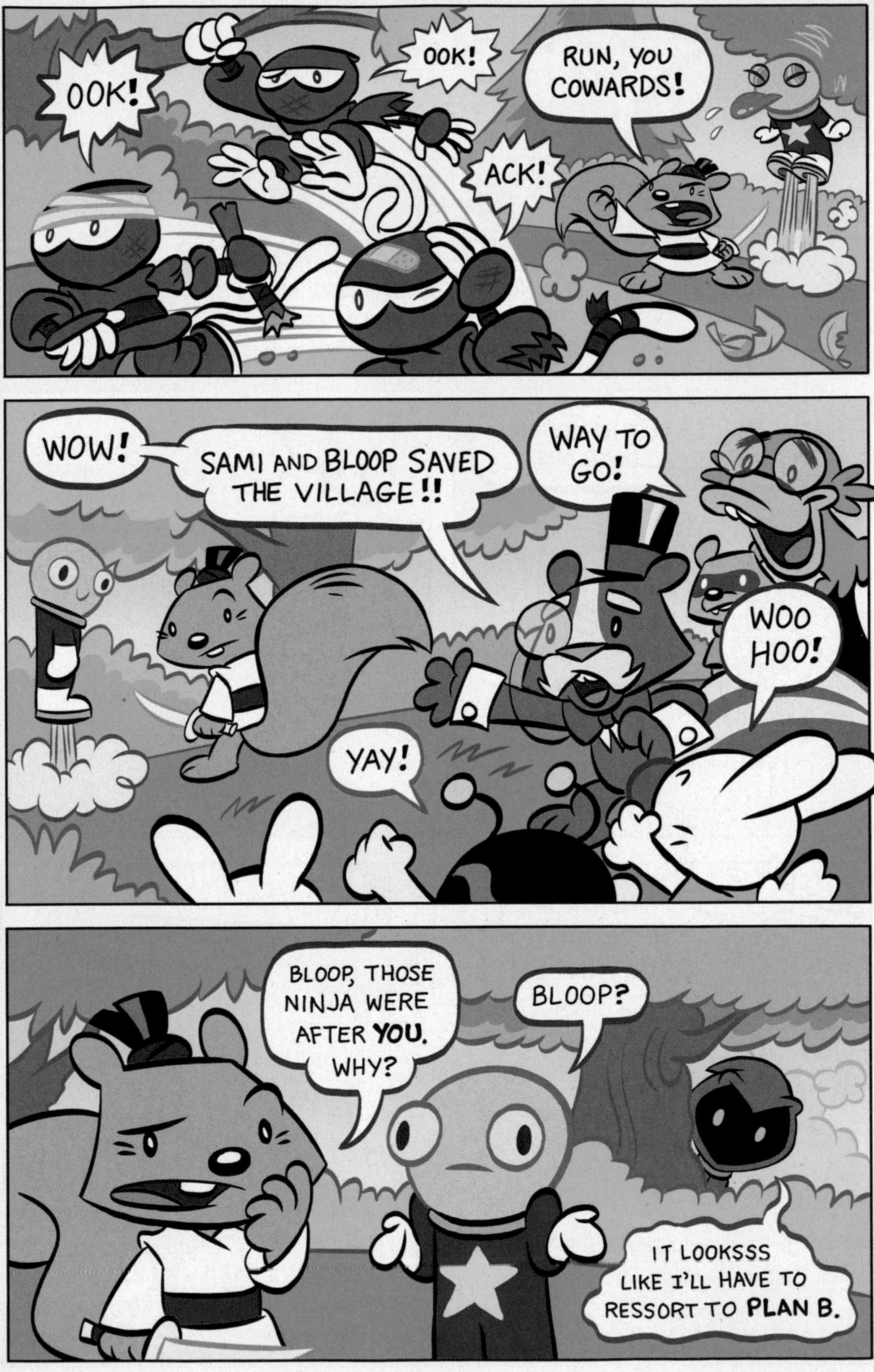
OOK!
OOK!
RUN, YOU COWARDS!
ACK!
WOW!
SAMI AND BLOOP SAVED THE VILLAGE!!
WAY TO GO!
WOO HOO!
YAY!
BLOOP, THOSE NINJA WERE AFTER YOU. WHY?
BLOOP?
IT LOOKSSS LIKE I'LL HAVE TO RESSORT TO PLAN B.

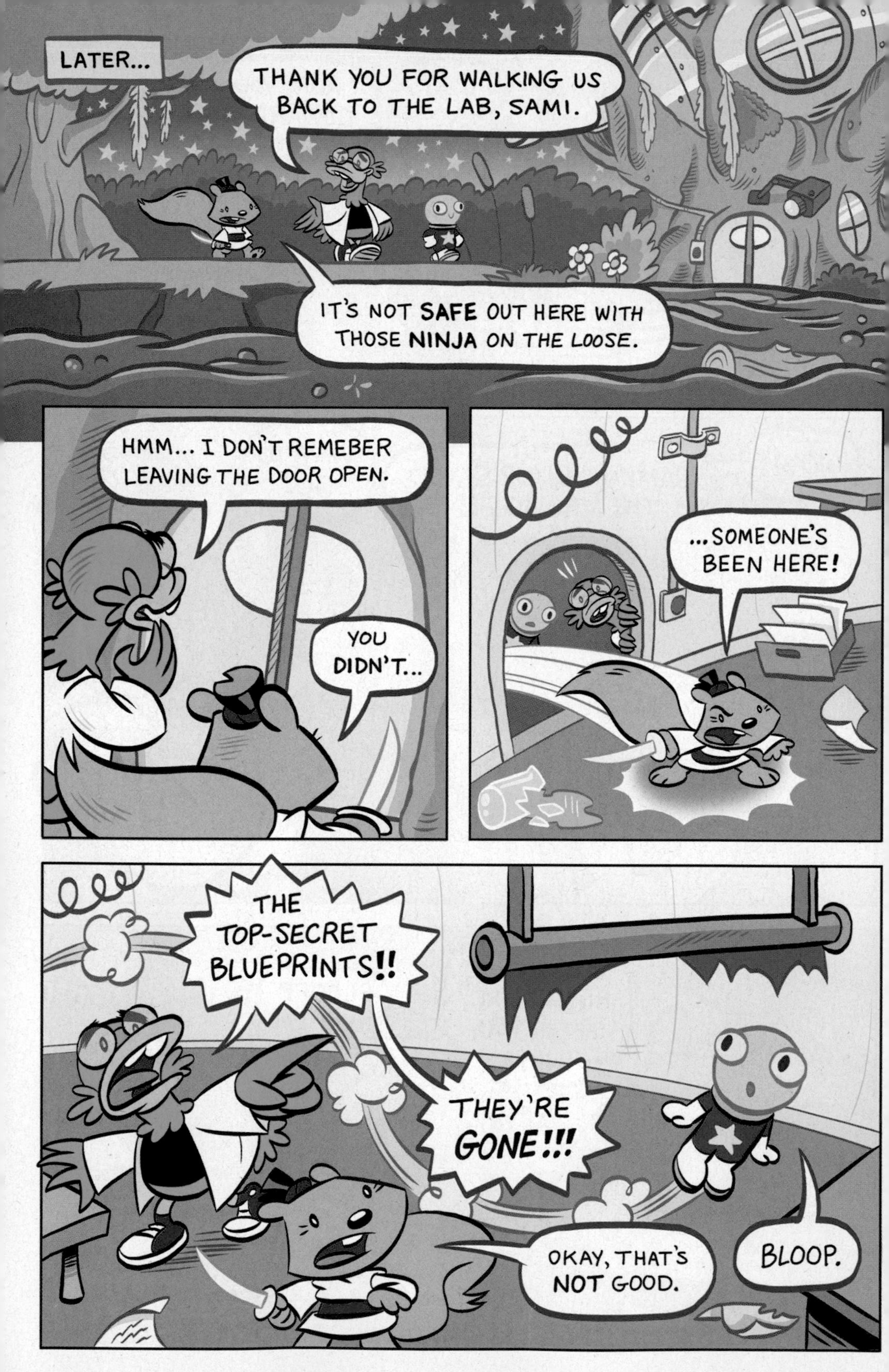
LATER...
THANK YOU FOR WALKING US BACK TO THE LAB, SAMI.
IT'S NOT SAFE OUT HERE WITH THOSE NINJA ON THE LOOSE.
HMM... I DON'T REMEBER LEAVING THE DOOR OPEN.
YOU DIDN'T...
...SOMEONE'S BEEN HERE!
THE TOP-SECRET BLUEPRINTS!!
THEY'RE GONE!!!
OKAY, THAT'S NOT GOOD.
BLOOP.

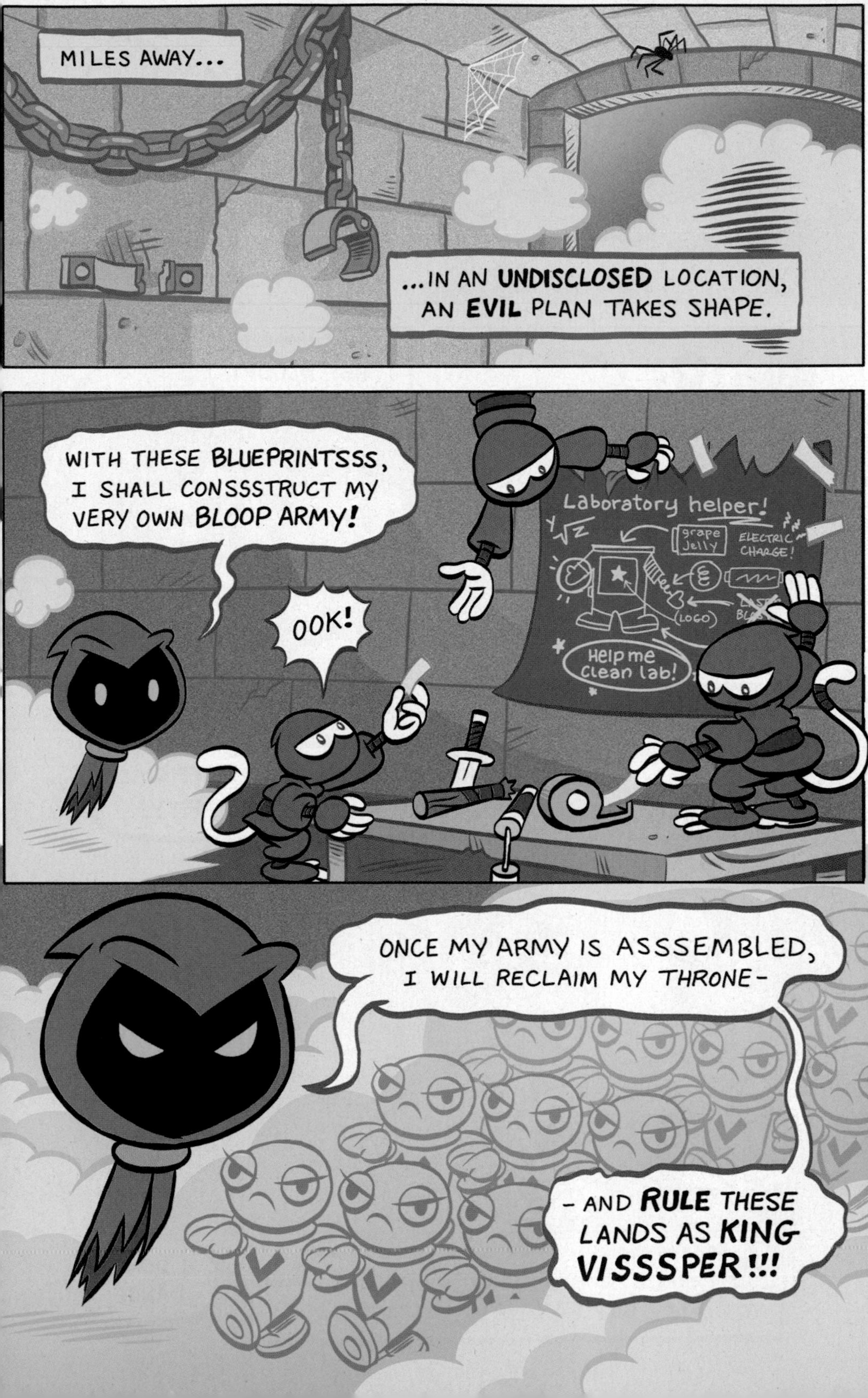
MILES AWAY...
...IN AN UNDISCLOSED LOCATION, AN EVIL PLAN TAKES SHAPE.
WITH THESE BLUEPRINTSSS, I SHALL CONSSSTRUCT MY VERY OWN BLOOP ARMY!
OOK!
Laboratory helper!
grape Jelly
ELECTRIC CHARGE!
(LOGO)
Help me clean lab!
ONCE MY ARMY IS ASSSEMBLED, I WILL RECLAIM MY THRONE-
-AND RULE THESE LANDS AS KING VISSSPER!!!

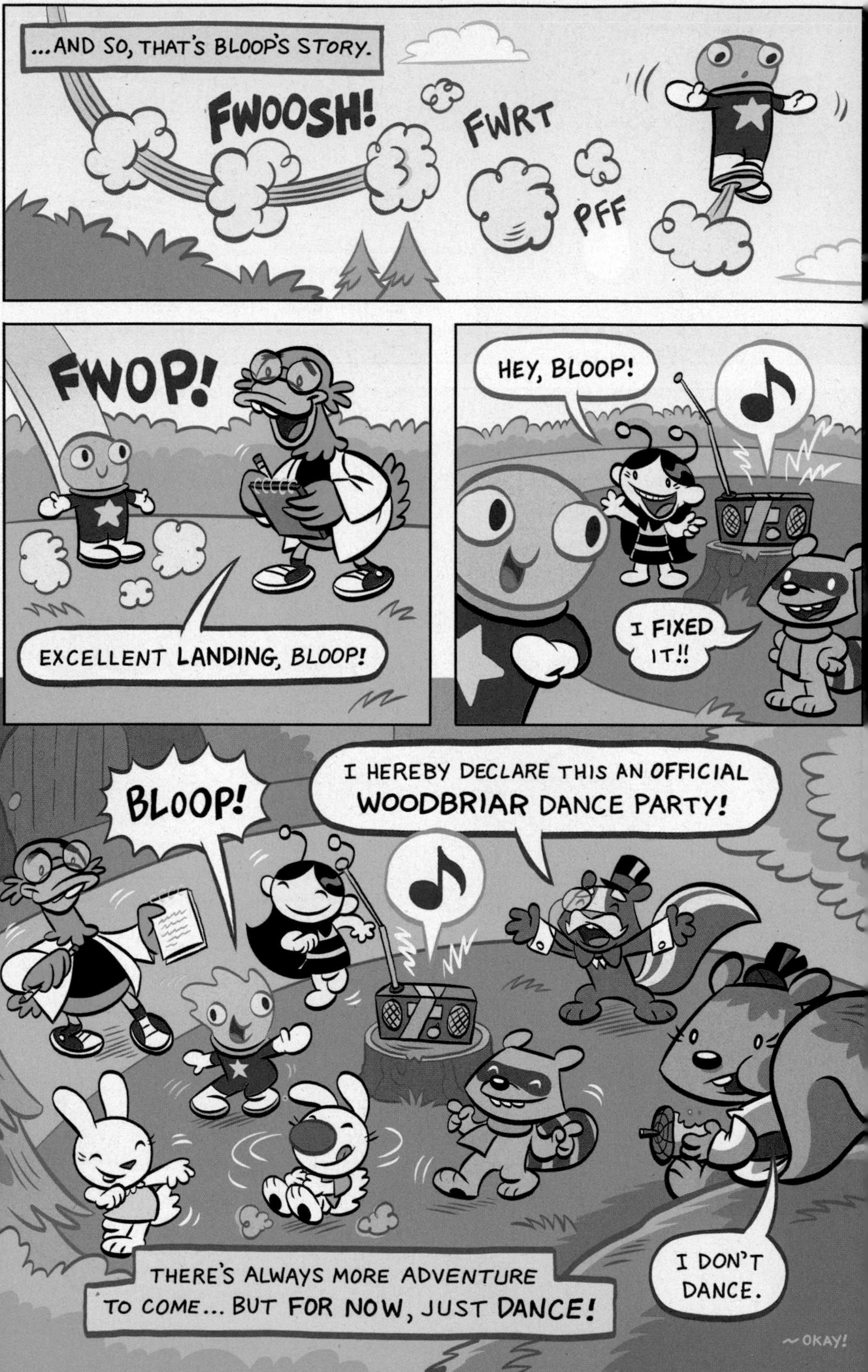
...AND SO, THAT'S BLOOP'S STORY.
FWOOSH!
FWRT
PFF
FWOP!
EXCELLENT LANDING, BLOOP!
HEY, BLOOP!
I FIXED IT!!
BLOOP!
I HEREBY DECLARE THIS AN OFFICIAL WOODBRIAR DANCE PARTY!
THERE'S ALWAYS MORE ADVENTURE TO COME... BUT FOR NOW, JUST DANCE!
I DON'T DANCE.
~OKAY!

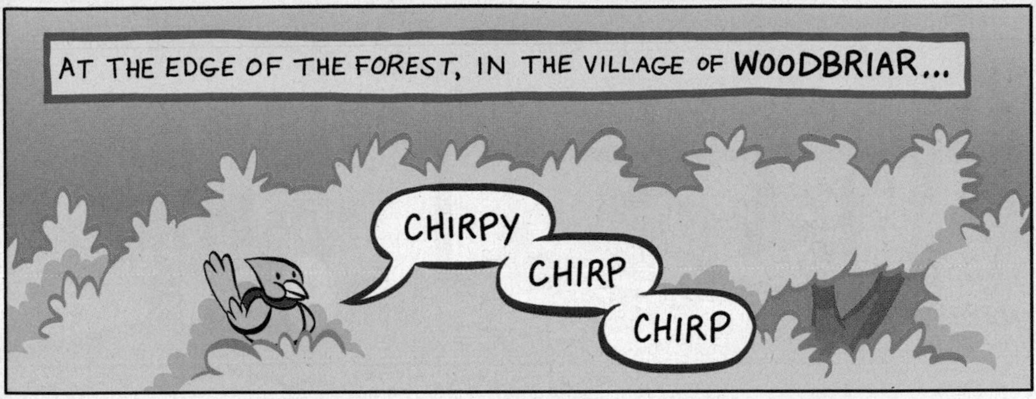
AT THE EDGE OF THE FOREST, IN THE VILLAGE OF WOODBRIAR...
CHIRPY
CHIRP
CHIRP

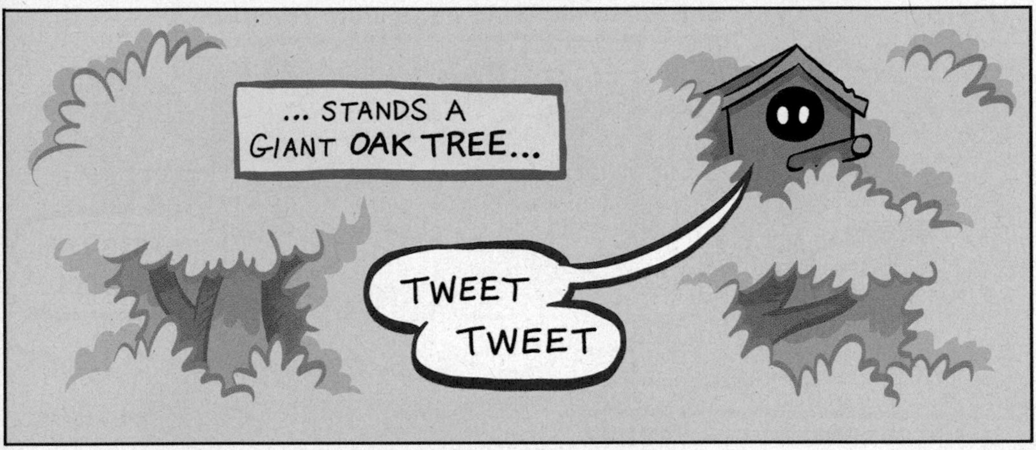
... STANDS A GIANT OAK TREE...
TWEET TWEET

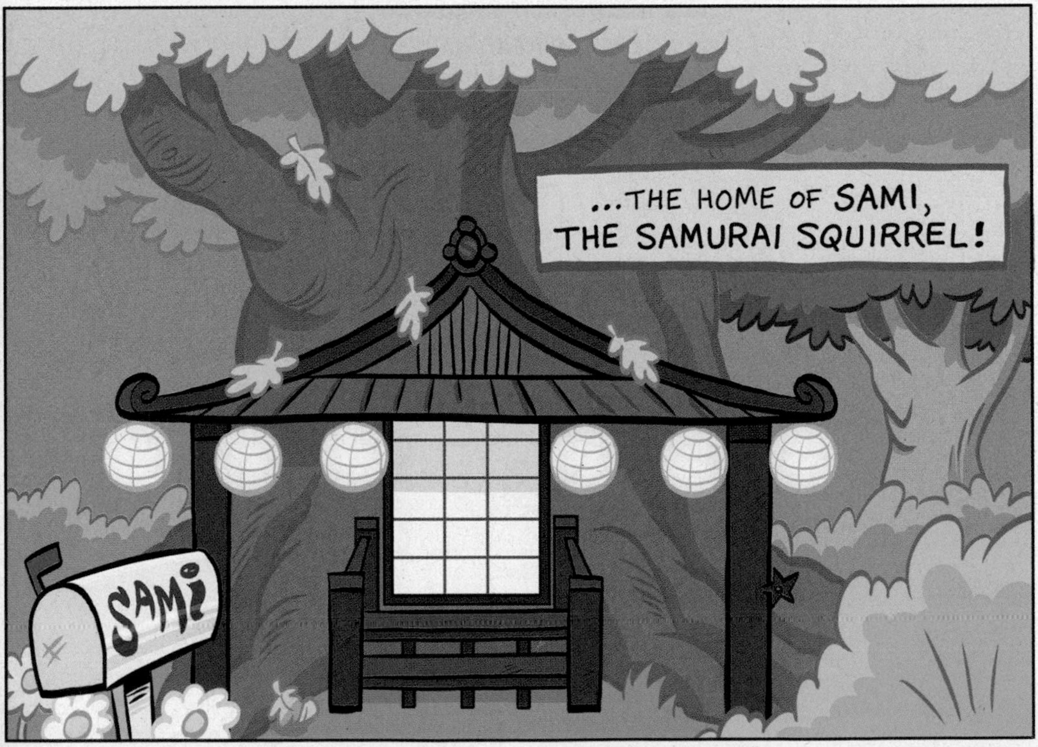
...THE HOME OF SAMI, THE SAMURAI SQUIRREL!
SAMI

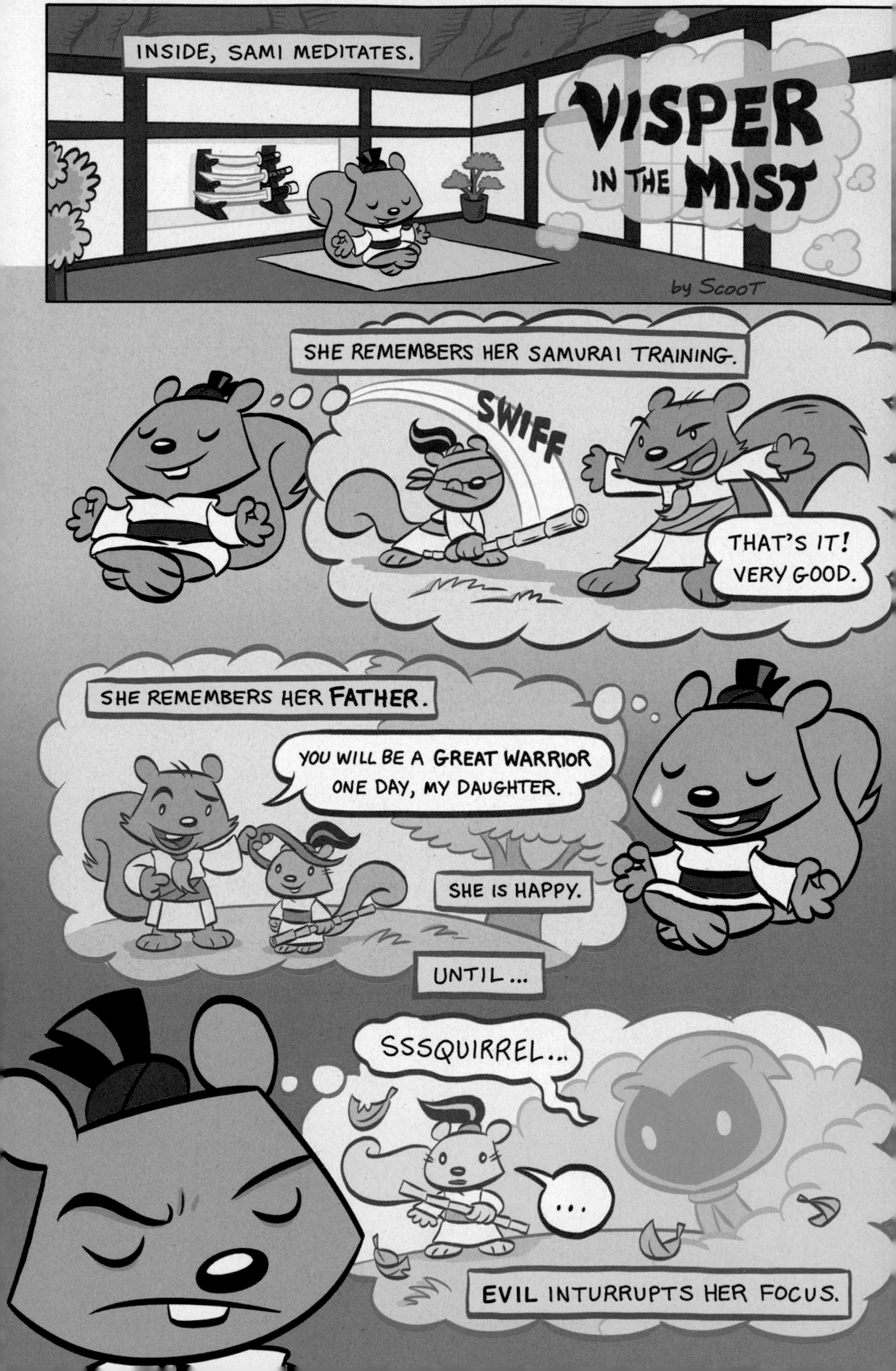
INSIDE, SAMI MEDITATES.
VISPER IN THE MIST
by SCOOT
SHE REMEMBERS HER SAMURAI TRAINING.
SWIFF
THAT'S IT! VERY GOOD.
SHE REMEMBERS HER FATHER.
YOU WILL BE A GREAT WARRIOR ONE DAY, MY DAUGHTER.
SHE IS HAPPY.
UNTIL...
SSSQUIRREL...
...
EVIL INTURRUPTS HER FOCUS.

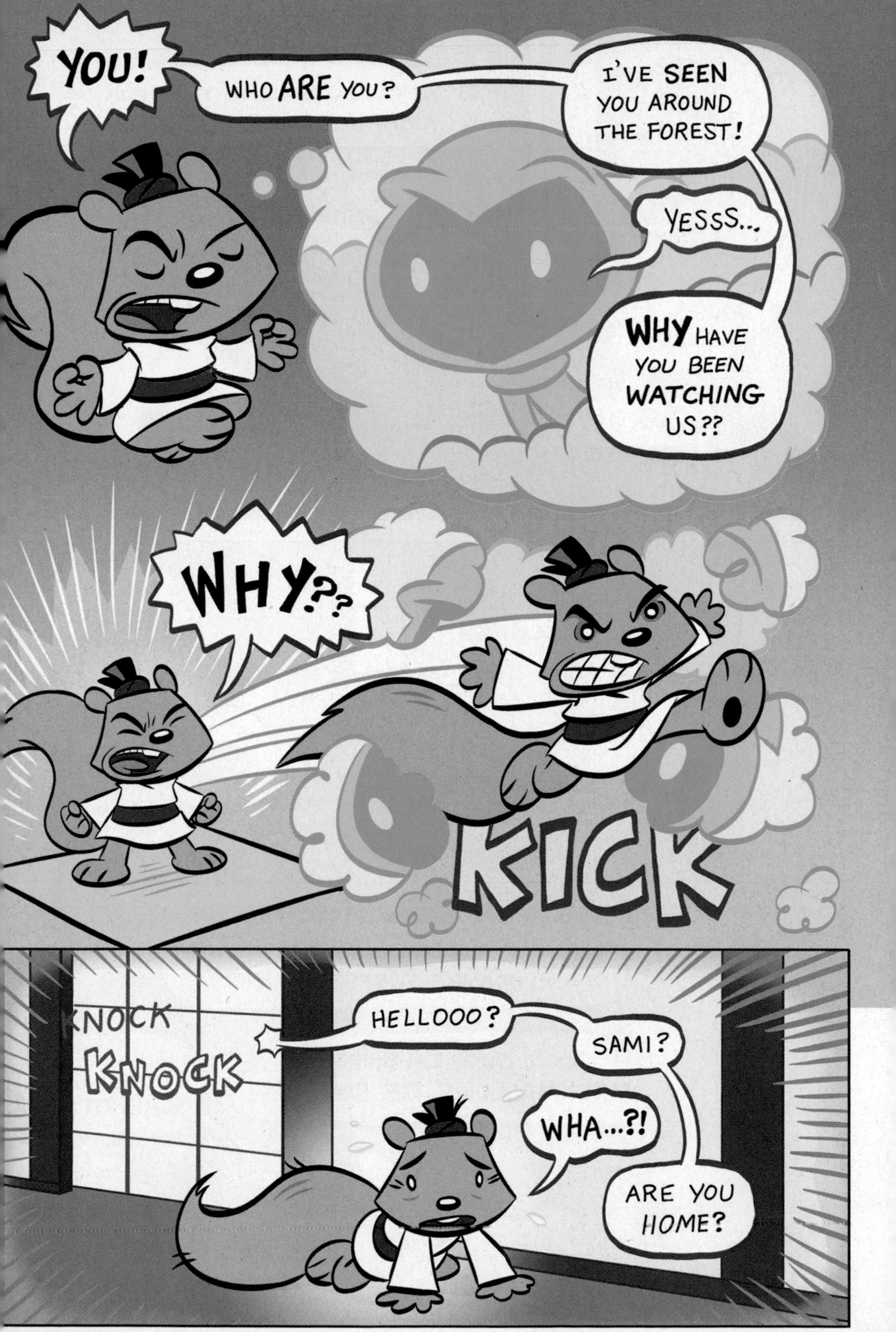
YOU!
WHO ARE YOU?
I'VE SEEN YOU AROUND THE FOREST!
YESSS...
WHY HAVE YOU BEEN WATCHING US??
WHY??
KICK
KNOCK
KNOCK
HELLOOO?
SAMI?
WHA...?!
ARE YOU HOME?

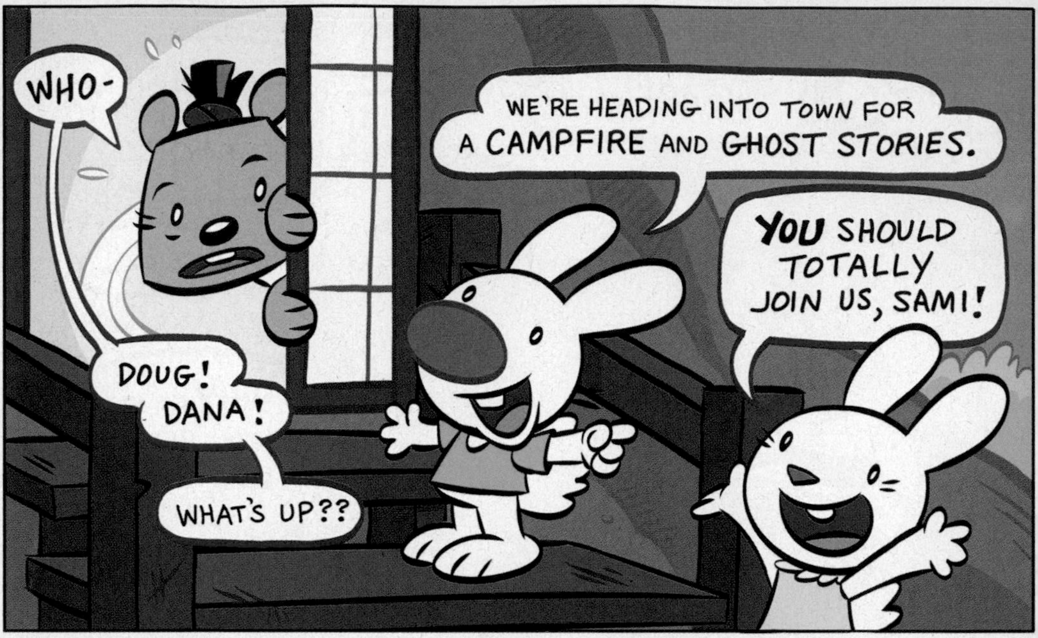
WHO-
WE'RE HEADING INTO TOWN FOR A CAMPFIRE AND GHOST STORIES.
YOU SHOULD TOTALLY JOIN US, SAMI!
DOUG! DANA!
WHAT'S UP??

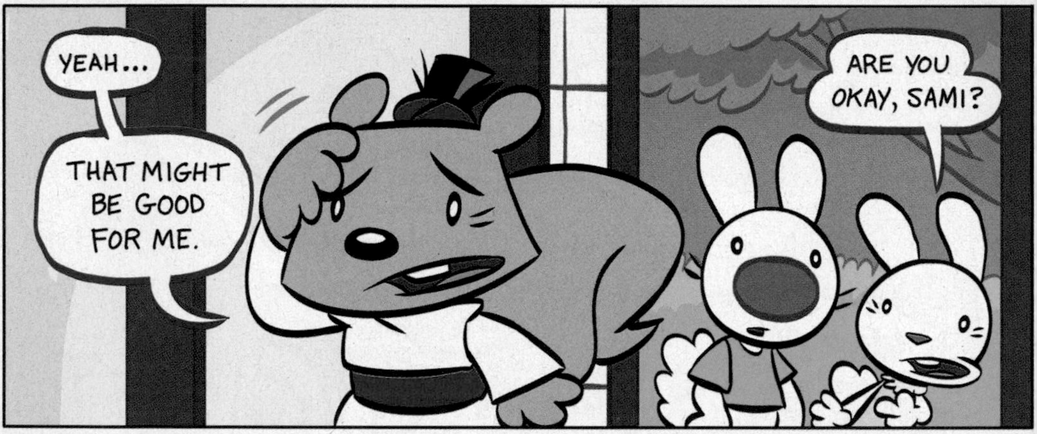
YEAH...
THAT MIGHT BE GOOD FOR ME.
ARE YOU OKAY, SAMI?

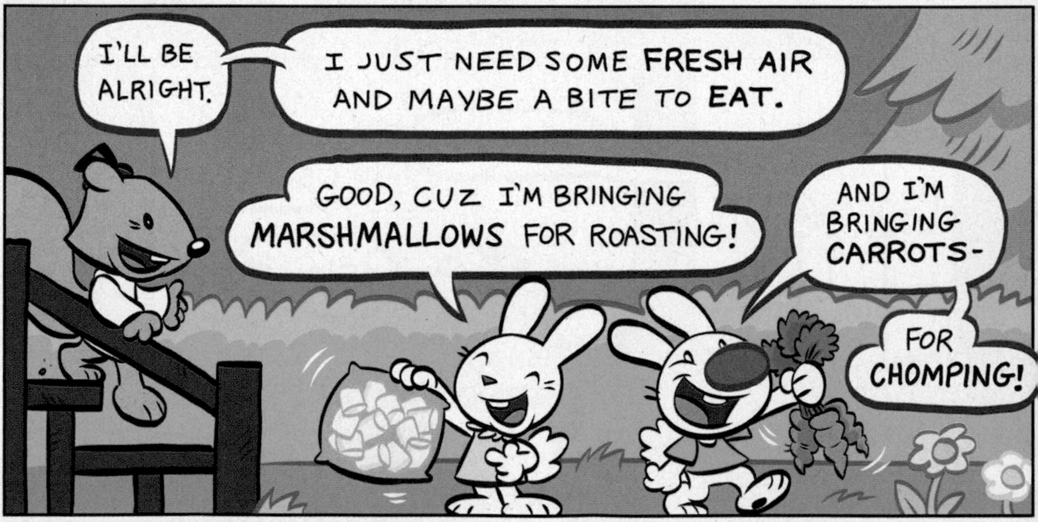
I'LL BE ALRIGHT.
I JUST NEED SOME FRESH AIR AND MAYBE A BITE TO EAT.
GOOD, CUZ I'M BRINGING MARSHMALLOWS FOR ROASTING!
AND I'M BRINGING CARROTS-
FOR CHOMPING!

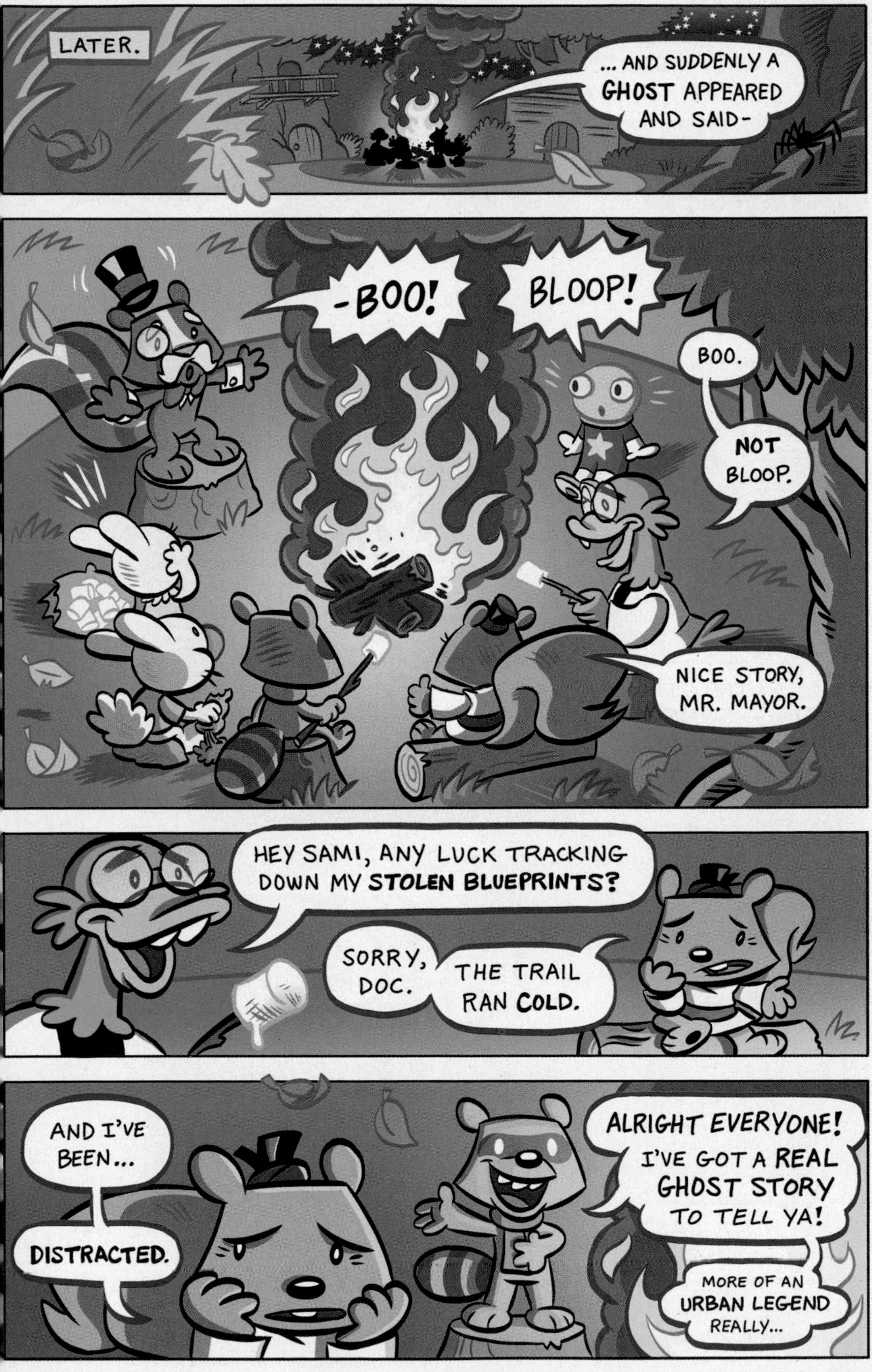

LATER.
... AND SUDDENLY A GHOST APPEARED AND SAID-
-BOO!
BLOOP!
BOO.
NOT BLOOP.
NICE STORY, MR. MAYOR.
HEY SAMI, ANY LUCK TRACKING DOWN MY STOLEN BLUEPRINTS?
SORRY, DOC.
THE TRAIL RAN COLD.
AND I'VE BEEN...
DISTRACTED.
ALRIGHT EVERYONE! I'VE GOT A REAL GHOST STORY TO TELL YA!
MORE OF AN URBAN LEGEND REALLY...

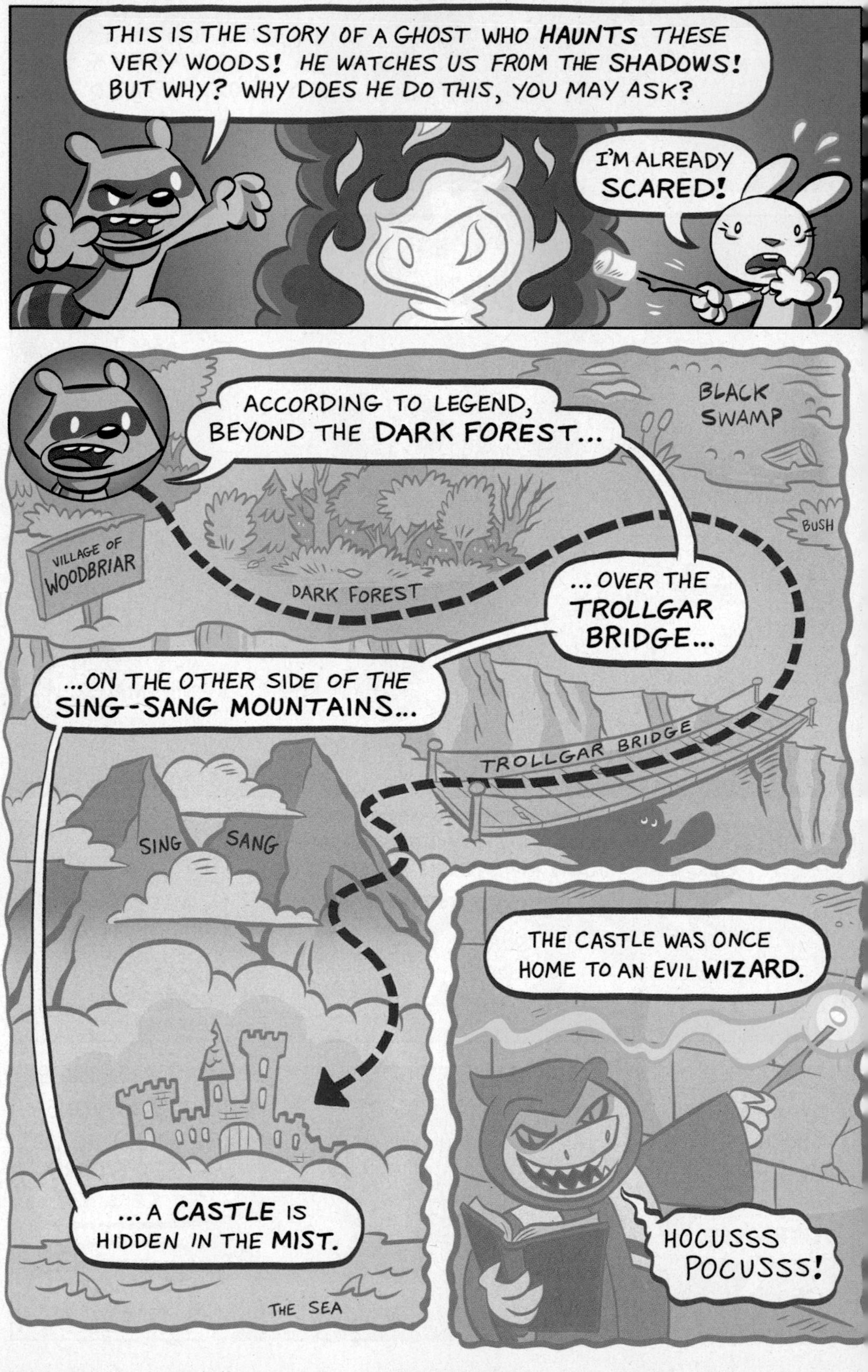
THIS IS THE STORY OF A GHOST WHO HAUNTS THESE VERY WOODS! HE WATCHES US FROM THE SHADOWS! BUT WHY? WHY DOES HE DO THIS, YOU MAY ASK?
I'M ALREADY SCARED!
ACCORDING TO LEGEND, BEYOND THE DARK FOREST...
BLACK SWAMP
BUSH
VILLAGE OF WOODBRIAR
DARK FOREST
...OVER THE TROLLGAR BRIDGE...
...ON THE OTHER SIDE OF THE SING-SANG MOUNTAINS...
TROLLGAR BRIDGE
SING
SANG
...A CASTLE IS HIDDEN IN THE MIST.
THE SEA
THE CASTLE WAS ONCE HOME TO AN EVIL WIZARD.
HOCUSSS POCUSSS!

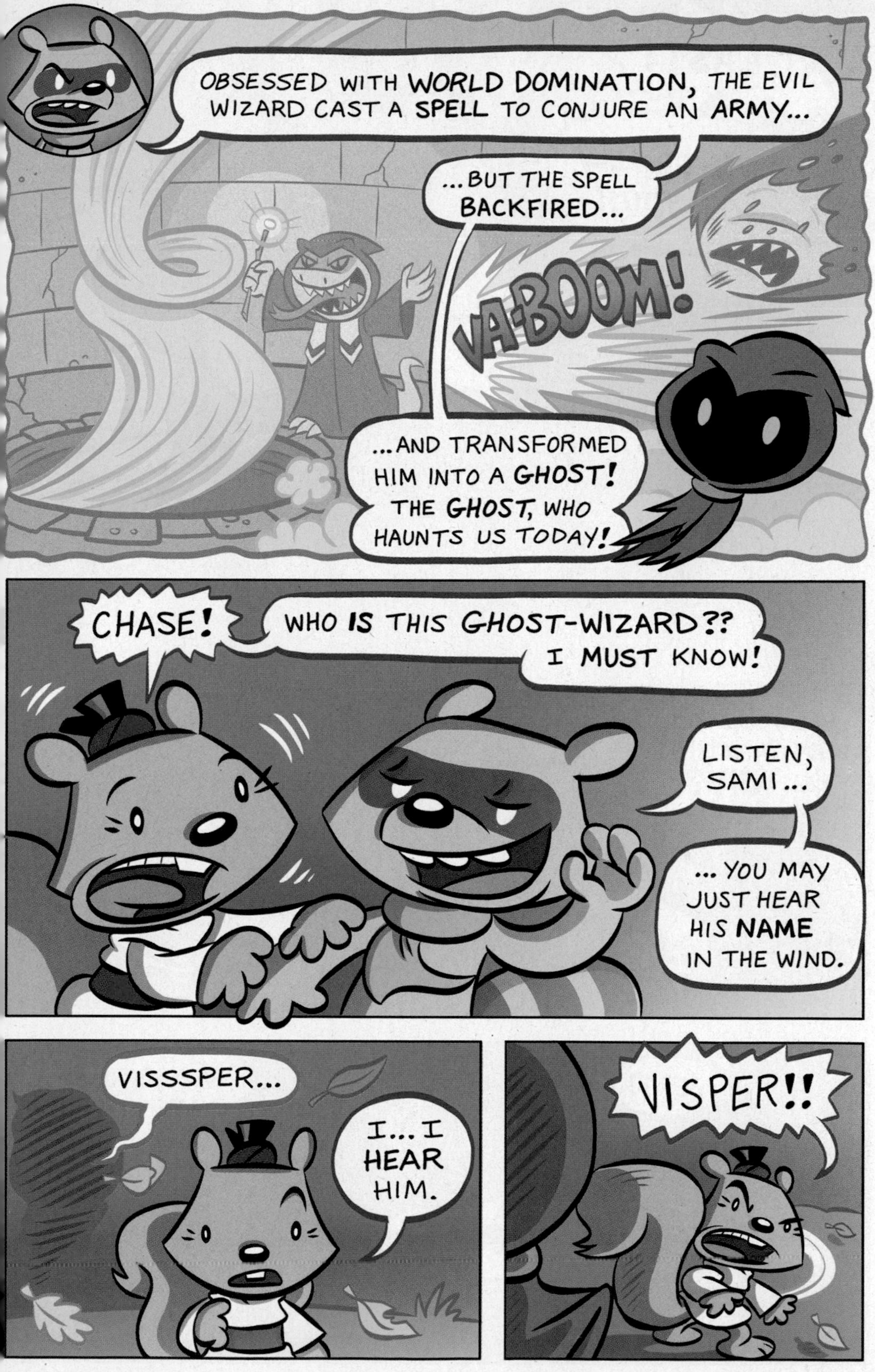
OBSESSED WITH WORLD DOMINATION, THE EVIL WIZARD CAST A SPELL TO CONJURE AN ARMY...
...BUT THE SPELL BACKFIRED...
VA-BOOM!
...AND TRANSFORMED HIM INTO A GHOST! THE GHOST, WHO HAUNTS US TODAY!
CHASE!
WHO IS THIS GHOST-WIZARD?? I MUST KNOW!
LISTEN, SAMI...
...YOU MAY JUST HEAR HIS NAME IN THE WIND.
VISSSPER...
I... I HEAR HIM.
VISPER!!

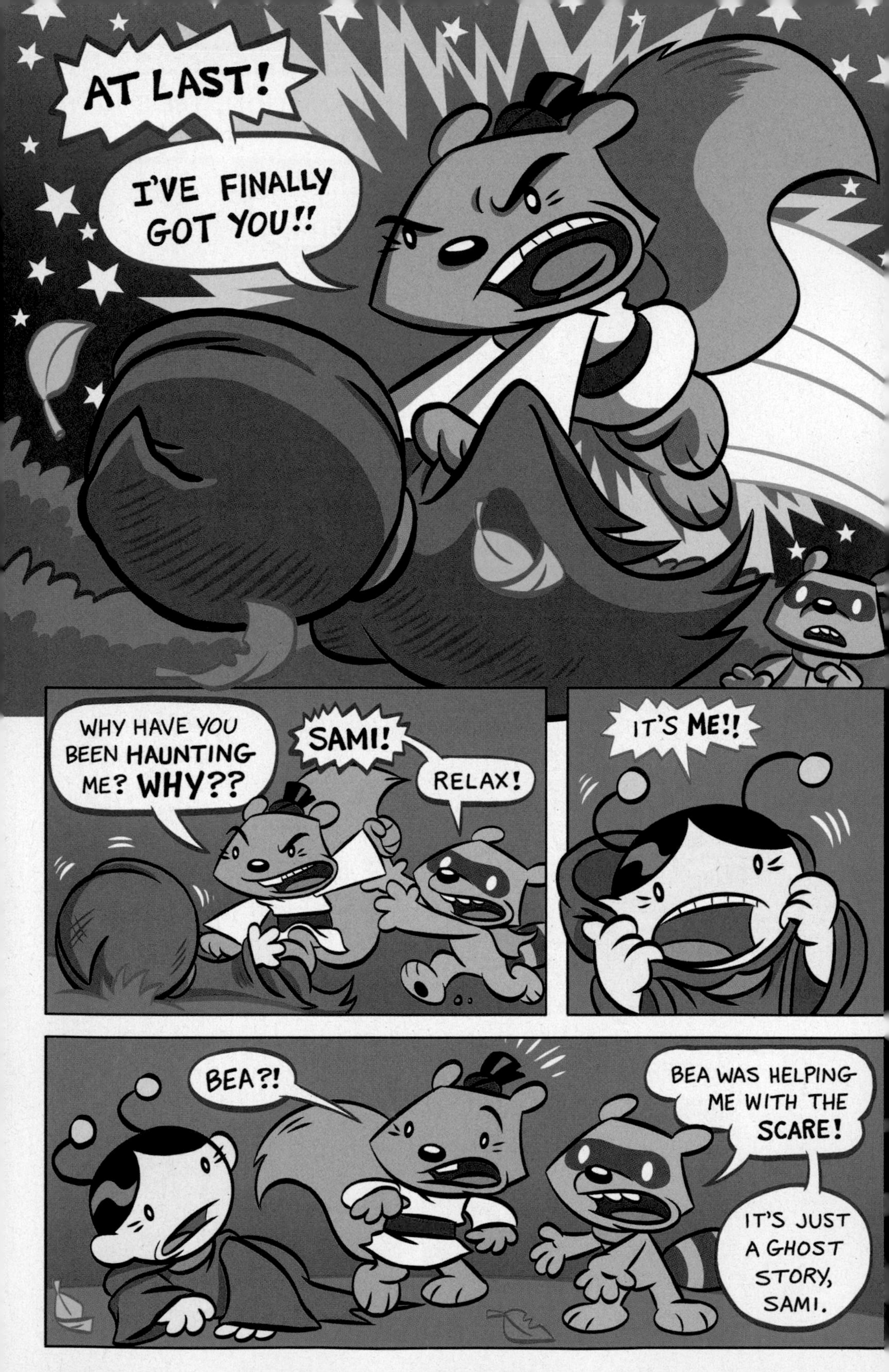
AT LAST!
I'VE FINALLY GOT YOU!!
WHY HAVE YOU BEEN HAUNTING ME? WHY??
SAMI!
RELAX!
IT'S ME!!
BEA?!
BEA WAS HELPING ME WITH THE SCARE!
IT'S JUST A GHOST STORY, SAMI.

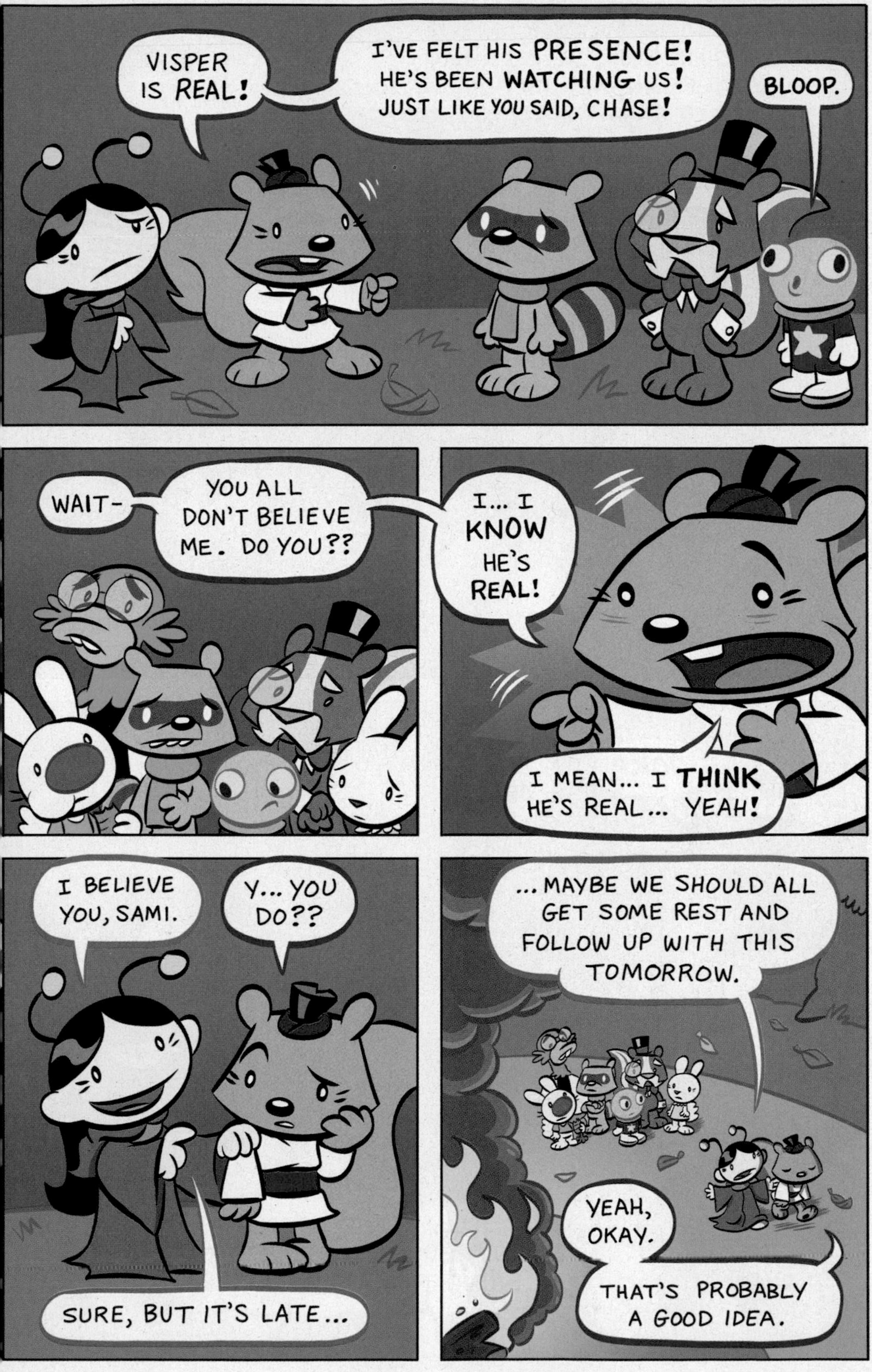
VISPER IS REAL!
I'VE FELT HIS PRESENCE! HE'S BEEN WATCHING US! JUST LIKE YOU SAID, CHASE!
BLOOP.
WAIT-
YOU ALL DON'T BELIEVE ME. DO YOU??
I... I KNOW HE'S REAL!
I MEAN... I THINK HE'S REAL... YEAH!
I BELIEVE YOU, SAMI.
Y... YOU DO??
SURE, BUT IT'S LATE...
...MAYBE WE SHOULD ALL GET SOME REST AND FOLLOW UP WITH THIS TOMORROW.
YEAH, OKAY.
THAT'S PROBABLY A GOOD IDEA.

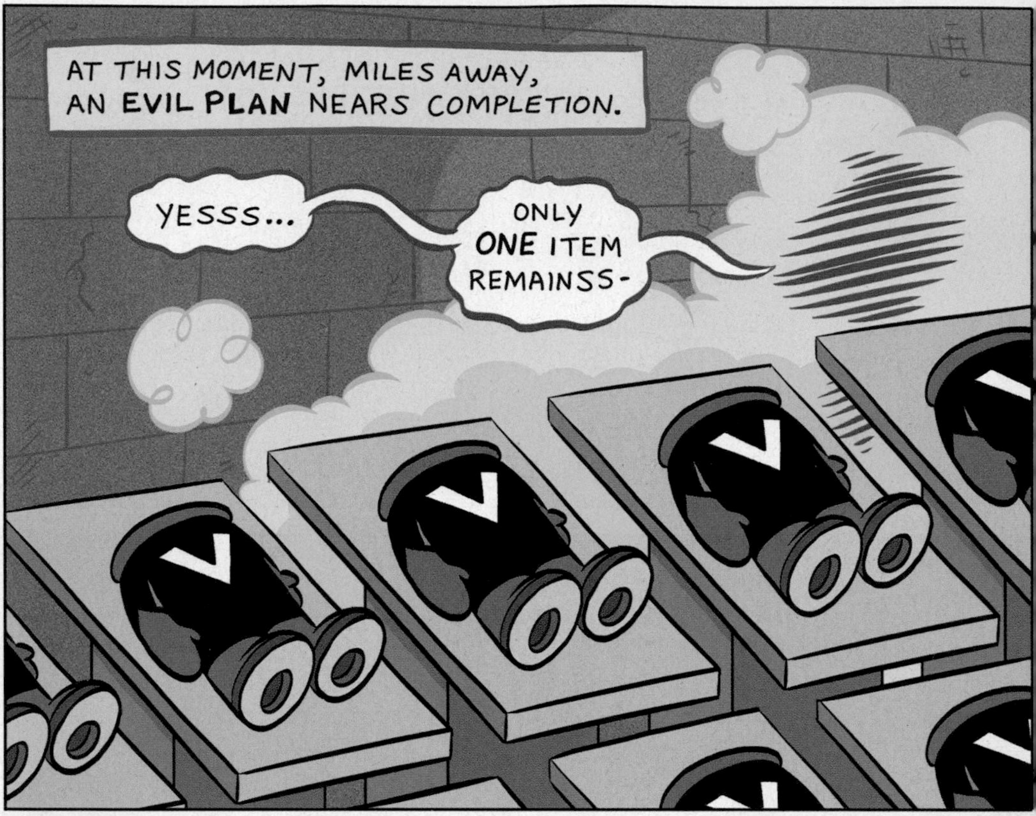
AT THIS MOMENT, MILES AWAY, AN EVIL PLAN NEARS COMPLETION.
YESSS...
ONLY ONE ITEM REMAINSS-

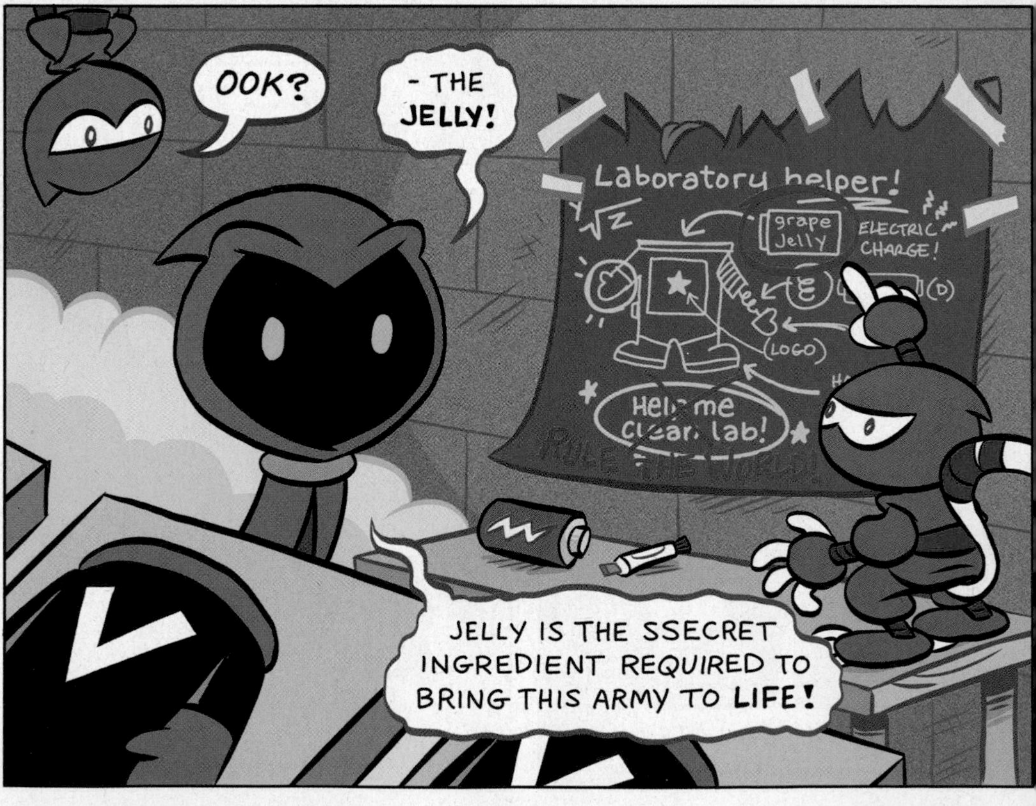
OOK?
- THE JELLY!
Laboratory helper!
grape Jelly
ELECTRIC CHARGE!
(LOGO)
(D)
Help me clean lab!
JELLY IS THE SSECRET INGREDIENT REQUIRED TO BRING THIS ARMY TO LIFE!

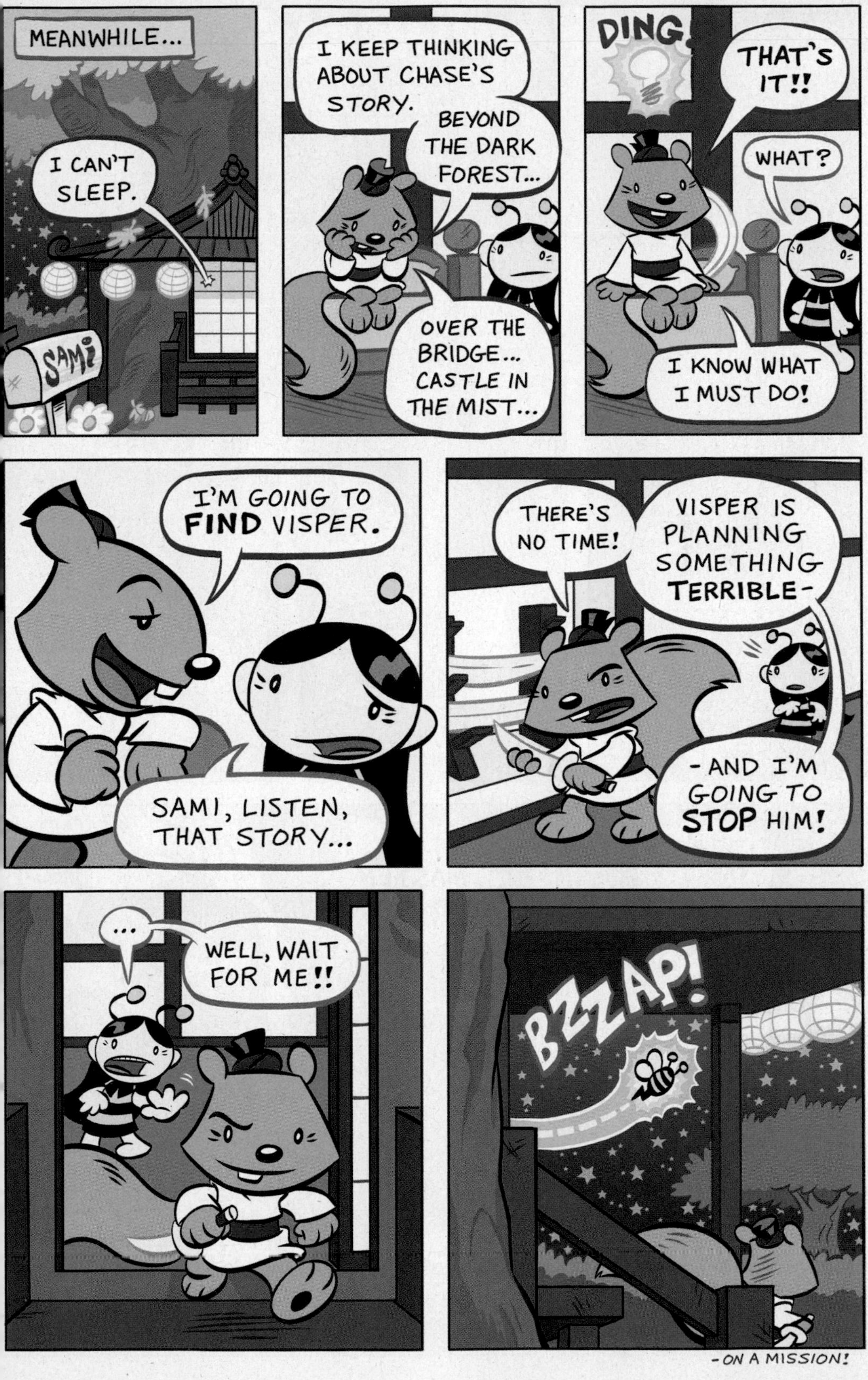
MEANWHILE...
I CAN'T SLEEP.
SAMI
I KEEP THINKING ABOUT CHASE'S STORY.
BEYOND THE DARK FOREST...
OVER THE BRIDGE... CASTLE IN THE MIST...
DING!
THAT'S IT!!
WHAT?
I KNOW WHAT I MUST DO!
I'M GOING TO FIND VISPER.
SAMI, LISTEN, THAT STORY...
THERE'S NO TIME!
VISPER IS PLANNING SOMETHING TERRIBLE-
-AND I'M GOING TO STOP HIM!
...
WELL, WAIT FOR ME!!
BZZAP!

-ON A MISSION!

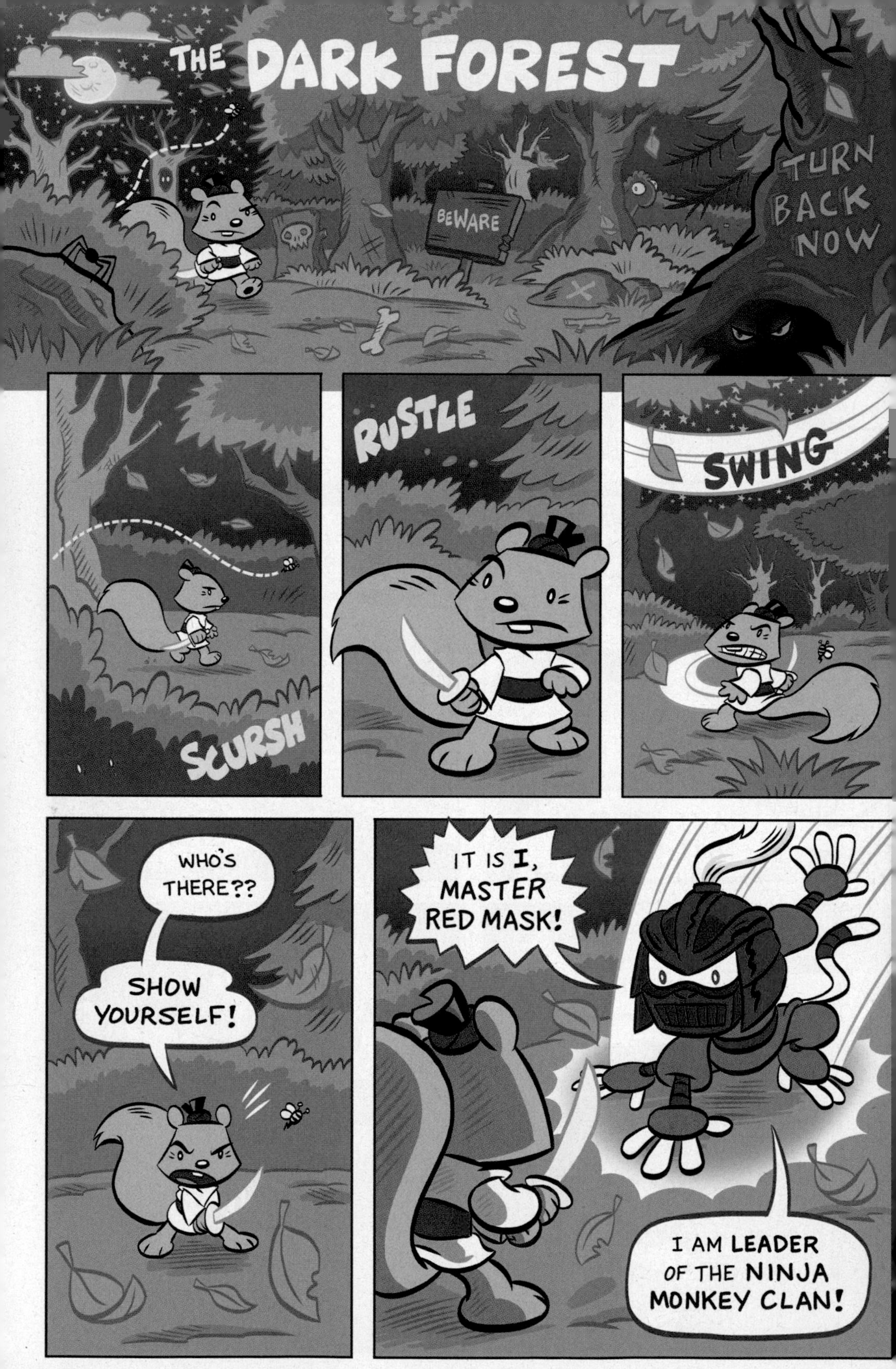
THE DARK FOREST
BEWARE
TURN BACK NOW
SCURSH
RUSTLE
SWING
WHO'S THERE??
SHOW YOURSELF!
IT IS I, MASTER RED MASK!
I AM LEADER OF THE NINJA MONKEY CLAN!

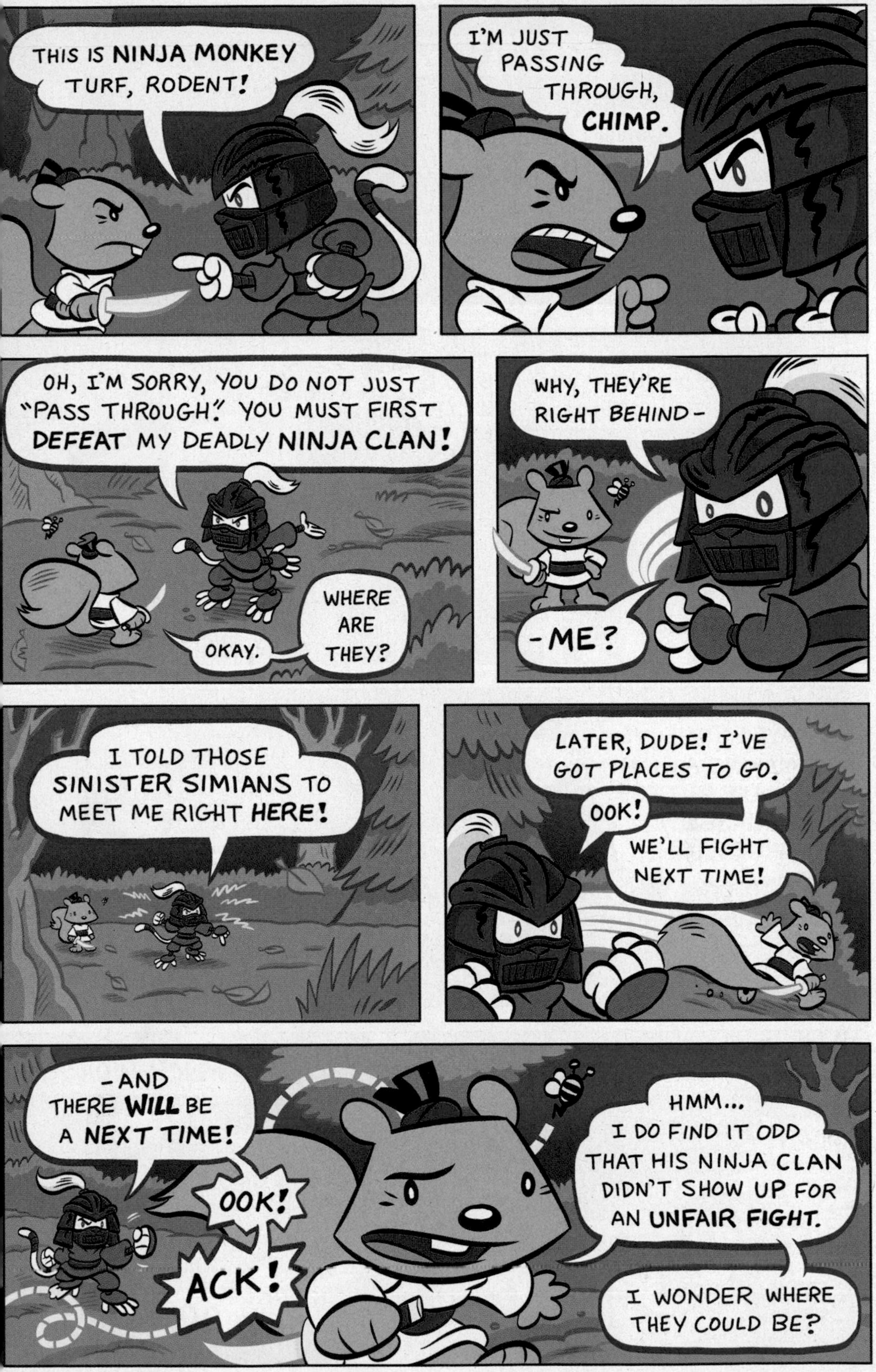
THIS IS NINJA MONKEY TURF, RODENT!
I'M JUST PASSING THROUGH, CHIMP.
OH, I'M SORRY, YOU DO NOT JUST "PASS THROUGH." YOU MUST FIRST DEFEAT MY DEADLY NINJA CLAN!
OKAY.
WHERE ARE THEY?
WHY, THEY'RE RIGHT BEHIND–
–ME?
I TOLD THOSE SINISTER SIMIANS TO MEET ME RIGHT HERE!
LATER, DUDE! I'VE GOT PLACES TO GO.
OOK!
WE'LL FIGHT NEXT TIME!
–AND THERE WILL BE A NEXT TIME!
OOK!
ACK!
HMM... I DO FIND IT ODD THAT HIS NINJA CLAN DIDN'T SHOW UP FOR AN UNFAIR FIGHT.
I WONDER WHERE THEY COULD BE?

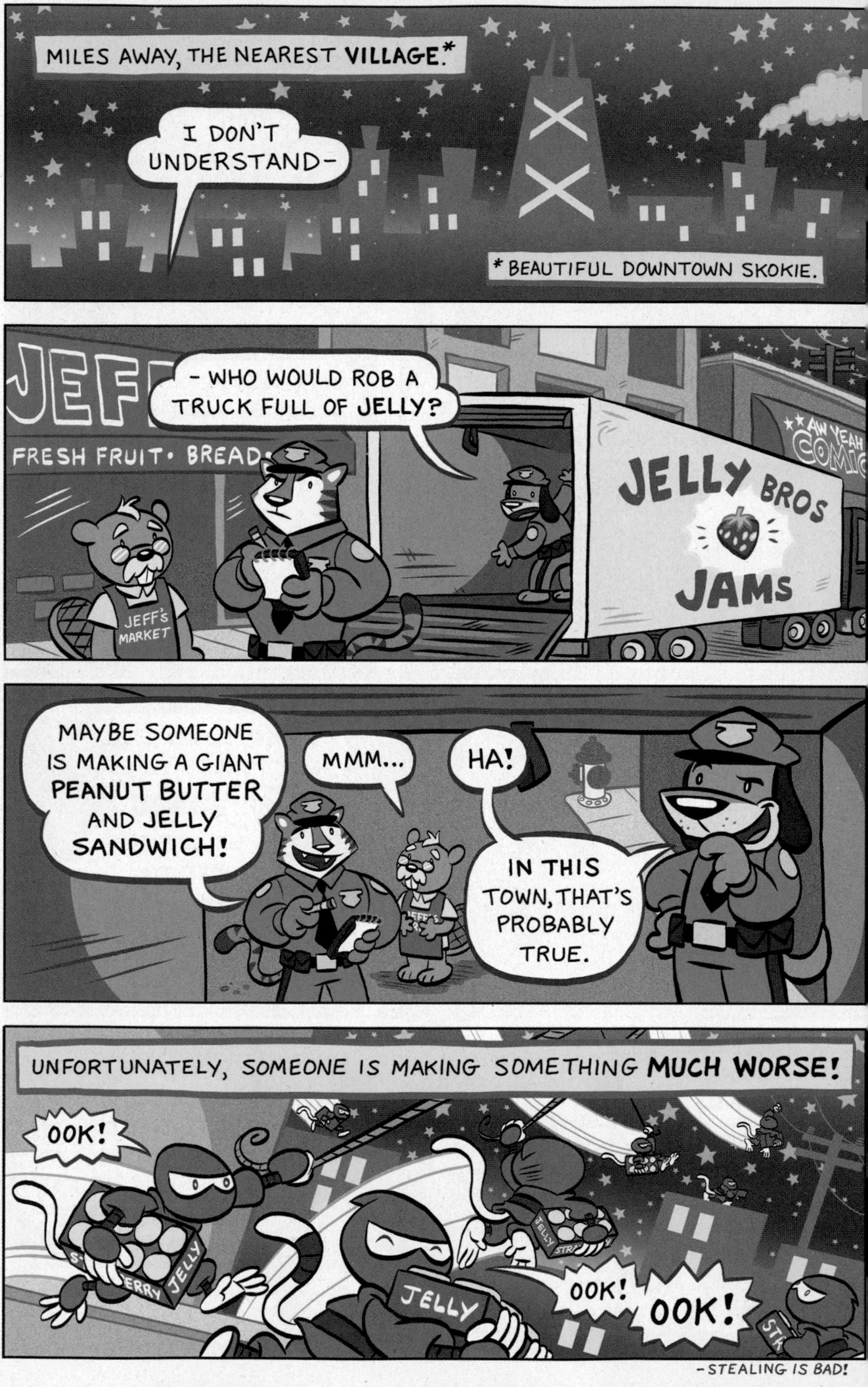

MILES AWAY, THE NEAREST **VILLAGE**.*
I DON'T UNDERSTAND-
* BEAUTIFUL DOWNTOWN SKOKIE.
JEFF
FRESH FRUIT • BREAD
- WHO WOULD ROB A TRUCK FULL OF **JELLY**?
JEFF'S MARKET
JELLY BROS JAMS
AW YEAH COMIC
MAYBE SOMEONE IS MAKING A GIANT **PEANUT BUTTER AND JELLY SANDWICH!**
MMM...
HA!
IN THIS TOWN, THAT'S PROBABLY TRUE.
UNFORTUNATELY, SOMEONE IS MAKING SOMETHING **MUCH WORSE!**
OOK!
JELLY
OOK!
OOK!

-STEALING IS BAD!

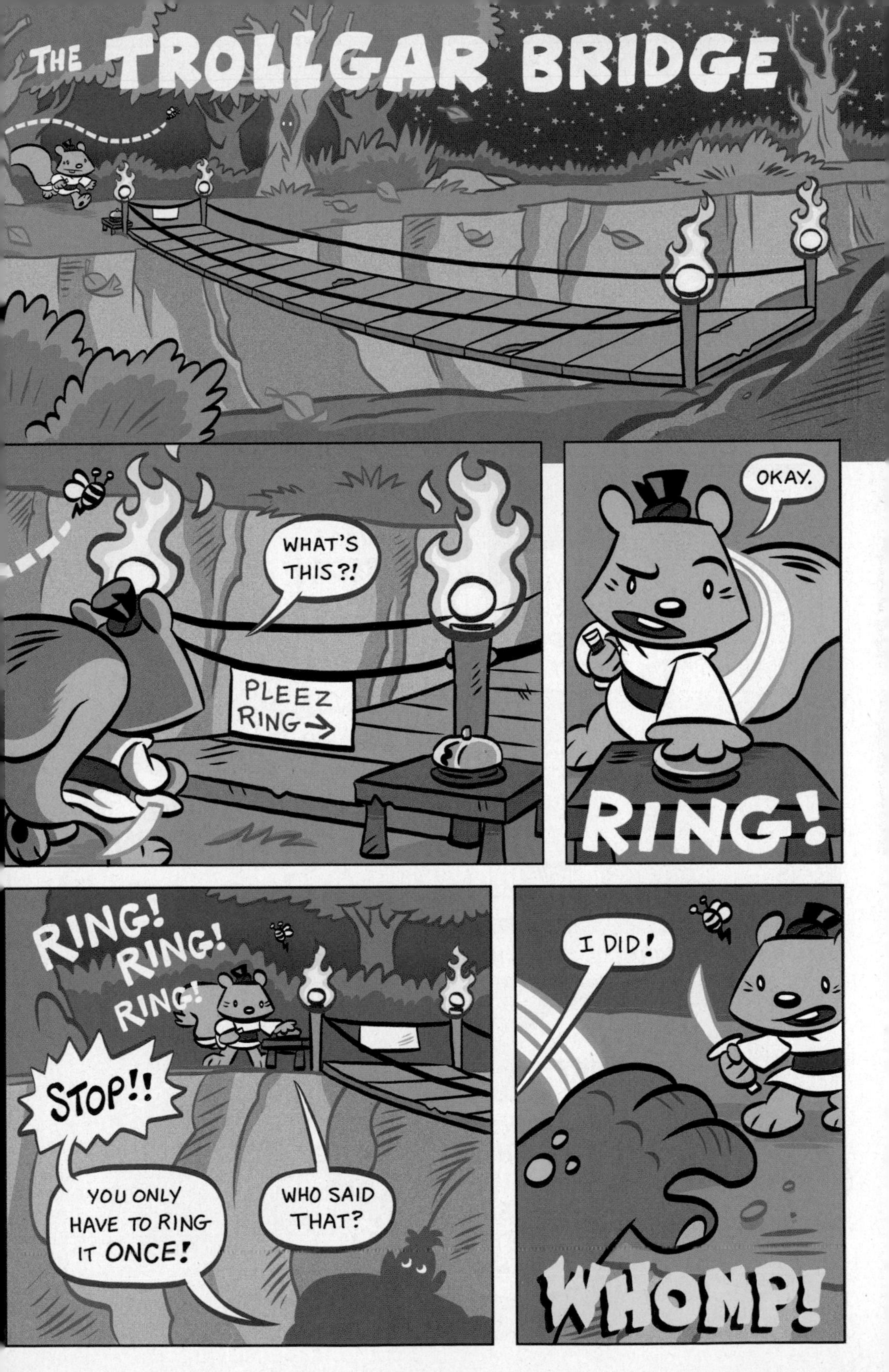
THE TROLLGAR BRIDGE
WHAT'S THIS?!
PLEEZ RING →
OKAY.
RING!
RING! RING! RING!
STOP!!
YOU ONLY HAVE TO RING IT ONCE!
WHO SAID THAT?
I DID!
WHOMP!

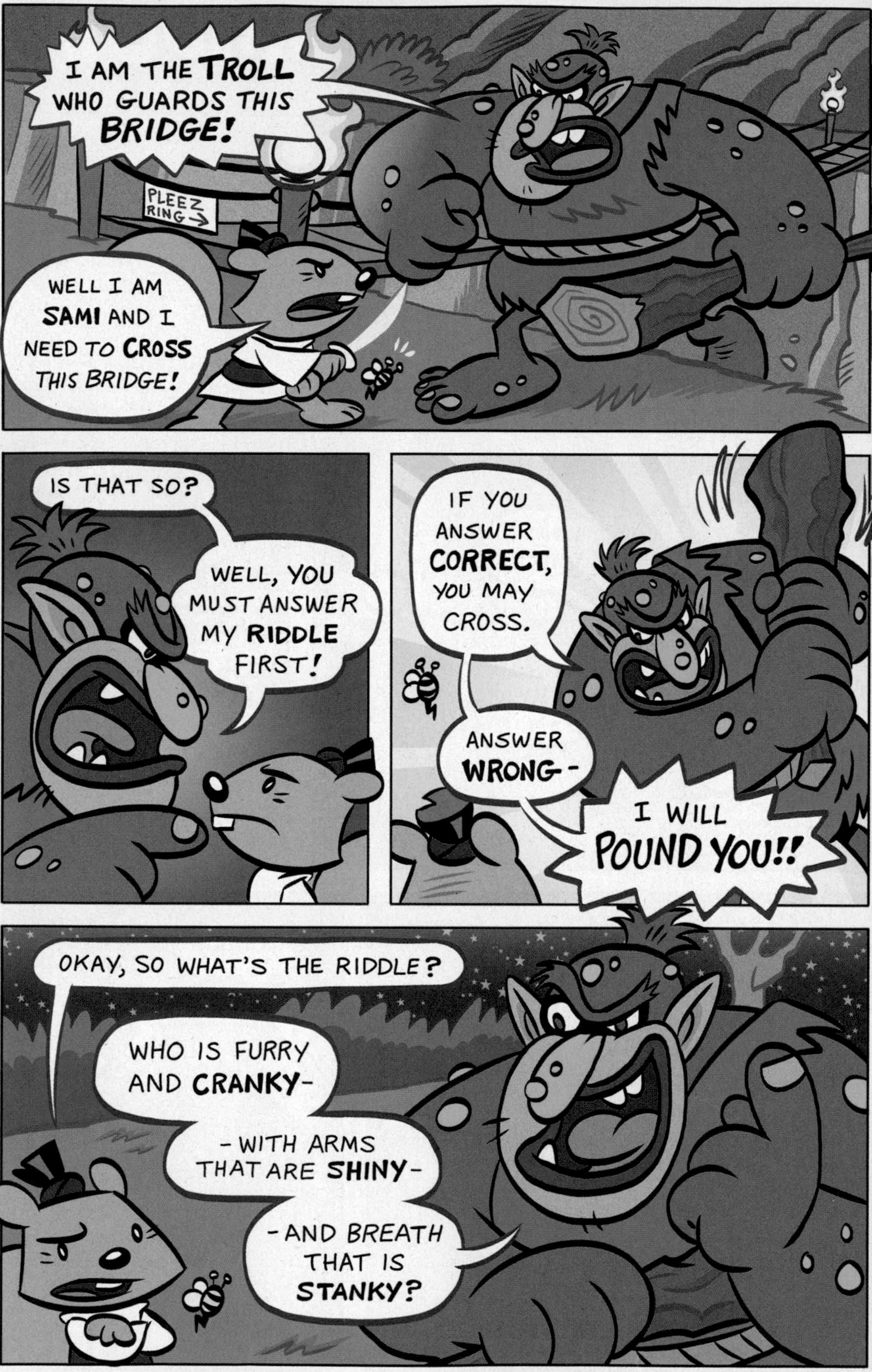
I AM THE TROLL WHO GUARDS THIS BRIDGE!
PLEEZ RING →
WELL I AM SAMI AND I NEED TO CROSS THIS BRIDGE!
IS THAT SO?
WELL, YOU MUST ANSWER MY RIDDLE FIRST!
IF YOU ANSWER CORRECT, YOU MAY CROSS.
ANSWER WRONG-
I WILL POUND YOU!!
OKAY, SO WHAT'S THE RIDDLE?
WHO IS FURRY AND CRANKY-
-WITH ARMS THAT ARE SHINY-
-AND BREATH THAT IS STANKY?

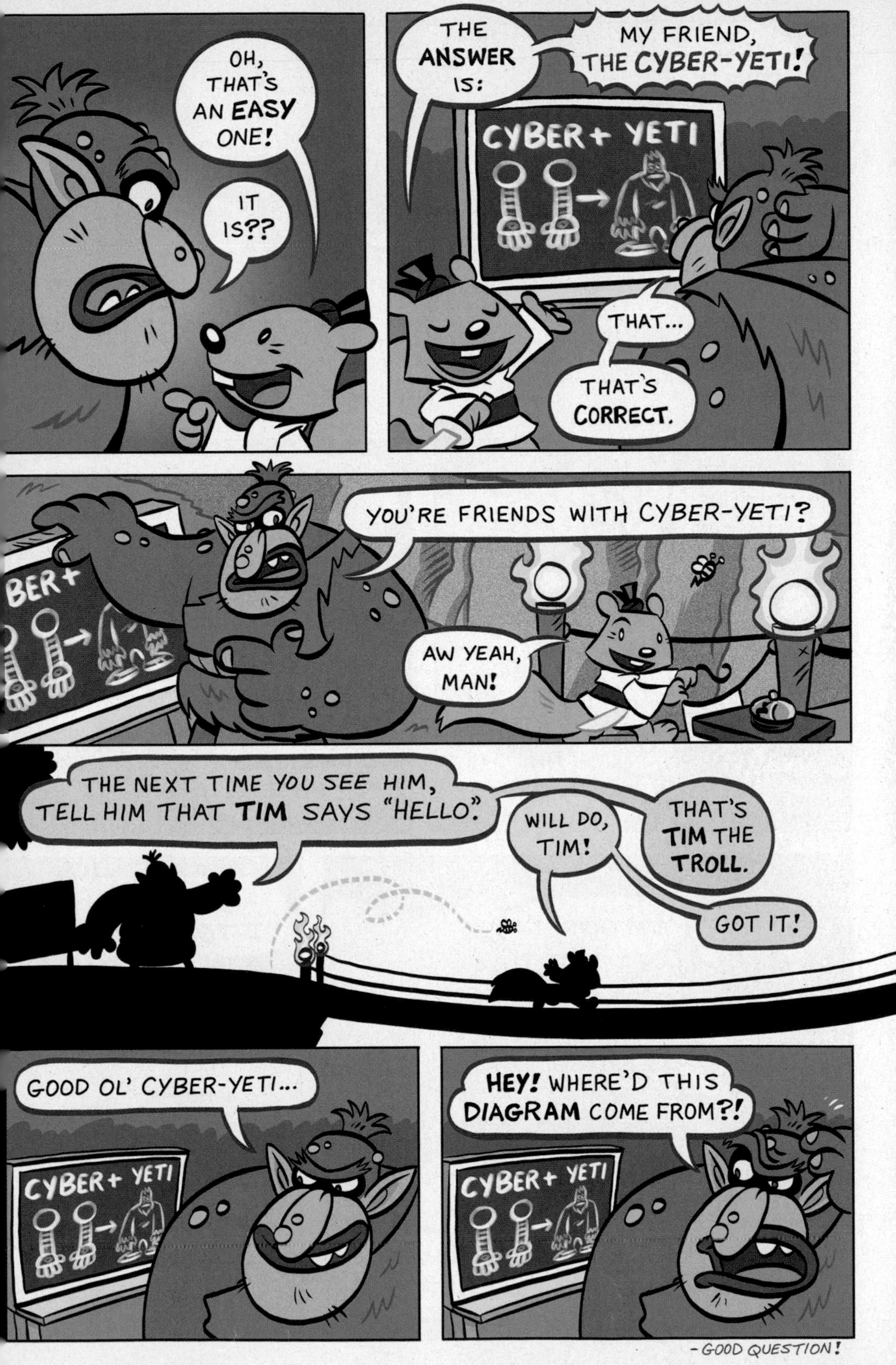
OH, THAT'S AN EASY ONE!
IT IS??
THE ANSWER IS:
MY FRIEND, THE CYBER-YETI!
CYBER + YETI
THAT...
THAT'S CORRECT.
YOU'RE FRIENDS WITH CYBER-YETI?
AW YEAH, MAN!
THE NEXT TIME YOU SEE HIM, TELL HIM THAT TIM SAYS "HELLO."
WILL DO, TIM!
THAT'S TIM THE TROLL.
GOT IT!
GOOD OL' CYBER-YETI...
CYBER + YETI
HEY! WHERE'D THIS DIAGRAM COME FROM?!
CYBER + YETI
- GOOD QUESTION!

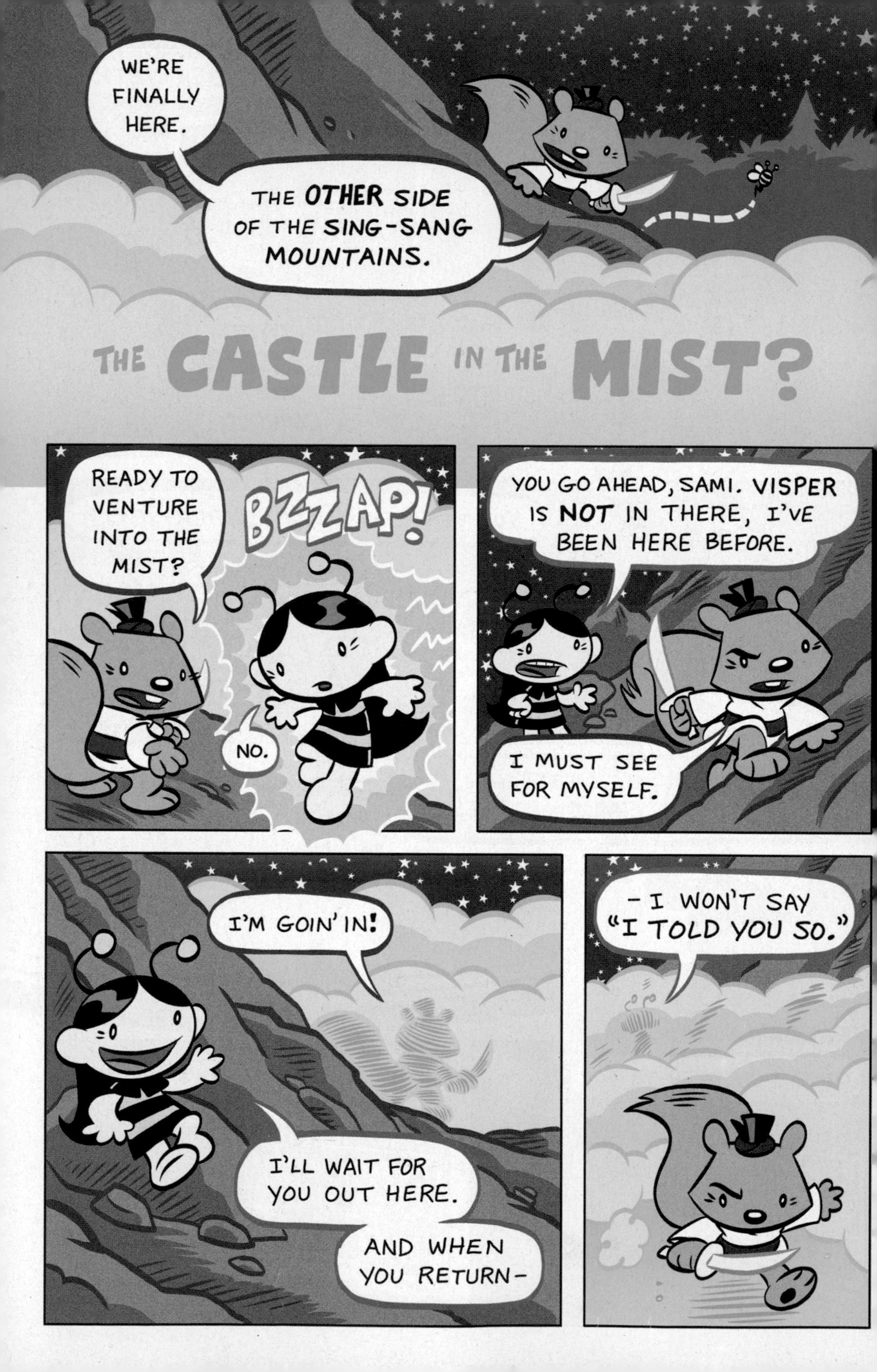
WE'RE FINALLY HERE.
THE OTHER SIDE OF THE SING-SANG MOUNTAINS.
THE CASTLE IN THE MIST?
READY TO VENTURE INTO THE MIST?
BZZAP!
NO.
YOU GO AHEAD, SAMI. VISPER IS NOT IN THERE, I'VE BEEN HERE BEFORE.
I MUST SEE FOR MYSELF.
I'M GOIN' IN!
I'LL WAIT FOR YOU OUT HERE.
AND WHEN YOU RETURN-
-I WON'T SAY "I TOLD YOU SO."

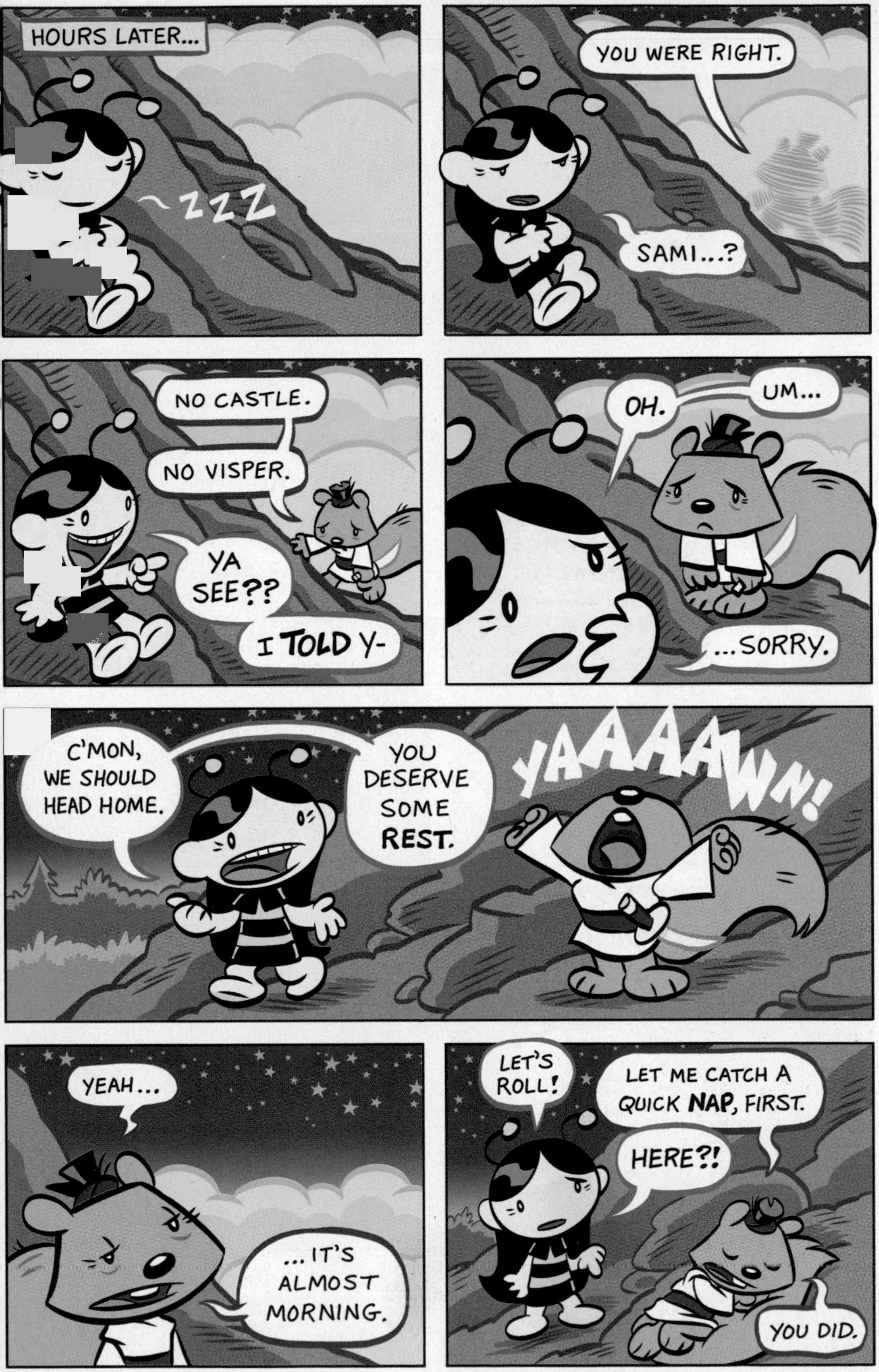
HOURS LATER...
~ZZZ
YOU WERE RIGHT.
SAMI...?
NO CASTLE.
NO VISPER.
YA SEE??
I TOLD Y-
OH.
UM...
...SORRY.
C'MON, WE SHOULD HEAD HOME.
YOU DESERVE SOME REST.
YAAAAAWN!
YEAH...
...IT'S ALMOST MORNING.
LET'S ROLL!
LET ME CATCH A QUICK NAP, FIRST.
HERE?!
YOU DID.

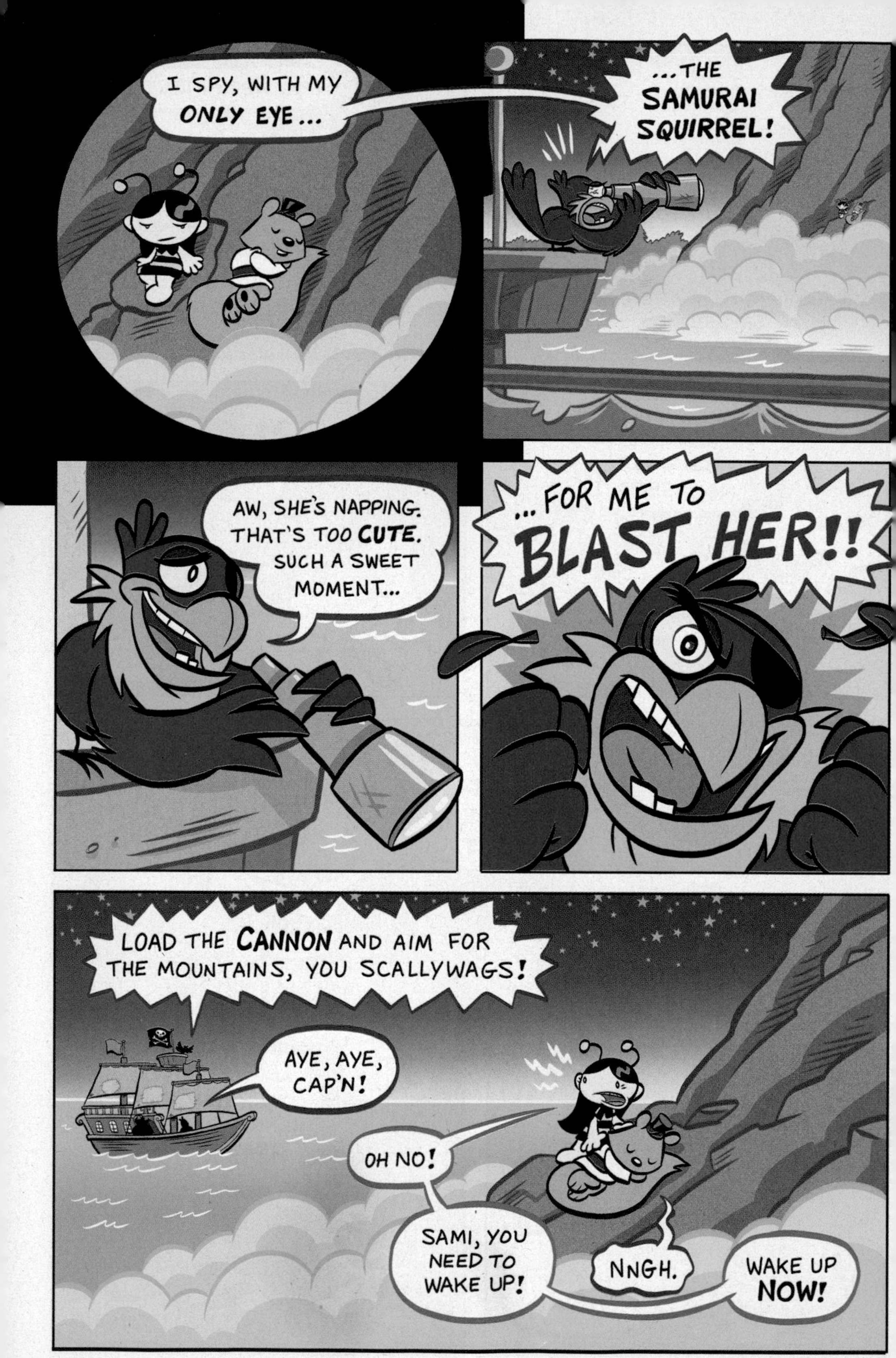
I SPY, WITH MY ONLY EYE...
...THE SAMURAI SQUIRREL!
AW, SHE'S NAPPING. THAT'S TOO CUTE. SUCH A SWEET MOMENT...
...FOR ME TO BLAST HER!!
LOAD THE CANNON AND AIM FOR THE MOUNTAINS, YOU SCALLYWAGS!
AYE, AYE, CAP'N!
OH NO!
SAMI, YOU NEED TO WAKE UP!
NNGH.
WAKE UP NOW!

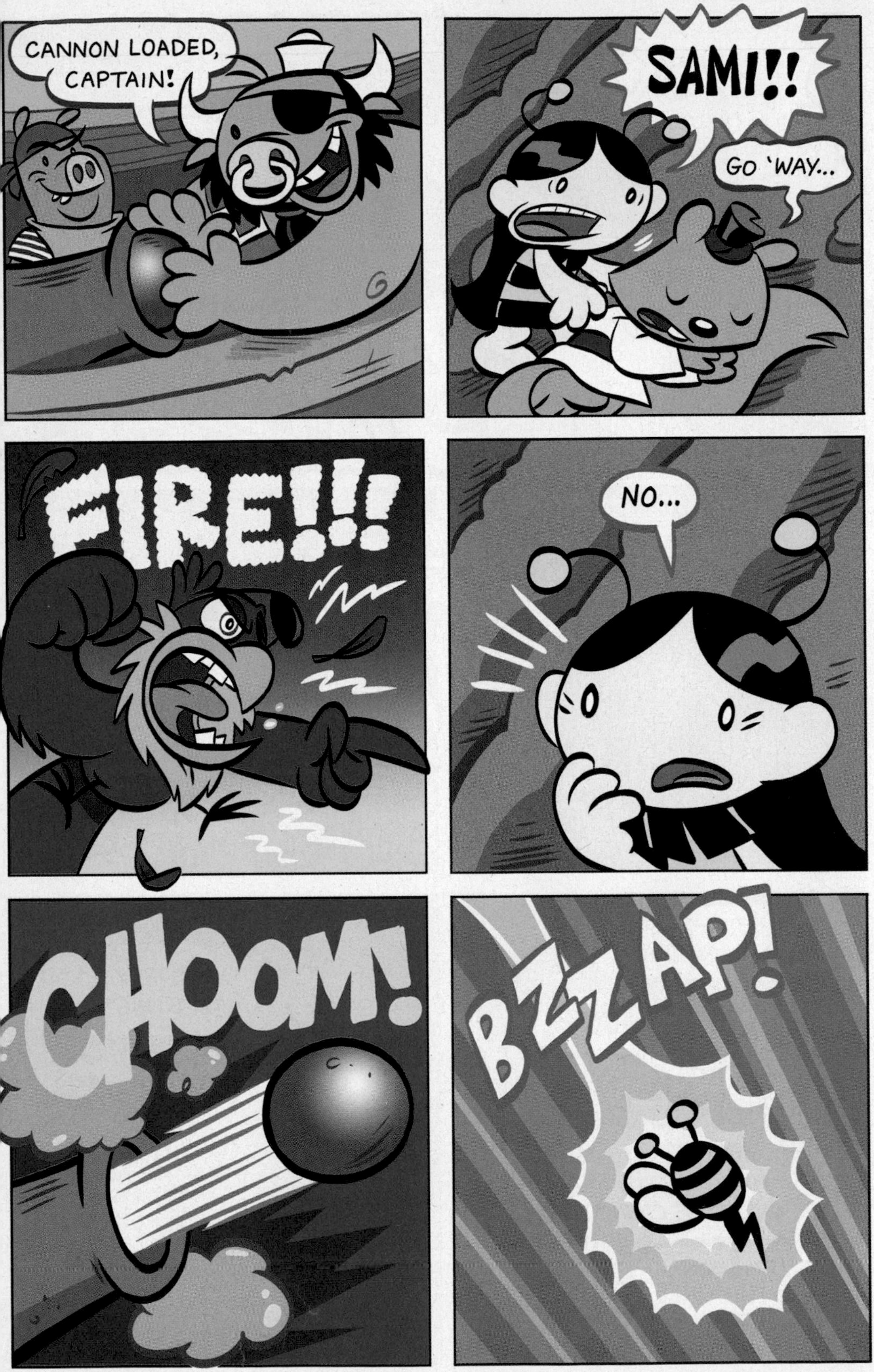
CANNON LOADED, CAPTAIN!
SAMI!!
GO 'WAY...
FIRE!!!
NO...
CHOOM!
BZZAP!

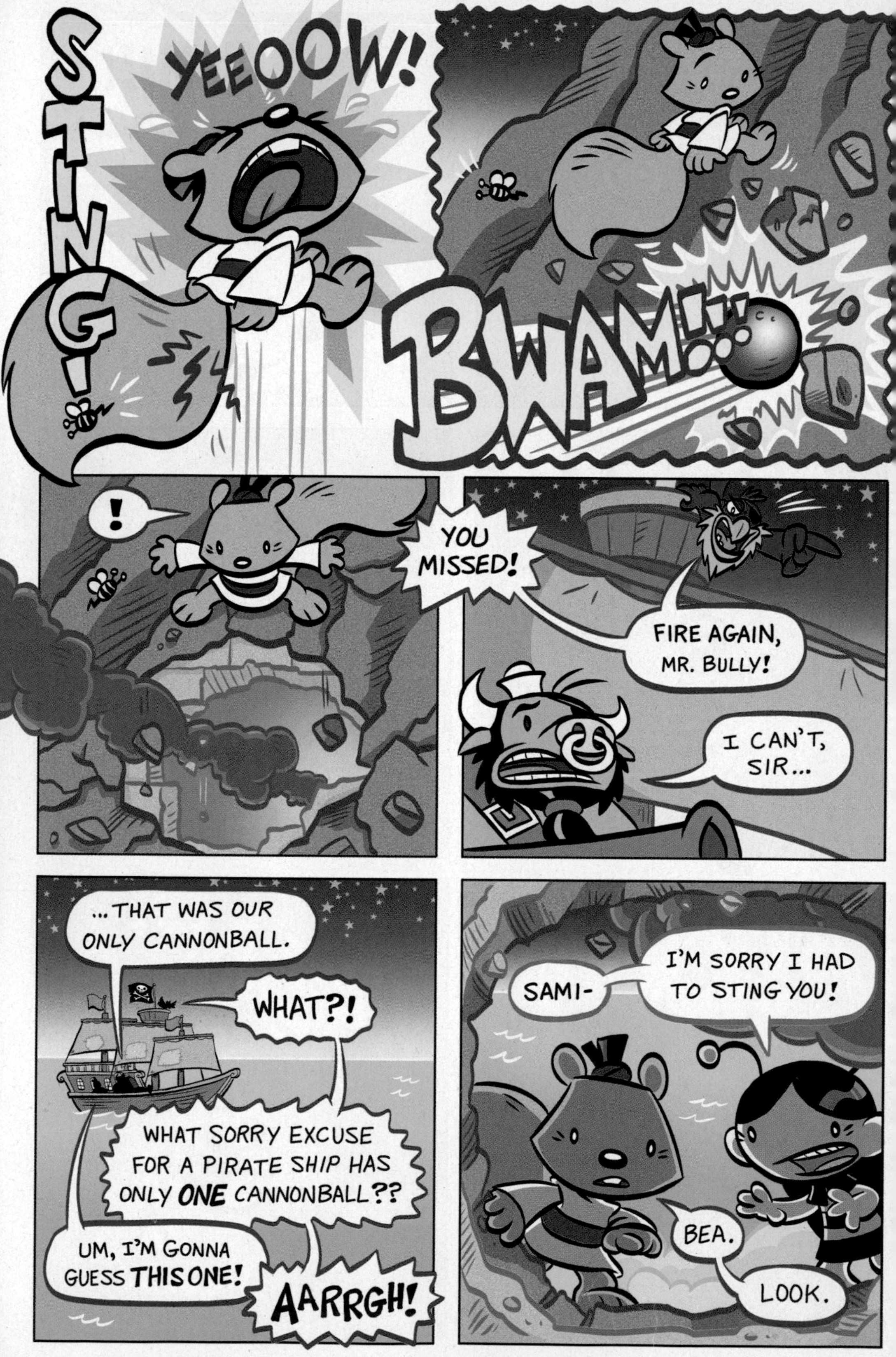
STING!
YEEOOOW!
BWAM!!!
!
YOU MISSED!
FIRE AGAIN, MR. BULLY!
I CAN'T, SIR...
...THAT WAS OUR ONLY CANNONBALL.
WHAT?!
WHAT SORRY EXCUSE FOR A PIRATE SHIP HAS ONLY ONE CANNONBALL??
UM, I'M GONNA GUESS THIS ONE!
AARRGH!
SAMI-
I'M SORRY I HAD TO STING YOU!
BEA.
LOOK.

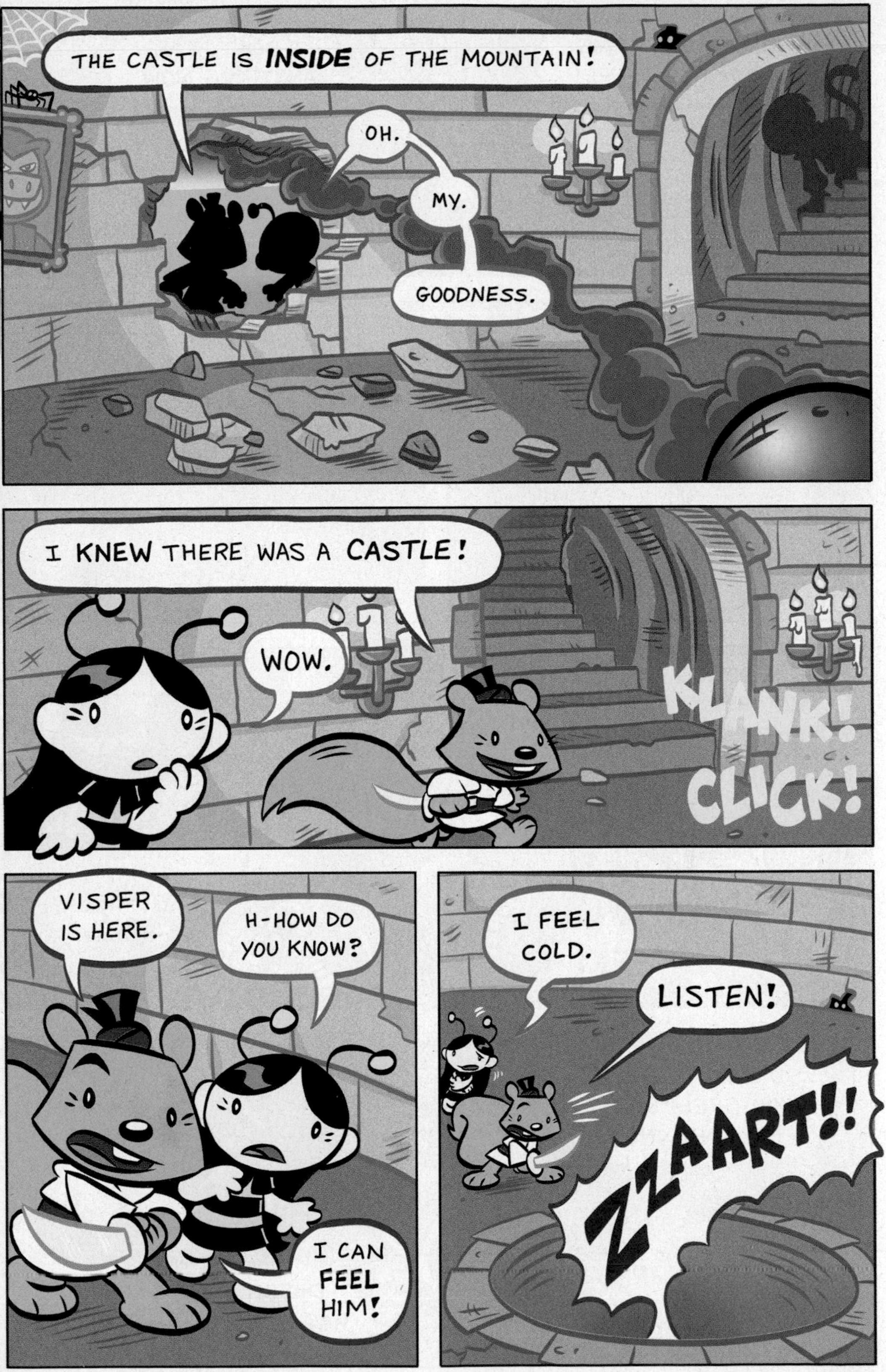
THE CASTLE IS INSIDE OF THE MOUNTAIN!
OH.
MY.
GOODNESS.
I KNEW THERE WAS A CASTLE!
WOW.
KLANK!
CLICK!
VISPER IS HERE.
H-HOW DO YOU KNOW?
I CAN FEEL HIM!
I FEEL COLD.
LISTEN!
ZZAART!!

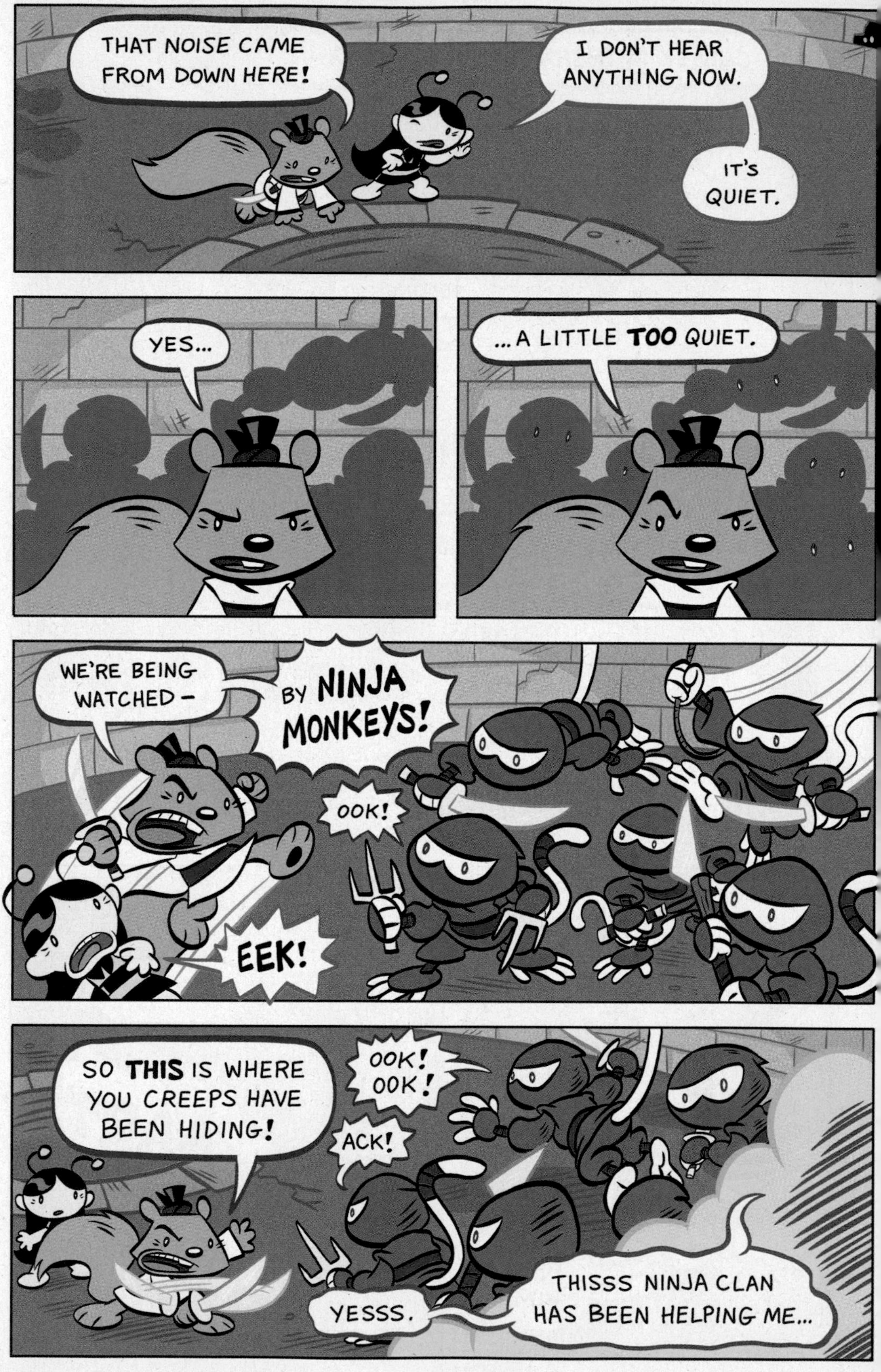
THAT NOISE CAME FROM DOWN HERE!
I DON'T HEAR ANYTHING NOW.
IT'S QUIET.
YES...
...A LITTLE TOO QUIET.
WE'RE BEING WATCHED—
BY NINJA MONKEYS!
OOK!
EEK!
SO THIS IS WHERE YOU CREEPS HAVE BEEN HIDING!
OOK! OOK!
ACK!
YESSS.
THISSS NINJA CLAN HAS BEEN HELPING ME...

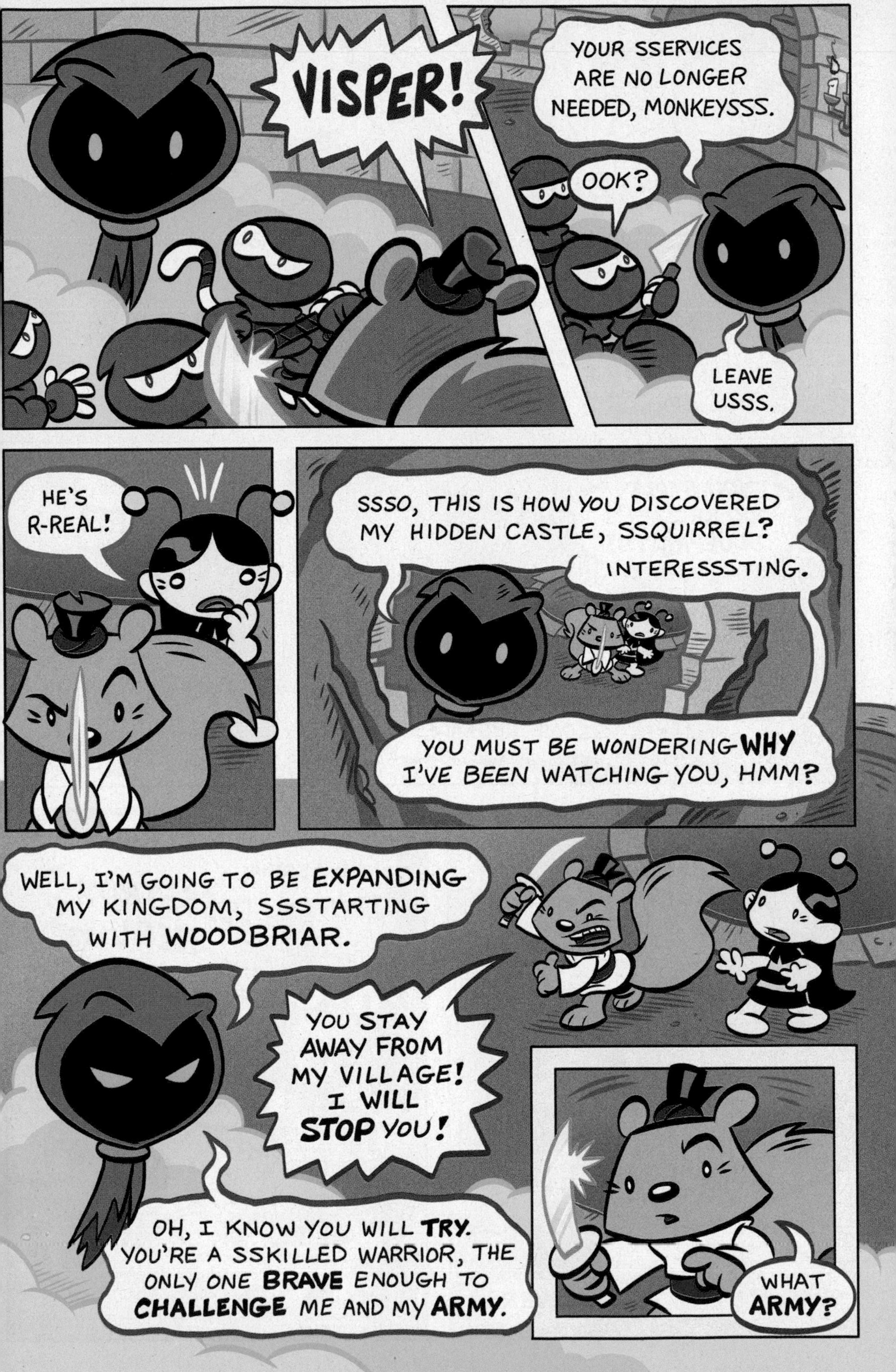
VISPER!
YOUR SSERVICES ARE NO LONGER NEEDED, MONKEYSSS.
OOK?
LEAVE USSS.
HE'S R-REAL!
SSSO, THIS IS HOW YOU DISCOVERED MY HIDDEN CASTLE, SSQUIRREL?
INTERESSSTING.
YOU MUST BE WONDERING WHY I'VE BEEN WATCHING YOU, HMM?
WELL, I'M GOING TO BE EXPANDING MY KINGDOM, SSSTARTING WITH WOODBRIAR.
YOU STAY AWAY FROM MY VILLAGE! I WILL STOP YOU!
OH, I KNOW YOU WILL TRY. YOU'RE A SSKILLED WARRIOR, THE ONLY ONE BRAVE ENOUGH TO CHALLENGE ME AND MY ARMY.
WHAT ARMY?

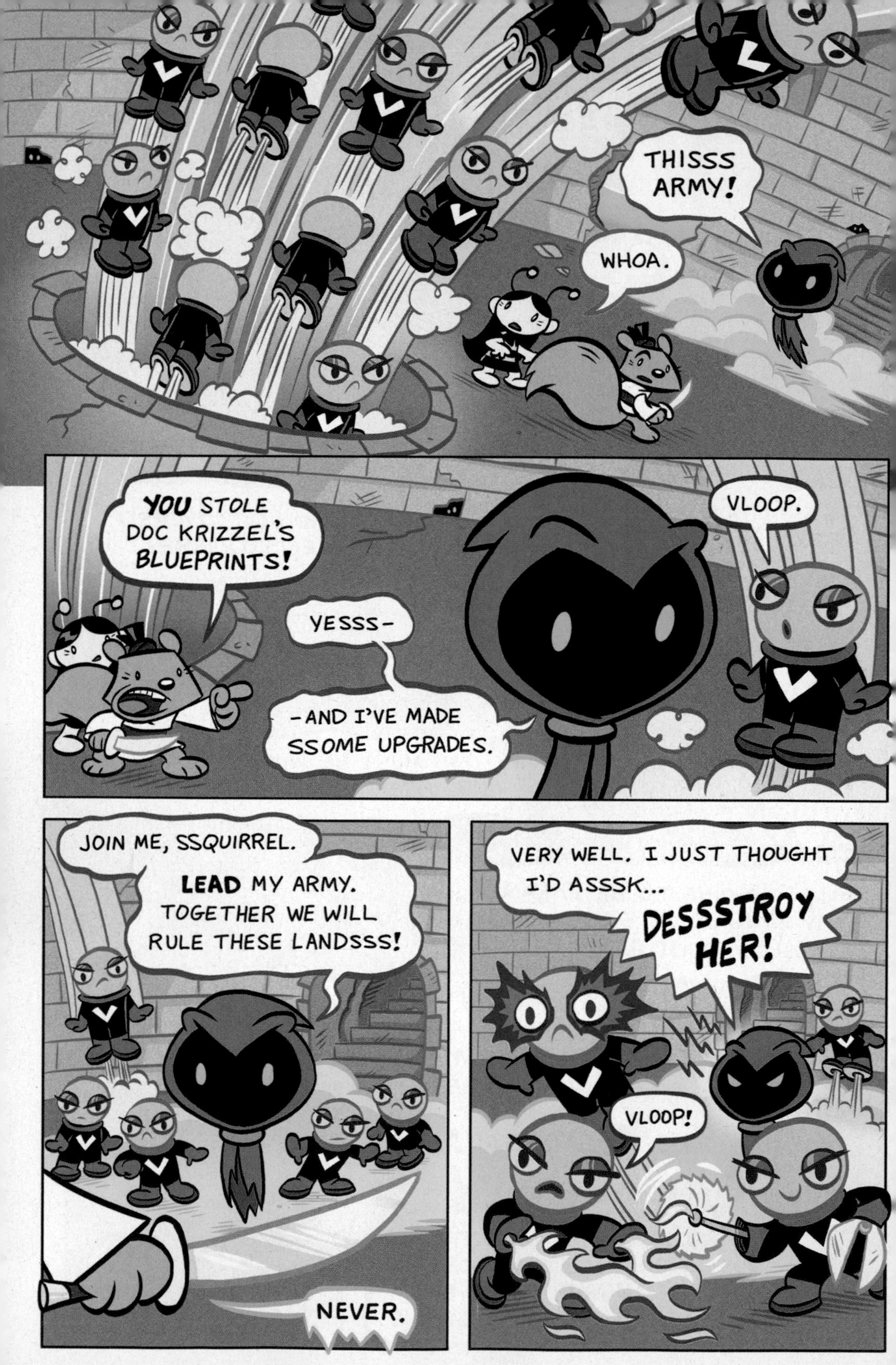
THISSS ARMY!
WHOA.
YOU STOLE DOC KRIZZEL'S BLUEPRINTS!
VLOOP.
YESSS-
-AND I'VE MADE SSOME UPGRADES.
JOIN ME, SSQUIRREL.
LEAD MY ARMY. TOGETHER WE WILL RULE THESE LANDSSS!
NEVER.
VERY WELL. I JUST THOUGHT I'D ASSSK...
DESSSTROY HER!
VLOOP!

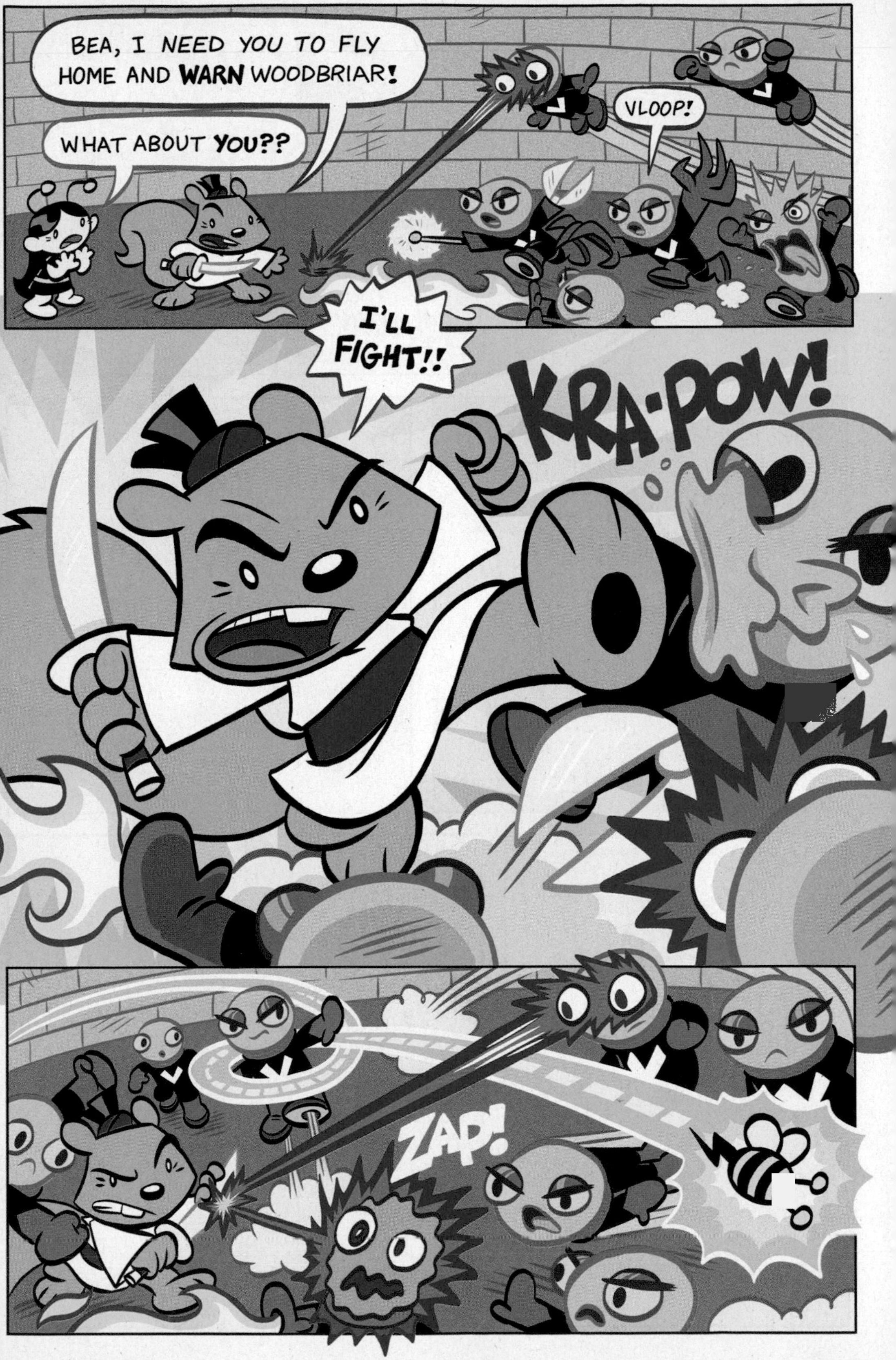
BEA, I NEED YOU TO FLY HOME AND WARN WOODBRIAR!
WHAT ABOUT YOU??
VLOOP!
I'LL FIGHT!!
KRA-POW!
ZAP!

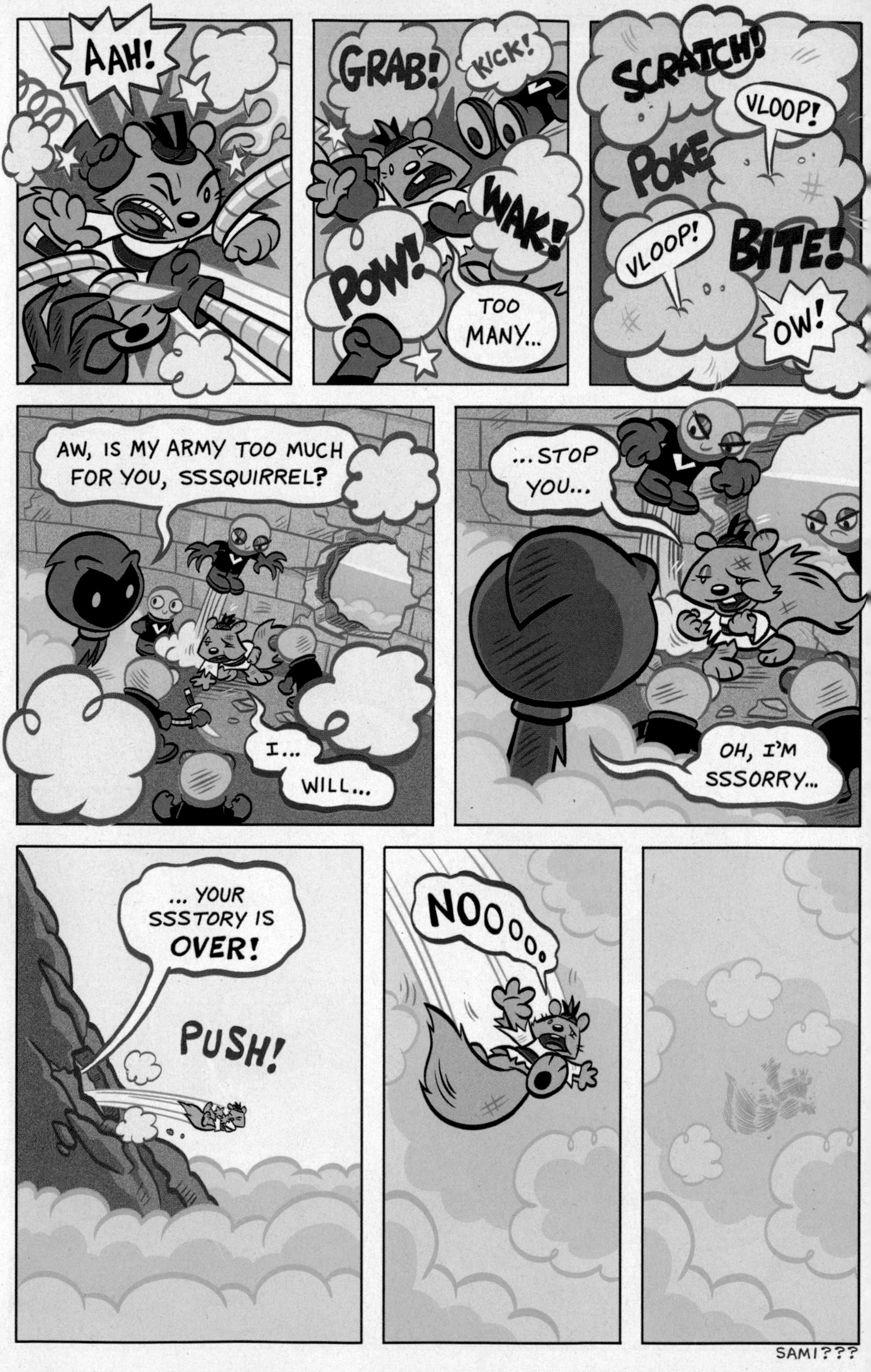
AAH!
GRAB!
KICK!
WAK!
POW!
TOO MANY...
SCRATCH!
VLOOP!
POKE
VLOOP!
BITE!
OW!
AW, IS MY ARMY TOO MUCH FOR YOU, SSSQUIRREL?
I... WILL...
...STOP YOU...
OH, I'M SSSORRY...
... YOUR SSSTORY IS OVER!
PUSH!
NOOooo
SAMI???

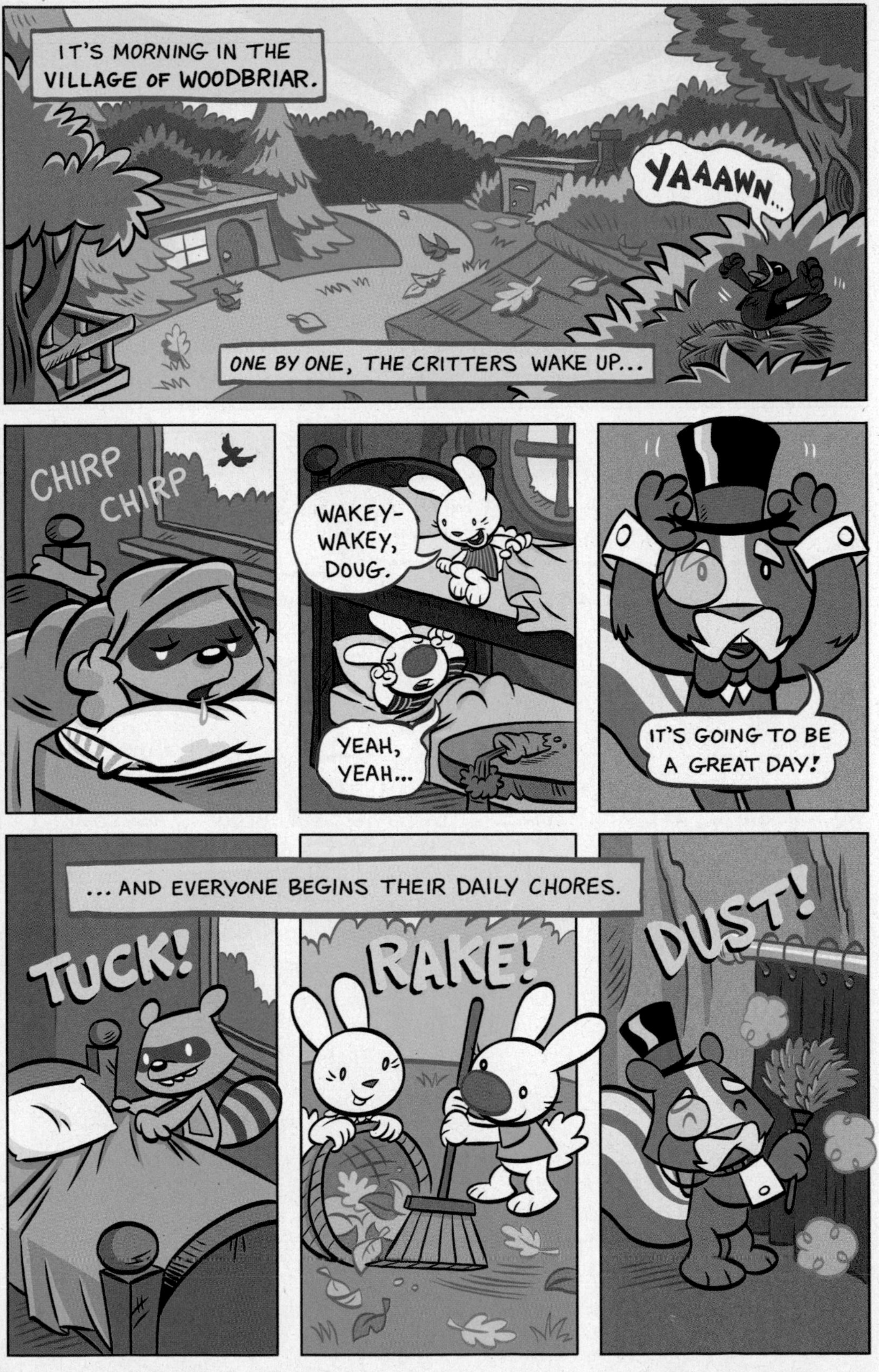
IT'S MORNING IN THE VILLAGE OF WOODBRIAR.
YAAAWN...
ONE BY ONE, THE CRITTERS WAKE UP...
CHIRP CHIRP
WAKEY-WAKEY, DOUG.
YEAH, YEAH...
IT'S GOING TO BE A GREAT DAY!
... AND EVERYONE BEGINS THEIR DAILY CHORES.
TUCK!
RAKE!
DUST!

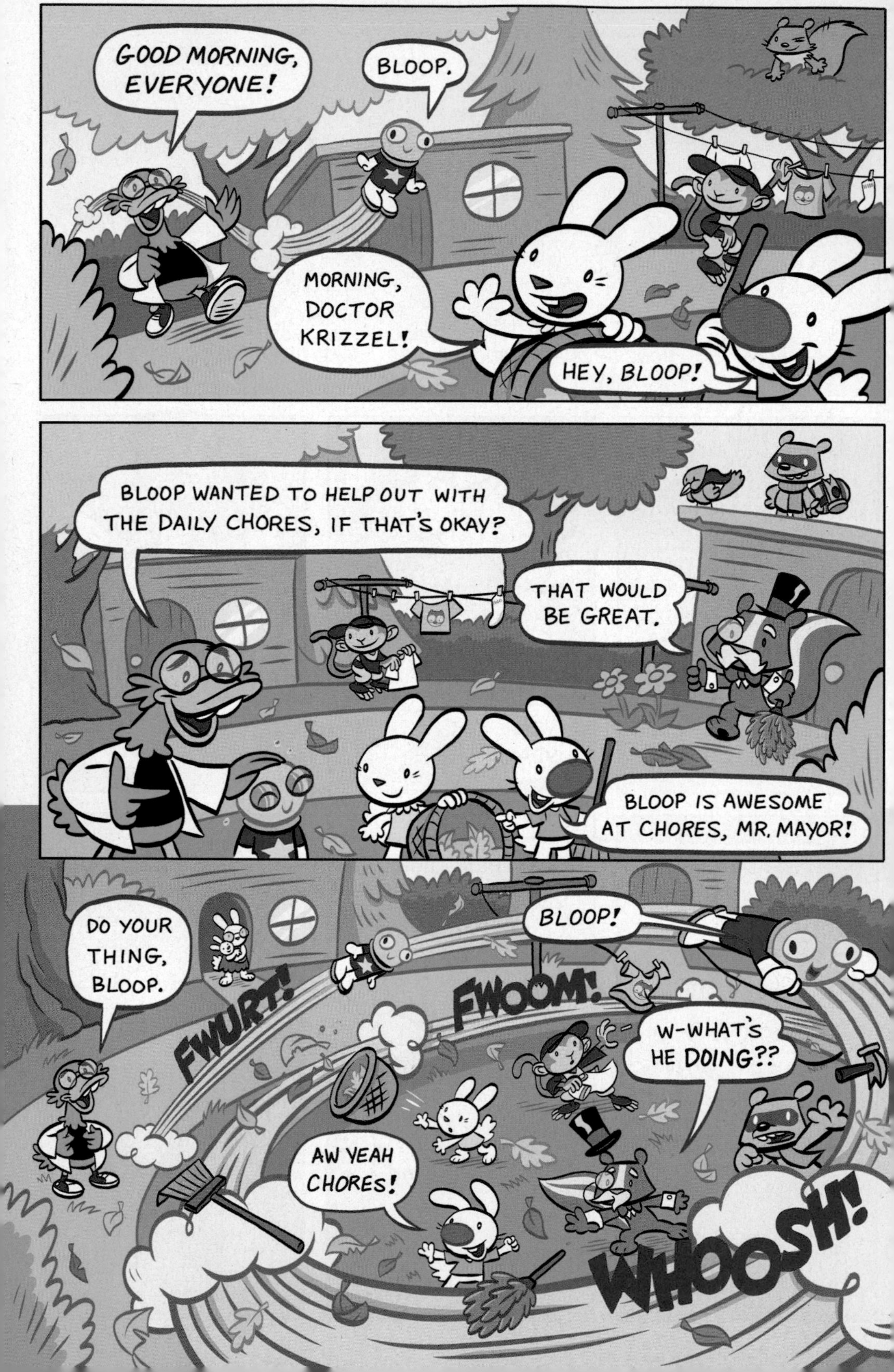
GOOD MORNING, EVERYONE!
BLOOP.
MORNING, DOCTOR KRIZZEL!
HEY, BLOOP!
BLOOP WANTED TO HELP OUT WITH THE DAILY CHORES, IF THAT'S OKAY?
THAT WOULD BE GREAT.
BLOOP IS AWESOME AT CHORES, MR. MAYOR!
DO YOUR THING, BLOOP.
BLOOP!
FWURT!
FWOOM!
W-WHAT'S HE DOING??
AW YEAH CHORES!
WHOOSH!

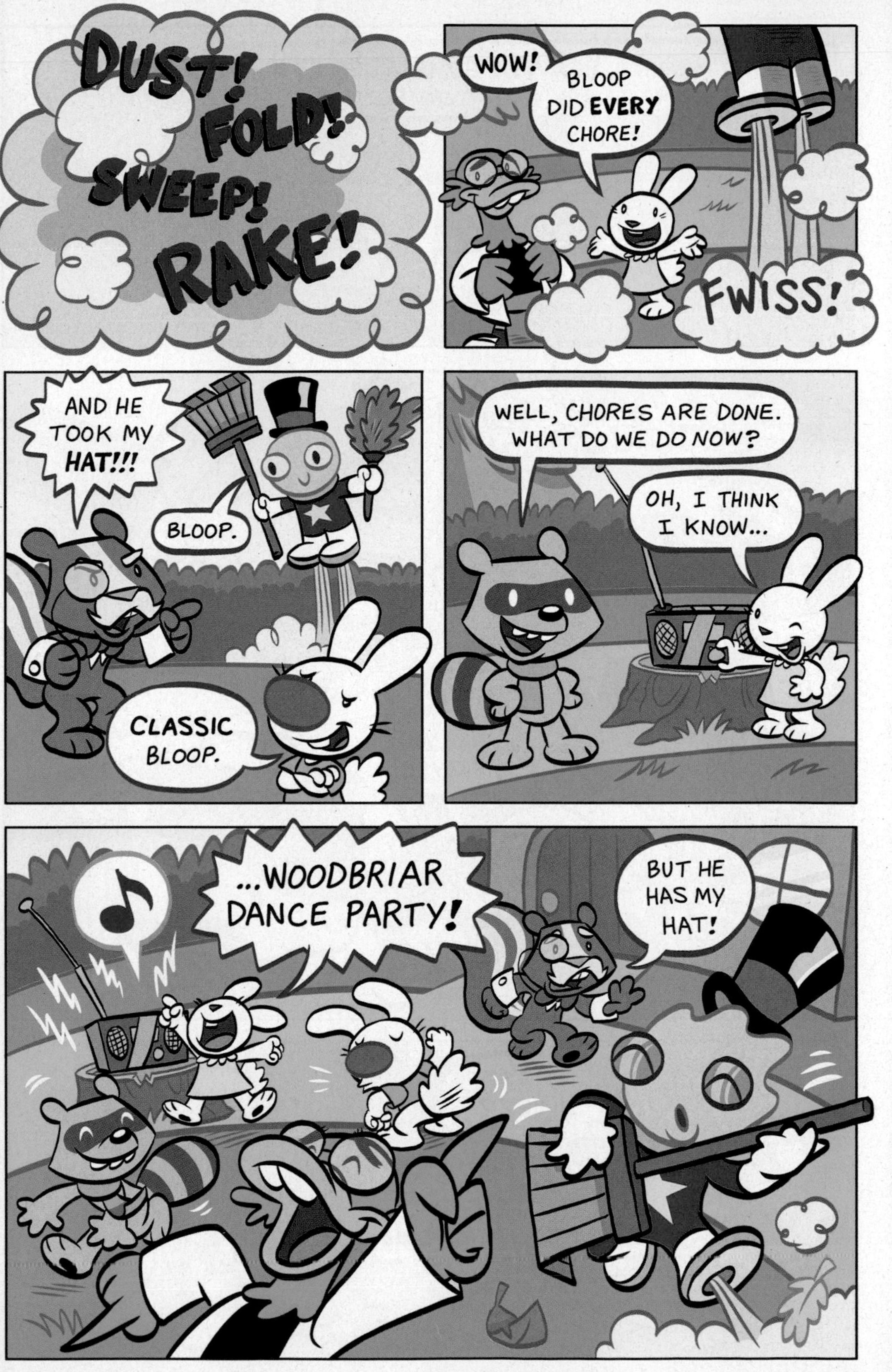
DUST! FOLD! SWEEP! RAKE!
WOW!
BLOOP DID EVERY CHORE!
FWISS!
AND HE TOOK MY HAT!!!
BLOOP.
CLASSIC BLOOP.
WELL, CHORES ARE DONE. WHAT DO WE DO NOW?
OH, I THINK I KNOW...
...WOODBRIAR DANCE PARTY!
BUT HE HAS MY HAT!

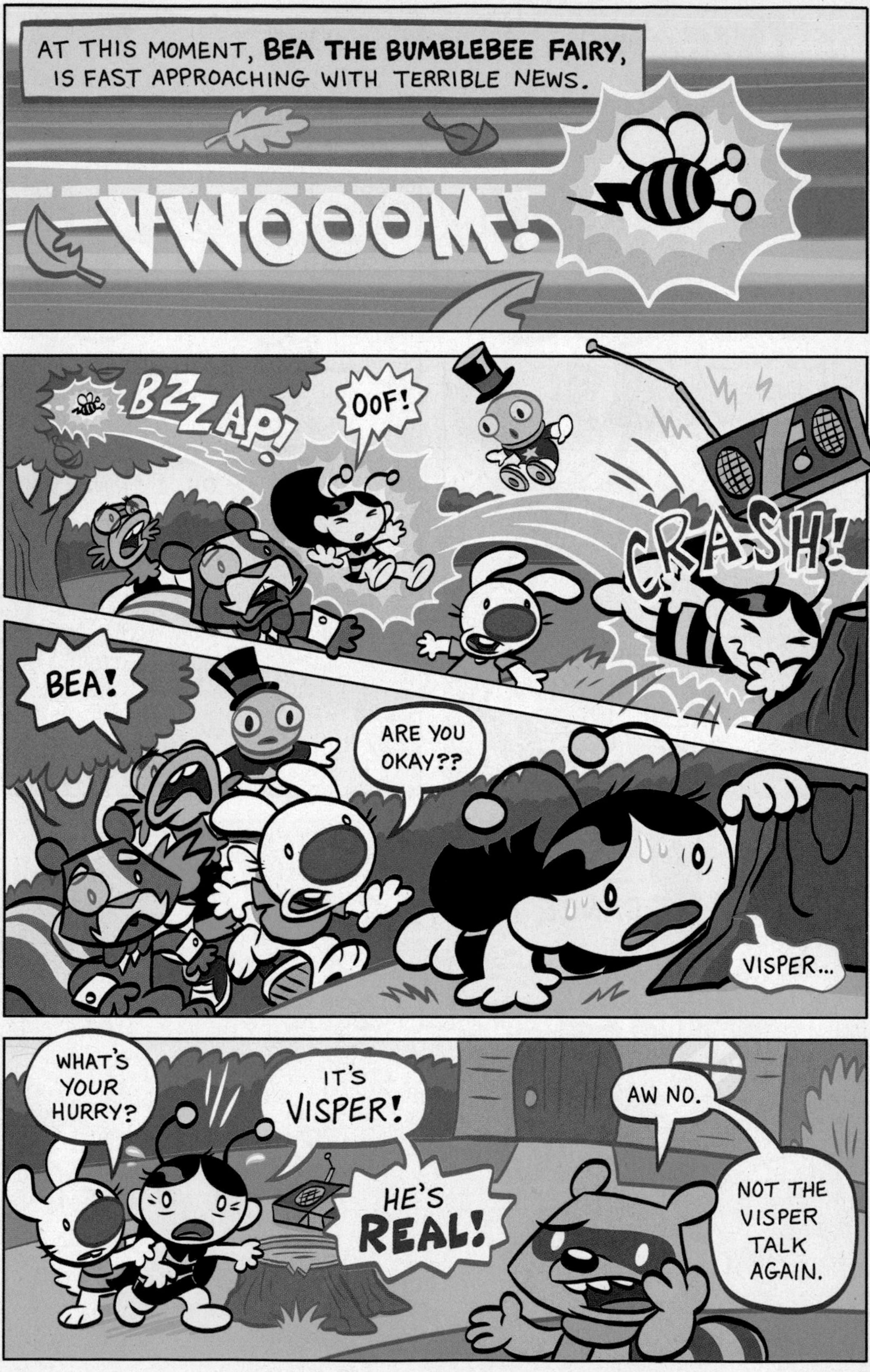
AT THIS MOMENT, BEA THE BUMBLEBEE FAIRY, IS FAST APPROACHING WITH TERRIBLE NEWS.
VWOOOM!
BZZAP!
OOF!
CRASH!
BEA!
ARE YOU OKAY??
VISPER...
WHAT'S YOUR HURRY?
IT'S VISPER!
HE'S REAL!
AW NO.
NOT THE VISPER TALK AGAIN.

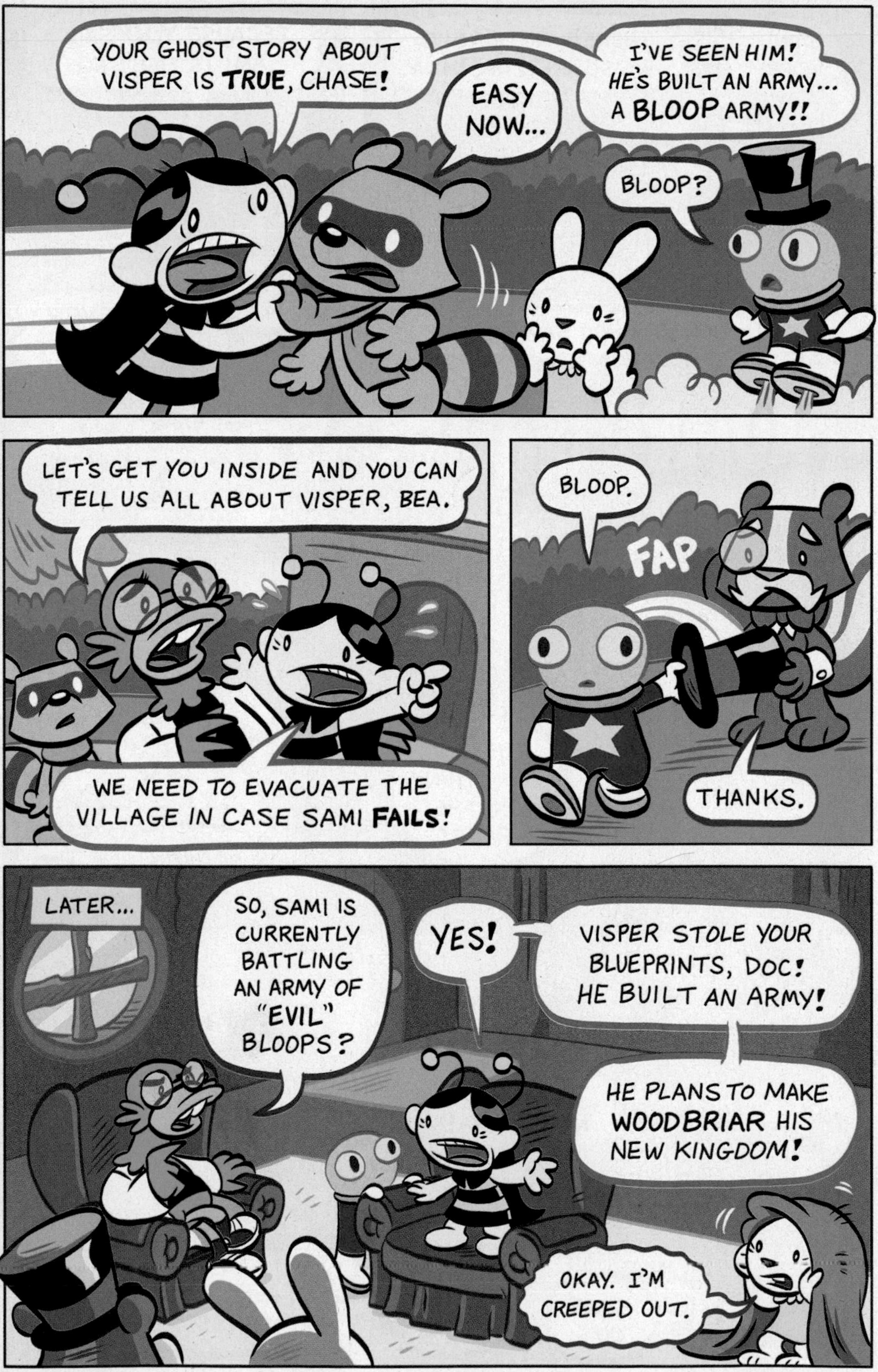
YOUR GHOST STORY ABOUT VISPER IS TRUE, CHASE!
EASY NOW...
I'VE SEEN HIM! HE'S BUILT AN ARMY... A BLOOP ARMY!!
BLOOP?
LET'S GET YOU INSIDE AND YOU CAN TELL US ALL ABOUT VISPER, BEA.
WE NEED TO EVACUATE THE VILLAGE IN CASE SAMI FAILS!
BLOOP.
FAP
THANKS.
LATER...
SO, SAMI IS CURRENTLY BATTLING AN ARMY OF "EVIL" BLOOPS?
YES!
VISPER STOLE YOUR BLUEPRINTS, DOC! HE BUILT AN ARMY!
HE PLANS TO MAKE WOODBRIAR HIS NEW KINGDOM!
OKAY. I'M CREEPED OUT.

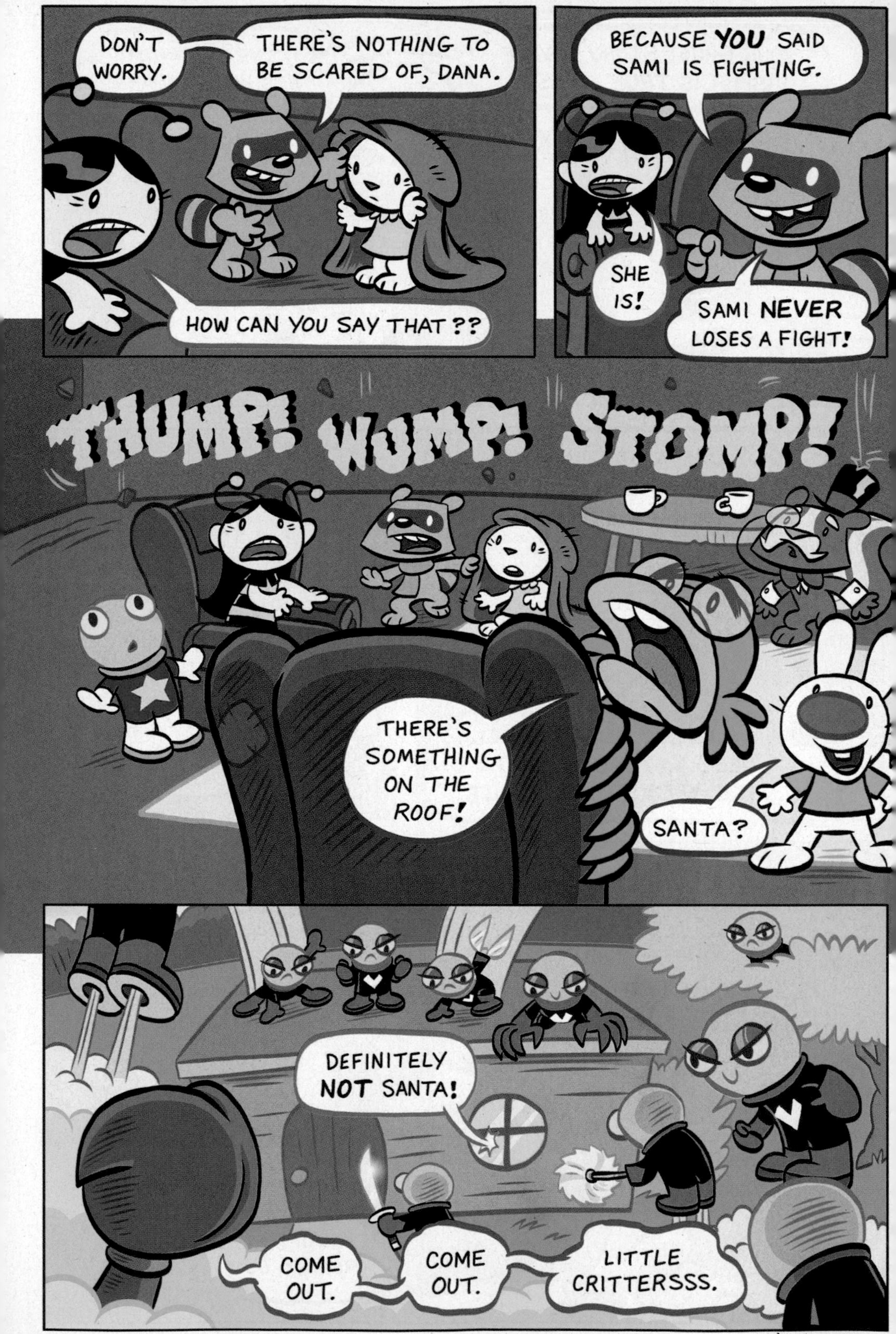
DON'T WORRY.
THERE'S NOTHING TO BE SCARED OF, DANA.
HOW CAN YOU SAY THAT??
BECAUSE YOU SAID SAMI IS FIGHTING.
SHE IS!
SAMI NEVER LOSES A FIGHT!
THUMP! WUMP! STOMP!
THERE'S SOMETHING ON THE ROOF!
SANTA?
DEFINITELY NOT SANTA!
COME OUT.
COME OUT.
LITTLE CRITTERSSS.

HE'S HEEERE...

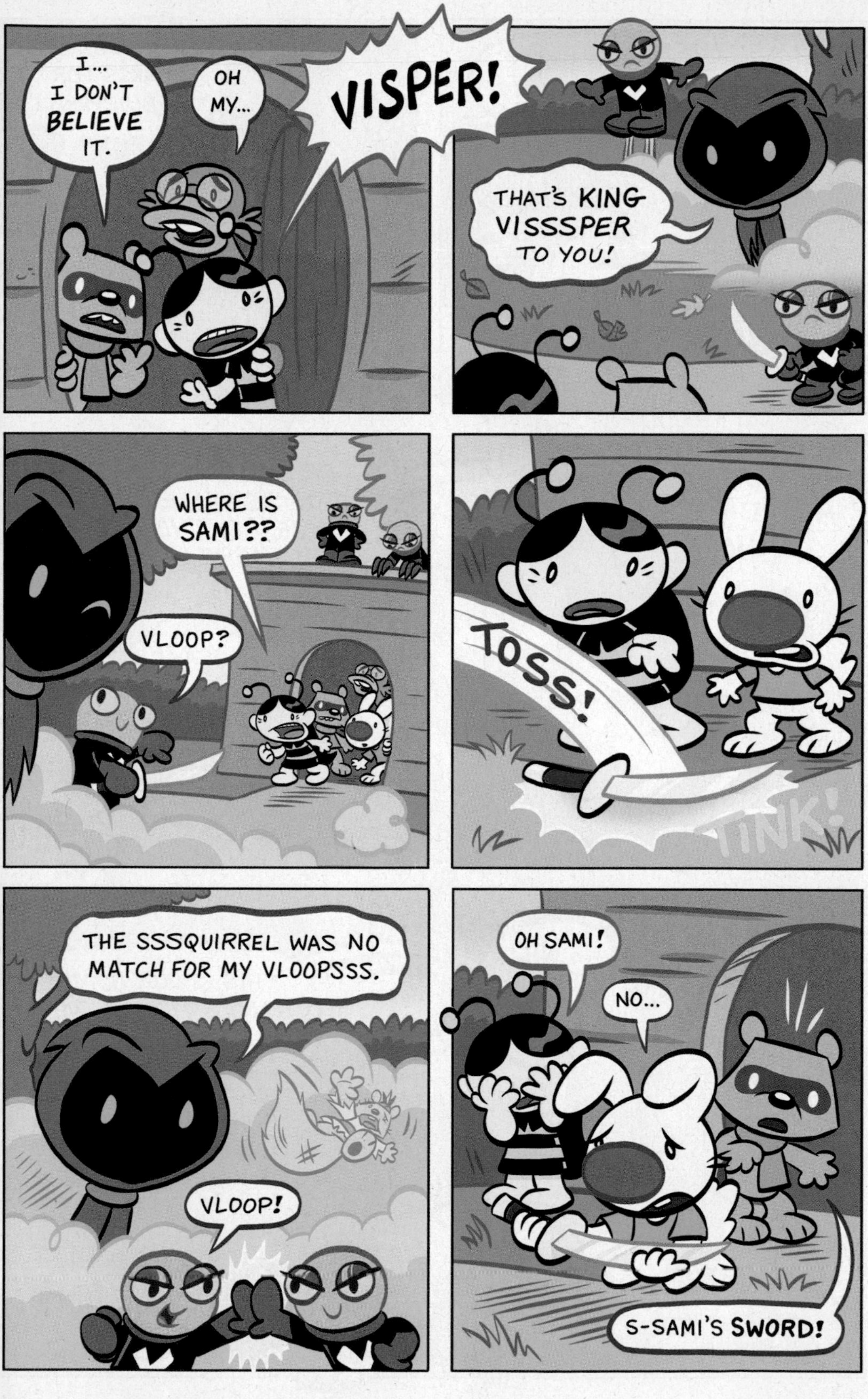
I... I DON'T BELIEVE IT.
OH MY...
VISPER!
THAT'S KING VISSSPER TO YOU!
WHERE IS SAMI??
VLOOP?
TOSS!
TINK!
THE SSSQUIRREL WAS NO MATCH FOR MY VLOOPSSS.
VLOOP!
OH SAMI!
NO...
S-SAMI'S SWORD!

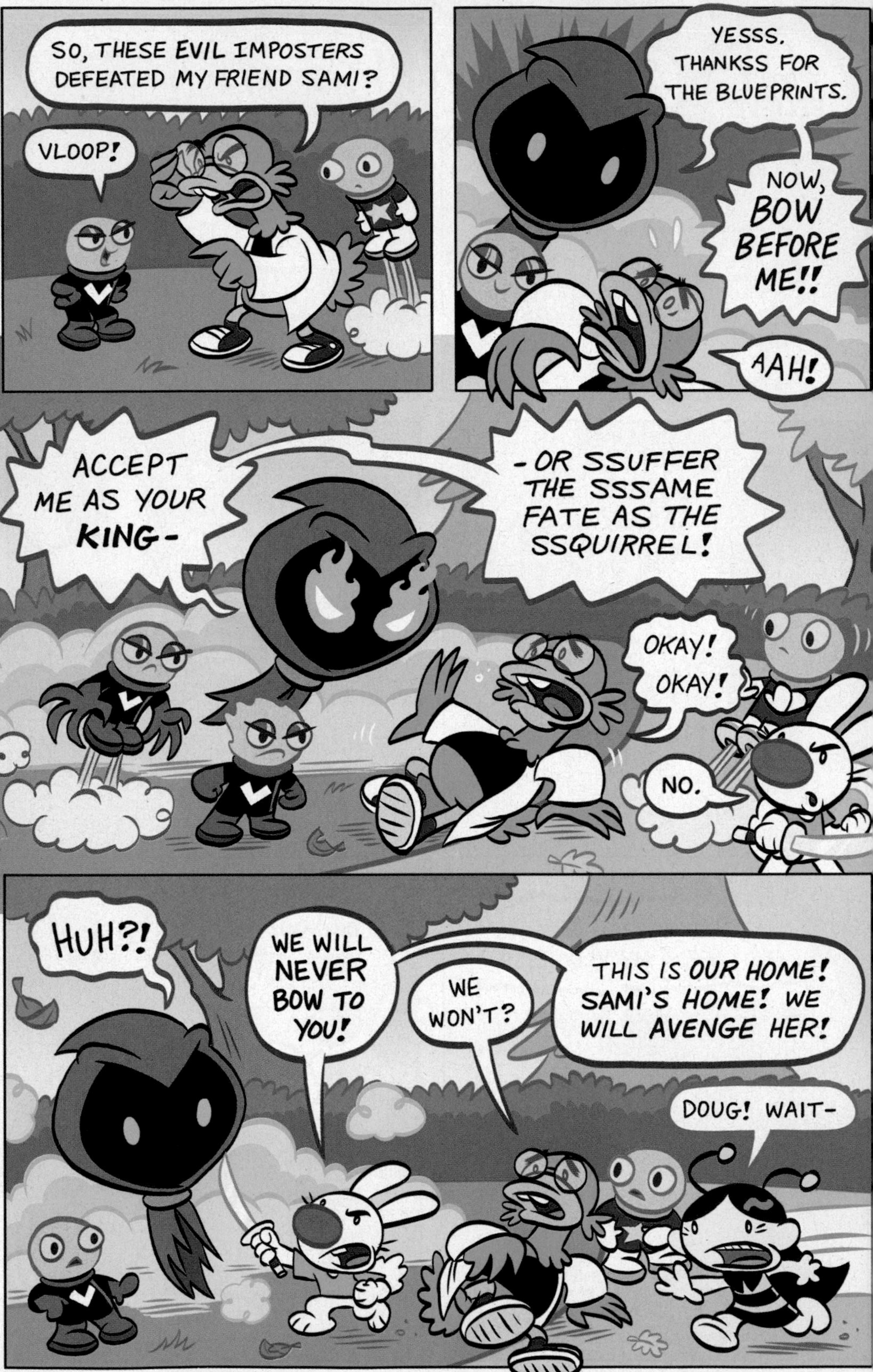
SO, THESE EVIL IMPOSTERS DEFEATED MY FRIEND SAMI?
VLOOP!
YESSS. THANKSS FOR THE BLUEPRINTS.
NOW, BOW BEFORE ME!!
AAH!
ACCEPT ME AS YOUR KING-
-OR SSUFFER THE SSSAME FATE AS THE SSQUIRREL!
OKAY! OKAY!
NO.
HUH?!
WE WILL NEVER BOW TO YOU!
WE WON'T?
THIS IS OUR HOME! SAMI'S HOME! WE WILL AVENGE HER!
DOUG! WAIT-

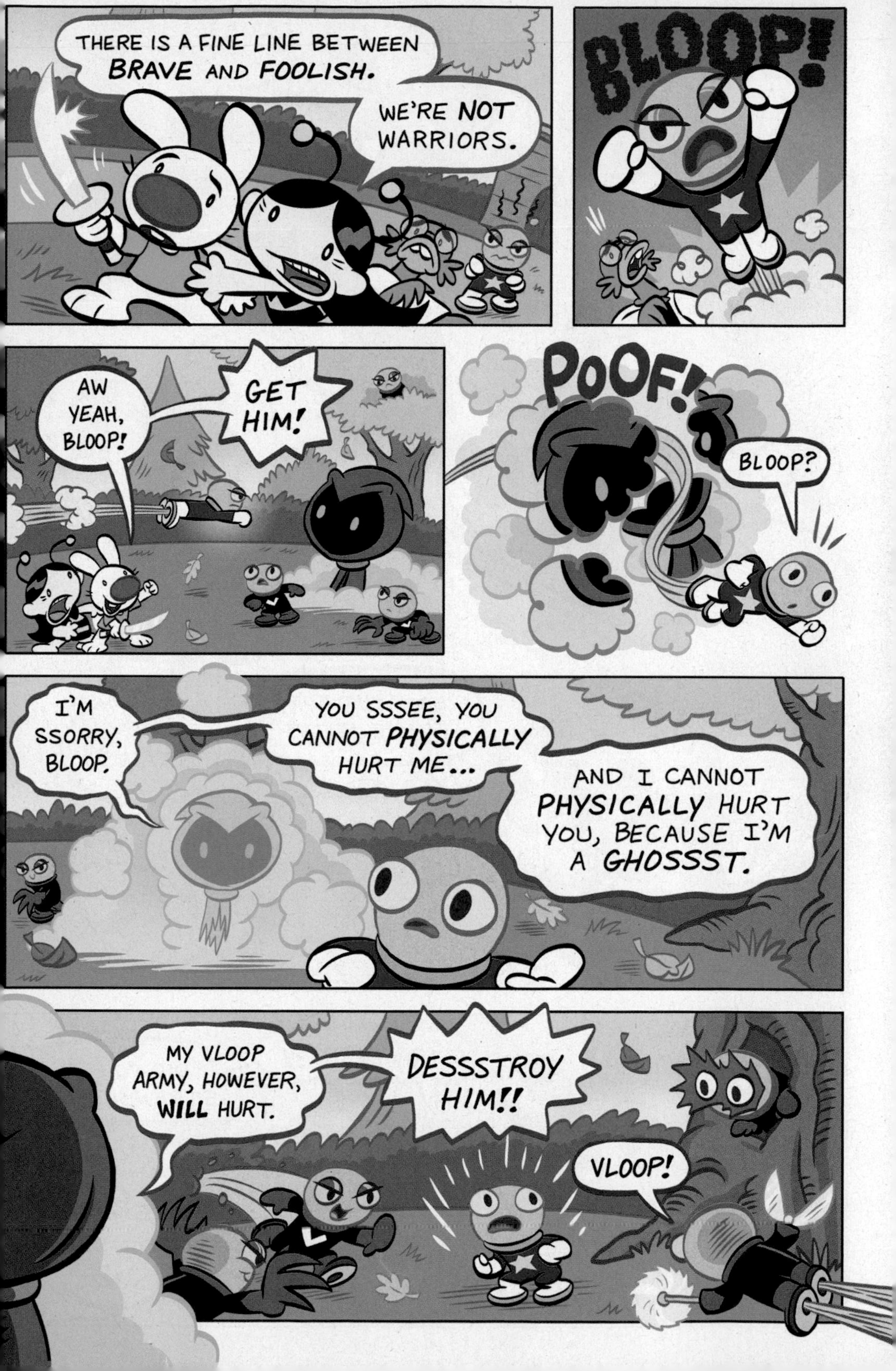
THERE IS A FINE LINE BETWEEN BRAVE AND FOOLISH.
WE'RE NOT WARRIORS.
BLOOP!
AW YEAH, BLOOP!
GET HIM!
POOF!
BLOOP?
I'M SSORRY, BLOOP.
YOU SSSEE, YOU CANNOT PHYSICALLY HURT ME...
AND I CANNOT PHYSICALLY HURT YOU, BECAUSE I'M A GHOSSST.
MY VLOOP ARMY, HOWEVER, WILL HURT.
DESSSTROY HIM!!
VLOOP!

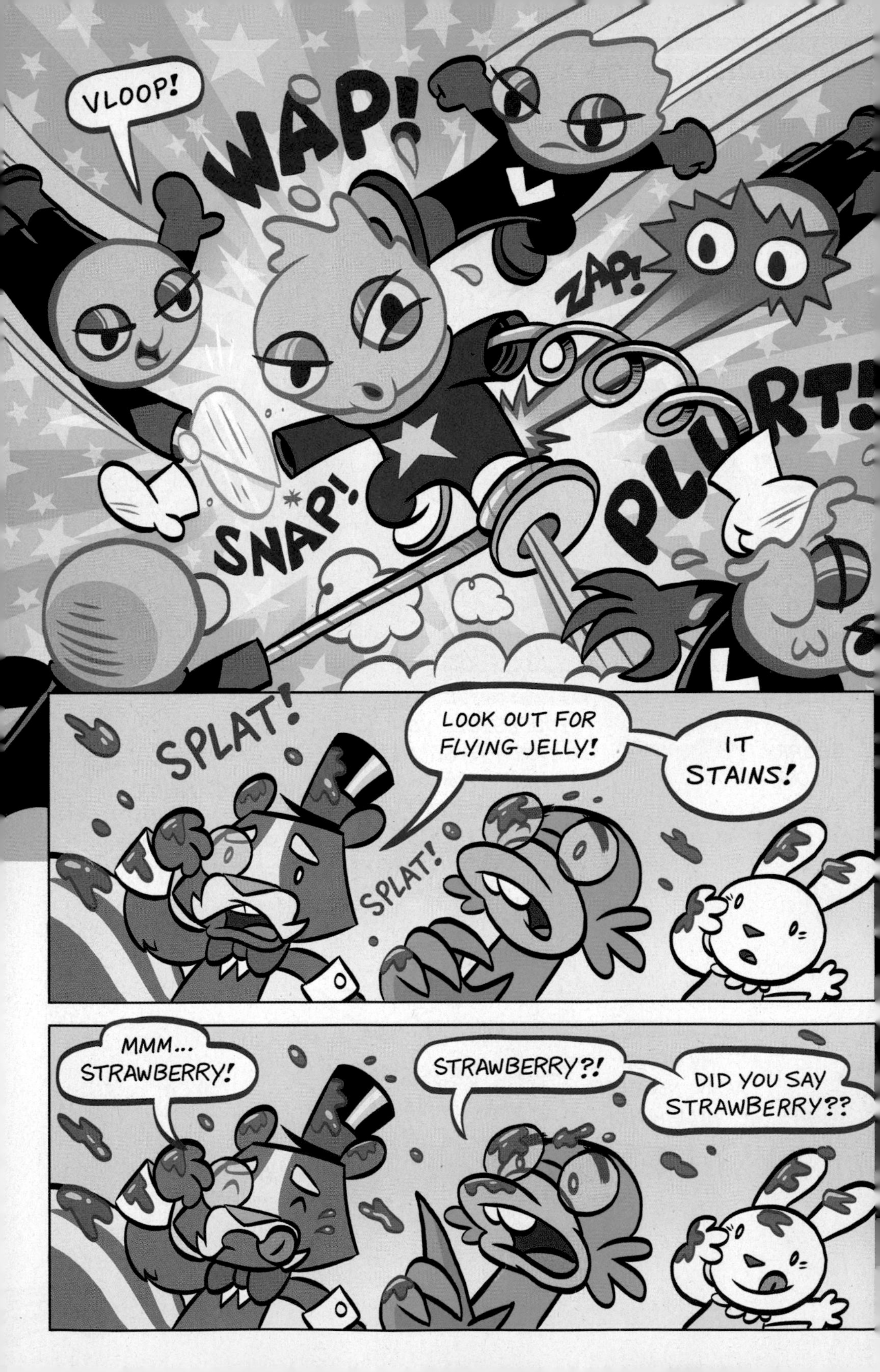
VLOOP!
WAP!
ZAP!
SNAP!
PLURT!
SPLAT!
LOOK OUT FOR FLYING JELLY!
IT STAINS!
SPLAT!
MMM... STRAWBERRY!
STRAWBERRY?!
DID YOU SAY STRAWBERRY??

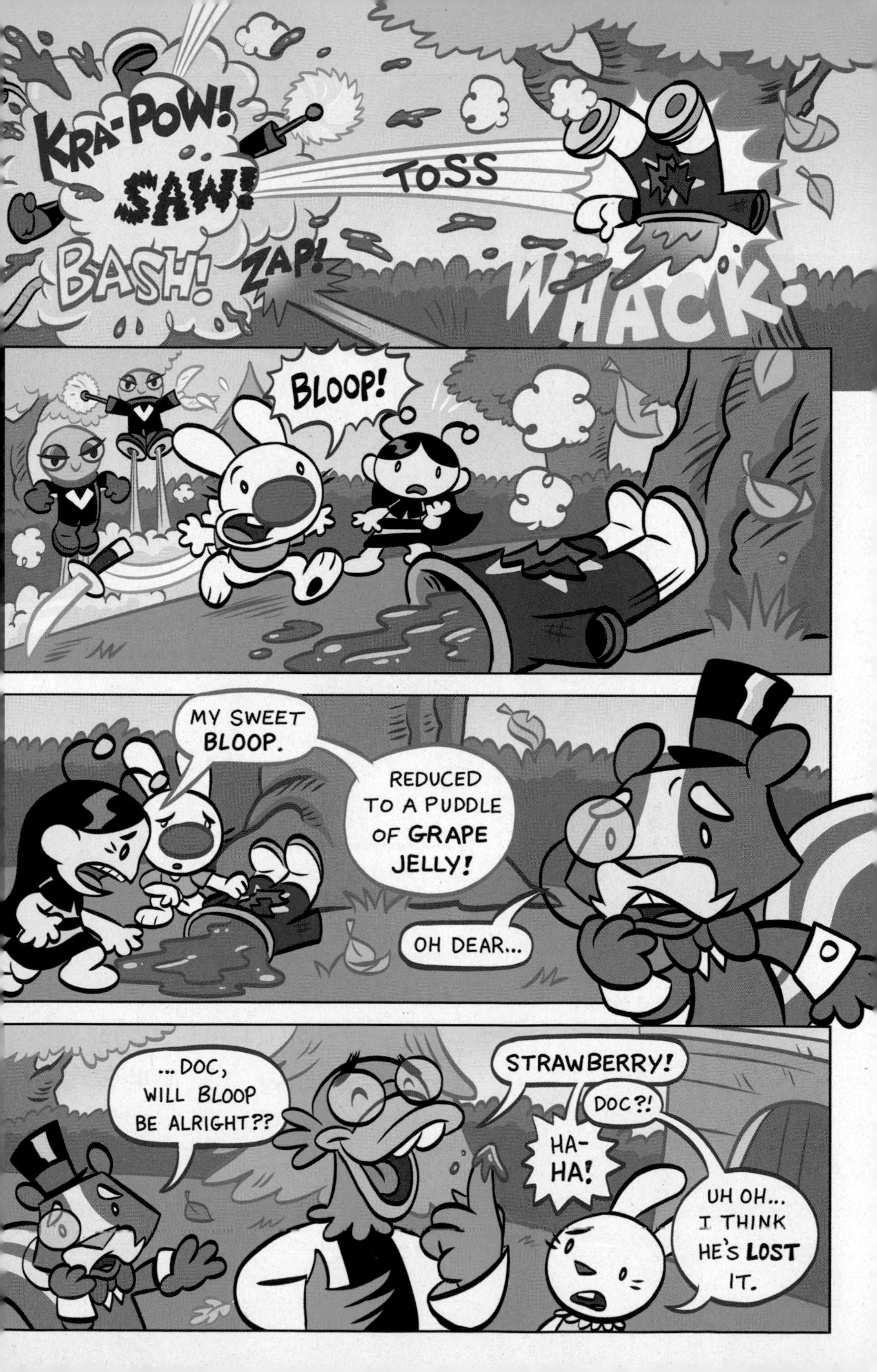
KRA-POW!
SAW!
BASH!
ZAP!
TOSS
WHACK
BLOOP!
MY SWEET BLOOP.
REDUCED TO A PUDDLE OF GRAPE JELLY!
OH DEAR...
...DOC, WILL BLOOP BE ALRIGHT??
STRAWBERRY!
HA-HA!
DOC?!
UH OH... I THINK HE'S LOST IT.

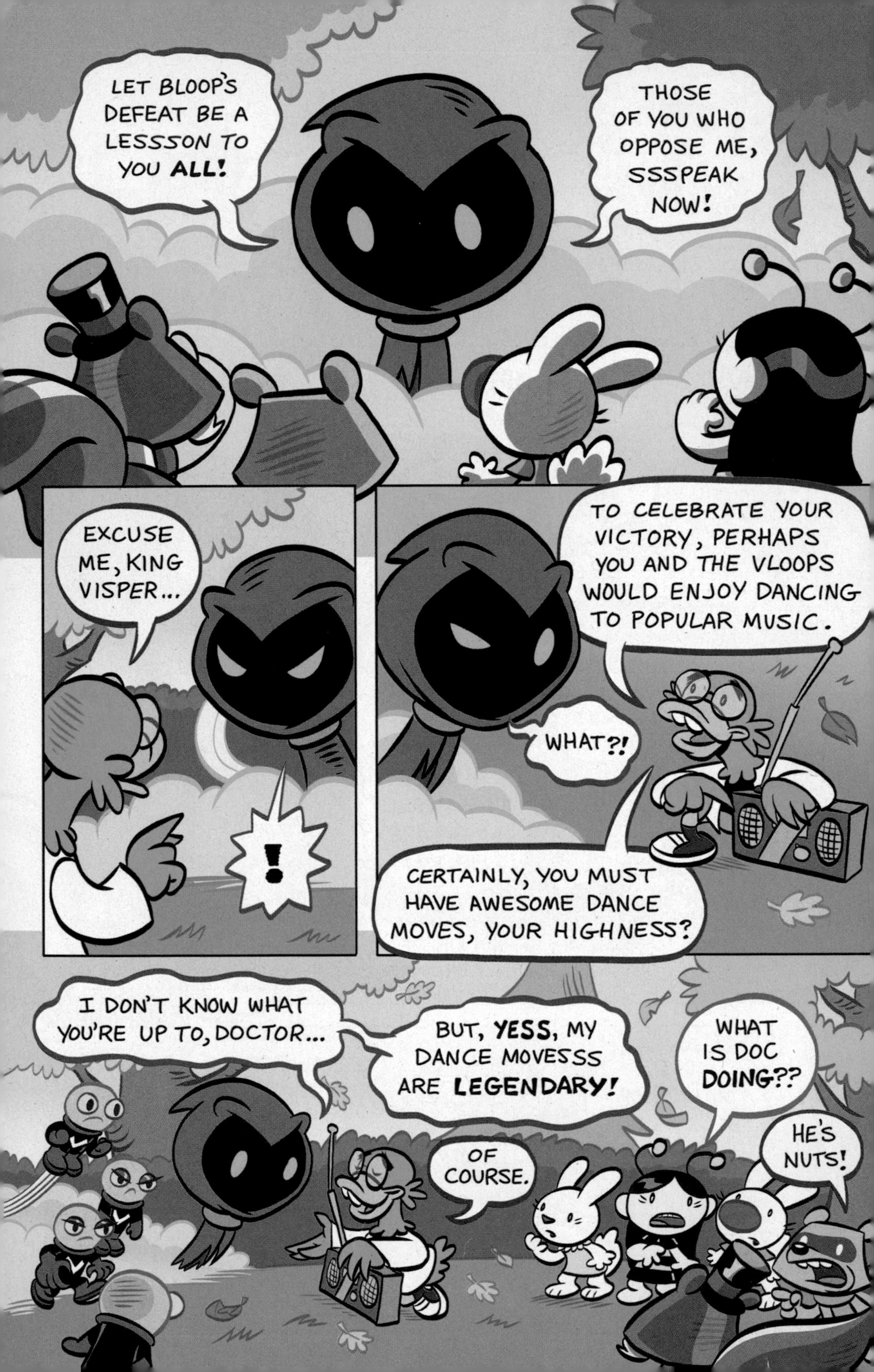

LET BLOOP'S DEFEAT BE A LESSSON TO YOU **ALL!**
THOSE OF YOU WHO OPPOSE ME, SSSPEAK NOW!
EXCUSE ME, KING VISPER...
!
TO CELEBRATE YOUR VICTORY, PERHAPS YOU AND THE VLOOPS WOULD ENJOY DANCING TO POPULAR MUSIC.
WHAT?!
CERTAINLY, YOU MUST HAVE AWESOME DANCE MOVES, YOUR HIGHNESS?
I DON'T KNOW WHAT YOU'RE UP TO, DOCTOR...
BUT, **YESS**, MY DANCE MOVESSS ARE **LEGENDARY!**
WHAT IS DOC **DOING??**
OF COURSE.
HE'S NUTS!

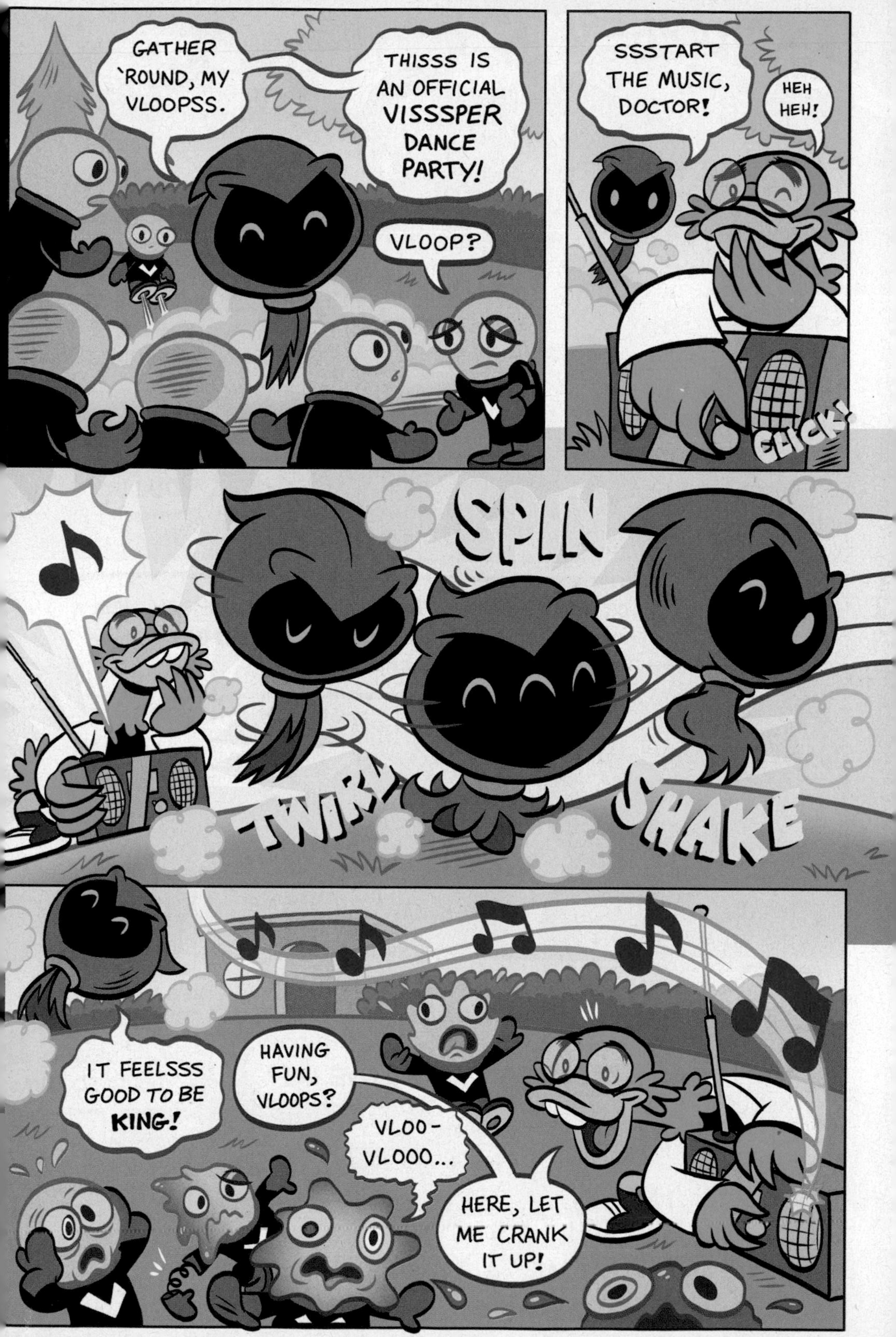

GATHER `ROUND, MY VLOOPSS.
THISSS IS AN OFFICIAL VISSSPER DANCE PARTY!
VLOOP?
SSSTART THE MUSIC, DOCTOR!
HEH HEH!
CLICK!
SPIN
TWIRL
SHAKE
IT FEELSSS GOOD TO BE KING!
HAVING FUN, VLOOPS?
VLOO-VLOOO...
HERE, LET ME CRANK IT UP!

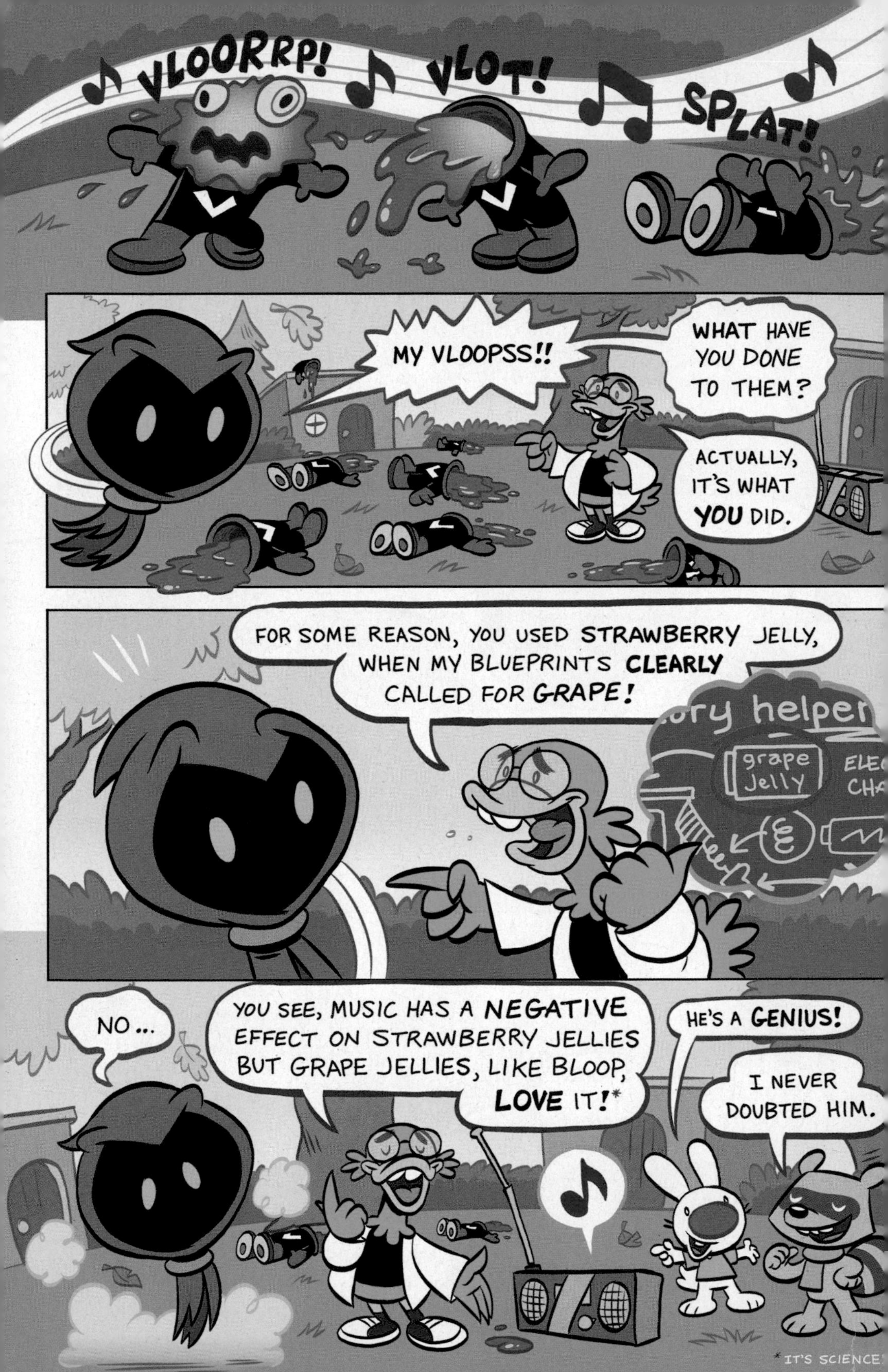
VLOORRP!
VLOT!
SPLAT!
MY VLOOPSS!!
WHAT HAVE YOU DONE TO THEM?
ACTUALLY, IT'S WHAT YOU DID.
FOR SOME REASON, YOU USED STRAWBERRY JELLY, WHEN MY BLUEPRINTS CLEARLY CALLED FOR GRAPE!
grape Jelly
NO...
YOU SEE, MUSIC HAS A NEGATIVE EFFECT ON STRAWBERRY JELLIES BUT GRAPE JELLIES, LIKE BLOOP, LOVE IT!*
HE'S A GENIUS!
I NEVER DOUBTED HIM.

* IT'S SCIENCE!

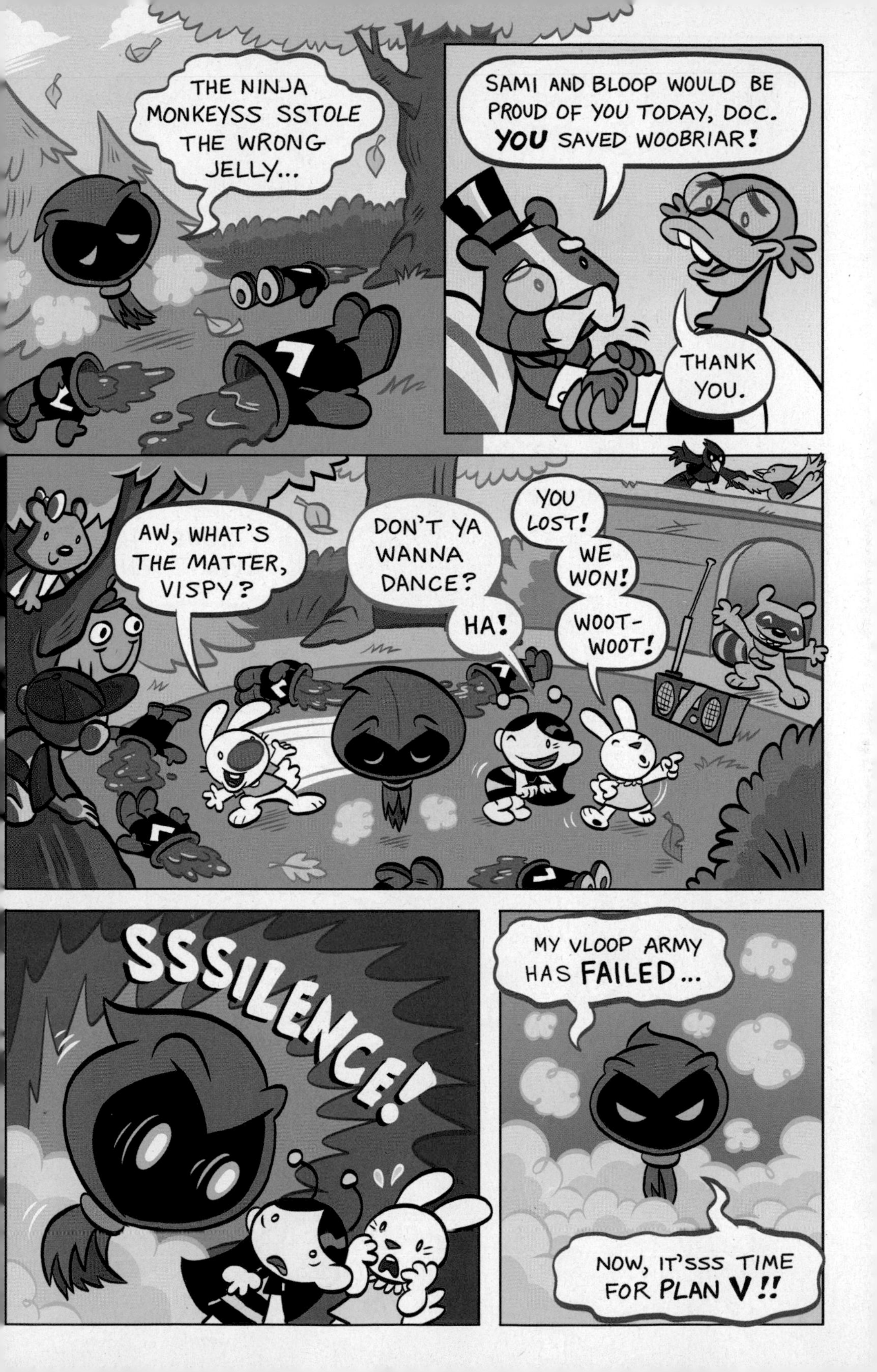
THE NINJA MONKEYSS SSTOLE THE WRONG JELLY...
SAMI AND BLOOP WOULD BE PROUD OF YOU TODAY, DOC. **YOU** SAVED WOOBRIAR!
THANK YOU.
AW, WHAT'S THE MATTER, VISPY?
DON'T YA WANNA DANCE?
HA!
YOU LOST!
WE WON!
WOOT-WOOT!
SSSILENCE!
MY VLOOP ARMY HAS **FAILED**...
NOW, IT'SSS TIME FOR **PLAN V!!**

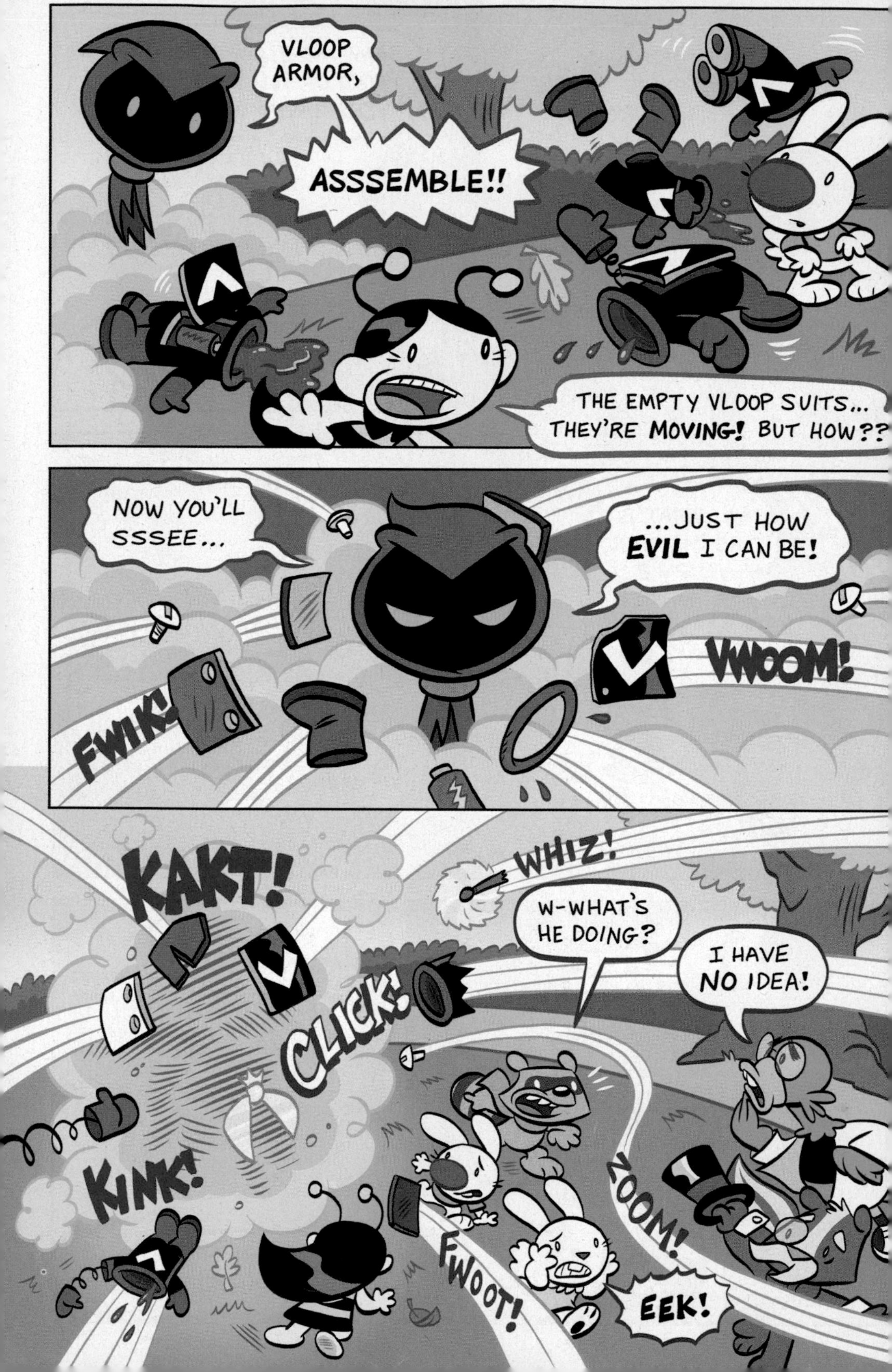
VLOOP ARMOR,
ASSSEMBLE!!
THE EMPTY VLOOP SUITS... THEY'RE MOVING! BUT HOW??
NOW YOU'LL SSSEE...
...JUST HOW EVIL I CAN BE!
VWOOM!
FWIK!
KAKT!
WHIZ!
W-WHAT'S HE DOING?
I HAVE NO IDEA!
CLICK!
KINK!
ZOOM!
FWOOT!
EEK!

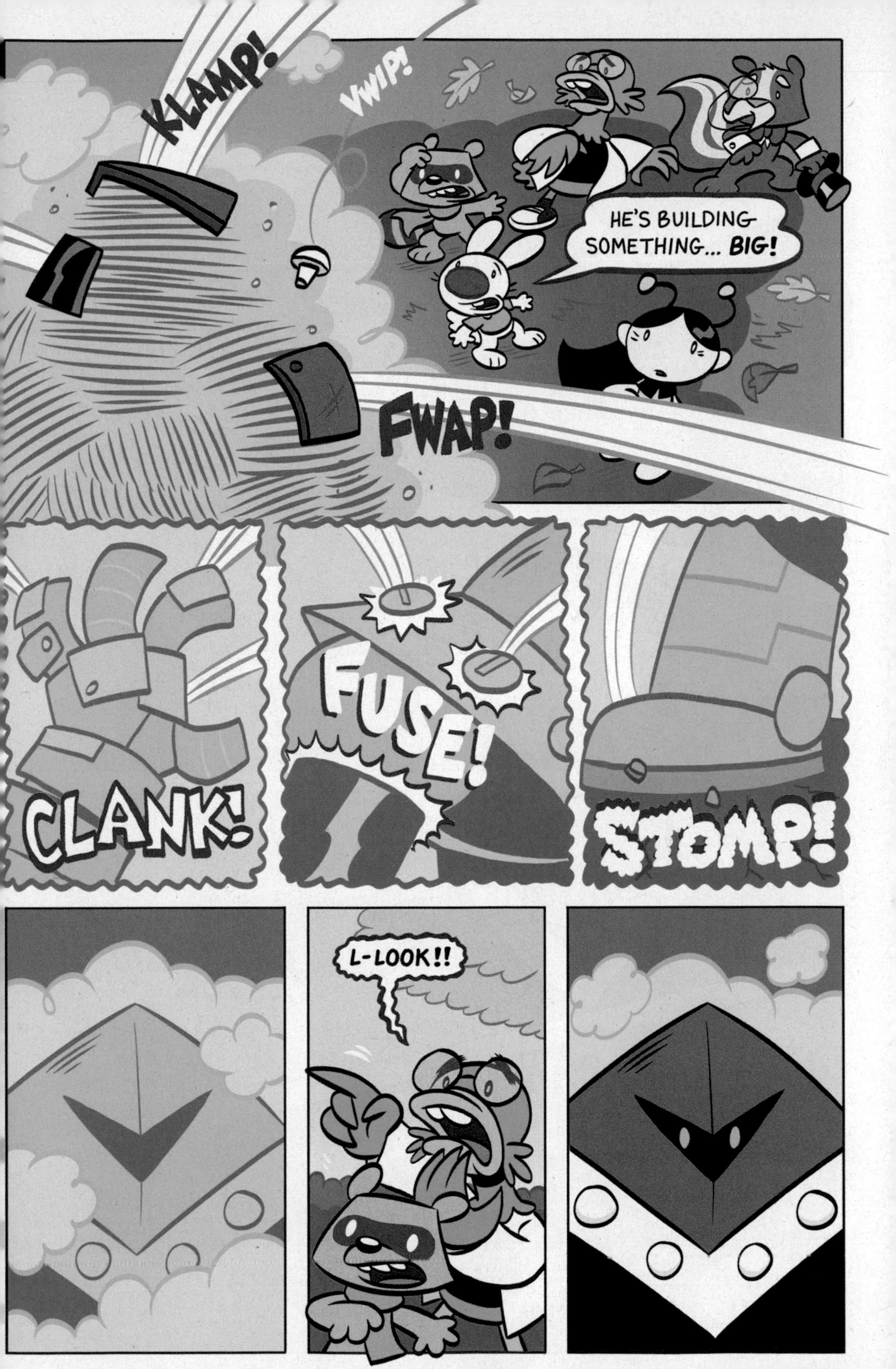
KLAMP!
VWIP!
HE'S BUILDING SOMETHING... BIG!
FWAP!
CLANK!
FUSE!
STOMP!
L-LOOK!!

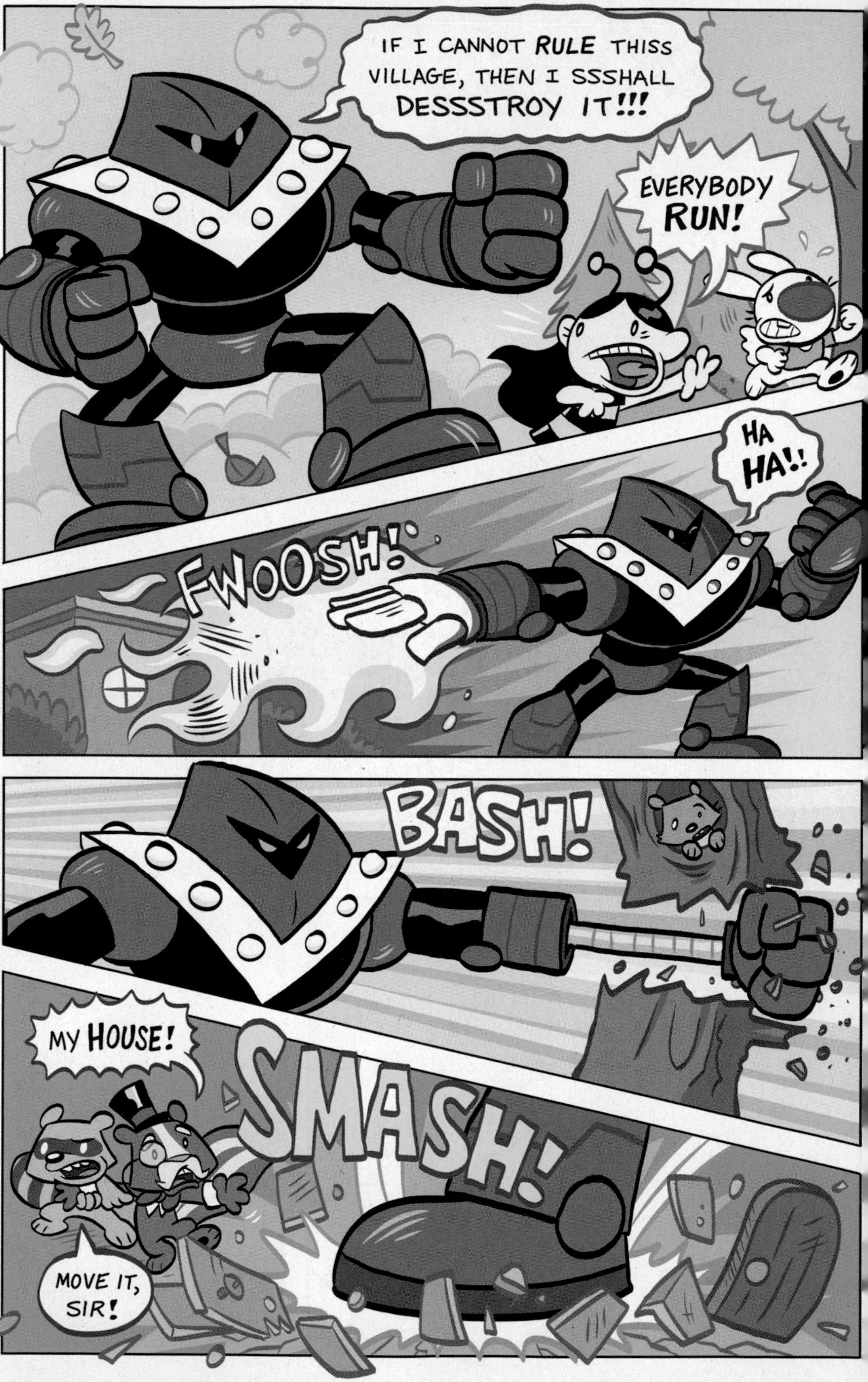

IF I CANNOT RULE THISS VILLAGE, THEN I SSSHALL DESSSTROY IT!!!
EVERYBODY RUN!
HA HA!!
FWOOSH!
BASH!
MY HOUSE!
SMASH!
MOVE IT, SIR!

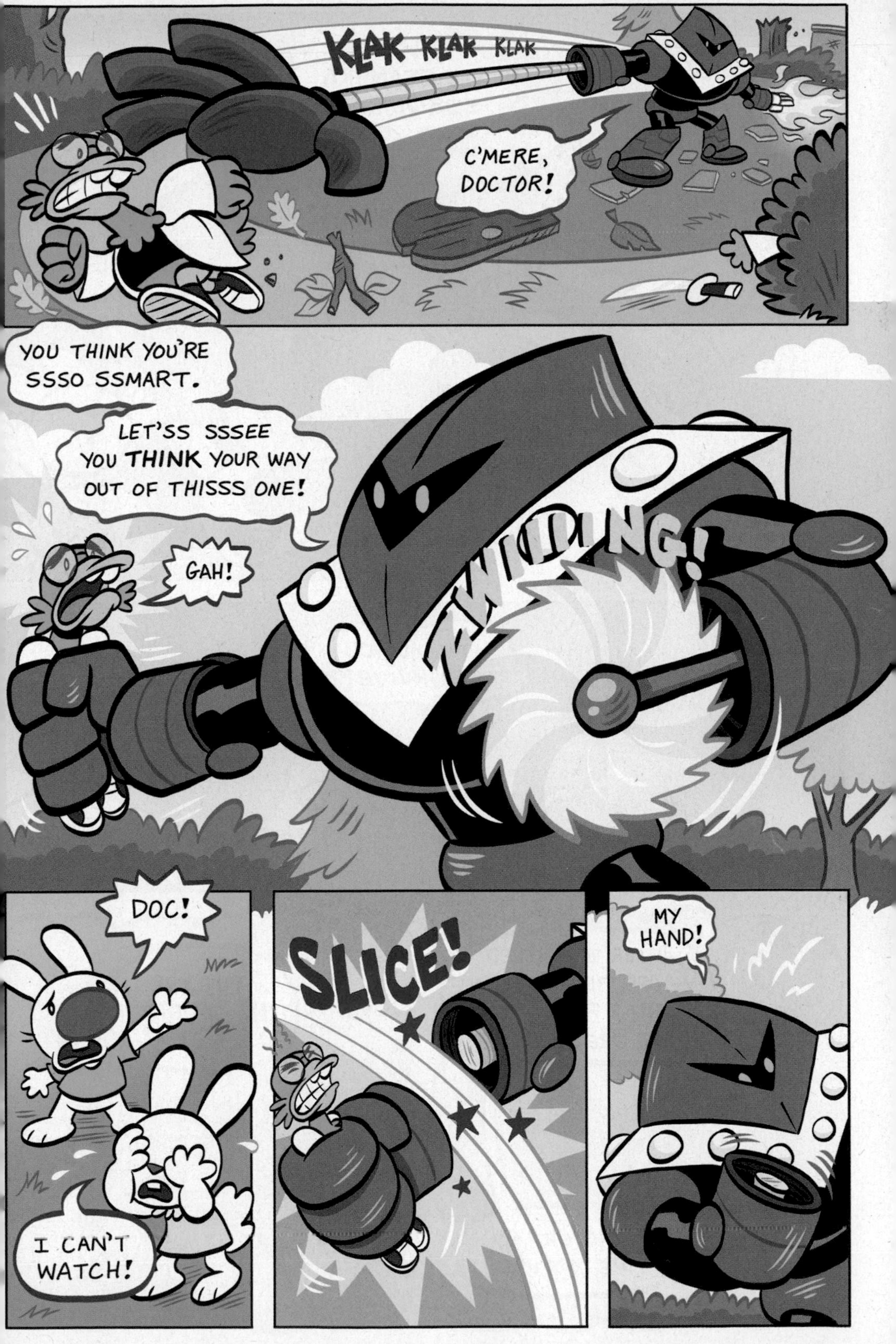
KLAK KLAK KLAK
C'MERE, DOCTOR!
YOU THINK YOU'RE SSSO SSMART.
LET'SS SSSEE YOU THINK YOUR WAY OUT OF THISSS ONE!
GAH!
ZWIIIIING!
DOC!
I CAN'T WATCH!
SLICE!
MY HAND!

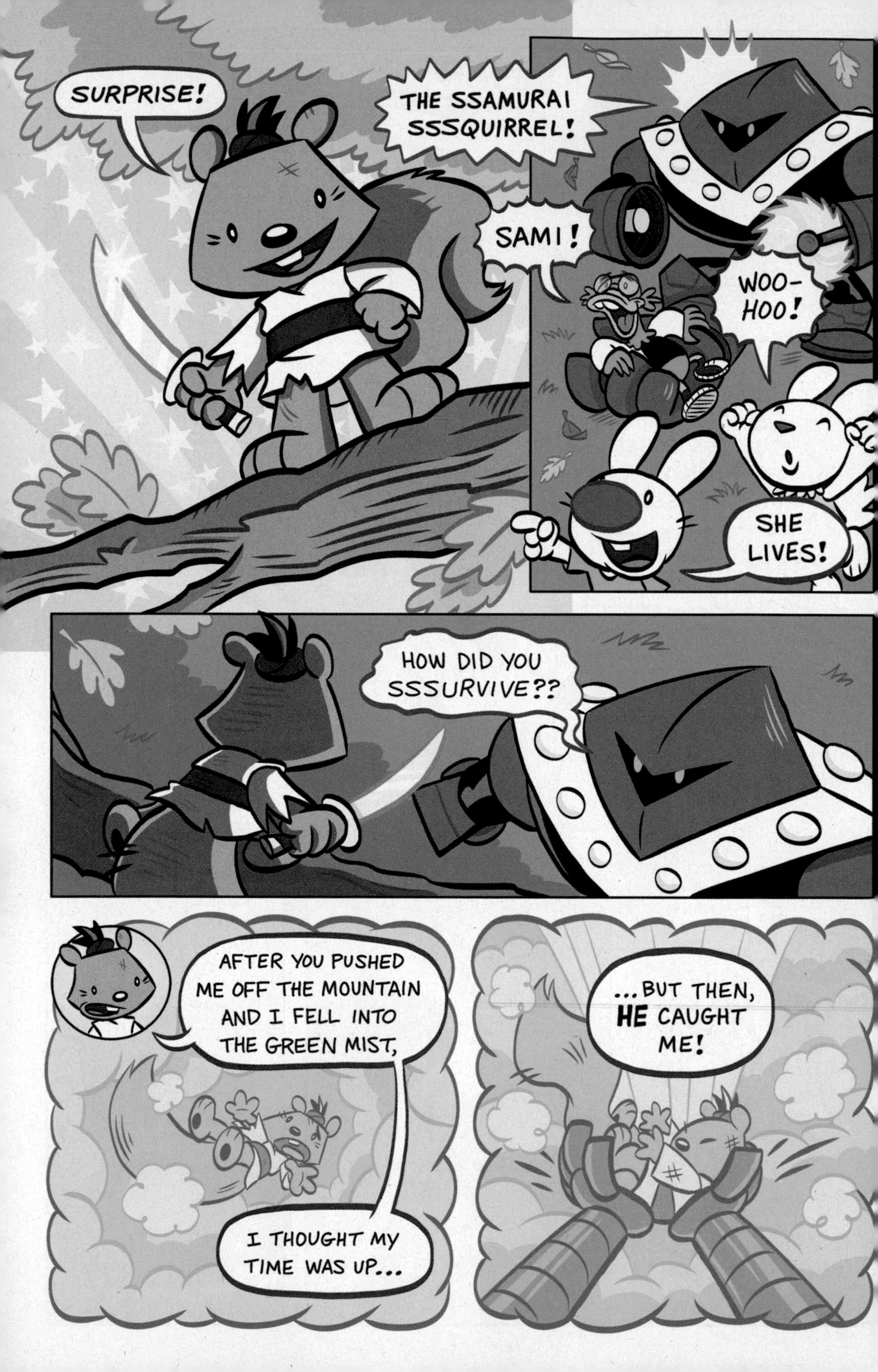
SURPRISE!
THE SSAMURAI SSSQUIRREL!
SAMI!
WOO-HOO!
SHE LIVES!
HOW DID YOU SSSURVIVE??
AFTER YOU PUSHED ME OFF THE MOUNTAIN AND I FELL INTO THE GREEN MIST,
I THOUGHT MY TIME WAS UP...
...BUT THEN, HE CAUGHT ME!

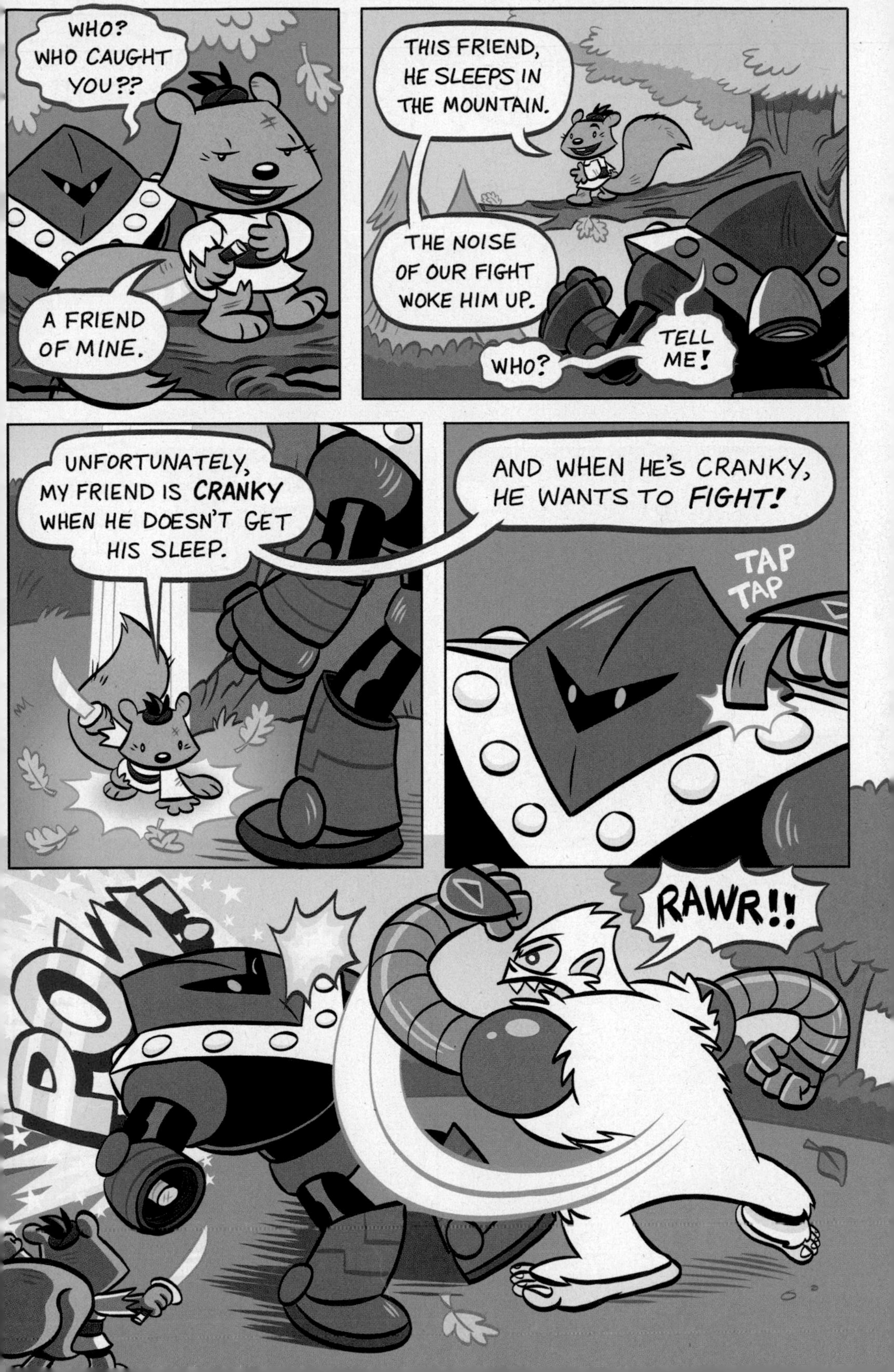
WHO? WHO CAUGHT YOU??
A FRIEND OF MINE.
THIS FRIEND, HE SLEEPS IN THE MOUNTAIN.
THE NOISE OF OUR FIGHT WOKE HIM UP.
WHO?
TELL ME!
UNFORTUNATELY, MY FRIEND IS CRANKY WHEN HE DOESN'T GET HIS SLEEP.
AND WHEN HE'S CRANKY, HE WANTS TO FIGHT!
TAP TAP
POW!
RAWR!!

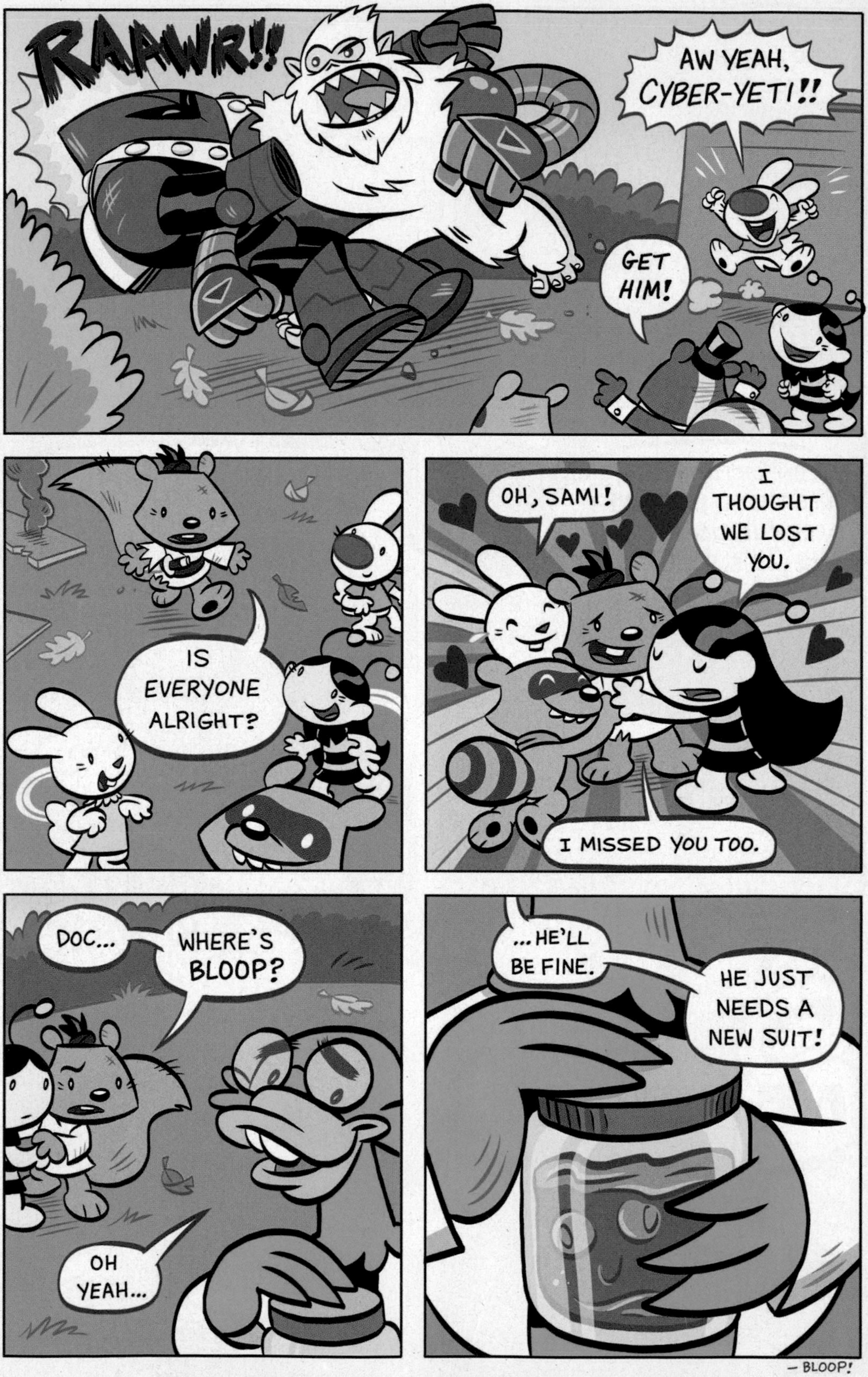
RAAWR!!
AW YEAH, CYBER-YETI!!
GET HIM!
IS EVERYONE ALRIGHT?
OH, SAMI!
I THOUGHT WE LOST YOU.
I MISSED YOU TOO.
DOC...
WHERE'S BLOOP?
OH YEAH...
...HE'LL BE FINE.
HE JUST NEEDS A NEW SUIT!
– BLOOP!

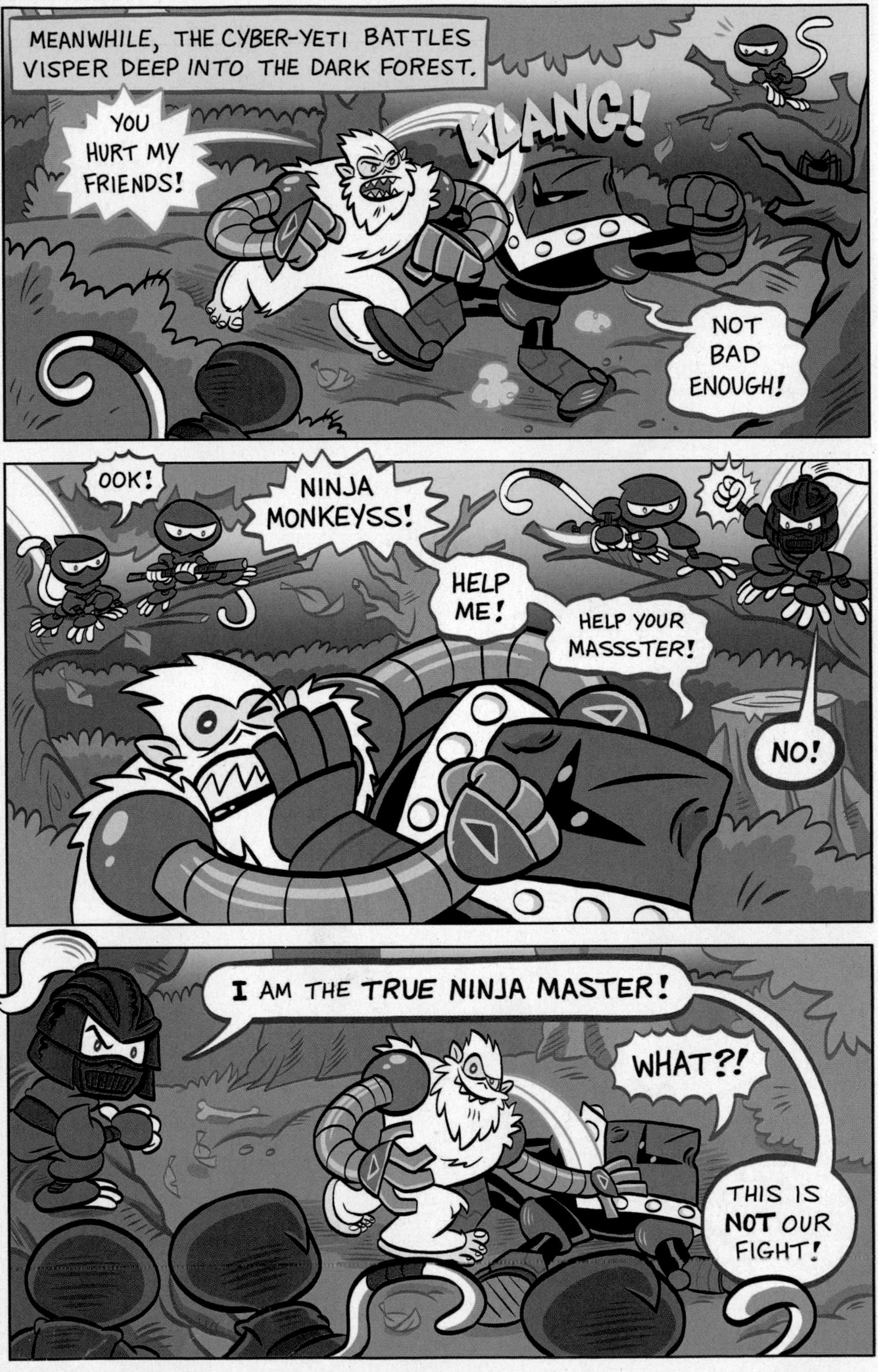
MEANWHILE, THE CYBER-YETI BATTLES VISPER DEEP INTO THE DARK FOREST.
YOU HURT MY FRIENDS!
KLANG!
NOT BAD ENOUGH!
OOK!
NINJA MONKEYSS!
HELP ME!
HELP YOUR MASSSTER!
NO!
I AM THE TRUE NINJA MASTER!
WHAT?!
THIS IS NOT OUR FIGHT!

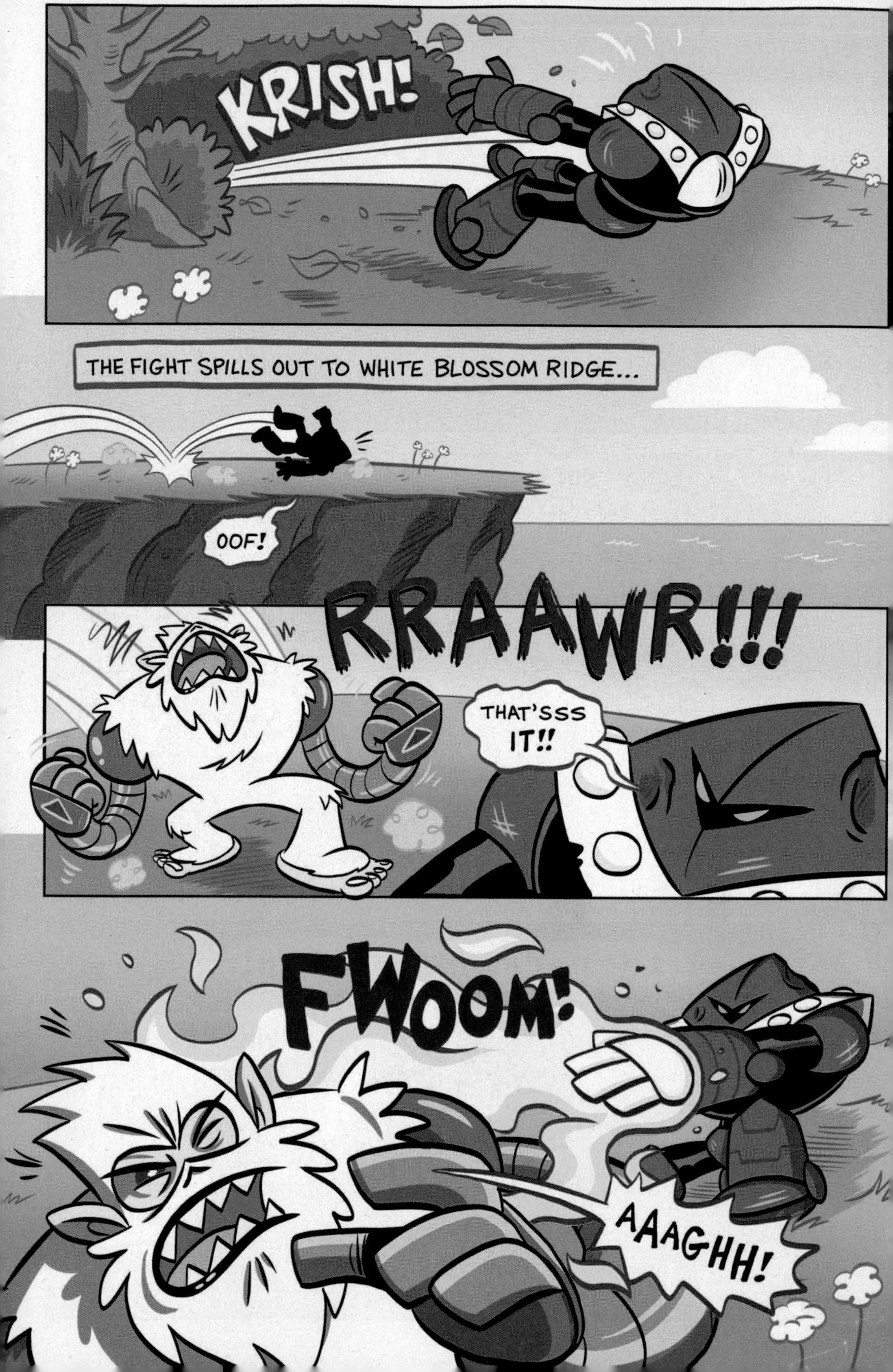
KRISH!
THE FIGHT SPILLS OUT TO WHITE BLOSSOM RIDGE...
OOF!
RRAAWR!!!
THAT'SSS IT!!
FWOOM!
AAAGHH!

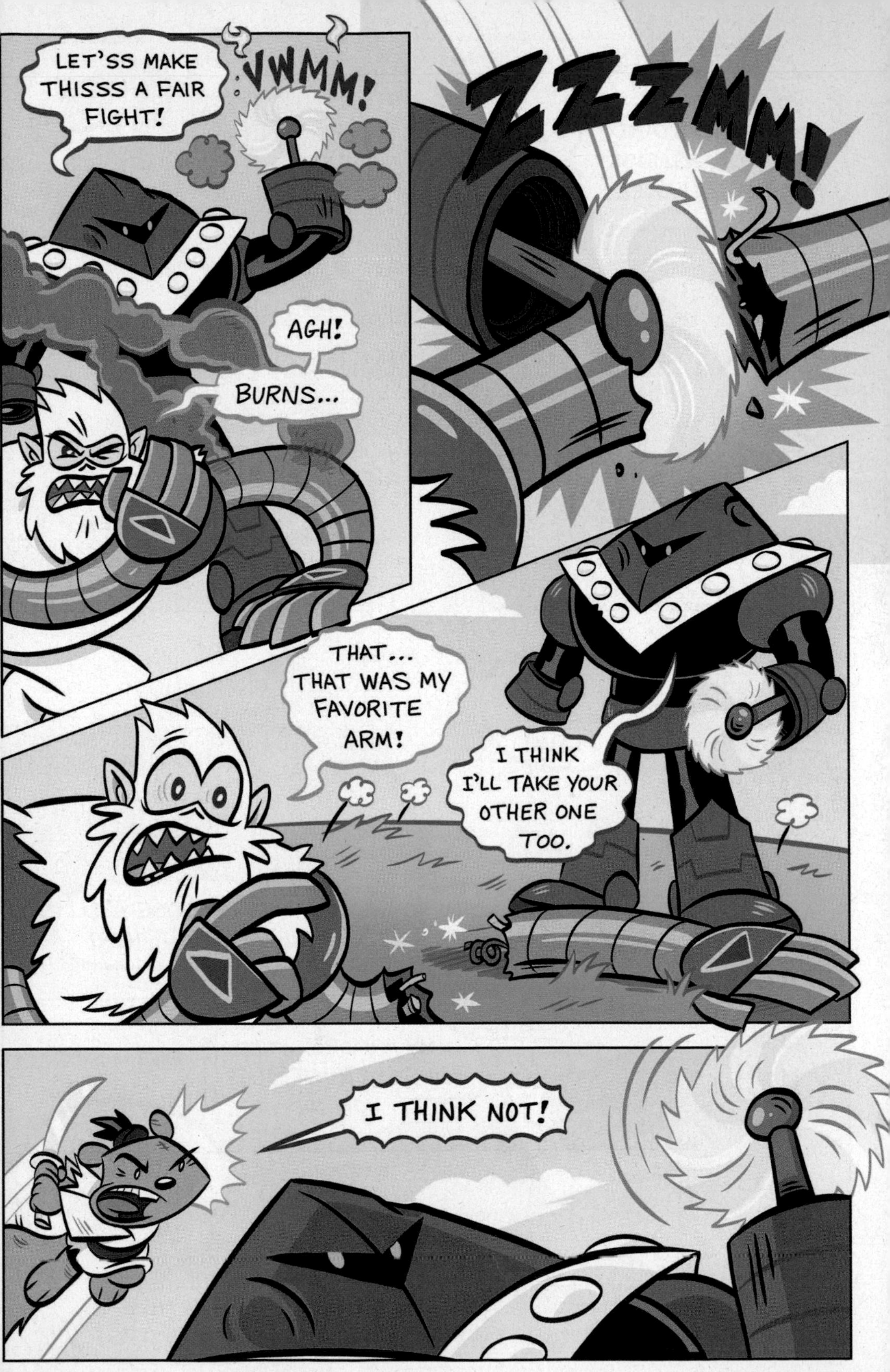
LET'SS MAKE THISSS A FAIR FIGHT!
VWMM!
AGH!
BURNS...
ZZZMM!
THAT... THAT WAS MY FAVORITE ARM!
I THINK I'LL TAKE YOUR OTHER ONE TOO.
I THINK NOT!

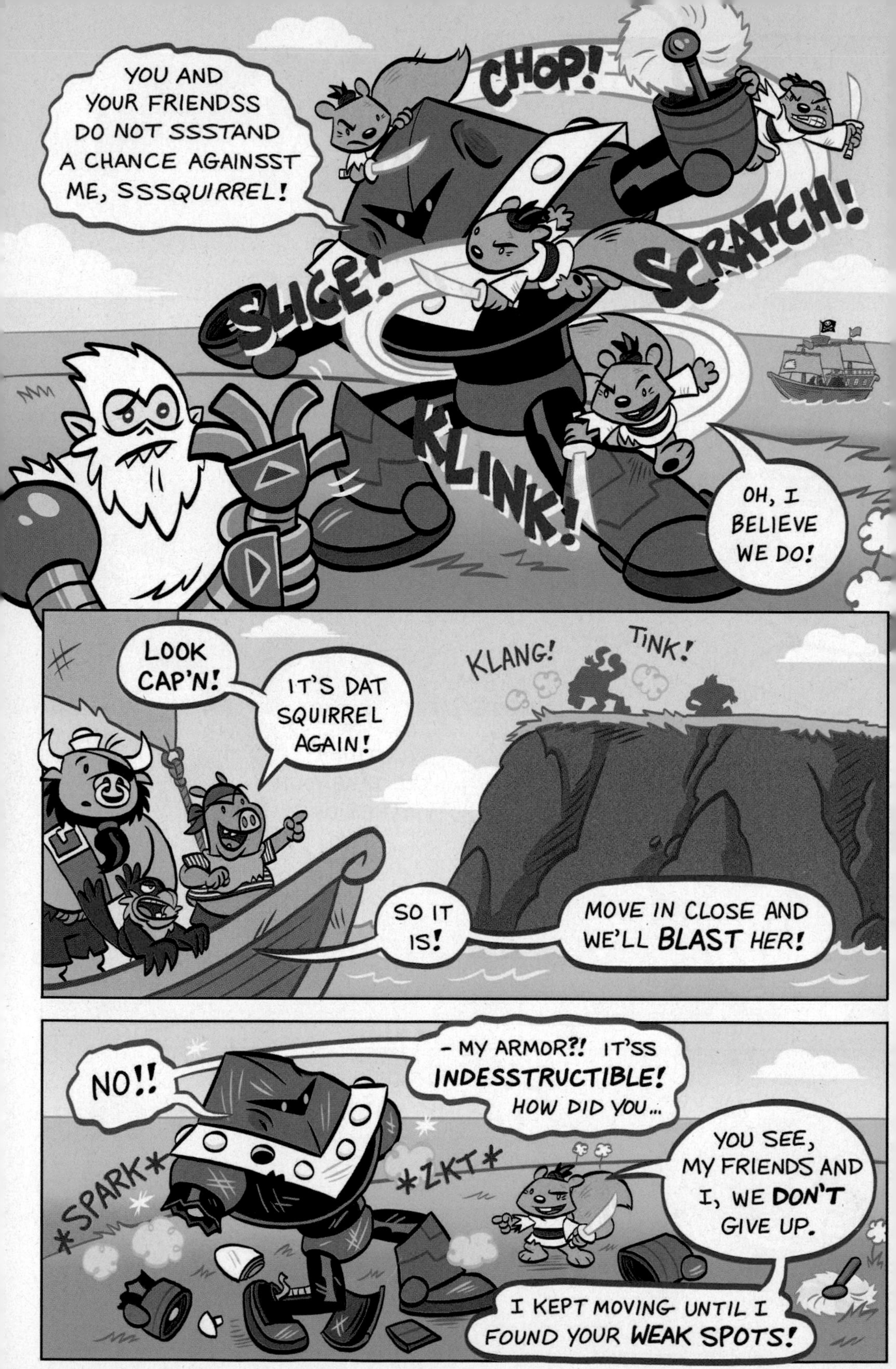
YOU AND YOUR FRIENDSS DO NOT SSSTAND A CHANCE AGAINSST ME, SSSQUIRREL!
CHOP!
SCRATCH!
SLICE!
KLINK!
OH, I BELIEVE WE DO!
LOOK CAP'N!
IT'S DAT SQUIRREL AGAIN!
KLANG!
TINK!
SO IT IS!
MOVE IN CLOSE AND WE'LL BLAST HER!
NO!!
- MY ARMOR?! IT'SS INDESSTRUCTIBLE! HOW DID YOU...
SPARK
ZKT
YOU SEE, MY FRIENDS AND I, WE DON'T GIVE UP.
I KEPT MOVING UNTIL I FOUND YOUR WEAK SPOTS!

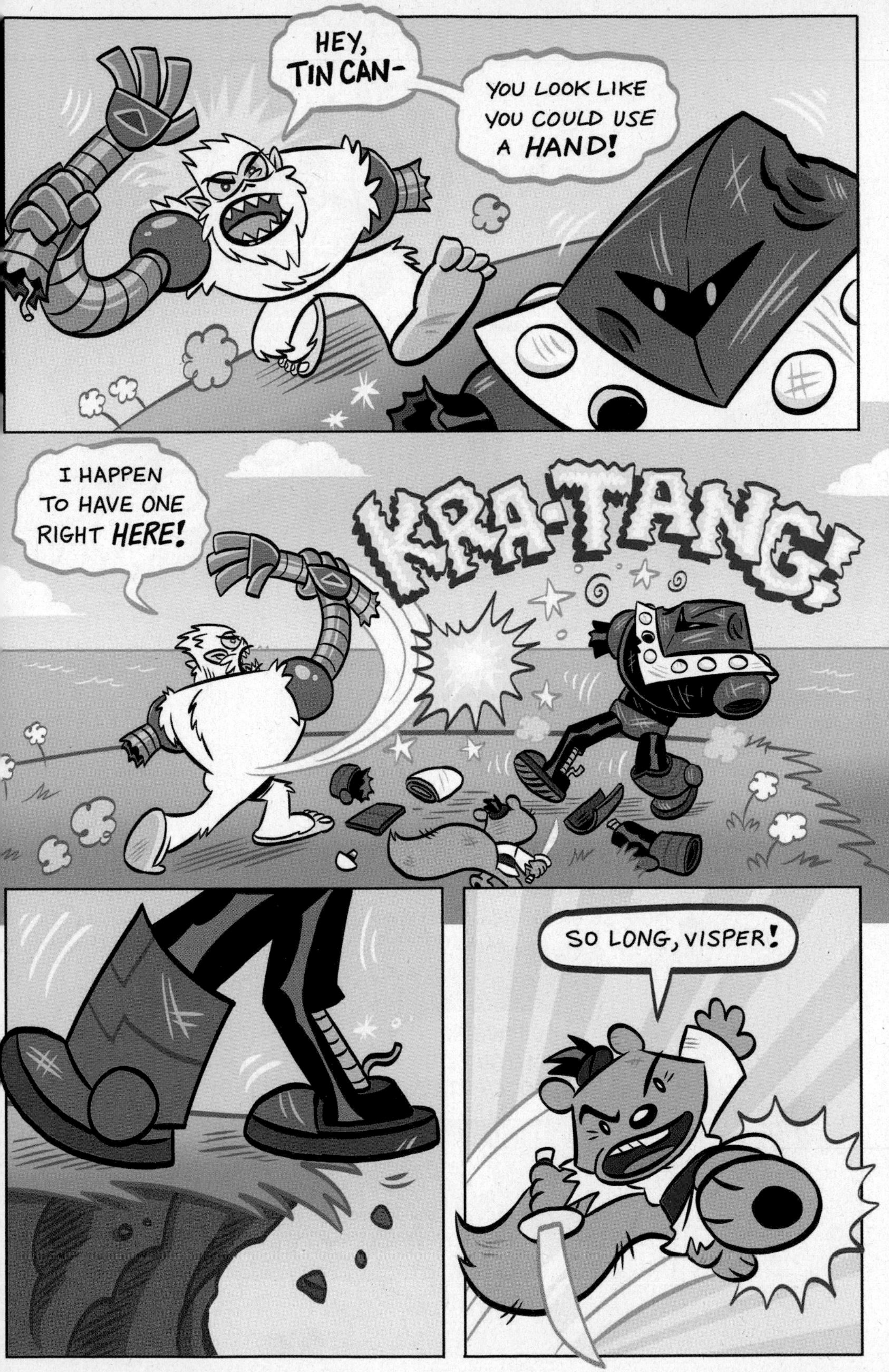
HEY, TIN CAN-
YOU LOOK LIKE YOU COULD USE A HAND!
I HAPPEN TO HAVE ONE RIGHT HERE!
KRA-TANG!
SO LONG, VISPER!

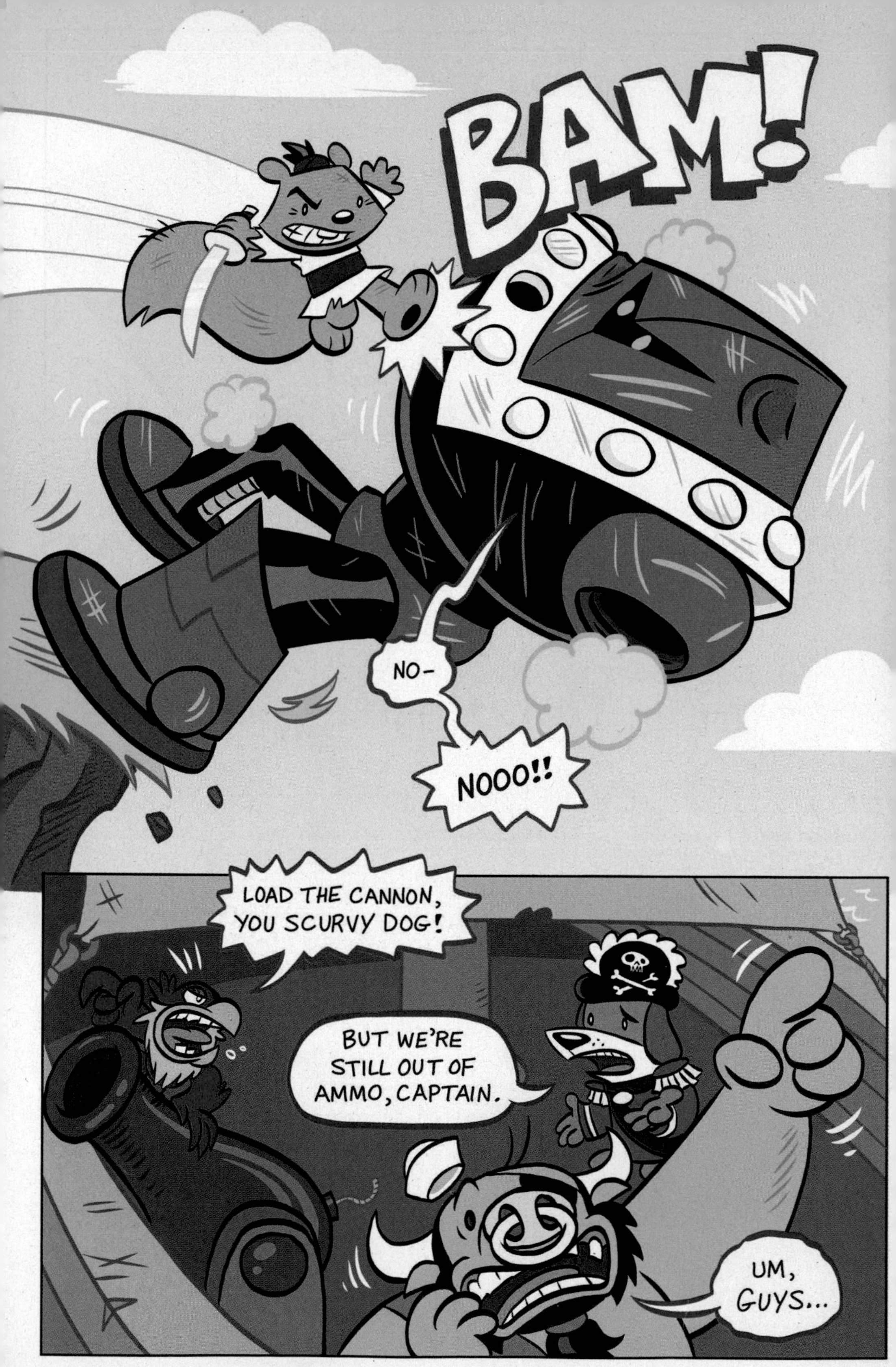
BAM!
NO-
NOOO!!
LOAD THE CANNON, YOU SCURVY DOG!
BUT WE'RE STILL OUT OF AMMO, CAPTAIN.
UM, GUYS...

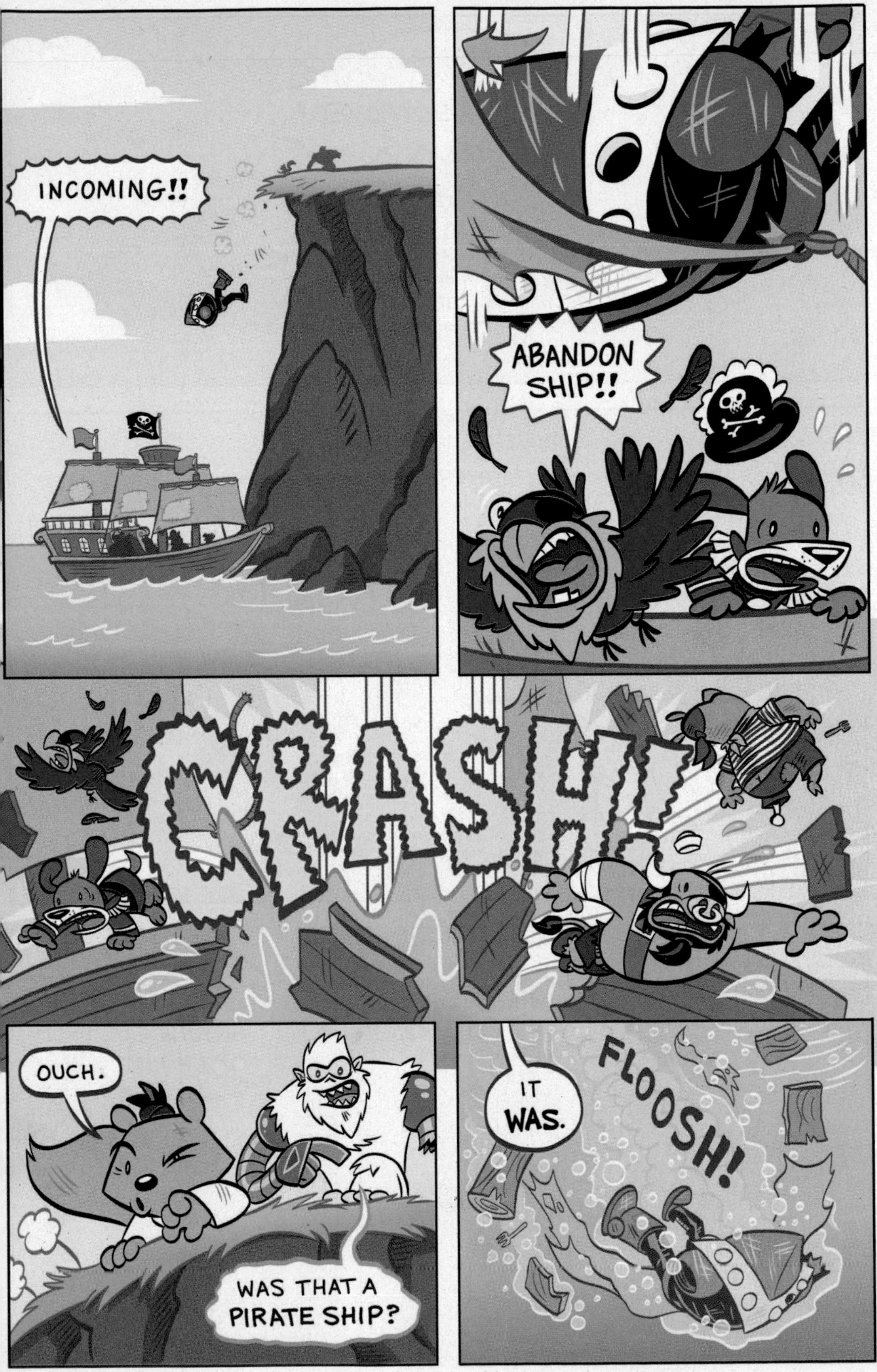
INCOMING!!
ABANDON SHIP!!
CRASH!
OUCH.
WAS THAT A PIRATE SHIP?
IT WAS.
FLOOSH!

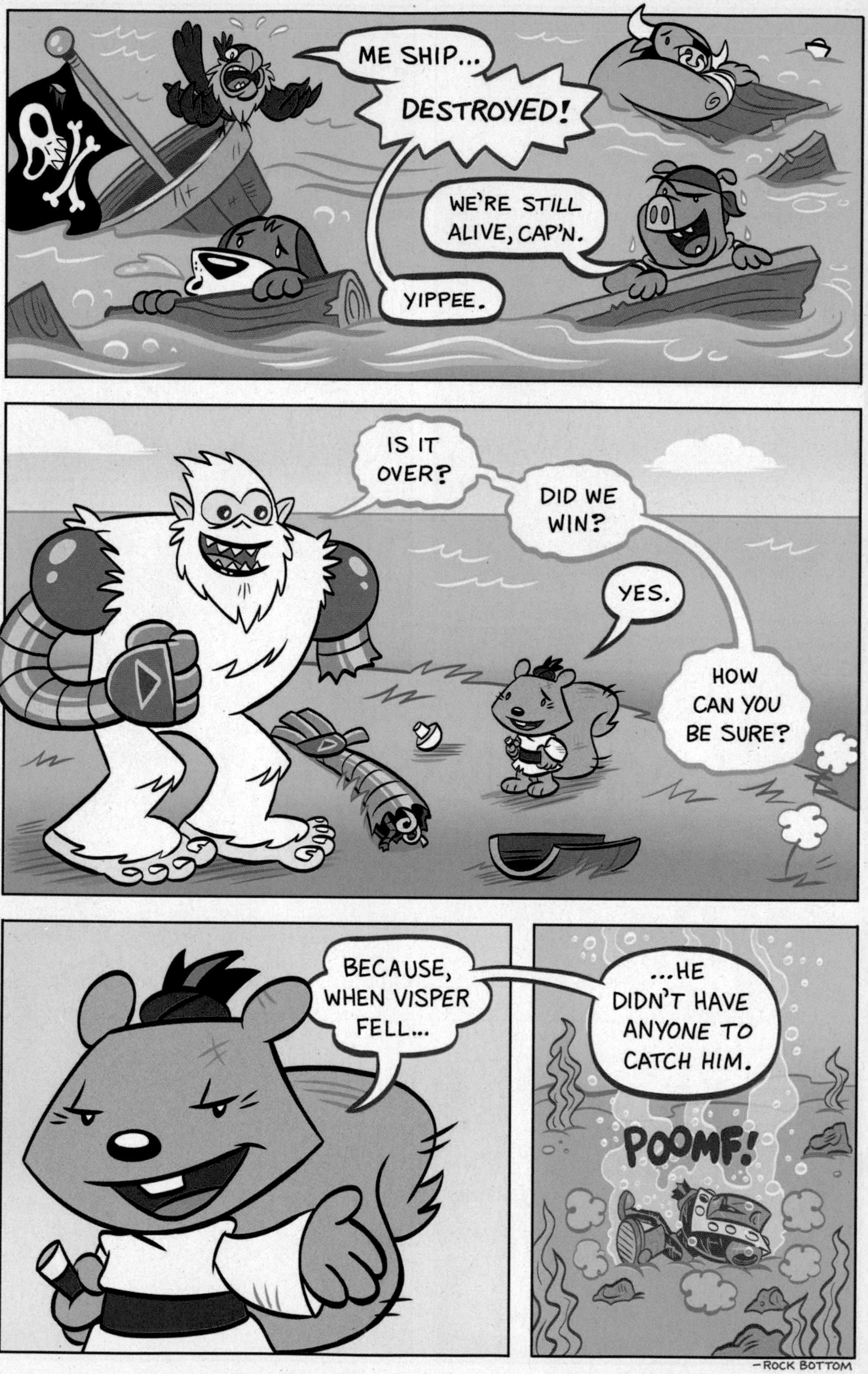
ME SHIP...
DESTROYED!
WE'RE STILL ALIVE, CAP'N.
YIPPEE.
IS IT OVER?
DID WE WIN?
YES.
HOW CAN YOU BE SURE?
BECAUSE, WHEN VISPER FELL...
...HE DIDN'T HAVE ANYONE TO CATCH HIM.
POOMF!

-ROCK BOTTOM

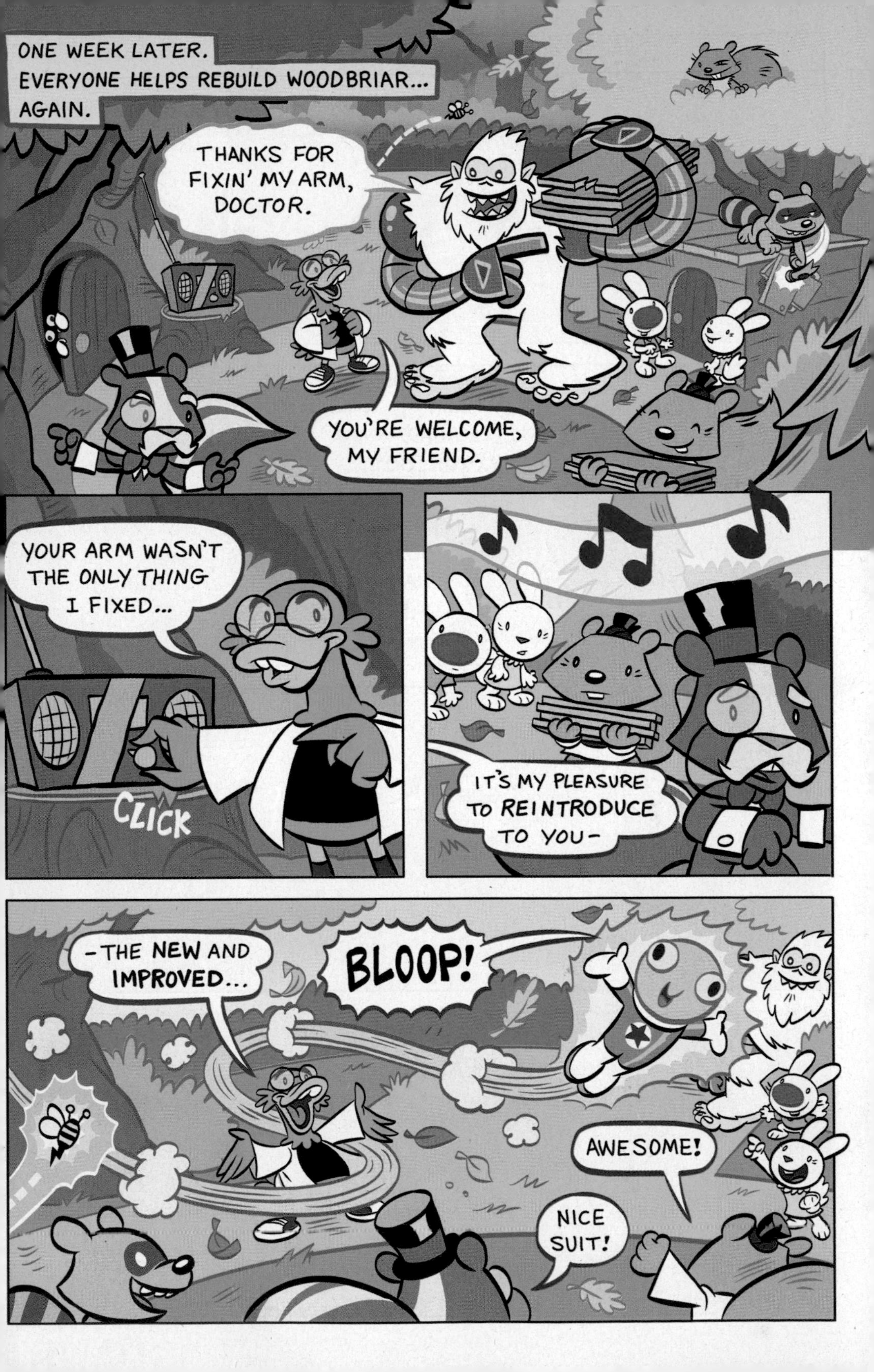
ONE WEEK LATER.
EVERYONE HELPS REBUILD WOODBRIAR...
AGAIN.
THANKS FOR FIXIN' MY ARM, DOCTOR.
YOU'RE WELCOME, MY FRIEND.
YOUR ARM WASN'T THE ONLY THING I FIXED...
CLICK
IT'S MY PLEASURE TO REINTRODUCE TO YOU-
-THE NEW AND IMPROVED...
BLOOP!
AWESOME!
NICE SUIT!

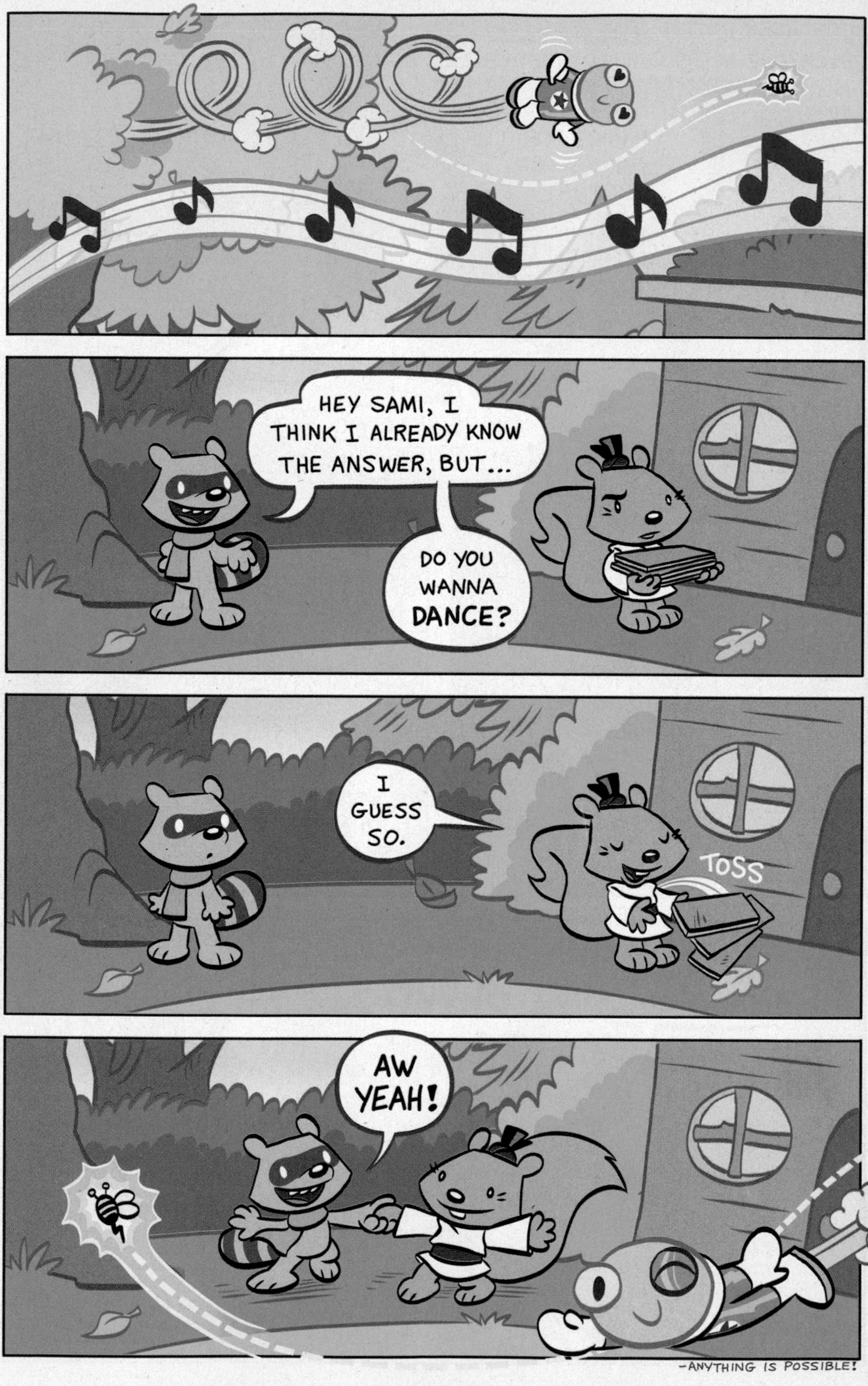
HEY SAMI, I THINK I ALREADY KNOW THE ANSWER, BUT...
DO YOU WANNA DANCE?
I GUESS SO.
TOSS
AW YEAH!

-ANYTHING IS POSSIBLE!

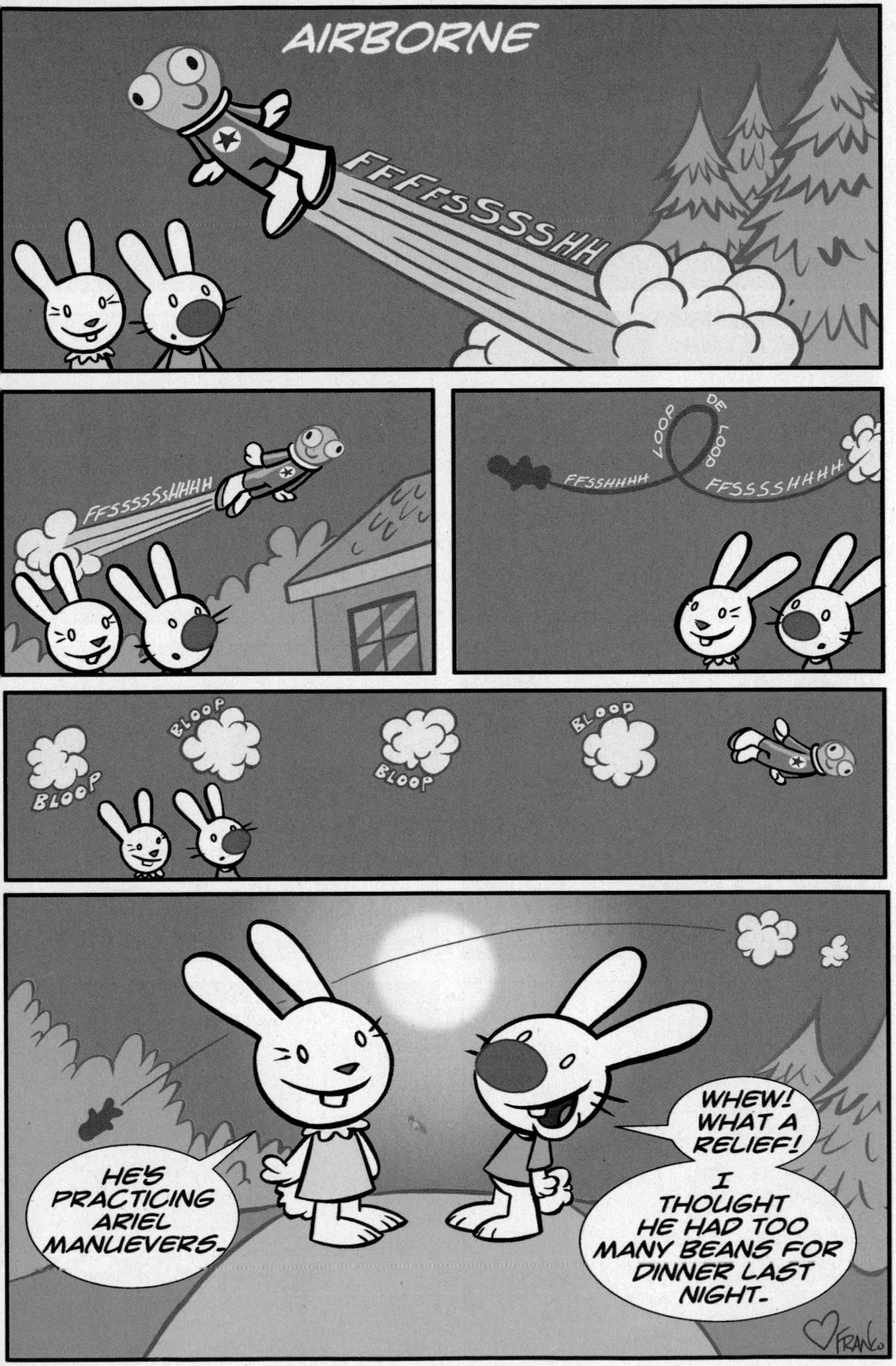
AIRBORNE
FFFFFSSSSSHH
FFSSSSSSHHHH
FFSSHHHH
LOOP DE LOOP
FFSSSSSHHHH
BLOOP
BLOOP
BLOOP
BLOOP
HE'S PRACTICING ARIEL MANUEVERS.
WHEW! WHAT A RELIEF!
I THOUGHT HE HAD TOO MANY BEANS FOR DINNER LAST NIGHT.
FRANCO

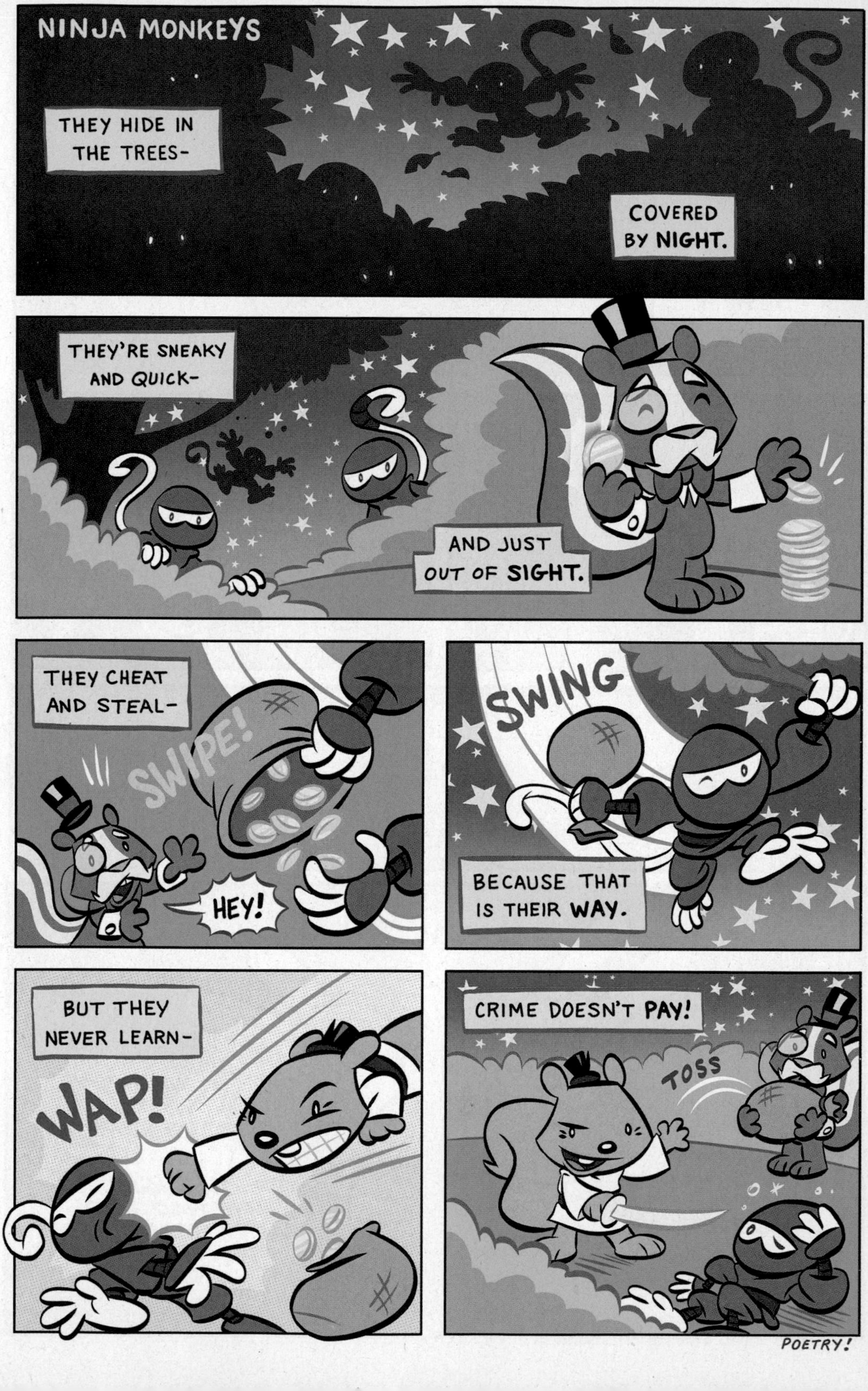
NINJA MONKEYS
THEY HIDE IN THE TREES-
COVERED BY NIGHT.
THEY'RE SNEAKY AND QUICK-
AND JUST OUT OF SIGHT.
THEY CHEAT AND STEAL-
SWIPE!
HEY!
SWING
BECAUSE THAT IS THEIR WAY.
BUT THEY NEVER LEARN-
WAP!
CRIME DOESN'T PAY!
TOSS
POETRY!

The SUPER NEW DEFENDERS of JUSTICE!

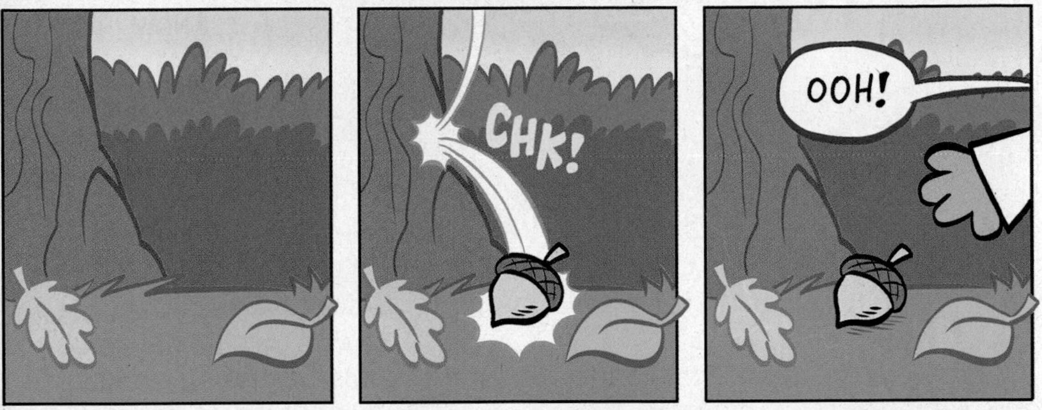
CHK!
OOH!

STORY & ART BY: SCOOT • ART BALTAZAR • FRANCO!

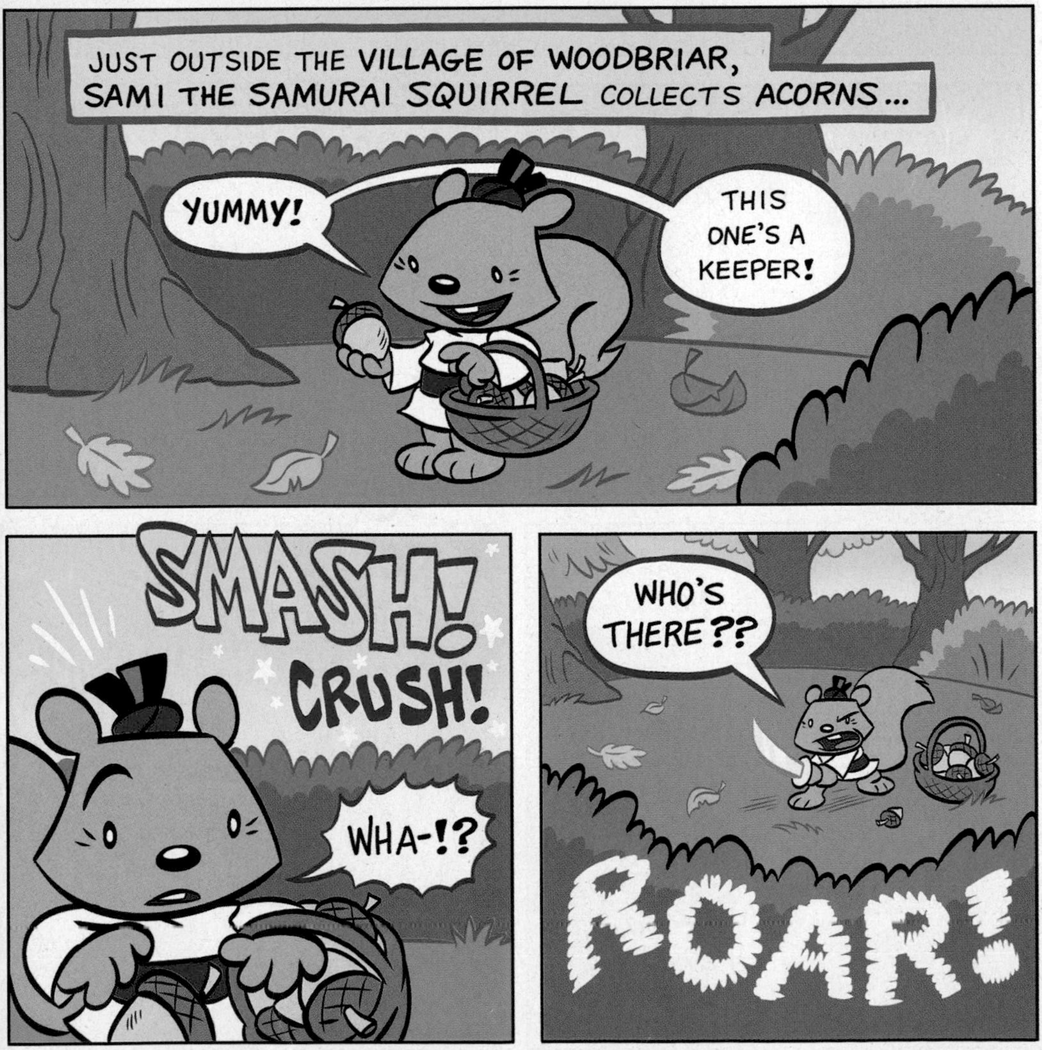
JUST OUTSIDE THE VILLAGE OF WOODBRIAR, SAMI THE SAMURAI SQUIRREL COLLECTS ACORNS...
YUMMY!
THIS ONE'S A KEEPER!
SMASH!
CRUSH!
WHA-!?
WHO'S THERE??
ROAR!

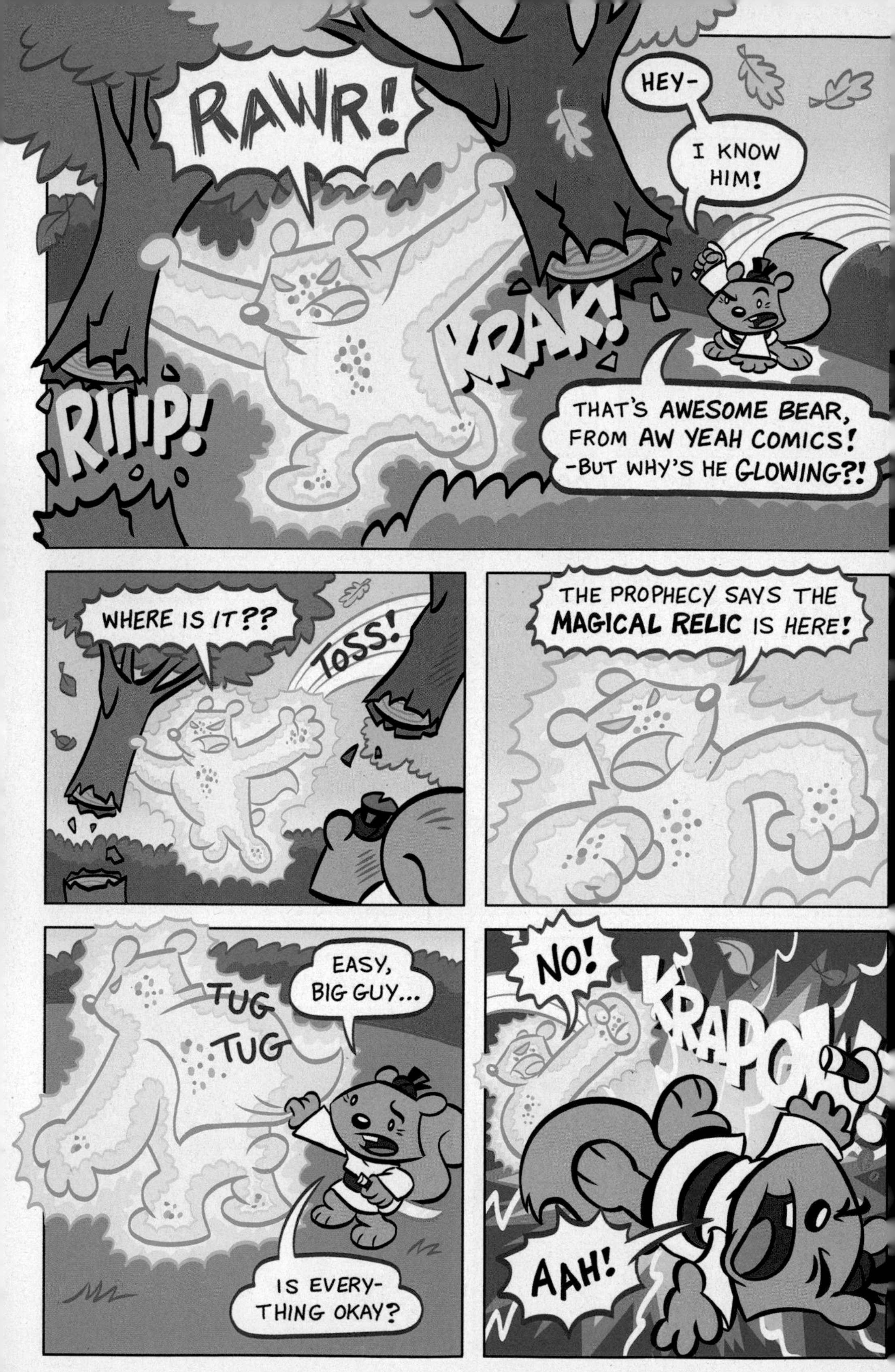
RAWR!
HEY-
I KNOW HIM!
KRAK!
RIIIP!
THAT'S AWESOME BEAR, FROM AW YEAH COMICS! -BUT WHY'S HE GLOWING?!
WHERE IS IT??
TOSS!
THE PROPHECY SAYS THE MAGICAL RELIC IS HERE!
TUG TUG
EASY, BIG GUY...
IS EVERY-THING OKAY?
NO!
KRAPOW!
AAH!

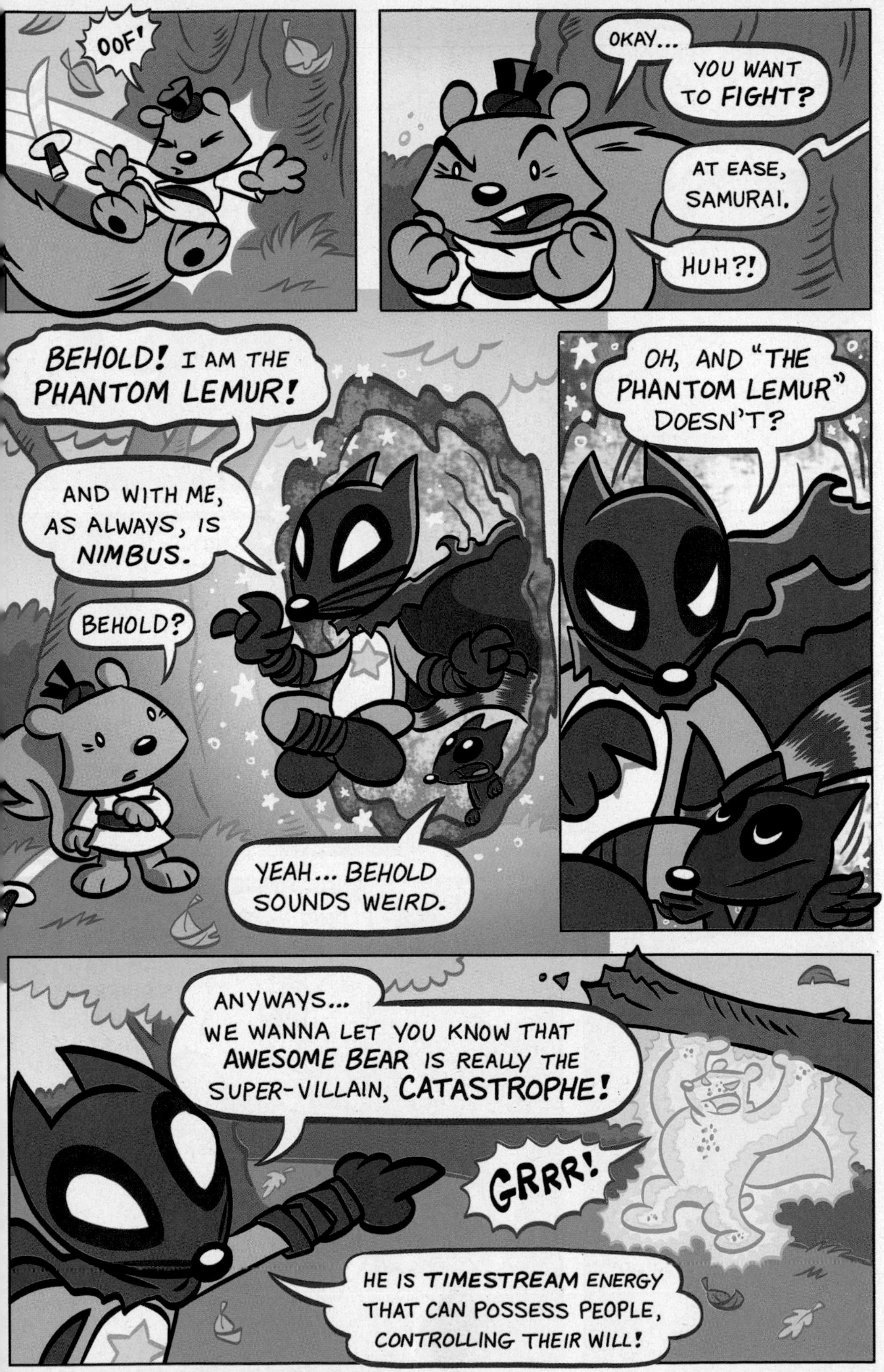
OOF!
OKAY...
YOU WANT TO FIGHT?
AT EASE, SAMURAI.
HUH?!
BEHOLD! I AM THE PHANTOM LEMUR!
AND WITH ME, AS ALWAYS, IS NIMBUS.
BEHOLD?
YEAH... BEHOLD SOUNDS WEIRD.
OH, AND "THE PHANTOM LEMUR" DOESN'T?
ANYWAYS...
WE WANNA LET YOU KNOW THAT AWESOME BEAR IS REALLY THE SUPER-VILLAIN, CATASTROPHE!
GRRR!
HE IS TIMESTREAM ENERGY THAT CAN POSSESS PEOPLE, CONTROLLING THEIR WILL!

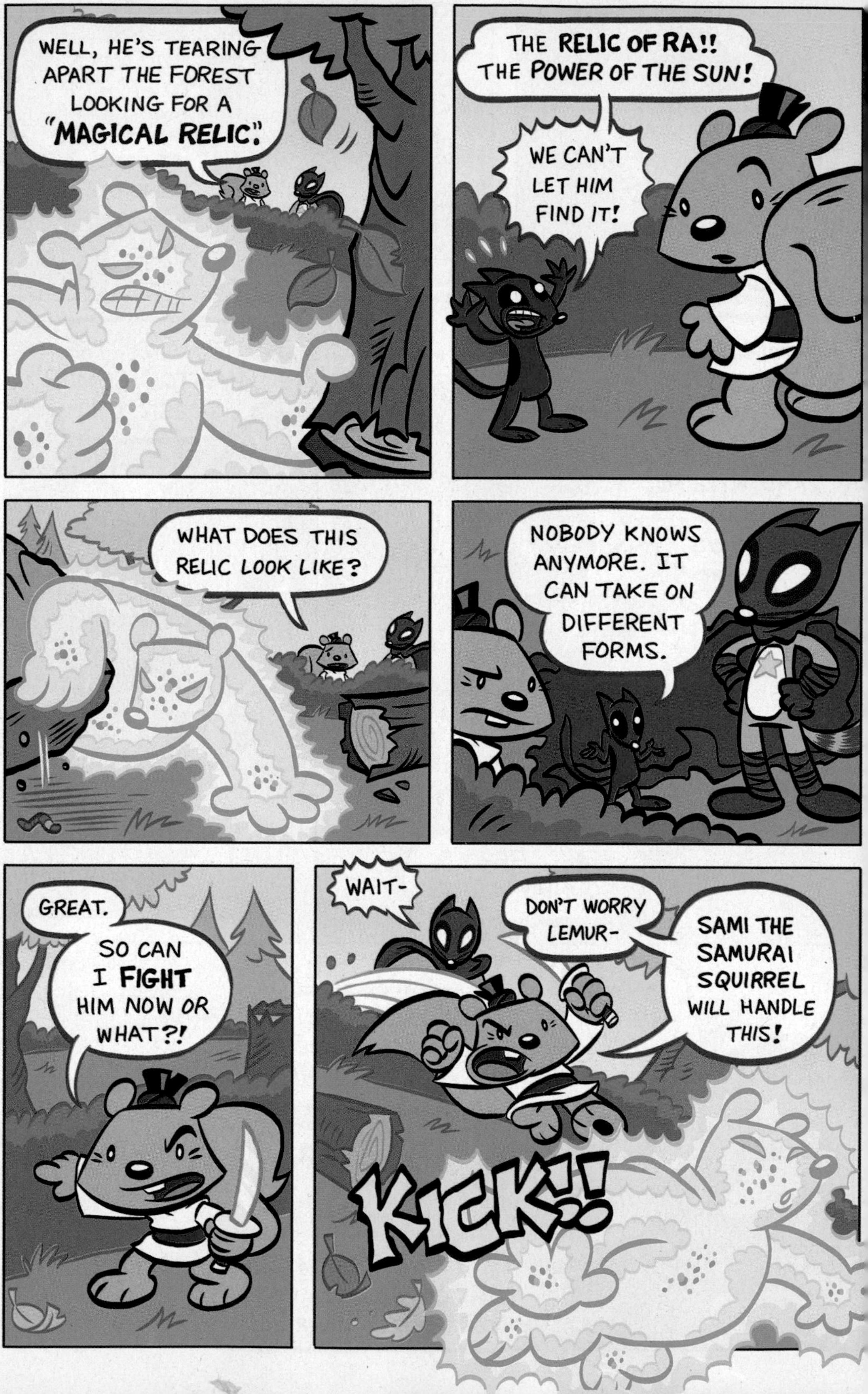

WELL, HE'S TEARING APART THE FOREST LOOKING FOR A "MAGICAL RELIC."
THE RELIC OF RA!! THE POWER OF THE SUN!
WE CAN'T LET HIM FIND IT!
WHAT DOES THIS RELIC LOOK LIKE?
NOBODY KNOWS ANYMORE. IT CAN TAKE ON DIFFERENT FORMS.
GREAT.
SO CAN I FIGHT HIM NOW OR WHAT?!
WAIT-
DON'T WORRY LEMUR-
SAMI THE SAMURAI SQUIRREL WILL HANDLE THIS!
KICK!!

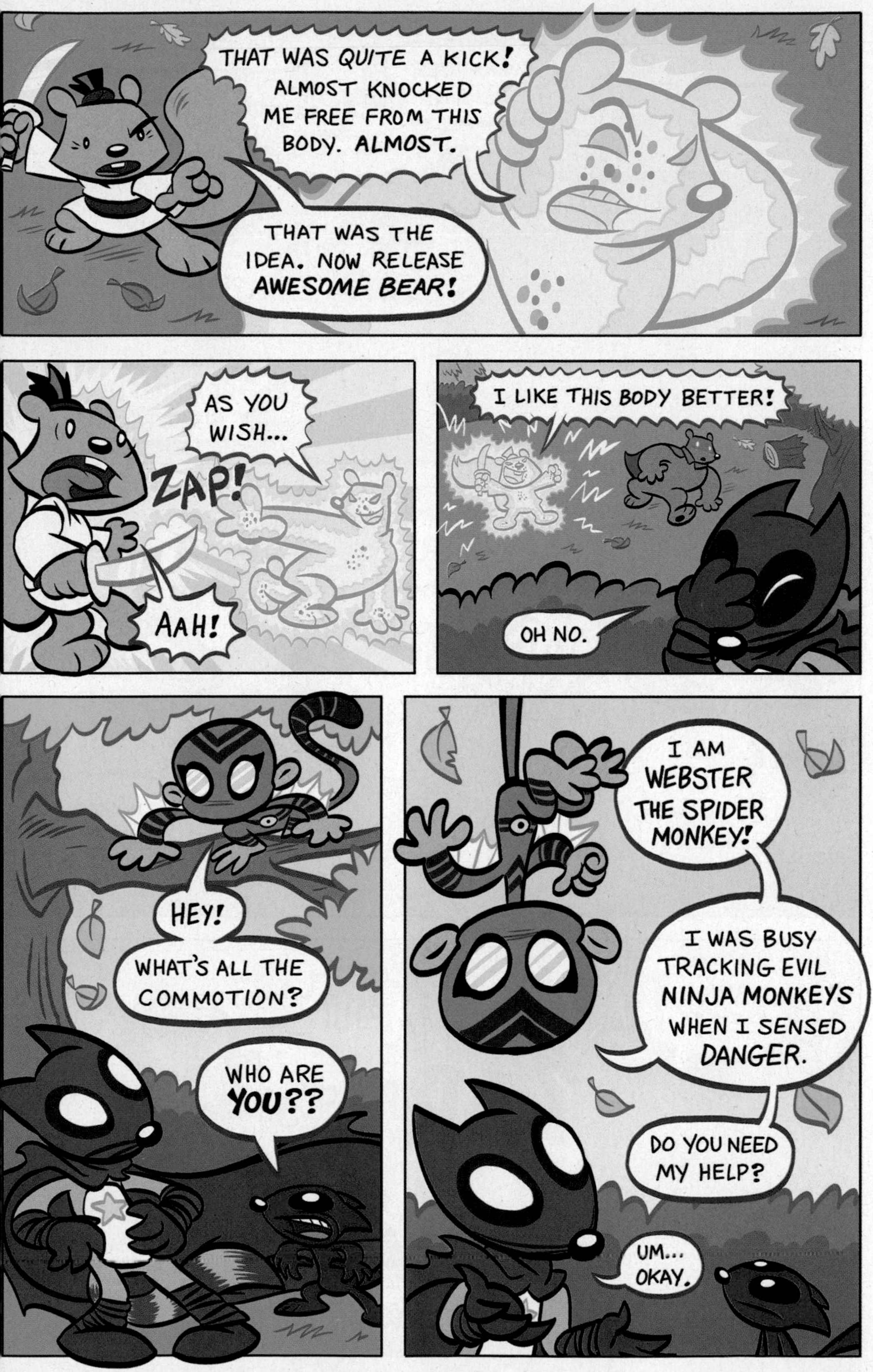
THAT WAS QUITE A KICK! ALMOST KNOCKED ME FREE FROM THIS BODY. ALMOST.
THAT WAS THE IDEA. NOW RELEASE AWESOME BEAR!
AS YOU WISH...
ZAP!
AAH!
I LIKE THIS BODY BETTER!
OH NO.
HEY!
WHAT'S ALL THE COMMOTION?
WHO ARE YOU??
I AM WEBSTER THE SPIDER MONKEY!
I WAS BUSY TRACKING EVIL NINJA MONKEYS WHEN I SENSED DANGER.
DO YOU NEED MY HELP?
UM... OKAY.

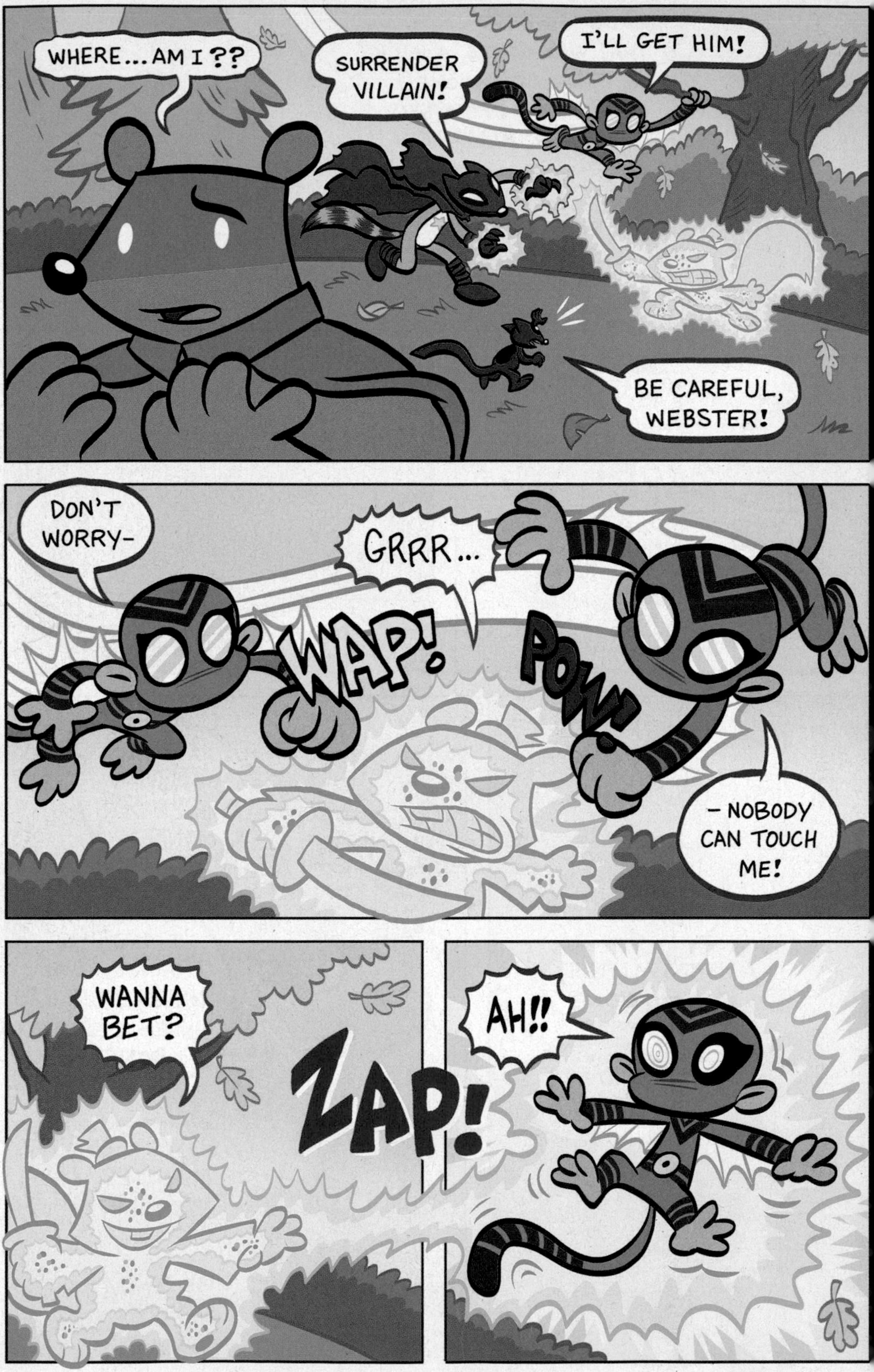
WHERE... AM I??
SURRENDER VILLAIN!
I'LL GET HIM!
BE CAREFUL, WEBSTER!
DON'T WORRY-
GRRR...
WAP!
POW!
-NOBODY CAN TOUCH ME!
WANNA BET?
ZAP!
AH!!

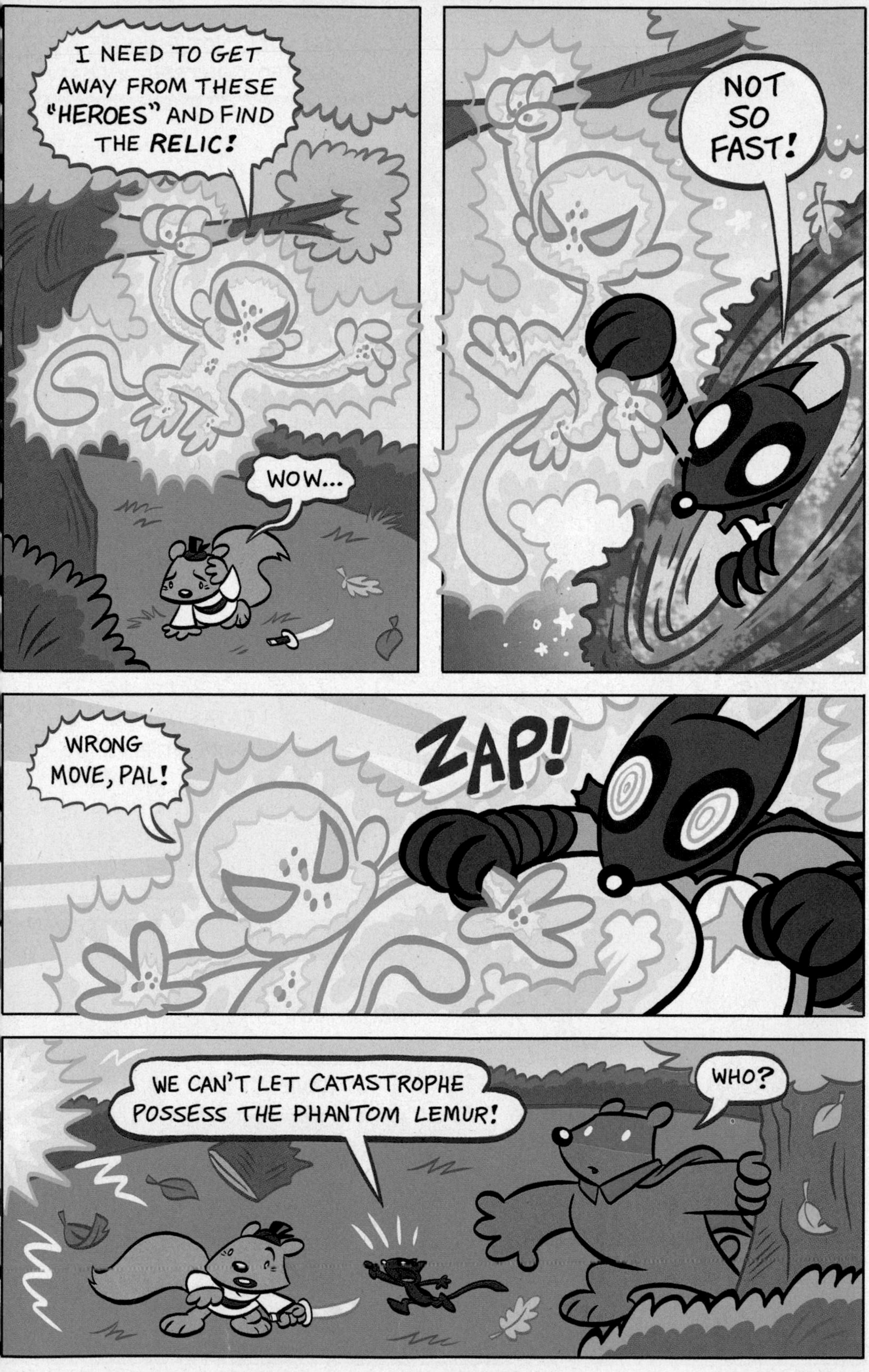
I NEED TO GET AWAY FROM THESE "HEROES" AND FIND THE RELIC!
WOW...
NOT SO FAST!
WRONG MOVE, PAL!
ZAP!
WE CAN'T LET CATASTROPHE POSSESS THE PHANTOM LEMUR!
WHO?

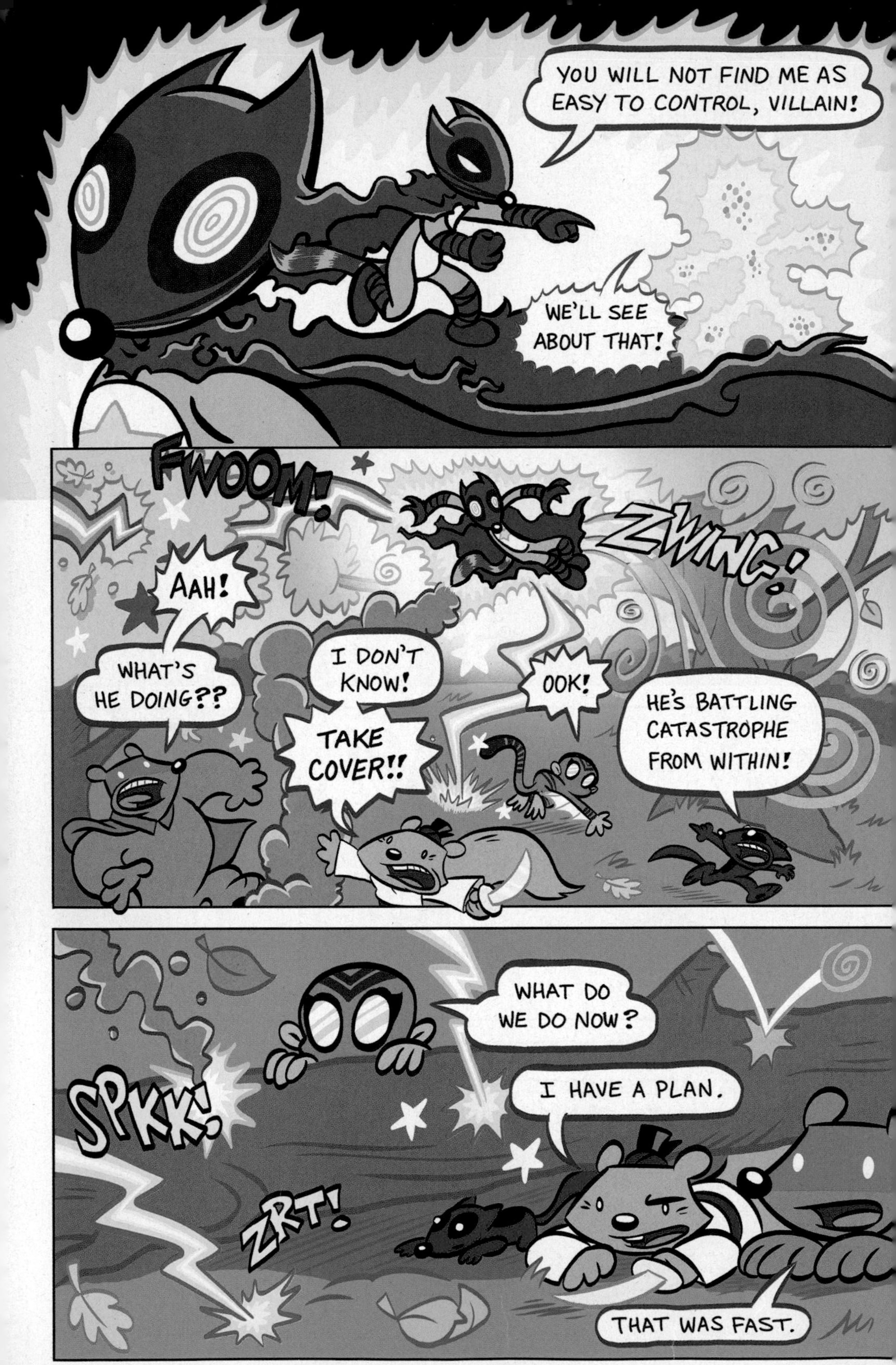
YOU WILL NOT FIND ME AS EASY TO CONTROL, VILLAIN!
WE'LL SEE ABOUT THAT!
FWOOM!
ZWING!
AAH!
WHAT'S HE DOING??
I DON'T KNOW!
TAKE COVER!!
OOK!
HE'S BATTLING CATASTROPHE FROM WITHIN!
WHAT DO WE DO NOW?
I HAVE A PLAN.
SPKK!
ZRT!
THAT WAS FAST.

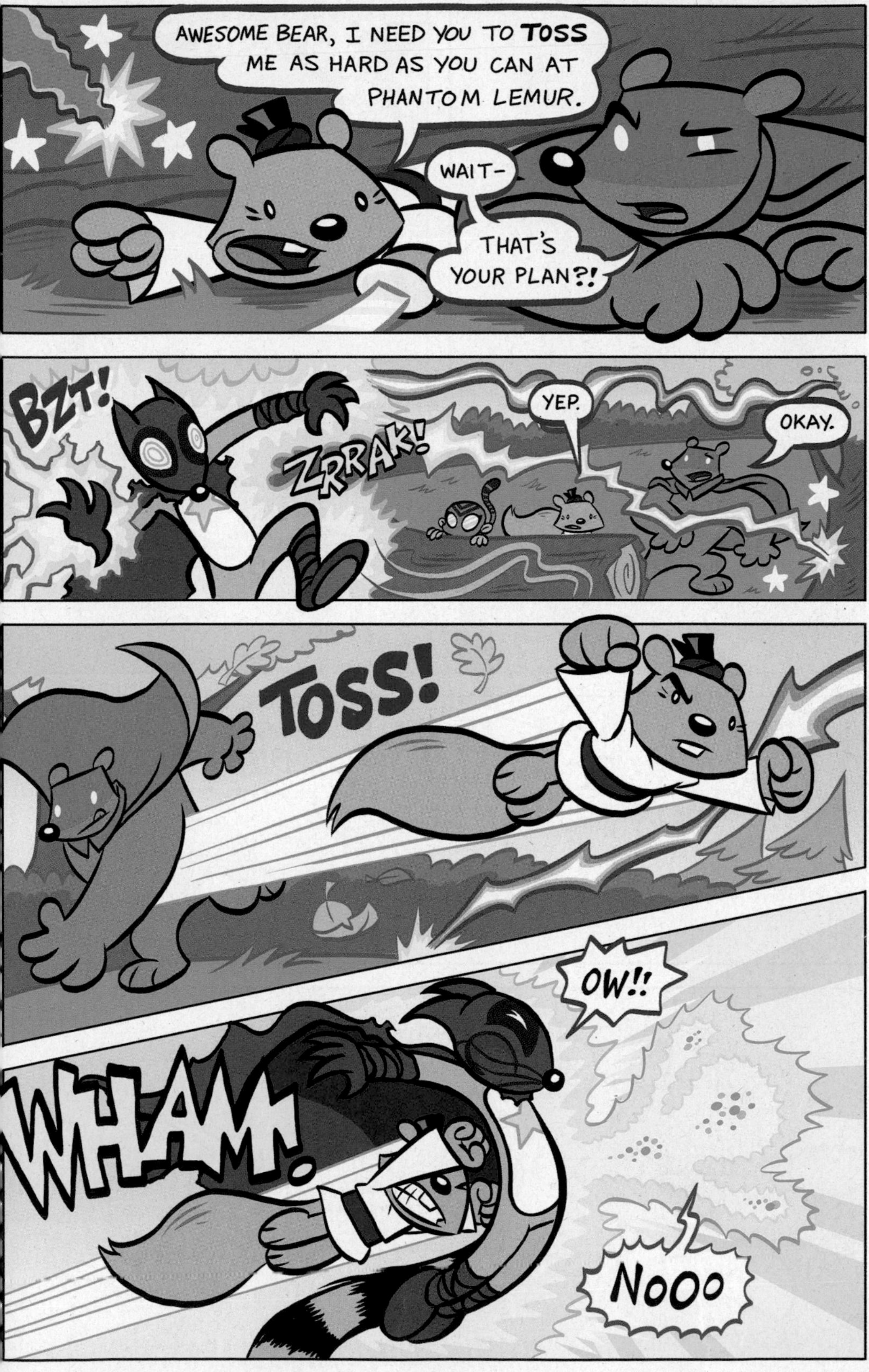
AWESOME BEAR, I NEED YOU TO **TOSS** ME AS HARD AS YOU CAN AT PHANTOM LEMUR.
WAIT-
THAT'S YOUR PLAN?!
BZT!
ZRRAK!
YEP.
OKAY.
TOSS!
OW!!
WHAM!
NoOo

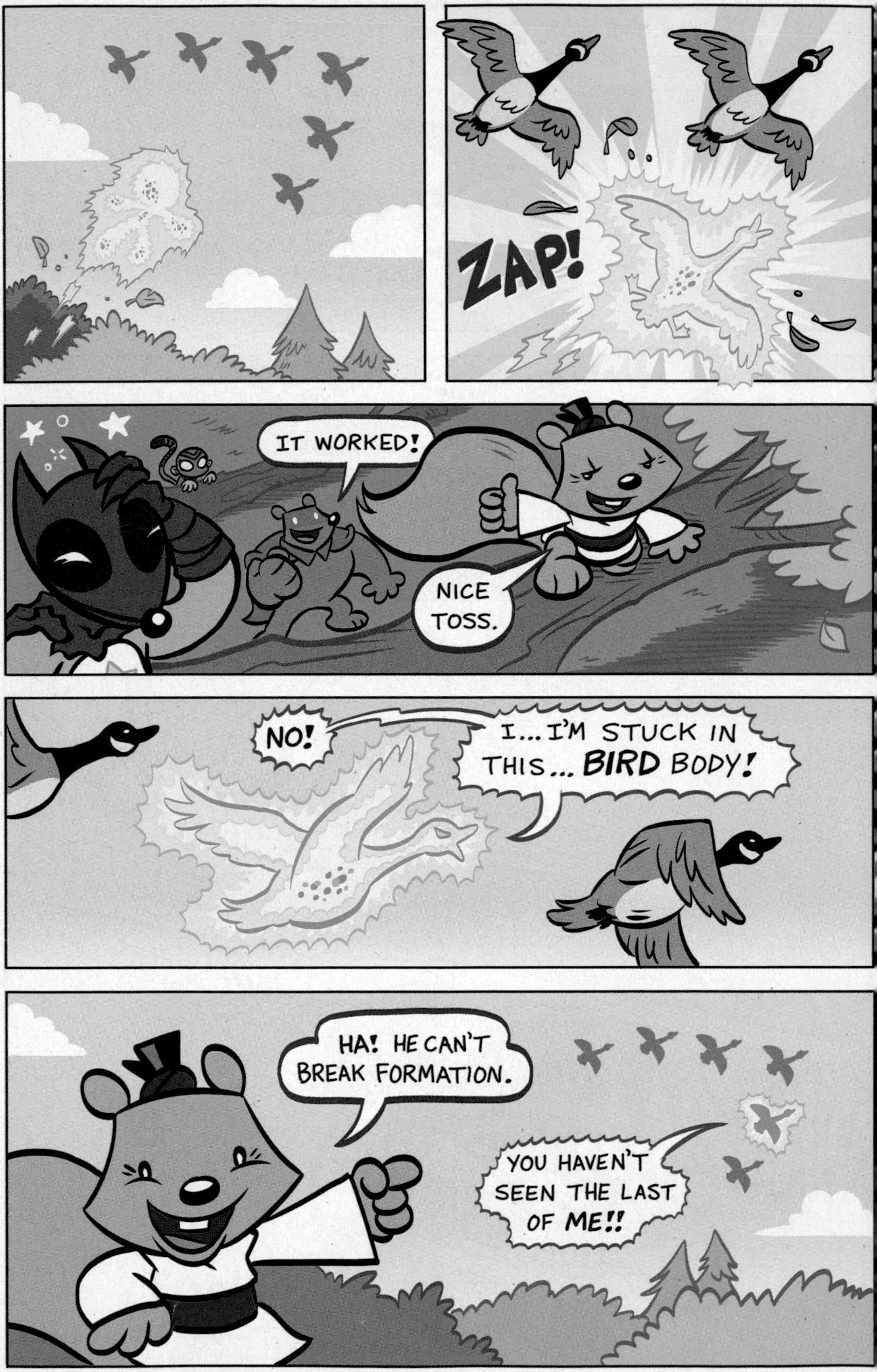
ZAP!
IT WORKED!
NICE TOSS.
NO!
I... I'M STUCK IN THIS... BIRD BODY!
HA! HE CAN'T BREAK FORMATION.
YOU HAVEN'T SEEN THE LAST OF ME!!

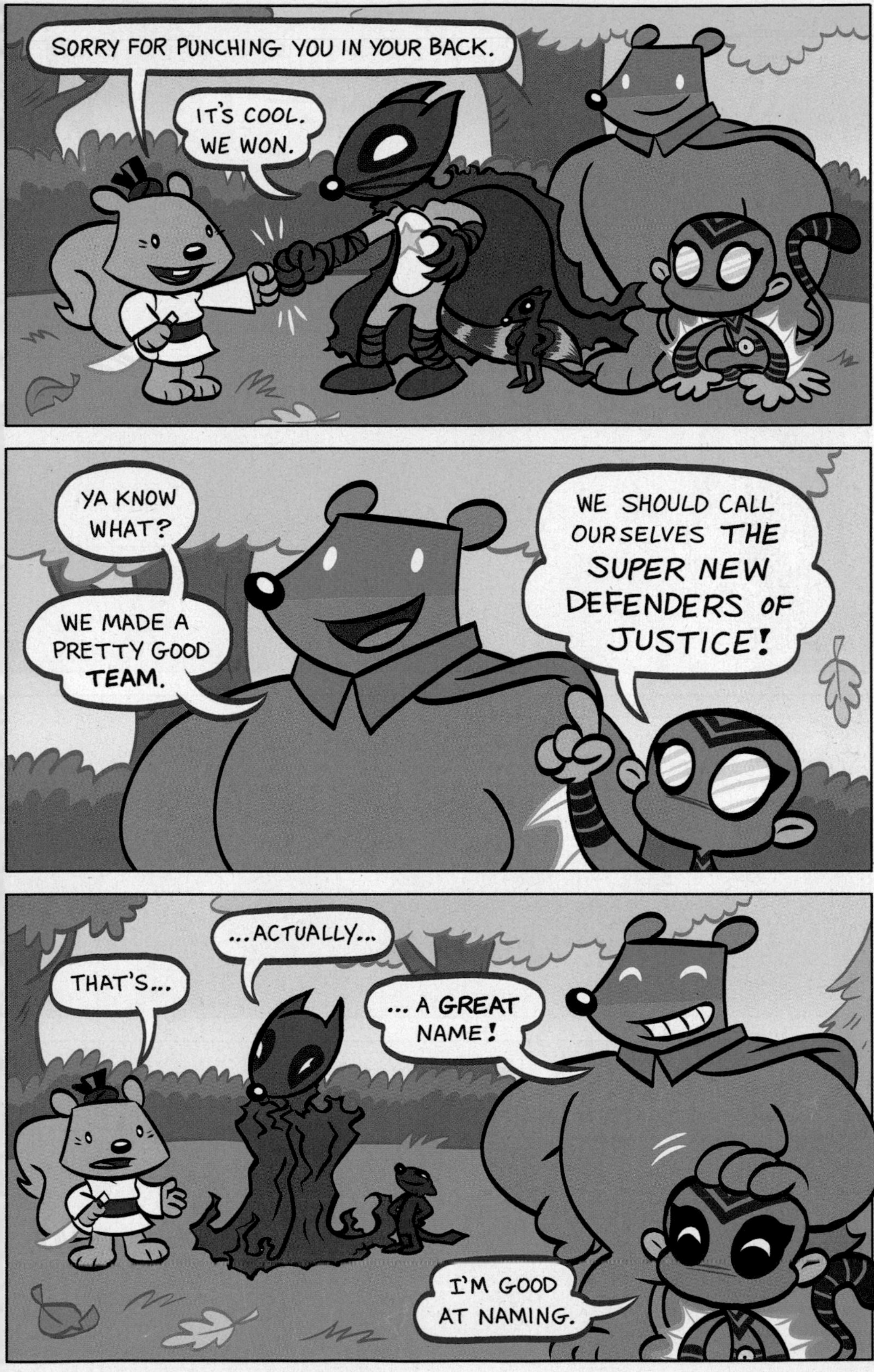
SORRY FOR PUNCHING YOU IN YOUR BACK.
IT'S COOL. WE WON.
YA KNOW WHAT?
WE MADE A PRETTY GOOD TEAM.
WE SHOULD CALL OURSELVES THE SUPER NEW DEFENDERS OF JUSTICE!
THAT'S...
...ACTUALLY...
... A GREAT NAME!
I'M GOOD AT NAMING.

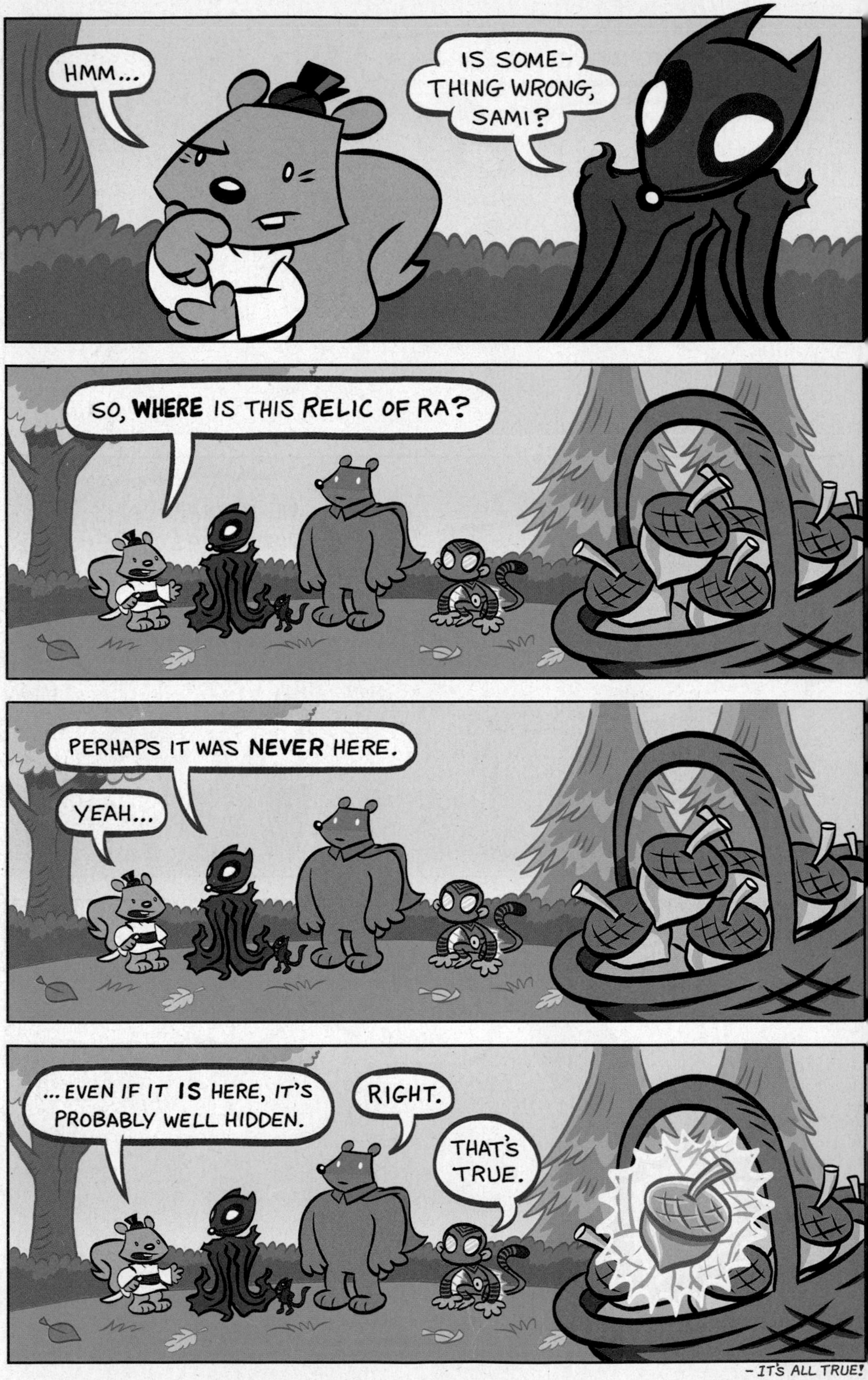
HMM...
IS SOME-THING WRONG, SAMI?
SO, **WHERE** IS THIS RELIC OF RA?
PERHAPS IT WAS **NEVER** HERE.
YEAH...
... EVEN IF IT **IS** HERE, IT'S PROBABLY WELL HIDDEN.
RIGHT.
THAT'S TRUE.

- IT'S ALL TRUE!